"THE STORM IS DYING. YOU ARE SAFE."

Adam fought the fire moving through him, fought his overwhelming desire to taste her and touch his lips to her hair, to her throat and her own soft lips. *Let her go*, he ordered himself. But he could not.

"I . . . thought lightning had hit the house," she whispered, her breath quickening. "I thought the roof was going to fall on us. That's the only reason I'm . . . where I am." She turned her head, listened to the distant thunder and to the wild beating of her heart. "Maybe the storm's coming back."

"Do you want it to?"

Alexandra met his gaze without blinking. "Aye," she said softly.

When he pulled her closer, she lifted her lips, felt him gently, gently brushing them with his . . .

Beloved Pretender

JOAN VAN NUYS

AVON BOOKS ◆ NEW YORK

*He is my Beloved. He is my Savior, my Warrior, my
Lover, my Protector. He is my Happiness and my
Heart. He is my Breath, my very Life. He is my
husband.*

BELOVED PRETENDER is an original publication of Avon Books. This
work has never before appeared in book form. This work is a novel. Any
similarity to actual persons or events is purely coincidental.

AVON BOOKS
A division of
The Hearst Corporation
1350 Avenue of the Americas
New York, New York 10019

Copyright © 1993 by Joan Van Nuys
Published by arrangement with the author
Library of Congress Catalog Card Number: 93-90330
ISBN: 0-380-77207-8

First Avon Books Printing: October 1993

AVON TRADEMARK REG. U.S. PAT. OFF. AND IN OTHER COUNTRIES, MARCA
REGISTRADA, HECHO EN U.S.A.

Printed in the U.S.A.

RA 10 9 8 7 6 5 4 3 2 1

Prologue

August 1762
Windfall, New York Colony

Adam was filled with the sheer, aching sweetness of having his wife in his arms once more. How wonderful it was to hear her laughter again and see her beautiful brown eyes melting with her love for him. How wonderful to feel her small body, all warm and soft and yielding, crushed against his and to feel her returning his hungry kisses. God in heaven, he could hardly believe his good fortune. His darling was still alive, and all of these dark days he had thought she was—

He sat up, eyes wide and staring into the shadows, skin damp, breath rasping in his lungs. He began to tremble, felt his heart shriveling as reality knifed through him. He had been dreaming. Sweet Jesus, it was only a dream. She was gone. He uttered a long, hoarse cry that rang through the great manor house in the wilderness, a terrible cry heard only by him, for Windfall was empty now.

He climbed to his feet, stumbled to the windows, drew open the draperies, and shrank as sunlight streamed into the drawing room. He had been sleeping there on the floor on the great bearskin robe the Mohawks had given him. Now he hauled it up—God, it was heavy—and laid it against the settee, and began to walk, numb and unseeing, through the other chambers

1

on the first floor. Kitchen, pantry, dining room, living room. He trembled as he sensed Eliza's presence. It was everywhere. It had been only two weeks since he had laid her to rest, her and their newborn babe, on a knoll that overlooked the Schoharie and this house.

She had loved Windfall. Adam, too, had loved it, but now he looked on it with a hundred regrets. If only his brother, the Duke of Dover, had never bought this land and never built the damned place. But he had. And when he'd been called back to England to attend to his many ducal estates there, Adam had been glad to manage Windfall in his absence—and he felt safe in bringing his new, young wife along because the manor house was here. He had known Eliza would have all the comforts of home. Now he cursed the day she had ever left England. If she had not come here, he brooded for the thousandth time, she might still be alive. He sank into a wing chair, moaned softly, and held his head.

God Almighty, how everything had conspired against them, yet how wonderful it had all seemed in the beginning. Eliza had adored the house, they both had come to care deeply for the Mohawks in the area, and Adam thoroughly enjoyed overseeing his brother's ten thousand wilderness acres and managing his tenants and collecting new ones. An added boon was that his cousin and best friend, Jared Pennburton, had made the trip from England with them and was in charge of Dover's trading post, a league downriver from the house. It had been Eden, and then . . .

Resuming his blind pacing, he reflected on how everything had begun to unravel when Dover had taken sick and was unable to return to Windfall when he had planned. And then Eliza had become pregnant. And it had killed her. *He* had killed her. When he planted his seed in her, he had killed her as surely as if he had placed the barrel of his musket to her temple and squeezed the trigger.

Why, why, why in the name of all that was holy had

he not taken her to New York City for the birth? It was an easy journey by boat. He had talked of it, and he had talked, too, of bringing a doctor to Windfall from the city for the last few weeks, the last month even. But Eliza had laughed and reminded him that Erich Gelber from the German settlement across the Schoharie was an excellent doctor. She would be fine. But the truth was that no one could have saved her. The finest doctors in the world could not have saved her. She never should have become pregnant.

Adam rose and, breathing heavily with the effort, climbed the stairs and walked aimlessly through the bedchambers. Their own bedchamber, however, was locked tight. He never wanted to see it again. But in his mind's eye, he saw his darling in the great canopied bed they had shared. He saw the two of them making love—and he saw her dying there. He thrust the image fiercely from his mind. Nay! He could not yet bear to think of her last moments. Not yet, maybe never. Instead he thought of her going about her daily chores, cooking, baking, sewing, polishing. He thought of her laughing, running, playing with the Indian children she adored . . .

He wanted to shake his fist, rail at Fate as he had so often these past two weeks, but he was too tired. Instead, he wondered, resented how the sun could continue to shine and the birds to sing when one of God's angels had fallen. He did not understand. The world, the very universe should have been plunged into darkness to grieve her loss.

As he was slowly descending the staircase to the foyer, he stopped and stared at the woman who was standing in the open doorway. He saw dimly that she was young and comely, with almond-shaped black eyes and one long ebony braid hanging down the front of her beaded doeskin tunic. When she smiled up at him shyly, Adam's dulled mind registered the fact that he knew her. She was Lark, from the Mohawk castle on the upper Schoharie.

"*Sekon,* Lord Adam."

"*Sekon* . . ."

"I knocked but you did not hear. I hope it is all right that I opened the door. May I come in?"

Adam nodded. He continued his descent in silence without another look at her and sat heavily on the bottom step.

Lark was shocked by the English lord's changed appearance. His dark skin had a waxy pallor, and his long black hair was dirty and tangled. He was bearded, and he had lost so much weight that his breeches and shirt hung on his once-powerful frame as if it were made of lodgepoles. But it was his beautiful black eyes, always so filled with curiosity and life, which worried Lark the most. They held neither light nor life nor hope, but were empty. In the two winters he had lived in this great dwelling-place, she had never seen him look so and her heart wept for him. She knew that her brother, the sachem, would be furious to learn that his good friend, Adam Rutledge, was in such a state. She realized now, too late, that they should have looked in on him daily, even though he had forbidden it. She asked quietly:

"How are you, *ion kiatenro?*"

Adam shrugged. "As you can see, I'm fine." His gaze was fastened unblinkingly on the grass and the sky beyond the open door. He would give anything, anything on this earth if only Eliza would come running toward him over the brow of the hill, laughing, with her long brown hair flying. He would sell his soul for such a sight.

A chill swept Lark. His deep voice that had always thrilled her was toneless and without depth, the voice of one who no longer cared. She said gently, "My people are worried about you, Lord Adam . . ." When he made no reply but rose and shuffled into the drawing room, she followed him. She watched wide-eyed as he threw his bearskin cloak onto the floor and then closed the draperies on two windows, placing most of the room in shadow. She frowned. "What are you doing?"

"I want to sleep," Adam muttered, lowering himself to the thick black fur. He was tired, so damned tired, yet sleep came to him only in snatches in the daytime.

Lark's heart pounded, seeing that the effort of lowering his body to the floor had made the nobleman tremble. Keeping her voice calm, she said, "My friend, when did you eat last?"

"It doesn't matter . . ." Adam closed his eyes. He wanted only to sleep. To dream.

Lark knelt by his side. In all of her eighteen winters, she had never seen a man suffer so over a woman. It was not the Indian way. Now she raised her voice. "Please, when did you eat?"

"I don't know. It's . . . been many days."

He had killed her, Adam thought. It was drumming, drumming through his head without cease. It would not leave him. He had killed her. Killed his darling. Her parents had placed her in his hands with complete love and trust, and he had killed her. His terrible message to them was on the high seas this moment while they, God help them, lived their lives and talked and ate and laughed and planned and did not know their only daughter was in the ground. God, God.

Adam opened his eyes and, gazing at Lark in the half-light, saw the fright on her face. She was such a beautiful little thing, so gentle, and he saw now that she was grieving for him as well as for Eliza. He did not want that. He smiled, reached out, touched her small hand. "Go home, *onkiatshi*. It's all right. I'm not hungry. Just—let me sleep."

Lark stared at him. When one of her people wanted life to end, he closed his eyes and willed Death to come. Seeing Death looking back at her from Adam Rutledge's black eyes, she felt her heart grow faint. She had claimed this man for her own from the first moment she had seen him, not knowing he was wed. He was strong and beautiful and kind to her, and for two years she had loved him in secret. Now he was not wed, and she was not going to let Death take him from her. She would not. She would ride like the wind back to the castle and tell her brother of this thing, and Silver Hawk would send men and a travois for him. And when his ordeal was over, she would help Adam to forget his sadness. She would make him laugh again, no matter how long it took. She was made of patience. But she feared greatly that he would slip into the Bright Land of Death before they could return for him.

"Adam . . ." She took his cold hand between hers, chafed it, blew her warm, moist breath on it. "Adam, do not sleep." When he did not answer, she lay down beside him on the bearskin, her head on his shoulder and her arm across his chest. "Adam?" His body felt so cold. She rose, found a wool blanket, lay back down beside him, and pulled it over them. "Wake up, *ion kiatenro*. Please . . ." Slipping her warm hands beneath his shirt and sliding them over his chest, she felt his cool skin prickle beneath her fingertips. He was still so cold, so cold. Somehow she had to warm him, breathe life into him, make him want to live. Great Sustainer, help her . . .

Knowing suddenly what she must do, Lark quickly stripped off her tunic and unbuttoned his shirt. Crawling back under the blanket, she enfolded him, pressing her warm breasts against his bare chest and breathing her hot breath against his face and throat and shoulders. She massaged his skin gently but deeply. "Adam, please, you must not sleep . . ."

Adam was exactly where he wanted to be—in a warm, dark cave. He could sleep there before his journey began. In truth, he wanted nothing quite so much as he wanted sleep, the sweet black nothingness of sleep. But feeling the warmth and softness of a woman's body against his own, he frowned, stirred. No woman should be here. He craved no woman, not where he was preparing to go—a land of blue skies and deep green grass which he could smell even now. But the feel of those soft, warm breasts pressed against him and her hot breath fluttering over his skin was kindling a small flame within him. As it began to warm the winter of his body and soul, he opened his eyes.

"Lark . . ."

"Do not sleep, my friend. You must not sleep. You will . . . die . . ."

Adam said simply, "Aye."

Only then did he see it was his intention. He was twenty-eight winters old, and he no longer had any reason to live. For him life was over. Yet the perfection of the maid's smooth, warm body was calling to him, stirring him—the dusky buds of her breasts, the gleam of her black hair, her mouth, so pink and moist and tempting. Adam could not help himself. He put his hand behind her head, drew her face toward his, and with darkness crowding him, he tasted her lips, felt her life and strength and vitality infusing him. He still had no reason to live. He did not love this woman. He knew only that this was not his day to die.

Chapter 1

April 1764
New York Colony

Adam watched the young Mohawk chieftain with admiring eyes as the calumet was passed reverently around the circle of braves. He was careful to hide his feelings behind his masked face and lowered lids—it would embarrass the sachem to be admired—but in truth, Adam had never known such a man. Silver Hawk was a warrior of deep pride and courage and determination, and he entered into all things with a fierce passion and eagerness.

From him, Adam had learned how to speak the Mohawk tongue and how to move through the forest as silently as a puma. He had gone from being Adam Rutledge, friend of the Mohawk, to being the Cougar, an honorary Mohawk. Silver Hawk had taught him, drilled him, prodded him endlessly with the love and patience of a brother. Yet in his heart, Adam knew that Hawk would be an implacable, unforgiving foe if the occasion ever arose. When he hated a thing, he hated as deeply as he loved—with every fiber of his being. And now he hated England and her king, and he threatened war. It seemed to Adam as if he himself were the only one trying to keep peace between their two peoples.

Silver Hawk watched his white brother with great calm. Not until he had taken several puffs of the calu-

8

met and passed it on did he speak to him in the Mohawk tongue:

"So. Your eyes hold a storm, *rikena.*"

"My news is not what I had hoped to bring you," Adam replied. He had spent the past week traveling and talking to the whites in the surrounding areas: Dover's tenants, the Dutch and German settlers, and other newly arrived settlers who were squatting on Indian land. "They won't stop hunting and fishing your land."

Silver Hawk's teeth, white against his dark skin, bared as he gave a bitter laugh. "Our friend Warraghiyagey, He Who Does Much, said it was the French who would strip us of our forests and streams. It was why we joined your great King George in driving them away. Now I ask, for what? We have only made it easier for you English to strip us." He gave Adam a baleful look and spat on the ground. "Your great and good king lied to us, *ion kiatenro.*"

At that moment, Adam was ashamed to be an Englishman, but he answered quietly, "The truth is, the king does not know what is happening. I live here, and only now am I learning the facts." He looked from Silver Hawk's unsmiling face to the grim countenances of the other braves. "Know that he values your friendship and has passed laws to protect your hunting and fishing rights, but the local officials and garrison commanders are not enforcing them."

Silver Hawk's lip curled. "The white man's greed is a worm that gnaws his gut. I pray that one day it will kill him. It is clear that this land, vast though it is, is not vast enough for our two peoples. Let the white devils move westward beyond the mountains."

Adam leaned forward. *"Raktsia,* they want to, but the English are forbidden to migrate beyond the boundary that the Crown has drawn. I have told you this."

Silver Hawk's brown eyes gleamed. "And because they themselves cannot forge westward, they will force us to move."

"Hen," Adam muttered. And the means brought to bear included claiming the Mohawks' land and overrunning their hunting grounds, thus reducing them to starvation.

"It has been said," Silver Hawk said quietly, "that they will even bring their diseases to kill us off."

"I . . . have heard that," Adam muttered. "But it will not happen, *raktsia.*" That rumor had come out of a garrison on the Hudson. Its commander, Wade Chamberlain, had talked about introducing smallpox to decimate the Indians, who were helpless against it. Adam had met the devil when he first came to New York Colony, and he'd never forgotten him. Chamberlain, a sour-faced colonel, had shown the utmost scorn and hatred for a great war hero, William Johnson—also known as Warraghiyagey. He'd called him a squaw-man.

Hell. He, too, was a squaw-man. Adam drew a sharp breath as the memory hit him. Lark. So soft and gentle and tender. Lark caring for him, comforting him, always there on his darkest days and his coldest nights. Lark giving him the hot, sweet pleasure of her young body when all he wanted was to die of his wretchedness and grief. Lark asking for nothing in return.

He raised his eyes and sought her. She was standing before her longhouse pounding corn, and she smiled when he caught her eyes, nodded, and quickly looked away. His heart warmed. She was as beautiful and as gentle as her name, and if ever he took another woman, it would be Lark. A man could do no better, and he would tell her so one day. She should know how he felt. But he could never love her, not after Eliza. He would tell her that also, and tell her that he would never again wed. He dragged his attention back to the sachem's anger.

"If your king does not know his laws are being disobeyed," Silver Hawk growled, "tell him. Tell him the French treated us far better than your people, who are destroying us with their crazy land and fur hunger. This has gone on too long and must stop, *rikena*. Your English king should know that we will strike back. There will be war. Tell him."

At this fresh threat, Adam's heart lurched in his fear for Eliza and then sank, as he remembered. Almost two dreary, endless years had passed since her death, yet he kept thinking she waited for him back at the hut he now shared with Jared. He thought he glimpsed her in the woods at twilight, thought he heard her soft laughter when the wind blew through the aspens. He died each time. It was his fault she had perished, he told himself for the thousandth time.

"*Rikena*, you have left us," Silver Hawk said gently.

Adam blinked as the pipe was placed in his hands again. He puffed on it, replied finally, "I was but pondering your words, *raktsia*. I will do my best to reach the king's ear. In the meantime, let us talk with Warraghiyagey." He had met Sir William Johnson earlier at a great gathering in Niagara and felt a strong camaraderie with the great Irishman.

"He is an old man now," Silver Hawk answered crisply.

"Forty-seven winters is not old among our people."

"He suffers greatly from his war wounds and other illnesses."

"He works without cease to quell the fighting on the western frontiers."

Silver Hawk received the calumet and drew on it before he said, "For that reason, we will deal with this problem ourselves. If he fights our every battle, the whites will no longer trust him, and he will be rendered useless to us."

Adam knew that Silver Hawk was right. He knew also that they were bent on war. And he was just as determined to avoid it. He said, "I have not the importance of William Johnson, but I am not without some voice among my people. I will send a message to the king as I promised, and I will go again to the white man's hall in Albany and tell them what you told me. I will rattle my saber as loudly as He Who Does Much."

Silver Hawk did not allow his mouth to smile, but instead studied his good friend thoughtfully. Adam, like the Irishman Johnson, was of two worlds now, and was a valuable link between the Mohawks and the whites who swarmed over them like locusts. In addition to being a hereditary leader among his people, he had learned Indian ways. He was no longer a fool in the forest, but moved through it now with the stealth and cunning of the cougar. It was how he had received his Indian name. He had earned it as surely as he had earned the Mohawks' great respect for his strength and courage these past four winters.

"My people do not want mere saber-rattling, *rikena.* They want to make war against those who wipe their feet on the Mohawks. Now."

Adam's heart beat harder. "I understand, but before you raise your tomahawks against England, remember, she has broken the back of France." Studying the braves' stony faces, he could already envision the carnage. And he could not let it happen. "I have given this much thought, *ion kiatenro,* and I think we may be able to frighten them into obeying the laws they now break. Listen to my words and tell me what you think . . ."

Jared Pennburton speared two more potatoes out of the embers, put them beside the heap of pan-fried fish on his plate, and frowned at this cousin as they hunched before their cookfire.

"What was decided finally? War? Will the local Mohawks go after them? It's not a half-bad idea, you know."

Adam shook his head. "There won't be war. Not yet."

"How did you manage?"

"I'm going to try talking some sense into the garrison commanders."

Jared snorted. "Not bloody likely."

Adam chewed and swallowed a mouthful of fish and potato. "Remember Chamberlain of the New York Seventh? The fellow we met at that bloody boring rout the day we landed in New York City?"

"Aye. He was the crusty old bastard who thought the whole country and everything in it belonged to England."

"He still does, yet he doesn't respect the Crown enough to enforce its laws. He's down at Tiyanoga and allows hunting and trapping all over the Indian land in his jurisdiction. I'll head for there tomorrow."

"The bloody bounder. Can't he see the danger?"

"He doesn't care," Adam muttered. His eyes darted to the woods as the wind stirred the treetops. There it was again. He would have sworn it was her soft laughter coming from the woods. And sometimes, sometimes he imagined he heard her weeping, and the babe crying . . .

Seeing that Adam's thoughts were drifting, Jared finished his meal in silence. If only Adam would talk about her. For until he did, there was nothing Jared or anyone else could do to help him. Jared rose, cleaned up the supper things, swept the store, and got things in order for the following day. When he was ready to turn in, Adam was still staring at the fluttering flames.

"Bedtime, old man," Jared said softly. Getting no answer, he touched Adam's bare shoulder. God, but he looked Indian sitting there cross-legged, glooming into the fire. For a fact, he was the Cougar; black hair falling over his shoulders, walnut-dark skin, black eyes glittering. It was uncanny. He had a sudden unsettling thought: Had Adam gone so completely Indian, so Mohawk that he was never going to mention Eliza's name again or even think of her? Hell, it wasn't civilized. He muttered, "Come on, man, it's late, and you have a long trip in front of you in the morn."

Without taking his eyes from the flames, Adam muttered, "If I hadn't come here, she'd still be alive."

Jared gave no hint of the thrill that shot through him. Adam was talking about it. He was talking about Eliza's death for the first time! Jared sank in silence to his heels beside his kinsman and watched as Adam buried his head in his hands. He heard his groan.

"Bloody hell and damnation. Why didn't I send her back to England as soon as I knew she was pregnant?"

Jared answered carefully, "Erich Gelber's a capable doctor. I think you know that." The man's only fault was that he could not perform miracles.

Adam raised his head, his eyes clouded with misery. He nodded. "I know it. It wasn't his fault. He's damned fine." It was that Eliza's slender body was not meant to bear children.

Unable still to think of the horror of her last hours, he turned his mind instead to old Dover, who was yet ailing back in England. It was three years since he'd first sickened, and Adam was damned worried. He wanted to go to him, but the duke forbade it. He did not want his valuable colonial property in any hands but Adam's. Adam did not force it, for this was not a good time to leave his Mohawk friends. They needed all the help he could give them. He got to his feet, yawned, and began to smother the fire.

"You're right, old man," he told Jared. "It's time I turned in. I want an early start."

Jared muttered, "I still say a good Mohawk rampage is what these greedy bastards need to see sense. Let some arrows fly."

"I agree."

Jared stared, seeing a familiar lazy smile on his cousin's face. It was a smile he had not seen for a long time. "Eh? I thought you said you'd talked them out of war."

"Out of war, aye. Let's just say some surprises will be forthcoming if reason fails."

Jared chuckled. "I like the sound of that. A warning of sorts?"

"Raids—to retrieve the stolen game." When Jared blew a soft whistle, Adam said, "Just a damned good scare, but no bloodshed."

"And how will you manage that, old man?"

"It will be in my hands," Adam replied quietly. "As of today, it seems I'm war chief of the Schoharie Mohawks."

Alexandra was shivering as she stood beside her mother at the prow of the sailing ship *Treasure*—but it was from excitement, not cold. She was feeling the same glorious, winging exhilaration she had experienced on their London–to–New York crossing even though this was a river trip. But then it was not just any river trip. They were plying the upper Hudson en route to her father's garrison at Tiyanoga. She had been begging to visit the fort ever since she and her mother had arrived in New York City almost a year ago, but he had always refused. He had said a garrison town was no place for a woman, and he'd visited them in New York twice a month instead. But then, completely out of the blue, he had summoned them to Tiyanoga for a two-week stay. It was a mystery.

"Are you chilled, darling?" Lydia Chamberlain asked. "You're shivering."

Alexandra's green eyes were glowing. "It's anticipation, Mum. Maybe Tiyanoga will be bristling with danger." Seeing her mother's bewilderment, she laughed. "I meant to say excitement."

She had been naive enough to think that something wonderful might happen to her in New York. Something so wild and wonderful and important that it would change her entire life—but she had been disappointed. After the sightseeing and the initial enchantment were over, it was almost as if she were back in England. Except in England, she'd had more freedom. Her father's regular visits had turned out to be nothing more than inspection trips to make sure she was behaving herself and meeting the proper suitors.

Lydia shook her head. "I will never understand you, Alexandra." The maid looked as placid as an angel with her pale gold hair, green eyes, and Botticelli face, but placid she was not. She was filled with curiosity and life and a hunger for adventure. She had actually gloried in their Atlantic crossing when a storm ripped one of the sails to shreds and they'd had to flee for their lives from pirates. Lydia had been terrified. "I hope you know, darling," she said firmly, "that Papa never would have summoned us to Tiyanoga if it were dangerous in any way. Disappointing as it may be to you, there will be no French about and the Indians are peaceful."

"That's not what he told Uncle Clarence. He said they were damned sneaky bastards who couldn't be trusted and they scalped and stole folks all the time."

Lydia compressed her lips. For years she had told Wade not to curse in front of Alexandra but he had, and this was the result. She said tautly, "That was on the Pennsylvania frontier, Alexandra." She had no idea where Pennsylvania or its frontier were. She could only trust her husband's wisdom.

Alexandra's eyes danced. "I guess you're right. But a gentleman I met at the Boswell rout said that Mohawk braves lust something fierce after white women." When her mother's pretty face blanched, Alexandra saw she had gone too far. She added quickly, "I'm sure he was only teasing, Mama. In fact I know he was—he was saying I should take him along for protection . . ."

For an instant, Lydia felt faint imagining Alexandra's being borne off into the deep woods on some dark shoulder, but then her anger flared. "How very coarse and ungallant of him to talk of such a thing to a young woman!" And for Alexandra to have repeated it—and to know what such a nasty word meant, even. Lust. Lydia could scarcely bring herself to think it, let alone say it. It stiffened the resolve that had been building within her these past few weeks.

She said suddenly, "I have decided we are returning to England."

Alexandra studied her mother's snapping green eyes and the sudden color in her face. "Does Papa agree?"

"He does not know. I will tell him when we see him. He said we were to come to the Colonies for six months, and it's been almost a year. It is time we went home."

Alexandra gaped at her, at the lamb turned lioness. "What if he says nay?"

"I will deal with that if it happens." Lydia had never disobeyed her husband before. She had never needed to or wanted to, but now the time was at hand. If this was a land where men could make free with such indecent talk to innocent maidens, it was no place for their daughter. In addition, there was her home to consider. She murmured, "I shudder to think what is happening at the Larches in our absence. The mice will play, you know."

"I'm sure they will," Alexandra replied gravely. She knew full well the servants would do as little as possible without her there to keep them in line.

She had discovered early on that her mother was a willow who bowed in the slightest breeze where the help was concerned. She was loved by them, aye, but after Alexandra's father had gone off to war, they ran the house. Lydia Chamberlain could not bear to hurt their feelings by pointing out cobwebs on the ceilings, smudges on the crystal, and egg on the forks. She thought they were doing the best they could when in fact they did very little. Alexandra smiled, recalling their surprise and dismay on the day she had first begun issuing orders.

"Not only is there the Larches to consider," Lydia

said, "but I fear your aunt and uncle are quite sick by now of our living with them."

"And I'm sick of it, too. They're stuffy."

"I agree. In truth, I don't see how my sister abides that man . . ."

Alexandra's earlier good spirits were rapidly dissolving. "Face it, Mum, Papa will never let us leave until he marries me off. You know that is why he brought us to the Colonies in the first place. He thought you weren't firm enough with me and my leash was too long."

The child was right, of course. Oh, dear, why did she have to be so terribly finicky? Lydia murmured, "You've met some lovely young men since you've been here . . ."

Alexandra made a face. "Too lovely." Her aunt and uncle had dragged her to a continuous round of assemblies to meet eligible men, and each party was more boring than the last. "If I see one more overdressed, overperfumed, bewigged male who thinks he's God's gift to women, I'll puke."

"Alexandra!"

"I will. I swear it."

"The two young gentlemen you met last week at the Chumleys' rout were not bewigged or perfumed. They were handsome and quite manly, I thought." And they had thought Alexandra was divine. A mother could tell.

Alexandra grinned. "They were quite nice, I agree, except we had naught to talk about."

Lydia stared at her only child in complete bewilderment and exasperation. "Naught to talk about? My dear Alexandra, since when have men and women ever had anything to talk about? Your father and I do not talk— unless it's about you. He has his war, and when he is at home he has his work. He has his politics and sports and clubs and gaming. I have my needlework and cards and the house and shopping—and I have my friends. Honestly, my dear, if you are looking for more, if you are looking for talk, and for a man to care what you think about anything whatsoever, you are asking for far too much. Men don't care tuppence about what's in a woman's head. I worry, in fact, that you have so much education. Men don't want learning in a woman. They say it curdles our brains."

Alexandra's laughter pealed out over the blue water and was carried off by the wind. "Goodness, that simplifies matters, then, doesn't it? With my curdled brains, no man will ever want me, and I'll have an absolutely glorious life. No lord and master, no restrictions . . ." Ages ago she had vowed that her life would not be cast in concrete like her friends'. She absolutely refused to be given to some pompous stranger and have her days filled with squalling babes and endless female duties. Her life was going to be different.

"Darling, you cannot be serious!" Lydia protested. "Every woman needs a husband to guide her and protect her." Although she doubted in her heart that the man existed who could guide this maid—or understand what the girl really wanted. She doubted Alexandra herself even knew.

Alexandra had grown quiet. She said finally, "I admit it would be nice to wed the right man and have a babe one day. But I'll not wed just to be wed, Mama, or to gain entry to the *ton*. I don't care a bean about a man's ancestry or wealth or if he belongs to the right club. I'm not like Sara and Justine. You know I'm not." Last summer, her two best friends had been wed, with much pomp, to dull, titled middle-aged strangers with whom they had nothing in common and to whom they had nothing to say. Alexandra could not imagine a more hideous existence.

Lydia said quietly, "They seemed wildly happy."

"They were. They are. They're in love with being wed and being the mistresses of their own manors. I want to be in love with a man, Mama." A man who would care about what was in her head and who would

like it that she knew more than needlework and how to
give parties and play cards. Sara and Justine had promised her that he was out there, and that her name was
carved on his heart—but she wondered . . .

Lydia hid her dismay. How on earth had all these
years slipped by without the two of them discussing
such an important thing? She had thought her little girl
was merely finicky about the appearance of her suitors.
She'd had no idea it involved so much more, and in
truth, she was not completely convinced it did. Perhaps
the child wanted to remain just that for a while
longer—a child. That made more sense than her talk of
love. Who on earth ever married for love nowadays?
Certainly no one she knew. Such things happened only
in books. She said carefully:

"Darling, perhaps you're just not quite ready yet for
the . . . responsibility of marriage. Perhaps you want to
remain in your papa's house awhile longer. And if you
do, it's perfectly all right. I understand. You may stay
as long as you wish within the safety and security of
the Larches. There will be no pressure on you to wed.
I'll simply not have it."

Alexandra smiled. "It's appreciated . . ."

Darling Mum. She said she understood, but she really didn't. Not even her friends understood Alexandra's hunger for freedom, the same freedom a man had
to go where he wanted and do what he wanted and
learn what he wanted. Freedoms that were denied
women. She'd had to fight a terrible battle with her private tutor before he'd consented to teach her history,
geography, literature, and German. When he had seen
finally that she was serious about learning, he taught
her eagerly and thoroughly even though he didn't approve of such learning for females. In return, Alexandra
had submitted to the morals, manners, and divinity
classes her father had insisted upon.

"What are you thinking about, darling?"

"School—and Piddington Pitts." Dear Old Piddy . . .

Lydia laughed. "I'll wager Master Pitts never had such a student before or since." She hoped devoutly that his thorough education of her daughter would be offset in a suitor's eyes by the needlework and dancing and music lessons Lydia had insisted upon. But it was a worry.

"I do hope, darling, that you brought along that lovely panel you've been embroidering to show Papa."

"I brought it."

Seeing her daughter's mouth twitch, Lydia murmured, "He'll be pleased. He's under such a strain up here in this awful place surrounded by savages—you know how he hates savages—that we must do all we can to make him happy."

Alexandra gave her an impulsive hug. It could not be easy, being the wife and mother of two such difficult people. "I do love you, Mum. I don't tell you often enough, I know."

Lydia laughed. "And I love you, my darling."

Actually, the child was quite right to wait for someone she cared for dreadfully to wed, but would it ever happen? And if it did not, was a life of loneliness preferable to one of boredom? But then, how could a woman possibly be bored with running a household and having babes? She herself had never been bored, but she saw keenly that she and her daughter were cut from different cloth. Alexandra would never be satisfied with the simple life that had satisfied Lydia.

It brought to Lydia full force the reason for this trip to Tiyanoga, but, of course, Alexandra had no idea. She watched as the child threw back her head so that the wind lifted her marvelous tangled mass of pale gold hair and sent it streaming out behind her. Lydia stared. She was so lovely. Exquisite, actually. So soft and pink and white and girlish . . .

"Dear, you really must not wear your hair like that around Papa. He doesn't like it in your eyes and tumbling about your face so—like a Gypsy, you know. Do tie a ribbon around it before we get there, and I so wish you had worn something more refined." Her eyes swept her daughter's plain white muslin gown. "He'll want you looking like a lady, not a kitchen maid. Do hurry with the ribbon now, darling. The captain says we'll be arriving soon."

Alexandra's golden brows drew together. "Why on earth are you fussing so over me?" It was the sort of thing Lydia did when a suitor was about to call. She froze as a terrible thought dawned on her. Blazes. Was that why Papa had decided so suddenly that they should visit his garrison after refusing her every request all year? She crossed her arms and studied her mother's too-pink face with narrowed eyes.

"Stupid me. Something's afoot, isn't it?"

"Now, darling . . ." How positively annoying. All she had to do was think a thing, and Alexandra sensed what it was.

"I can't believe this—" Alexandra's heart was pumping harder. "He wants me to meet someone, doesn't he?"

"Darling, please, don't get upset. It's just that he wants what's best for you. As he says, he c-could go at any time here in this awful place with so many savages about, and he wants you settled."

"Who is it?" Alexandra asked in an awful voice.

Lydia clutched her shawl about her more tightly. It simply was not fair that she was the one this had fallen to when it was all Wade's idea. She murmured, "Lord Adam Rutledge."

Alexandra's eyes glittered angrily. "*Lord* Adam Rutledge?"

Lydia looked miserable. "Aye, darling. Lord." She knew how very much Alexandra abhorred the idea of wedding into the nobility, and understood completely her distaste, although her husband never would. It was crass, somehow. As if one were trying to climb the social ladder, so to speak—a case in point being those two old men, both barons, to whom Alexandra's little friends had been given. She would never let on, of course, but she had definitely not approved. One fellow had a face like a pudding, and the other a prune. What a pity. Both maids were such lovely young things. So very English . . .

"This is disgusting," Alexandra muttered. "I'll not meet him."

"Now, darling, you must, really. You'll disgrace your papa otherwise. He's arranging a grand party for tomorrow evening and inviting the entire town to meet us."

Alexandra felt impossibly trapped. How damnable, being a dutiful daughter. "Who is this person, and what in the world is an English lord doing at Tiyanoga?" She could see him now. Plump, leering, bald under his periwig, and with a stained satin vest stretched disgustingly over his fat belly. He would be too jovial, too smooth, too important, and hideously determined, of course, that she know it. She felt ill.

"He is the brother of the Duke of Dover," Lydia answered, "and he is here overseeing the duke's property, although I cannot imagine why the duke himself is not here—or why an Englishman, titled or otherwise, would find it necessary to accumulate land in such a place . . ." Her disapproving gaze swept the impenetrable wilderness on either side of their blue waterway. It was all so very unlike England, so uncultivated and uncivilized. So very strange and savage. She could not suppress a shiver.

Seeing it, Alexandra misunderstood its cause and relented. "Very well, I'll meet him. But only so Papa won't go on and on about it to you. I'll not have you miserable over such a silly thing."

"Thank you, darling, and you can always say nay to—to anything, you know." She was vastly relieved that Alexandra would not make a fuss, and hoped against hope that she might actually like the man.

Her husband's letter said he had met Lord Adam four

years ago, and he had assumed Adam had long since returned to England. He had been shocked and delighted to learn His Lordship was still in New York Colony overseeing his brother's land, and it was only appropriate that he meet Alexandra. It all tended to make Lydia decidedly uneasy. She had told the girl she could say nay, but she knew in her heart that Wade would not allow it. Not if His Lordship was interested . . .

Chapter 2

Fort Tiyanoga

Alexandra sat gazing out the window of her father's study, quill in hand and her journal open before her. She had been about to record her impressions since arriving at Tiyanoga three days ago, but her father's strident voice coming from the drawing room scattered her thoughts. Bother. He was always angry about something. This time it was probably Lord Adam Rutledge's not attending the party and not even sending his regrets.

Smiling, Alexandra dipped her quill into the inkpot and wrote: *... and so I didn't have to meet Old Rhubarb after all. Cheers! Is it possible my reputation has preceded me and he doesn't want a female with curdled brains? Blazes, whoever would have thought my education would be so beneficial?*

Alexandra's gaze returned to the scene that stretched beyond the window: the fort, forbidding and almost hidden within its high palisade ... the artillery ... the warehouses and bark-roofed huts of the Lower Town ... the small, neat houses of the Upper Town, and behind them all, the River Hudson gleaming like a copper snake in the sunlight. It was all completely different from what she had imagined. She dipped the quill, put it to the paper, wrote:

I have two new friends, Mary and Jane Hatch. They call themselves Mayjay, and they could be Justine and Sara, they're so like them. They say no one lives in the

25

fort (blast!) unless there are Indian hostilities (which there aren't) so that Tiyanoga nowadays is nothing more than a peaceful little town clustered around the palisade and sitting on the edge of the wilderness.

I should mention our house. It's on a hill apart from all the others and in comparison looks like the Taj Mahal. I'm embarrassed. Why does Papa do these things? We have china and crystal, a damask cloth on the table, and a drawing room huge enough for dancing. It's where the party was held, and fourteen people squeezed in, all officers and their wives. No one from the Lower Town was invited, since Papa says it's named for the morals of its inhabitants. Mayjay pointed out some of the women who live there, and said they were for rent!!! Also I saw the one Indian who lives there. His name's John Stargazer. How I'd love to meet them all!

Alexandra raised her head, frowning, as her mother's usually gentle voice rose above her father's.

"—has been almost a year now," Lydia declared, "and really, Wade, I must protest. I want to go home. It is not at all good for Alexandra to be away from England so long and I fear, I really do, what must be happening to the Larches. I do not want it abused. As for Violet and Clarence, it is unfair for us to be imposing on their hospitality for such an extended period. Their home is not their own anymore and—"

"Go then!" Wade snapped.

Lydia gazed at her husband with those green eyes so like her daughter's and told herself to be patient. "My dear, I did not mean we should trundle off without you. I mean simply that you might indicate to the Crown that you have served well and faithfully for many years, and is it not time, perhaps, that you were sent home to enjoy your golden years with your family? Is that not reasonable?"

"Bah!"

Lydia blinked. He looked like a wet, cranky old rooster. "I beg your pardon?"

"I do not want to go home."

Her spine stiffened. "Indeed? And why is that, pray? Is there another woman?"

Wade gave a snort. "For Godsakes, what rot. Where would I find a woman other than a squaw or one of those disgraceful hangers-on in the Lower Town?" He shook his crisply barbered gray head. "Don't go female on me, Lydia. It does not become you."

"If not a woman, then what? Lydia demanded.

"If you must know, it's these damned savages. They will not accept the fact that we won the war and they are subject to the laws of the conqueror."

"I thought they were our allies. I thought—"

"Kindly refrain from thinking and discussing matters of which you are ignorant. The entire Mohawk nation is headstrong and arrogant and must be taught a lesson." And Adam Rutledge must be taught a lesson.

He paced, thought grimly of how delighted he'd been to see the fellow, popping up out of the blue as he had two weeks ago, and then, to discover why he had come to Tiyanoga! His blood boiled, recalling the young devil's accusing him of flouting the Crown's laws—and then making those outrageous demands on the Mohawks' behalf.

What did the Crown, safe and sound and warm back in the comforts of London, know of life here in this black, howling wilderness? He had settlers and traders and his own men to pacify. Their needs came before those of any damned Mingoes. But he had swallowed his outrage as something far more important that Mingoes had come to light: Adam Rutledge was widowed. Realizing that Adam must meet Alexandra, Wade had invited him to a party on the spot. The devil had accepted, and then had proceeded to snub him soundly by not attending. The damned young hound had not even sent regrets.

Lydia stared at the man she had married so long ago. "My dear old fool," she said softly, "you are fifty-five

now, and I am close behind. I am tired and I want to return to England, and I want my husband with me."
He'd had good sense once, and as she pondered what had become of it, there came a knock on the front door. She heard Alexandra answering it, and moments later, Alexandra appeared in the drawing room with the daughters of Lieutenant Hatch in tow.

"Mama and Papa, may I visit Mayjay now?"

"Of course, darling," Lydia answered. "Run along. Enjoy yourselves, and I trust you will be home for dinner. Girls, do come back and join us."

The girls nodded their gleaming heads. "We'd be pleased ma'am," Jane replied and dropped a curtsy.

As they departed, Wade called after them: "Alexandra, wait!" He had the damnedest uneasy feeling suddenly . . .

"What is it, Papa?"

He said gruffly, "Stay in the Officers' Area and out of the Lower Town, and don't go into the woods. Can't tell who's hanging about nowadays."

Alexandra's face burned. Would he never stop treating her like a child? A heated retort trembled on her lips, but then she saw her mother's eyes. They reminded her to think before she spoke. He had always been protective, and he was not used to her being nineteen years old. To his mind, she was still going on fourteen, the age she'd been when he'd gone off to war. She answered gently, "You needn't worry, Papa. We're just going to their house."

Her father cleared his throat and said uneasily, "Since I want to see the lieutenant anyway, I'll walk down with you."

Alexandra was mortified. It was clear to all that her father expected Mayjay to lead her astray. In silence, they walked down the hill, through the Upper Town and the Officers' Area to the Hatches' modest cabin. They were about to ascend the stone pathway leading to the front door when Alexandra heard hoofbeats. Turning, she caught her breath. Indians! Indian braves riding out of the woods, all bare dark gleaming skin and flying black hair and feathers. How absolutely marvelous! She had feared she would return to New York City having seen only John Stargazer from a distance. As she stopped to look at them admiringly, Mayjay shrieked, caught her hand, and tried to pull her toward the house. Her father drew his sword.

"For Godsakes, run!" he shouted. "Get into the house!"

When she finally saw the danger, Alexandra could not leave him there. She could not. She hesitated, and in that one instant she was lost, swept up by a pair of hard dark arms onto the back of a pinto pony. In a daze, she saw that her friends, too, had been seized.

"Father!" She saw his terror for her, saw the color drain from his face, and as the ponies raced back toward the woods, she turned for one last glimpse of him. She screamed, seeing that he had fallen, the head of a tomahawk buried in his ribs. "Papa! Oh, Papa! They've killed you! Oh, God . . ."

Adam gave his head a sharp shake. He had been asleep in the saddle again. For over two weeks he'd been traveling from fort to fort and village to village. He had warned the garrison commanders of the danger of their folly, he'd encouraged the Iroquois to retrieve their stolen game, and he'd gone to Albany, where he reported the state of things to the commissioner of Indian Affairs. But as he headed toward home, his heart was heavy. It was too little—and the military men he'd met were as stiff in their thinking as that Old Grayhead, Chamberlain.

He snapped his fingers. Hell, the party! The old boy had invited him to a party, and he'd accepted because he thought he'd be back in the area by then, and because it was another chance to badger the old devil—and he'd forgotten completely. Damnation. But then it was no great loss. Doubtless Chamberlain had forgotten he'd ever invited him. Seeing the dignified approach of a familiar figure, Adam raised a hand in friendship. It was Kaga, sachem of one of the Mohawk tribes in the area.

"We heard you were coming, *rikena,*" Kaga said in his own tongue. "It is good to see you again."

"It is good to see you, *raktsia.*"

"Your visit is well-timed. A band of Oneidas are just now passing through our village with three white women. They stole them in Tiyanoga two days ago."

"I see." Adam masked his shock. Sweet Jesus, that was the last thing that was needed, with tensions already running high.

"Since none of us speaks the white man's tongue, it is well you are here, Cougar. You must tell the women to stop their whining. They belong to the Oneidas now."

Adam drew a steadying breath, wondering how in God's name he could free them. "Take me to them."

He followed Kaga through the open village and past longhouses and barking dogs to the edge of a crowd that had gathered. In its center were the women. Two of them had sunk to the earth and were weeping into their hands. The third was standing, her head high, but Adam saw that she trembled.

Alexandra was feeling rage as well as fear. They had been blindfolded for two days, and when the cloths had been removed from their eyes, their captors, grinning slyly, watching them, raised their breechclouts and voided, seeing who could wet the farthest. The sight sent Mayjay into a weeping huddle on the ground. Alexandra gritted her teeth and turned away from the disgusting spectacle. It was far better to look at the people crowded about them even though their savage appearance shook her to her depths.

Both men and women were half-naked, and the men wore their hair like a brush from forehead to nape.

There was paint on their bodies, and tattoos, and their dark eyes were filled with hostility. But there was a small blessing—their captors had moved off for the moment. Alexandra rubbed her wrists and arms, saw the dark bruises the brave had left. In truth, she had never been more terrified, but her pride would not let it show. And she simply had to communicate with these people.

She called out, "Does anyone speak English?" When there was no reply, she cried, *"Parlez-vous français? Sprechen sie Deutsch?"* When the crowd parted for two braves, Alexandra looked on them hopefully. "Do either of you . . . gentlemen speak English? *Français? Deutsch?"* She masked her despair with a look of disgust. "But of course you don't. I'm sure you're all as stupid as you look!"

Turning to her weeping friends, she said low, "Mayjay, please, please don't bawl so." She was close to tears herself. "These are ignorant savages. You're Englishwomen! Hold up your heads and be proud." When her words fell on deaf ears, she said, "Blast it, uncover your eyes and see how silly they look!" Her own gaze swept the gathering with disdain, but inside she was quaking. "How any man," she muttered, "can expect to be taken seriously when his hair looks like a clothes brush, I'll never know. And the women"—she carefully avoided looking at the bare breasts of the squaws—"have no shame."

Adam did not allow himself to smile, but gazed down on her stonily. What a little hellcat. The maid was scarcely fifteen or sixteen winters, and without even speaking their tongue, she had managed to insult an entire tribe of Mohawks. That took courage. Or was she completely unaware of the danger she was in? He stepped closer.

"I speak English," he said quietly, and saw her cheeks turn fiery. She was roughly the same size as Eliza, but he had to admit, God forgive him, she was more beautiful. Never in his life had he seen such a perfect face or eyes so green, and her hair . . . He was taken aback by the masses and masses of silky curls the color of bleached wheat framing her oval face like an aureole of sunshine laced with moonbeams. Her green muslin gown, soiled and ripped at one shoulder, exposed white flesh that was as smooth as satin. She was a beauty, aye, but a haughtier, more arrogant little baggage he'd never had the misfortune to meet.

He pulled himself up short. Who the bloody hell was he to judge her? She and the other two maids had just come through a horrifying ordeal that was not over yet. In fact, he was not at all sure he could wrest them from the Oneidas.

Alexandra's cheeks stung as she blinked up at the brave towering over her. If he spoke English, why in blazes hadn't he said so before? But she felt a perverse gladness that he had heard her insults, because for his people to have stolen them was an outrage. Her country had won the war, after all. England was the conqueror and these people were conquered. She remembered then that certain Indians had fought for England—but surely not these. These looked so hostile . . .

Her heart bumping against her ribs, she met the jet-black eyes of the English speaker. He was taller than the other braves and his features were sharper and finer. There was no paint on his bronzed skin, only several tattoos on his arms, and two wide silver bands. His hair was long and straight, not in a ridiculous brush atop his head, and he carried himself with easy authority. She sensed instantly that he was intelligent, but she was frightened by the hot glitter in his eyes. No man in her safe, small world in England would ever have harmed a woman, but these were not Englishmen. These were savages. In truth, she did not understand why the honor of the three of them had been spared thus far.

"You should know," she spoke slowly and clearly as she would to a child, "That my father was the commander at Fort Tiyanoga." Her tears welled, but she or-

dered herself not to weep. She was damned if she
would show weakness before them. "He was slain by
the beasts who stole us, and I fear for all of you if we
are not released immediately."

Her news hit Adam like lightning. This was Chamberlain's daughter? And the old boy was dead? Sweet
Jesus, if that were the case, it would be futile for him
to plead the Indians' cause any further. He turned to
Kaga. "She says her father was slain. Is that so?"

Kaga grunted. "The Oneidas say the Grayhead was
but wounded in the ribs. He will recover to plague us
further."

Adam's relief was great as he turned to the spitfire.
"Your father lives. He was only wounded."

Alexandra bit her lip so it would not tremble. She
had seen her father fall and heard his awful strangled
cry. He was dead. They wanted merely to pacify her.
Well, she would not be pacified. She said stiffly:

"I don't believe you. Murder has been done, and you
have added to the crime by abducting us." Mayjay wept
louder.

"I?" Adam's mouth tilted. He had not seen such a
spunky maid since Eliza.

"You." Alexandra glared at him. She pointed a finger
at him and waved her arm at the grim-faced assem-
blage. "All of you are guilty, and I fail to see anything
amusing about the situation. Terrible punishment awaits
you from the Crown." She hoped to goodness it was so.

Adam's gaze moved over her lovely, frightened face.
He said quietly, "This is a Mohawk village, lady. It was
Oneidas who injured your father and took the three of
you." As he spoke, he saw the culprits striding toward
them.

"Mohawks, Oneidas, what's the difference? An Indian is an Indian." It was what her father had always
said, and now more than ever she had no reason to
doubt him. Seeing her captor pushing his way toward

her, she clenched her teeth against the expected pain. It came as his dark hand cruelly seized her upper arm.

"She is mine," the brave warned Adam in Mohawk.

Adam answered easily, "I never doubted it, my friend, but I would like to buy her from you."

The brave laughed. "For this one, it would take gold."

"I have gold."

The Oneida studied with narrowed eyes the tall brave with the quiet voice. He spoke as the Mohawks spoke and he carried Mohawk weapons, but he was not Mohawk. "Who are you?" he demanded.

"I am called the Cougar," Adam said.

A faint smile curved the Oneida's mouth. "I am called Mojag, and I have waited long to meet the Cougar." He turned to his comrades as they arrived. "This is the one of whom we have heard."

As Adam greeted the others in the band, he was met with the same warm camaraderie he always received in the villages. But he had sensed instantly the difference in Mojag. He was hostile. Adam understood it well. Adam was a threat. He wanted the Oneida's woman.

Mojag put on a false smile and clapped the Cougar's shoulder. "I have heard tales of your strength and your skill in fighting, my friend."

Adam said quietly, "They will have grown with each telling."

"I would see for myself, Cougar. A contest between us would do me great honor."

Adam deliberated quickly and carefully. Mojag was six feet tall, over several inches shorter than Adam, but he had more meat on his bones. He would be a strong opponent and eager for glory. But glory was not the prize Adam sought were he to win such a battle. What he sought was far more important.

"The honor is mutual, my friend," he replied gravely. "You will be a formidable opponent—but the prize must be worth the battle. I will have the women if I am victor."

Mojag answered sharply, "That is not possible. I will join with the Gold Hair when we reach our village."

Adam gave a slow smile. "It would seem you fear losing . . ." When the brave's dark eyes shuttered, Adam knew he had him. By God, he had him.

Mojag breathed a deep breath. "We will fight for the women then, but I will not lose. As for those two—" he looked with scorn to where Mary and Jane Hatch huddled on the ground, red-eyed and weeping. He grunted. "They are howlers, and you are welcome to them, win or lose. Our women would not permit them to live."

Adam suspected he was right. Indian women gave no mercy to the weak, men or women. "So be it. The three are mine after the battle."

Mojag said nothing. He skinned back his teeth in a smile and flexed his muscles.

Alexandra had watched with wide eyes as her Oneida captor confronted the tall Mohawk who spoke English. There was anger between them, she saw and felt it, so she was not surprised when it became apparent that they were going to fight. But she wished she knew why. She watched uneasily as they removed their weapons and began circling each other slowly, warily, their arms extended and their dark gleaming bodies crouched to spring. The crowd shouted when they closed finally and began to grapple.

"Alex . . ." It was a whisper from Jane Hatch. "What is happening? Wh-why are they fighting?"

"I don't know," Alexandra murmured, although an idea had come to her mind. Perhaps the Mohawk had taken heed of her words. Perhaps he was battling the Oneida to have them returned to Tiyanoga! Her heart pounded to think of it.

"But you suspect something . . ." Mary choked, her tears flowing anew.

"Nay." Alexandra shook her head. It was best not to raise any hopes that could be cruelly dashed.

Looking back toward the two panting, sweat-streaked warriors, she saw that the battle between them had grown brutal. And the Mohawk was winning. He was tall and strong and quick, and he fought so cleverly with his fists that her captor never had a chance. The battle ended almost before it had begun as the Oneida was sent sprawling with several terrible blows to his face and body. After the final blow, he struggled painfully to his feet, only to collapse when a breath of wind touched him.

Alexandra hid her jubilation. Now if only she were right. If only this Mohawk with the intelligent black eyes would return them to Tiyanoga. Oh, Lord, please let it be so, please. Closing her eyes, she said it over and over and over.

Adam had seen immediately that Mojag was not the great fighter he supposed himself to be. Adam could have downed him easily and painlessly, but when the Oneida tried to strike him below the belt, he knew he could not be gentle with him. If he were disabled by a low blow, the women would be in Mojag's power, and he could not risk it. Adam trounced him. After the short-lived battle, he extended a hand. Mojag, his face and body bloodied, ignored it. He climbed to his feet and moved off with his brethren in silence, but his eyes spoke. Adam was pondering their message when Kaga came to him.

"He is not a credit to his people, that one. You have done well, *rikena*. The Gold Hair will make you a fine squaw."

Adam knew the maid was watching him. He had seen her relief when he'd downed Mojag, but now he saw uncertainty in her eyes. "To wed her is not my purpose," he said, wiping the blood from his face.

"Then I will buy her from you," Kaga said.

"*Raktsia,* she is not for sale. I . . . have a use for her."

Kaga laughed, his dark eyes knowing. "Ah. What man would not?"

Adam allowed it to pass. There was no need for any but himself to know of the plot that was just now struggling to take shape in his brain. It was so hazy and fast-changing, he did not know what direction it would finally take. He considered and quickly discarded using her as a bargaining chip with her father—it was too distasteful. It seemed more reasonable to try to touch the heart of this maid by showing her the plight of his Mohawks. And if she reacted as he hoped . . . *Iah!* He would not think ahead that far. For now he would just show her the way things were.

"What of the other two?" Kaga asked.

Adam grinned. "I will show you." Motioning the sachem to follow, he strode toward the women. "You—" He spoke gruffly in English to the brown-haired weepers. "You will be given food and returned to Tiyanoga. You will not be harmed." At his words, the two gave a joyous shriek and fell into each other's arms.

Alexandra observed the tall Mohawk through a mist of happiness. She had prayed for them to be returned to the fort, and her prayers had been answered. Yet when he turned to her she shrank inside. Why was he looking at her so strangely? As if he were studying her. Her mouth was suddenly so dry from fright, she doubted she could make a sound, but she must. She must thank him for what he had just done. She did not want him to think they were ungrateful.

Adam's eyes flickered over the maid's beautiful face and body. Good Christ, if he had not been in this particular place at this particular time, she and her friends would have been carried westward to an Oneida village where they would have been made to run the gauntlet. He doubted the two weepers would have survived, just as he doubted this soft, golden city girl could have survived for long as the squaw of Mojag. He had seen the evidence of his harsh treatment of her in those ugly bruises on her white skin. He watched, enchanted, as she nervously pushed her wild mane of cornsilk hair out of her eyes and walked over to him.

Alexandra said simply, "We thank you for returning us." She blushed under his frowning scrutiny.

"Not you," Adam said crisply. "Only they go."

She stared up at him, and absolutely forbade herself to faint. "I—beg your pardon?" She saw that he was not listening. His black eyes had swung back to Mayjay.

"You will tell the commander of Tiyanoga that his daughter is safe," Adam ordered the maids.

"The commander of Tiyanoga is dead!" Alexandra cried. "I have told you—my father was slain!"

Adam ignored her outburst and continued to address the others. "He is to abandon all efforts to find her, for they will be fruitless. She will be returned at a time of my choosing, and she will be unharmed. Assure him of that. Do you understand?"

Jane hiccoughed and looked at Alexandra guiltily. "Aye."

Mary asked, "Who is th-the message from? Who are you?"

"I am the Cougar. Go now with the women. They will feed you before you depart."

"Thank you!" Mary gasped. "Thank you so very, very much—but we couldn't possibly leave without Alexandra!"

"Then you will not leave," Adam said.

Jane quavered, "We'll do everything you say, never fear."

Alexandra planted herself in front of the brave, her eyes sparkling with fury. She put her hands on her hips. "Why am I to stay?"

"We will talk later, you and I," Adam said. He turned to Kaga. "Now that this small matter is concluded, there are things of importance to discuss. I have been to Albany and I have—"

Alexandra stepped between them. "You can't do this! You simply can't keep me here against my will. I'm a subject of the Crown!"

Adam crossed his arms and gazed down at her. He saw that the color had drained from her face and fear had widened her green eyes. Her breath came in small pants through her rosy lips. He felt a pang of real regret at what he was about to do, but it was the only way he could protect her.

"You are in Mohawk country now, Gold Hair," he replied brusquely. "I fought a battle for you and I won it. You belong to me."

Alexandra felt herself sway. She shook her head as she looked up at his handsome dark face and hooded eyes. She said faintly, "Really, you . . . can't do this. I'm not some object to be won or lost or bought or sold. I'm . . . an Englishwoman. I . . . belong to myself!"

"You belong to me," Adam said. "You are mine."

"Please, nay . . ."

"It is so," the Cougar said. "I have said it."

Chapter 3

It was a nightmare, Alexandra thought, watching as her two friends were led to waiting Mohawk ponies and blindfolded. They were leaving—and she was being left behind with a savage who claimed he owned her.

"Are you still there, Alexandra?" Jane's voice was disgustingly cheerful.

"Where else would I be, pray?"

"Goodness, do keep up your spirits! Everything is going to be fine."

Mary said gently, "Look on the bright side, Alex. Your papa is alive and—"

"I doubt that very much," Alexandra snapped.

"Do try to think the best now. I am sure he is alive, and the Cougar says you will be returned to him."

"The Cougar also says I'm his. That doesn't inspire confidence."

"I . . . think you would be wise not to aggravate him, dear," Jane offered. "He seems a-a nice man."

"Hah!"

"She's right, Alex. Do placate him, and everything will be fine. If I were not so certain of it, I wouldn't leave you. And rest assured, we will tell your papa exactly what the, er, Cougar told us to tell him."

Angry and resentful as she was with them for their naiveté, Alexandra could not help but feel sorry for them. She saw that they were as terrified as she despite their good fortune. Jane was shaking, and Mary's teeth

40

were chattering noticeably. Alexandra went to her, embraced her, and whispered, "Goodbye—and good luck."

Mary clung to her tightly. "G-goodbye, a-and do take heart."

"I will." Alexandra embraced Jane next. "Goodbye, and go with God."

"Oh, Alex, I do hope you don't hate us for this. Y-you'll be fine, I know you will."

"So will you, and do assure Mama for me. She mustn't worry."

"We will, we promise. We'll tell her we're not a bit worried about you! Oh, Alex, I do wish you were coming with us . . ."

As they jogged off at the center of a band of silent braves, Alexandra's wrists were bound together by two women who then tethered her to a post. Left alone, she lowered herself to the ground, leaned against the post, and watched sullenly as the women returned to their chores, and the men seated themselves in a circle about the fire. She closed her eyes and breathed a deep breath. She had been counting on a miracle, but no more. This was the way things were. Her father was dead, and she was trapped in this impenetrable wilderness of foliage, wild animals, and savages, without the faintest idea of which direction to flee even if she had the chance. She was trapped and without her friends.

She sank her teeth into her lower lip and ordered herself not to think of it. If she did she would break down. She would think instead of Mojag and how much she hated him, and of how lovely it had been to see him sprawled on the ground spitting blood. It served him right, the beast.

For what seemed like hours, she leaned against the post with her eyes closed. Opening them, she saw that the men were still sitting around the fire, talking in low voices, and passing a foul-smelling pipe. The women were still working. Seeing them yoked to water buckets and struggling under large bundles of brush on their backs, Alexandra felt a flicker of pity. Why didn't the men stop their stupid talking and help them? As she glared balefully at the braves, the group disbanded and the Cougar strode toward her. He freed her abruptly from the tether and untied her hands.

"We are leaving."

Alexandra gave him a scathing look. "For Tiyanoga, I trust. For your sake, it had better be."

"Abandon the thought," Adam replied gruffly.

Outrage swept her. How dare he treat her this way? Yet who was to stop him? If her father were alive, he would leave no stone unturned to find her. But he was dead. Dead! Her throat burned with the hot, aching lump that would not leave. For two days now, she had been torn between wanting to weep her eyes out and not allowing herself to dwell on the tragedy. She sensed that these people would savor her sadness and terror and hold it as a victory. She said quietly, "You will be hanged, you know."

Adam declined to reply. He was studying her torn green gown and the fragile slippers on her small feet. She could not travel farther in such clothes. She would be up on Anoki with him, and those yards and yards of cloth would be one hell of a hindrance. He beckoned to a group of squaws who stood nearby staring at them, and spoke in Mohawk.

"Have you garb to spare for the maid, my friends?" When they nodded, he said, "Take her then, and dress her properly. In helping her, you help me and your people."

As the women approached, Alexandra shrank from them. And when they caught her arms and began to drag her with them, she cried out to the Cougar, "Where are they taking me?"

"You are dressed for the white man's house, not the wilderness. They will garb you in something more suitable." He took care that no trace of England sounded in his speech.

"I won't wear it."

"You will wear it."

"I will not!" She was on the verge of a tantrum, a thing she had not done in years.

"Then you will go naked."

Alexandra's face flamed. She gasped. "You'll pay for this!"

She went with the squaws, her golden head held high, and with silent dignity, she suffered them to strip and dress her in leggings, a shirt, and strange-looking shoes. She resented hugely that the garb felt soft against her skin and was not displeasing to the eye, decorated gaily as it was with feathers and beads. When she was returned to the Cougar, she felt so light on her feet, it was as if she were floating. Even so, she said icily:

"I suppose my own clothes have been stolen."

As she spoke, one of the women handed her a familiar bundle: her gown, petticoat, and chemise rolled neatly about her shoes and tied with a strip of rawhide. She thanked her crisply and then clutched the bundle tightly to her breasts, thinking, grieving that it was the only thing that remained of her life as she had known it. The only thing. Her torn clothes and muddied shoes. She stared sullenly at the ground.

Adam studied the maid's new attire approvingly. There was room aplenty for the two of them now on the black, and her weight could not be more than that of a feather. A cloud. What a fragile thing she was to have such spirit. Into his thoughts came the image of another fragile maid of spirit, that one laughing and brown-eyed. A maid he loved with all his heart and who had so loved him, she had come to this uncharted wilderness to be with him. Such a vise of pain clamped his heart, he clenched his teeth.

"We will go now," he said sharply, striding toward where Anoki grazed. When the girl did not move but stood staring at him defiantly, he snapped his fingers. "You, Gold Hair, come. We are leaving." He untied his mount.

Alexandra shot him a blazing look. "My name is not Gold Hair, it's Alexandra, and I'm not a dog for you to snap your fingers at me!"

Adam suppressed his amusement and reminded himself she was a child. A angry, frightened child who had been through hell. It was not her fault she was the seed of a bitter, small-minded man with the heart of a tyrant. He ordered himself to be patient with her and to soften his tongue. He held out his hand, said quietly, "I am leaving, Alexandra. Are you coming, or would you rather stay here? The chieftain of this tribe has offered to buy you from me." He watched as her wonderful green eyes widened.

"I-I'll come." Alexandra forced her lips to form the hated words, forced one foot in front of the other until she was standing beside him.

She shivered, hating that she felt so small and helpless next to him, and that his height and near-nakedness were making her skin tingle so pleasurably. And she hated it that he was the very picture of what she had imagined an Indian should look like—strong, formidable, with a lean hard body, a nose that was positively regal, his skin dark and polished, his long hair and eyes and brows jet-black. Blazes, how beautiful he was, but he was also a savage. And he said he owned her. And there was nothing she could do about it except write down everything he said and did so that he could be properly punished when he was caught.

Oh, aye, write it down—but with what, pray? And what made her think she would ever be found in this awful wilderness? It was more likely that she would be with this man until the end of her days. She would never see her mother again or her friends or the Larches or England. In fact, losing Alexandra on top of the death of her husband would surely kill Lydia Chamberlain. Oh, Mama . . .

Adam was pleased when Alexandra came to him willingly. While he had threatened to sell her to the sachem, it was never even a possibility. She was not his to sell. She was her own woman. Grasping the maid about her slim waist, he lifted her easily onto the deerskin tied on his stallion's back. She was as feather-light as he'd suspected. After leaping up behind her, he collected the reins and raised his hand in a farewell to the watching Mohawk. His black eyes found Kaga.

"I am glad we had this talk, *ion kiatenro*. Let yourselves bend with the winds until you hear from me again. I think you will be rewarded for your patience."

Kaga lifted his hand, his nod of assent nearly imperceptible. "Do not make us wait too long, *rikena*. Our patience is as limited as the game they leave us."

It was twilight as the black neared the Duke of Dover's trading post and the shack Adam shared with Jared. Aside from several stops to tend their needs, the maid had sat as stiff as a lodgepole and as silent as a stone within his arms. It was all right. He had nothing to say to her, either. Not just yet. After he took on fresh supplies and told Jared his plans, they would catch some sleep and then leave for the first village. He had decided night travel was safest, and one month was a sufficient length of time to show her the hardships inflicted on the Indians by bastards like her father. He'd been allowing himself to dream that she might have a heart, and that her pleas might move Chamberlain . . .

Suddenly he was overwhelmed with the impossibility of the thing. It would never work. From all he had seen, she was a cold, spoiled little wench with a heart of granite. And he ran the risk that some settler might stop by the trading post and spy her—and any who saw Alexandra Chamberlain would never forget her. Not with that incredible mop of blond angel-hair and that sensuous yet innocent face of hers. To boot, no white man, not even Jared, had seen him in his breechclout and moccasins. It was his habit to change his clothing before entering a village or returning to the store. Damnation, he'd not used his head at all in his first wild euphoria. As the trading post came into sight, he knew his first task was to get Jared alone. He dismounted, tethered Anoki to the rail, and addressed the maid sternly:

"Do not think of escape, Alexandra. Night is upon us and there are bears in these woods. And rattlesnakes." Seeing her blink, he knew his message had reached her. Even so, he did not go into the store but called to his cousin from the stoop: "Jared, it is the Cougar."

Jared Pennburton had been taking inventory when he heard Adam calling from outside. He frowned, noting his cousin's voice was not quite his own but was slightly accented, the careful way an Indian spoke English. He smiled. So. The Cougar, was it? This was carrying the Indian bit too far. It was all right for him to play Mohawk when he was with Mohawks, but not with him. After tossing down his quill, he strode to the door.

"Man, it's all right to—" He gaped at the sight that greeted him. Adam in breechclout and moccasins, a bow and quiver slung over one shoulder, a dark finger to his lips, and behind him aboard the black, a woman. A very blond, very beautiful, very frightened woman in Indian garb. What in God's name? Picking up on Adam's cue, he quickly got his face under control. "Greetings, uh, Cougar. How can I help you, my friend?"

"We need lodging for a few hours. Can you put us up?" Then Adam said low, "Put your eyes back in, old man, it's not what you think."

"What is it then, old boy?" Jared muttered, but raised his voice to go along with the game: "You I can always accommodate, my friend, if you're not too picky."

"I am not picky—I can sleep anywhere, but the child needs a bed." He added in a whisper, "I won her from an Oneida. It was a damned good fight . . ."

Jared's astonished gaze returned to the exquisite creature on Adam's mount. Child? He said under his breath, "Have you looked at that *child* closely, old man?"

Adam turned, felt his heart thud. Was this the same female he had lifted onto Anoki back at the Mohawk village? She had been beautiful, aye, sullen and wasp-tongued though she was, but he'd thought she was a young maid. He would have sworn it. But this vision was no child. The last slanting rays of the sun etched the fullness of each breast and emphasized the soft lines of her doeskin-clad thighs against the gleaming black barrel of his mount. Her lips were full and pink and soft, her chin and cheeks and throat white and rounded, the frightened green eyes wide and luminous. He stared. This was a woman, aye, and more beautiful by far than he had remembered. Her hair was a corona of dazzling white-gold framing her face, and the pale, delicate brows arching over her gold-lashed eyes were winged perfection. He turned back to Jared, whispered:

"Sweet Jesus."

"I agree." Jared gave the vision a smile and made a sweeping bow. "Welcome to my humble abode, my lady. What's mine is yours. What repast may I prepare for your delectation? You have but to—"

"Please," Alexandra cried, "save me from this savage!" She had been too terrified to speak or move, realizing she had two men to contend with as darkness fell, but this was an Englishman! It seemed he owned this store and lived in the small hut beside it, and from his sleek blond head and neatly trimmed beard to his well-polished boots, he looked a gentleman. Decent and honorable and—and normal. What a relief! "Sir, I beg you, don't let him take me from here. Keep me with you! Please, I beg you. This beast"—she gave the Cougar a look of loathing—"thinks h-he owns me."

Jared gave Adam an uneasy glance. "Well, now, little lady, I'm sure he'll treat you well . . ."

Alexandra's mouth fell open. "You dare to say you'll not help me? And you an Englishman?" He looked so wretched, it gave her hope. "Sir, I throw myself on your mercy."

Adam bent to his cousin's ear, growled. "She's old Chamberlain's daughter. The Oneidas wounded him, not badly, I hear, and stole her and two other women. I've sent the others back to Tiyanoga, but before this one goes back, she's damned well going to see how my Mohawks have to live."

Jared blinked. "Upon my soul, what a stroke of luck. D'you think it'll work?"

"I doubt it, but I have to try."

Seeing the two with their heads together, Alexandra felt her heart tremble. It sank when the Englishman returned his somber gaze to her. "Sir, I beg of you. If you have a mother, a sister . . ."

Jared said brusquely, "I'm sorry."

For one shining moment, she had thought he was an honorable man, an ally, but he was neither. "In truth, *sorry* describes you well," she flared. "You're not only a coward and a traitor to our country, you're a bloody Indian-lover!" Hearing herself, Alexandra was shocked. She sounded just like Papa . . .

As she had watched Mayjay greedily gobbling the food the Mohawk women had offered them, Alexandra had vowed she would starve rather than eat with the enemy. Now she was ravenous, and the Englishman, traitor and coward though he was, had a way with meat and potatoes and onions, frying them all together in a heavy skillet over the flames. She had hoped he and the Cougar would talk during the meal so she might get some idea of where this place was and what was going to happen to her, but she was disappointed. They had eaten in silence. Now, sitting around the fire with the dark pressing in on them, she could stand it no longer. Putting her tin plate and fork on the ground, she looked across the glowing embers at the brave.

"Why?" she demanded. "Why did you let my friends go home and not me?"

"There are things I would have you see . . ."

Adam had kept his gaze on the fire as he ate. Looking at her was too painful. It reminded him that she was not Eliza, and that until now, no woman but Eliza had sat at their cookfire sharing food with them.

"I can't imagine what could be so important that I personally have to see it," Alexandra retorted. "I've seen all I care to, believe me." Her flesh crawled as a sudden deep snarl erupted from the black woods surrounding their small haven of light and warmth. It was hideously near and sounded like a giant cat. She lay a hand on her heart. "Wh-what is *that?*"

"Puma," Jared said. Seeing that she did not understand, he added, "It's a mountain lion. A cougar. They're all one and the same."

A cougar? Alexandra's frightened gaze went to the brooding Mohawk brave named Cougar who sat hunched before the flames.

"You needn't worry," Jared continued easily. "It's just a mother cat who's been hunting the area these past few nights. She doesn't stay. She doesn't like the fire."

Adam abruptly got to his feet. "It is time we turned in."

"Right." Jared collected the plates and started for the hut. "I'm clearing out for a bit. The night's young and I've my lady to visit—but first I'll shake the bedding for you."

"Not on my account!" Alexandra called after him sharply and climbed to her feet. "I'm not sleepy." If they thought she was going to get into a bed and shut her eyes for one instant with that beast of a savage looking on, they were badly mistaken.

Adam shrugged. "As you wish, but you will join me while I sleep." He saw that her eyes had turned from green to gold with reflected firelight.

Alexandra's flesh crept as his dark gaze moved over her. "So that's what this is all about. You want to bed me ..." The words popped out so unexpectedly, she shocked herself. Idiot! If the thought had not entered his head, she had just put it there. In addition, ladies did not say such things. But since she had been so gauche as to say it, she might as well say the rest of it. "Know this. If you touch me, if you dare, I'll slay you! Nothing less will suffice."

Adam chuckled. "In that case, Gold Hair, I will certainly not touch you." He did not like the little wench, but by God, her honesty was refreshing. He would always know what she thought, for she would not hesitate to tell him. He pointed to the woods. "Tend to your needs, Alexandra. Do not tarry."

Alexandra stared at the blackness and then back at him. "The ... cougar is there ..."

"She is gone. There is only this Cougar." He tapped his chest. "I will be here waiting for you."

Bed. It was as narrow as a post and twice as hard, but it was his own and it had never felt so good to Adam. He did not intend to sleep. He wanted only to stretch out his tired legs and rest for a while. Yawning deeply, he looked over to where the spitfire sat stiffly in the other bed, arms and legs crossed and her back against the clay-chinked wall.

"Sleep, Alexandra," he said quietly.

She made no reply. In the candle's soft glow, he saw the hatred burning in her eyes. And the disgust. When he'd finally had to grasp her arm and rough-march her into the shack, he had seen and felt her inward shrinking as she looked about her at the small bed-sitting chamber he and Jared shared. It was clear she was too fine a lady to inhabit such a place even for a few hours.

Adam's lips curved as he remembered Eliza's childish delight at her first sight of the corncob mattresses and packed-earth floor and small hearth. She had said it was cozy. And she had made the little red curtain that still brightened the window, and with her own small hands she had pieced together with colorful scraps of cloth the two coverlets on the beds. She had wanted it to look nice for Jared.

Adam rolled onto his side, his heavy-lidded gaze fixed on the daughter of Wade Chamberlain. She would sleep soon. He had seen the signs of her exhaustion as they ate. And when she slept, he would close his own eyes for just a short time. His cousin would have returned from visiting his German sweetheart by then. He sighed, thinking what a pleasant sight Alexandra was in comparison to old Jared in his nightshirt—her hair a flaxen cloud framing her face, her feminine curves delightfully obvious in the dancing shadows. How in God's name, he wondered sleepily, could he have thought she was a child? He yawned deeply. No matter. All that mattered was that she had a heart.

When he turned onto his back again, his eyes lit on the dreamcatcher hanging from the rafter over his head. It was a small willow hoop holding a net of grass and decorated with beads and feathers. Lark had given it to Eliza, explaining how bad dreams were caught in the net while the good ones slipped through the hole in its center. When Lark had cared for him those four lost months after Eliza's death, her own dreamcatcher had hung over his head each night. Now, gazing up at Eliza's and remembering how she had treasured it, Adam felt his body turn to stone. He stretched, yawned, flexed his muscles, but stone he remained. Numb, without life or feeling. He sighed. It was a thing he had grown accustomed to.

* * *

Alexandra sat very still as the brave tossed on his narrow bed. Each time his eyes sought her, she knew terror. They were alone, they were in beds, and he was naked—or might as well have been. The doeskin that covered him in the front and back was scarcely decent. When he rolled onto his back again, seeming to study the strange circular object that hung from the rafter over his head, her frightened green eyes never left him. He was like some great golden animal lying there, its dark skin gleaming in the half-light. And when he yawned and stretched, bringing every muscle and sinew into play, Alexandra's heart leaped. Blazes. What a crying shame that he was a savage. Why did the men in England and New York City not look like that?

She watched, breathless, as his heavy lids closed, opened, and then closed ... opened ... closed. And remained closed. She sat motionless, afraid to move or even to breathe, and wondered, Had he fallen asleep? Could she be so lucky? She listened, heart thundering, to his breathing. It was slow and deep and even. Oh, God, he was asleep. He was! He had actually fallen asleep, and the Englishman was still gone. She had not heard him return. Should she try to escape? For this might be her only chance. Certainly it was the first chance she'd had since she was stolen. She could take his horse. It was in a small enclosure beside the store.

Fresh trembling seized her as she realized she did not know where the bridle was, nor could she take the time to look for it. Yet did she dare go on foot as well as unarmed into those woods that were filled with snakes, bears, mountain cats, and Indians? She decided instantly that anything was better than waiting in terror for the Cougar to awaken and come to her. Anything. Having seen the sun set, she knew east from west and north from south, and the river she had seen earlier in

the day was surely the Hudson. She had only to find
and follow it south to end up eventually at Tiyanoga.
Silently she slid from her bed, crossed the earthen floor,
and slipped out into the night.

Chapter 4

A dam opened his eyes abruptly. Seeing the dreamcatcher spinning and its feathers stirring, he suspected that a breeze blowing through the small open window had awakened him. Damn, he had never meant to sleep. He hadn't a doubt the spitfire would take off like a rabbit if she got the chance. But then she was probably sound asleep by now and— He froze, seeing the other bed empty. He quickly got to his feet.

"Alexandra?" Nothing. He slung his quiver over his shoulder and took up his bow. Moving swiftly through the kitchen to the front door, he saw that the cot that stood there was empty. Jared had not yet returned.

He went out into the night, his eyes scanning the clearing and the woods beyond. The moon was huge and so bright, he saw easily that Anoki was still in the paddock. The stallion raised his head, nickering softly. Adam did not hear him. His every sense was alerted to the dangers for the woman. She was too fragile a thing and too inexperienced to be fleeing through these black woods on foot and unarmed. She was also a fool. But then perhaps she had just gone out to relieve herself and was close by. Heartened by the thought, he called softly, "Alexandra . . ." There was a long silence before her voice came, small and choked with fright:

"I'm here. Please . . . help me . . ."

A low growl told him that the cougar had returned

and had found her. As he rapidly strung his bow, he called to her, "I'm coming. Keep talking so I can find you." He was as angry with her as he was fearful for her. He had never killed one of the big cats, nor did he want to, but if it was necessary in order to save her, he would not hesitate. Damn the woman.

Alexandra was backed against a great oak, and not more than ten feet away was the cougar. For what seemed an eternity, the creature, its tail switching, had lain gazing at her. Now it blinked its tawny eyes, yawned, licked its huge chops, and gave another deep, hollow-sounding growl.

"She . . . doesn't seem too hungry," Alexandra quavered, obeying the brave's command to keep talking. "She's just . . . lying here . . . looking at me . . . a-and yawning." Her flying heart shook her entire body. Her legs simply would not have supported her had the tree not been there. "But do hurry, please! Except—oh, dear, you're not going to kill her, are you? I don't really want her hurt . . . She's so beautiful . . . and if she has babies . . . Oh, dear." She made a small helpless noise, half hiccough, half sob, imagining the big cat slain and its cubs without a mother. And all because of her.

Suddenly the Cougar was there, charging the astonished beast, shouting in his deep voice, and waving his arms and his bow to frighten it. By the time Alexandra realized what had happened, the beast had bounded into the woods and disappeared. She was close to weeping in her relief that everything was all right. The mother would go home to its babes and she herself was alive. The Cougar had saved her. Quite impulsively, she threw her arms about his neck.

"Thank you so much! Oh, thank you . . ."

Feeling his tall, hard body against hers, Alexandra leaped back. What a stupid, stupid thing to do. He would misunderstand. Besides, this whole horrible thing was his fault. If he had sent her back to Tiyanoga with the others, it never would have happened.

Adam's nerves were as taut as his bowstring. It had been a close thing. In another moment, the cat might have sprung, and he would have slain it. He had no choice. But his anger toward Alexandra was gone. Her childish gratitude had touched him, and her soft breasts and body pressed so unexpectedly against him was a thing he would not soon forget. And she had surprised him with her gentle heart for animals. But what about people? Could he open her heart toward his Mohawks?

"Are you all right?" he asked gruffly. When she nodded, not looking at him, he resisted lecturing her on what a foolish thing she had done. Her chattering teeth told him that she knew already. They returned to the shack in silence, and in the candlelight, Adam saw the purple smudges under her eyes and how tired she was. "It is several hours yet before we leave. We can still get some rest."

Alexandra watched, astonished, as he began to drag her bed across the earth floor. "What are you doing?"

He parked it beside his. "Making sure you do not sleepwalk again." He went into the small kitchen, found a length of rope, and returned.

Her breath caught when she realized that he meant to tie her to the bed. "Nay!" her voice rose to a shriek as he approached her. "Stay away from me!"

Ignoring her small fists pummeling him, Adam deftly slipped the rope around her waist and knotted it. Alexandra tried frantically to pick the knot loose, but he had tied it too tightly. "Damn you!"

Adam kept his temper. He was remembering that she had not wanted him to kill the cougar and leave its cubs motherless. He said softly, "Lie down, Alexandra."

"I won't!"

"Lie down and be quiet, or I will see that you do. Choose."

Seeing the look in his eyes, Alexandra swallowed the venomous reply she wanted to make. She lay down, her face turned away from him, but she knew he was wrapping the other end of the rope about his own waist and knotting it. Her fear nearly smothered her, but at least he had not bound her to the bed, rendering her helpless. It was small comfort. She heard his bed creak as he, too, lay down, so close she could feel the heat from his body.

She clenched her teeth, ordered herself not to think of his blasted body—and saw it immediately in her mind's eye: tall, powerful, those long dark arms and legs . . . She swallowed. Very well, admit it! Go ahead. He was virile and comely even though he was a savage. In fact, every other man she had ever known looked like a schoolboy in comparison. A pale, puny, piddling schoolboy. It simply was not fair. And it was hideous that she should be here alone with him in this wild black wilderness—and tied to him.

Again fear caught her by the throat. If she moved, he would know it. He could hear her every breath, just as she heard his. And if he moved his hand the slightest bit to the left, he would touch her thigh. Slowly, silently, Alexandra drew in a shaky breath and let it sigh out. He had been warned; if he touched her, she would slay him. Somehow, someday, somewhere, she would slay him. But more immediately, she had teeth and nails and she knew where and how to kick a man who needed kicking. Her blood ran faster at the thought. She almost wished he would lay a hand on her. He would get the surprise of his life.

Knowing she was not defenseless relaxed her enough so that she yawned several times, and then slowly, cautiously, she turned her head toward him. He was on his back, his eyes closed. Through lowered lids, she studied him. The scant breechclout; a hard, flat belly; polished

...k skin; his thick ebony hair spread over one brawny shoulder; and that magnificent nose, like a triangle jutting out from his face.

Oh, my . . . A soft sigh slipped past her lips. He was absolutely stupefying, and Sara and Justine would goggle if they could see him. Whoever would have dreamed when she told her mother about Indians stealing white women that it would actually come to pass? And that she would be the one stolen—and her father slain. The heavy feeling of despair settled over her again. It came every time she thought of him, but it seemed lighter this time somehow. Perhaps she was almost ready to believe the Cougar's assertion that he had only been wounded—or perhaps she was too weary to think clearly.

Her eyes, heavy-lidded now, were still fastened on the brave. So he was marvelous-looking. So what. It did not eliminate the fact that he was a tyrant who demanded her obedience. And if he thought for one instant that she was going to submit meekly, he was sorely mistaken. She was going to make him sorrier than sorry that he'd not sent her back to Tiyanoga with Mayjay. She would make his life miserable. And just as soon as she could, she was going to attempt another escape. And the next time she would not leave unarmed; she would steal his knife. A yawn interrupted her thoughts, and then another and yet another as she pondered what he would do if he caught her fleeing again . . .

She was still brooding over it when she realized she was no longer in bed, but was wandering through a forest shrouded in mist. How strange, yet how wonderful. She had just been thinking of escape, and now here she was, free. But she sensed that the woods were filled with danger. Someone, or something, was lurking out there and was moving toward her. Mojag? Was it Mojag? Oh, God . . .

Alexandra held her breath, listening over the roaring of her heart to the snapping of branches and the sound of breathing. Her skin crawled. She knew suddenly that it was not Mojag coming for her. It was the Cougar, and she had to get away from him. Mama was waiting. She tried to move her legs, to run, but she could not. It was as if she were wading against a strong tide. She opened her mouth and screamed and screamed, but no sound came.

Suddenly a figure loomed out of the mist before her . . . A man, tall and shadowy . . . a man who held out his hand to her. Alexandra clutched it, knowing as she did that she would be safe with him. He was a haven. Sanctuary. The awful nameless threat behind her in the mist could no longer harm her. She did not know who her savior was, she could not see his face, but when he opened his arms, she stepped within them. And when they closed about her, she knew she had come home.

His hands were warm and protective as they moved over her, and when his lips met hers in a long hungry kiss, her first kiss, she felt as if every bone in her body were melting. It was a thing she had never experienced before, and she craved more. She wanted him to kiss her again and again; she wanted to feel his strength and warmth and the fire he was stirring within her forever.

"Alexandra . . ."

The deep whisper was close to Alexandra's ear, and it filled her with delight. How astonishing that he knew who she was!

"Wake up, Gold Hair."

Alexandra clutched her unknown savior to her more closely. "Please, not yet. Just hold me . . ." She lifted her hungry mouth for more kisses.

Adam smiled, gave her shoulder a gentle shake. "There is no time for me to hold you. We must leave."

lexandra's eyes flew open. Seeing the dreary little room and the Cougar bending over her, she felt a rush of emptiness and loss. Oh, nay. It was a dream! Her wonderful savior was only a dream. She sat up, dazed, and rubbed her eyes. In the half-light, she saw that the rope which had joined them was no longer tied about his waist, only her own. She plucked futilely at the knot with fingers that were weak from sleep.

"Come, Gold Hair. Be quick and be quiet."

She blinked. Beyond the window, the sky was black. "It's still night . . ."

"That is so. Come." When she got to her feet too rapidly, she swayed. His hands went quickly to her shoulders, steadying her.

Alexandra pushed them away, whispered furiously, "Don't touch me!"

Adam clenched his teeth. The contrary little wench. He said crisply, "Untie the rope."

Alexandra tried. "I can't!" The knot was as beastly tight as when he'd tied it.

"Then I must touch you." His strong fingers quickly undid it, and then he coiled the rope and laid it on her bed. "Come," he said softly, sliding his quiver and bow over his shoulder and taking up the candle.

As they moved through the tiny kitchen, Alexandra noticed that the Cougar now wore pale leggings and a tunic. She saw, too, that the beast of an Englishman had returned and was sleeping there. Following the brave into the adjoining store, she gazed about in surprise. The walls were filled with shelves, and the shelves were laden with goods. This small trading post in the middle of nowhere had more wares than she had seen even in London shops.

"I have already gathered supplies for our journey," the Cougar said. He placed the candle on the counter, where it filled the low-raftered room with soft light and shadows. "Do you see anything you need?"

Alexandra crossed her arms and looked at him stonily. "My need is to be returned to Tiyanoga."

"Forget Tiyanoga," Adam replied curtly. Seeing the sudden high color in her cheeks, he wondered for the first time if a man was waiting for her back at the fort. If so, he felt sorry for him. The poor devil would be going out of his head with worry. "We will be traveling hard this next month or so—"

"This next month!"

"I have said it. You will be with me for at least a month, perhaps more, so look around. If you want or need anything, get it now."

A month or more . . . Alexandra shook her head. The thought made her absolutely ill. "The only thing I want," she choked, "is to be back with my mother."

"So be it," Adam said brusquely. "If you want nothing here, we will leave now." He bent to blow out the candle.

"Wait!" Alexandra had seen a familiar sight on one of the shelves. "Is that writing paper?"

Adam gave one nod. *"Hen."*

She looked about, confused, half-expecting to see a chicken appear. "What do you mean, *hen?"*

Adam did not smile. *"Hen* means aye. That is writing paper."

"Then I want it." She drew closer. It was a tablet of foolscap. She could write a whole book on it. Frowning at the other wares in the dimness, she said, "And I want quills and ink." She told herself to be calm; she was appearing far too eager.

Adam scowled at her. "What would a woman do with such things?"

"The same as a man," she replied sharply. "Write. I've always kept a journal." And in addition to the journal, she would leave behind her a trail of messages that someone was sure to find. She watched in secret triumph as he collected three bottles of ink, several quills, and the foolscap. Hallelujah!

"It is good." Adam gave her a look of approval. In truth, he knew of no woman other than Eliza who had ever bothered to learn to write or read. "In your talking papers," he said, "you can tell of the things I will show you. I will keep these supplies for you, of course." Seeing her face fall, he smiled, said softly, "*Iah,* Gold Hair, you will not be leaving any messages behind you."

Alexandra said nothing, but she yearned to kick him. How could he have guessed so exactly what she'd meant to do? She watched glumly as he put her writing things in a buckskin bag that lay on the counter.

"You have no other needs?" Adam asked.

The devil nudged her. "I have many needs. Soap, a comb"—her eyes flew over the shelves—"that blanket and knife, this cup and that little mirror—" His big hand closed about her arm, silencing her. She gave him a glare that could kill.

"Soap and a comb are sufficient," he said, and added them to his bag. He blew out the candle. "Come."

Alexandra followed him reluctantly. They stole past the snoring shopkeeper and went out into the chilly April night, where he easily hoisted her aboard his horse and mounted behind her. She tensed as his arms slid about her once more and his dark hands took the reins. The hardness of his chest and his warmth pressed against her back and caused her to recall instantly, vividly, the heady memory of her dream and her savior. He'd been so gentle and protective, so passionate and hungry—and so real. He was a man she could have loved. Remembering his tall, shadowy form, and remembering the way he had made her feel, Alexandra could not stop the silent prayer that came from her depths.

Dear God, please . . . Please let there be such a man . . . Let him come galloping out of the woods right now . . . Let him take me from the Cougar and

*return me to Mama ... and let him kiss me all the way
back to Tiyanoga ... Please ...*

Alexandra felt her entire body burning with embarrassment. She was awful, wasting a prayer on such a
stupid thing as a dream and kisses. It did not deserve to
be answered. Her mother would be appalled, and so
would her father. She shuddered and mentally lashed
herself for forgetting, even for an instant, that he was
gone. Papa was gone, no matter what this brave said.

They had not ridden far through the cool, moon-
dappled woods when the Cougar stopped his mount.
Gazing where he pointed, Alexandra felt her skin crawl.
Something large and glistening was obstructing their
path. Something dead. Things were moving upon and
within it.

"Wh-what is it?" she gasped.

"Bear. Some greedy white has done this. They want
only the fur, and leave the carcass to rot."

Alexandra was horrified, but she bristled at the accusation. "Why do you think it was a white man? Why
not an Indian?"

"No Indian would take the meat from the mouths of
his children," Adam muttered. He signaled Anoki to
move on.

Adam had been enjoying holding Alexandra's slender
body within the circle of his arms. Secretly he had
brushed his lips over her wild, silky mane of hair when
its lavender scent taunted him beyond endurance. He
imagined burying his face in its fragrance and between
her white breasts. He remembered well their softness
and fullness from when she'd hugged him so unexpectedly. God knew, he was stirred by her and wanted to
make love to her, but he knew the pleasure would be
short-lived. It would serve only to remind him further
of how empty his life had become. His hunger for Eliza
had been bound so tightly to his love for her that hunger alone for a woman held little temptation for him
anymore.

Thinking of it, he sat straighter so as not to touch the body of the maid sitting before him. He grimly pointed out yet another bear carcass to Alexandra, and then another. Moments later, they came to a pond. Heaped about it were the carcasses of ten skinned beavers left to rot.

Alexandra bit back her tears. At the Larches and in her aunt's household in New York City, servants did the marketing, a cook prepared the food, and other servants placed it on an elegantly appointed table for them to eat. She was unused to the idea of killing animals to survive, although she understood the necessity of it, but this—all of these poor animals slain for their fur and just tossed aside. It was dreadful, but she hid her distress from the Cougar.

"This is what you wanted me to see?"

"Among other things."

"But why? What has it to do with me?"

"Your country has laws forbidding whites to hunt on Indian land."

"Well then?"

"Your father and others ignore the laws."

Alexandra turned her head to give him an icy stare. "My father?" He might as well have accused him of murder—or of cheating at cards.

"He is one of the worst offenders."

"My father is dead!" Her voice broke. "He was slain by your people!"

"He was wounded by Oneidas, not Mohawks," Adam replied, not too patiently, "and he will be around to torment us for years to come."

"Why do you speak of him so cruelly? What has he ever done to you?"

Adam reined and indicated the black woods surrounding them. "This was Mohawk land long before your people came from across the sea. We would gladly have shared it with you, and shared the water and the game, for there is plenty for all. But your people will share with no one. They squat on our land, fence it, and are now stripping it of game. Not out of need but for the hides. Hides and pelts mean money, and it is important for the white man to have more and more money so he can live better than his neighbor."

Alexandra was enraged by his unfairness. "Are you blaming my father for the greed of every white in New York Colony?"

Adam raised a wall between him and the heat of her fury. Her loyalty to the man was only natural, and she could not understand until she had seen more. Perhaps even then she would not understand. He said quietly, "Your father is the commander of a large garrison and responsible for enforcing the law. Instead he looks the other way."

"How dare you make such an accusation when he's g-gone and can't defend himself!"

Adam set his jaw. To argue would be a waste of breath. There was no way to get it into that beautiful head of hers that Wade Chamberlain was alive and was the meanest bastard in the land. For the next hour they rode in simmering silence under a high bright moon. During a brief stop, he gave her a piece of jerky and a small handful of pemmican, for there would be no cooked food en route.

Alexandra's lip curled. "What, pray, is this?"

"It is food," he growled. "Eat."

Alexandra knew very well that it was food, and in truth she was famished. But her hatred for the Cougar was stronger by far than her hunger. She looked at his offering as if it had legs and had crept from beneath a rock. "In my country," she said stiffly, "we give our dogs food that looks better than this." She hurled it to the ground.

Adam gazed at her with shuttered eyes. "Lady," he said low, "it has taken more patience than you will ever possess for our women to make the food you have just thrown away. I will not share it with you so freely from now on. That is a promise." After lifting her onto Anoki's strong back, he mounted behind her and gave the horse his heels. But he wished he had paddled her rump first, the spoiled-rotten little witch.

Chapter 5

The other women in the lodge were up and about when Lark crawled out of the bedshelf in her family's compartment. Walking out into the soft, cool air of the April dawn, she saw that her mother had a pot of cornmeal already bubbling over the fire.

"Good morning, my mother. I did not mean to sleep so late."

"You were restless last night," Fox Woman said, filling a bowl and handing it to her.

Lark thanked her and seated herself on her mat before the fire. "I am sorry if I disturbed you."

She had yearned for sleep to rescue her from her worrisome thoughts of the Cougar, but all the night long her mind had sought his image and the remembered sound of his voice. So far, she had been too shy to tell her mother about him. She was too shy even to look at the Englishman when he came to their village, except for an occasional stolen glimpse. But when he came last, he had smiled at her, and she wondered, Was he remembering that they had made love? Had it meant anything to him at all? Her heart went louder and faster, remembering how they had fit into each other's arms, but at the same time she shivered, contemplating telling Fox Woman that she wished him for a husband. And she feared even more telling Old Father and her brother, the chieftain.

It was not that they did not respect and admire the Cougar, she told herself as she ate the cornmeal. *Iah*. It

67

was that she herself was so lacking in worth. All would wonder at her presumptuousness in asking for a man of such high standing when she was not the true daughter of this royal Mohawk family with whom she dwelt. She was a nobody. Long ago, Akando the Seneca had slain her own family, stolen her, and taken her into slavery. Lark sighed and continued eating. She did not want to think of that now. She wanted only to think of the sign she had received that the Cougar was going to be her man. Three nights in a row, she had dreamed that they were wed.

Fox Woman gathered her blanket more tightly about her thin shoulders and gray head. She hid her curiosity, seeing the flood of pink touching Lark's cheeks and the way her eyes had brightened. It was a look she had noted many times in young women, but she had despaired of ever finding it on the face of this girl of hers.

"My daughter, what is it?" When Lark hid her face in her hands and shook her head, Fox Woman chuckled. "Perhaps you have settled on a husband." Seeing the maid's blush deepen, she knew she was right. She stroked Lark's petal-smooth cheek. "Is it so, child?"

Lark's tongue had never been forked, and she could not bring herself to lie now. "*Hen,* my mother."

Fox Woman's heart sang for her, and her wrinkled face lit with a smile. Ever since Silver Hawk had brought her home to them, a frightened, ragged Ojibwa maid of thirteen winters whom he had won in a game of hand, Fox Woman had sought to make her life a happy one. And she had prayed to the Great Creator again and again that Lark would find such happiness as she herself had found with her own old one.

"Who is he?" she asked softly, her brown eyes twinkling.

Again Lark shook her head. Her cheeks grew pinker than ever. "My mother, I cannot tell you. Not yet. Forgive me."

Fox Woman frowned, wondered, Had this to do with

Silver Hawk? Her chieftain son was tall and comely and powerful with the women, drawing them to him the way honey drew flies, but he tired of them easily and had never joined. He had shocked Fox Woman recently by admitting he wanted Lark for his woman. She refused him outright. Lark knew him only as a brother, and such a union could harm her greatly. In addition, it would create a fine scandal for certain gossiping old women who had by now forgotten the girl was adopted. But if Lark herself wanted Silver Hawk, if she loved him, it was a different matter. She nodded, whispered:

"There is nothing to forgive, my daughter, and it will be as you wish. We will not speak of this now."

"Niawen," Lark murmured.

She finished her meal hurriedly and fled into the darkness before her mother could change her mind. She bathed in the nearby stream, combed and braided her hair, and quickly scoured the breakfast bowls and spoons. All the while her thoughts were filled with the Cougar. He was coming. Her body always sensed it before her eyes and ears grew aware of it. It had been that way since she had first set eyes on him. She was connected to this man in a way she did not understand and had never heard of before.

"I will water the horses now, my mother. What would you have me do next?"

"As soon as it is light, you can begin hoeing for the next planting. After, help the others to remove the rocks and roots from the south field."

"I will do it."

Lark's heart had wings as she filled the water buckets, fastened them to the yoke across her slender shoulders, and bore them back to the thirsty horses. He was coming. Her beloved was coming. Usually he came in order to discuss matters of importance with the men, and when men talked, women remained silent. But perhaps this time she would say hello to him, and he would say hello to her. Perhaps this time he would accept food and she could serve him and their fingers would touch. Her heart continued to fly as she poured the water into the troughs and carried the buckets back to the stream and lowered them. He was coming . . .

It was then, as the sky was turning pearl-gray, that she saw a flicker of movement and heard a faint sound in the woods across the stream. She knew it was the Cougar even before she discerned the gleaming black coat of his mount and saw its tall rider. But the sun fell from her sky as Lark saw that he was not alone but had a woman sitting before him. The most beautiful woman she had ever seen. As Lark gazed at her, she felt a great hot lump fill her throat. It was as it had been on that day when Adam had brought Her She Could Not Name to their castle and said she was his wife. Was this his new wife, then? She could have wept, but instead she held her head high and stood waiting as they drew near. She would not allow her tears and her tongue to dishonor her.

Alexandra had made the entire journey in wintry silence, but she had simmered inside all the way. She had been relieved when the Cougar did not try to bed her, aye, but it was fast followed by outrage. To think, he expected her to incriminate her own father by writing down all the terrible things he'd presumably caused to happen. Oh, aye. The Cougar, in his wisdom, had decreed that her poor papa was the villain behind every woe that had ever befallen his people. Never mind that he had been slain. In the Cougar's mind, he was alive, and evil. The most evil man in the Colonies.

She got all hot inside just thinking of the quiet scorn in the brave's voice and eyes when he spoke of Wade Chamberlain. He despised him. Well, she despised the Cougar! And no matter what he might do to coerce her, she would never destroy her father's memory or stain his reputation. Never. She started as he spoke suddenly, his deep voice close to her ear:

"We are coming to a Mohawk castle, Gold Hair. It is a larger village within a palisade."

Alexandra pressed her lips together. She yearned to tell him that a castle was a great, brooding stone dwelling with towers and turrets and parapets and a moat. In England, a castle looked the way a castle should. She wanted to thwart and insult and infuriate him, but common sense told her she did not dare. She was in his power, and if she wanted to see her mother again, she could not criticize every small thing he said, or lash out at his slanderous comments about her father. Yet how could she not defend the man who had lost his own life in her defense? Besides, this savage was not without intelligence. For her to go from defiance to meek acceptance would surely arouse his suspicion. She sighed, thinking of the fine line she must walk, and wondering if she could walk it.

As they emerged from the woods and Adam saw Lark waiting for them, his heart swelled with the affection he felt for her. He never saw her without thinking of her many kindnesses to him and to Eliza. He raised his hand and spoke in her tongue.

"Greetings, my very dear friend." He saw her blink of astonishment, saw her golden skin blush with pleasure.

"Greetings, my ... very dear friend," Lark replied. Her gaze went to the beautiful stranger-woman sitting within the circle of the Cougar's arms.

"Her name is Alexandra," Adam said, "and I won her in a fight." Seeing Lark bow her head, he felt it necessary to add quickly, "Not for myself. Her father is a man of importance among my people. I would have her see the hardship the People suffer so that she might tell him." Seeing her black eyes widen, he realized that a brave would never discuss such a thing with a squaw. He said gently, "I need your help, *onkiatshi*. This woman feels the sting of salt now. She and her friends were stolen by Oneidas and she saw her father struck down."

Lark knew the feeling well. In truth, she still thought too much of the past and of how Akando had slain her folk and stolen her. She asked softly, "Does the old one breathe now—or is he in the ground?"

"He will breathe for a long time to come," Adam replied. "I have sent her friends back to him saying she is safe and will be returned eventually."

Lark's gaze lingered on the Cougar's long dark arms at either side of the woman's slight body. She herself would have died content could she have sat for the space of one breath, one heartbeat, within them. And his big, square dark hands grasping the reins—had the stranger-woman touched them? Her hands were so white and small and soft, he surely would have wanted to hold and kiss them. Such pain gripped her at the thought, she could scarcely bear it. Unable to look at his face, she murmured:

"So you have brought her to . . . see how the Mohawks live?"

"*Hen.*" Into Adam's thoughts came the sunny picture of Eliza and Lark together, laughing, learning from each other, enjoying each other. He shoved it into a far corner of his mind. "It would be helpful if she could spend some time with you."

Lark's masked face did not reveal her distaste. "If it is your wish, I will do it."

Adam dismounted, went to her. He said low, "She is not to know who I am."

"I will say nothing." His nearness flustered Lark. She had not been this close to him since his illness, and her heart was so filled with the hot pleasure of it, it nearly smothered her. She looked at the ground, said faintly, "Will she . . . be your woman one day?"

Adam saw on her face and heard in her voice the thing he had long suspected. She cared for him deeply. He said gently, "She will not be my woman, *onkiatshi.*"

He was filled with guilt suddenly. Had the maid been waiting for him all these many moons because he had made love to her once? He had intended to talk to her long ago and tell her how he felt, but there had never been time. Nor was now the right moment, not with Alexandra glowering at them. Hell, there would never be a right moment. But in all fairness to Lark, he must speak of it so she could get on with her life. There were many men who would crave her for a wife.

He said gruffly, "For many moons I have wanted to talk to you . . ."

Hardly daring to breathe, Lark met his black gaze. "About what?"

"Many things. But first, I will never forget that I owe you my life."

Sensing the gravity of the moment, she waited, her heart roaring like storm-thunder.

"You are beautiful and giving," Adam continued, "and your heart is tender. I regret I have not told you sooner of my admiration for you. Know, my friend, if ever I were to wed again, it is you I would ask for." Seeing that her eyes shone with sudden tears, he added softly, "But I will never take another wife. Know that also, *onkiatshi* . . ."

Holding his gaze, Lark lifted her small, sleek head. "You honor me. Know that I would have been proud to call you husband . . ."

They walked to the awakening village then, Adam carrying Lark's water buckets yoked to his shoulders, and Lark leading Anoki, his stallion. None saw her triumph. Her head was spinning with his praises. He had said he admired her, and he thought she was beautiful and giving and her heart was tender—and if he married again, he would choose her. It was more than she had expected in her wildest dreams. For certain, he would be hers although he did not know it. He did not know of the sign she had received . . .

* * *

Alexandra had stared openly at the graceful, doe-eyed young woman speaking with the Cougar. Blazes, but she was beautiful. She had a lovely oval face, golden skin, and a body as straight and slender as a young sapling. One long, shining braid hung down over her bare, shapely breasts to her waist. But Alexandra's admiration was dampened when the maid flashed her a brief hostile glance before returning her attention to the Cougar.

The woman hated her, she thought with resentment, but it was all right; Alexandra hated her, too. She hated all savages at this moment. She watched as the Cougar handed her the reins of his mount, and then carried her water buckets toward a fenced field which held horses. The young woman followed, leading Anoki with Alexandra still upon him. At the field, Alexandra slid to the ground. The girl then led the stallion within the enclosure and unbridled him. The Cougar emptied the buckets into two troughs and returned to Alexandra.

"This is Lark," he said. "She will help you while we are here."

Alexandra muttered, "As if she could . . ." Blast, there she went again. She simply could not keep her mouth shut.

Adam said to Lark dryly in Mohawk, "She is determined to be miserable. Perhaps we should not disappoint her."

"She is a guest," Lark protested, "and one of your own people. We must show her our best hospitality."

Adam smiled. "I know well of the Mohawks' great hospitality, *onkiatshi,* but this one does not consider herself your guest, nor do I want her pampered." He did not add that Alexandra would turn up her nose at their hospitality.

Lark said quietly, "Whatever you decide, I will do."

"Good." It still rankled him that Alexandra had thrown away food. Part of his plan now was for her to learn that most folk in this new world, aye, on this earth, lived by the sweat of their own brows. They did not have servants to turn down their beds and wash their clothing and cook their food. He said, more crisply than he intended, "You will help Lark during our stay here, Alexandra."

Again Alexandra yearned to kick him. It was a frequent occurrence now. She crossed her arms. "I'm not your slave to order about."

Adam's hand once again itched to paddle her backside. "All are required to work for the food they eat."

Alexandra's eyes glittered. "I have perceived that. I don't need to be told. I'm perfectly willing to help, but I'll not be ordered about like a servant."

Adam's mouth twitched when he saw Lark's look of astonishment. For a certainty, she had never seen such a firebrand as this. No Indian maid in the land would ever talk back to a brave that way. He said to Lark in her own tongue, "It is as I said; she is bitter. I know your patience is great, but do not allow her to insult you. Come to me if she does."

Lark watched him stride off. He was very tall and strong, this man of hers, with wide muscular shoulders and a copper-skinned body that was as lean and hard as the cougar for whom he was named, but she saw that he was exhausted. His weariness showed in his step. She nearly called after him that he needed time in the sweat lodge, but she bit her lip. It was not her place to tell a brave what to do.

She turned a placid gaze on the white woman. So. This was Alexandra who had been stolen by Oneidas and won by the Cougar and who was tasting much bitterness at her fate. Lark had sensed that her man wished for friendship between the two of them although he had not said it. She drew a deep breath. She no longer felt jealousy toward the woman—Alexandra would never be Adam's wife—but she did not like her. The maid was too beautiful, and her tongue was of a boldness

that did not become a woman—but there was nothing
in this world Lark would not do for her beloved.

She frowned, seeing suddenly what she had not seen
before: the trembling of Alexandra's soft mouth and her
quickened breathing. She was frightened. The maid was
frightened nigh unto death and hiding it with boldness.
Ever mindful of how it had been to see her own family
slain and herself carried off, Lark said gently, "I would
be your friend, Alexandra."

Alexandra blinked. "You speak English?"

Lark smiled. "Aye."

It was a wonderful surprise, but the friend part Alexandra could not believe. It was a trick. Since she and
the Cougar seemed to know each other, he had probably told her what to say. Be her friend, indeed. What he
wanted, the beast, was to confuse her so she would feel
sorry for these people. He wanted her to think of Indians, all Indians, as poor, sad, ill-treated folk rather than
the bloodthirsty savages they were. Savages who
thought nothing of abducting women and children and
slaying His Majesty's officers.

"Doubtless you are weary if you have ridden half the
night," Lark said. "Perhaps you would like to rest
awhile. I will show you where—you will be staying in
our longhouse."

"I'm fine," Alexandra said shortly.

"Then perhaps you are hungry and thirsty." Looking
at the maid's defiant green eyes, Lark thought how
strange they were, yet how very beautiful. She had
never seen such a color before, like a forest pond with
sunlight glittering over its surface. "Come with me to
our lodge and have some food," she urged softly. "It is
nothing grand, but it is filling."

"Thank you," Alexandra replied stiffly, and followed
her. In truth, her stomach had been growling for hours.
It had been a mistake to throw away the food the Cougar had given her. Also, it had angered him.

After she had met Fox Woman, Lark's mother, and

eaten a bowl of thick yellow porridge and maple syrup, Lark gave Alexandra a hoe and took her to a long, narrow plot near the village.

"This field belongs to my family," Lark said, "but it has never been planted. We grow corn and beans and squash and potatoes, but first we must ready the earth for the seed. Have you ever used a hoe, Alexandra?"

Alexandra looked without enthusiasm at the hard, flat black earth stretching out before her, and shook her head. "Nay, I've never used a hoe." She made no mention of her mother's gardeners who hoed and dug and planted things the day long to keep the Larches looking beautiful. The memory stabbed her. How beautiful her home had been with its lovely, quiet, beautifully furnished rooms and cared-for grounds—and how she missed it. And she missed Justine and Sara and old Piddy. What would he think if he could see her now . . .

"It is very easy to use," Lark said. "You just take it in both hands like this and . . ." She demonstrated.

As the sun climbed into the sky, the two of them hoed side by side breaking the hard-packed earth into smaller and smaller clumps. Alexandra's hands were covered with blisters by the time they moved to a different chore in another field. There, the womens' labor was backbreaking—prying great rocks and roots from the earth and rolling or dragging them to the side of the field. Alexandra hauled and struggled for some time before her anger got the better of her. She straightened up, rubbed her aching back, and pushed her damp, streaming hair behind her ears.

"I have a question." She was breathing hard from exertion and her flaring temper.

"Hen?"

"Why is it that Mohawk women do all the work while your men do nothing but sit and smoke and talk all day?" She knew it for a fact. All morning and afternoon, the Cougar and the other braves in the castle had sat in a circle about the fire talking and smoking their

stupid pipe. She could see them while she and Lark and
the others had slaved away. It had been exactly the
same in the village they had left. The men sat, talked
and smoked while the women worked. "It's not fair,
you know."

Lark wanted to ask angrily what white men did all
day that was fair, but she held her tongue. The Cougar
had said she had great patience, and so she did. She
would not disappoint him. And she had seen, too, that
this Alexandra was younger than she. She had a woman's body, *hen,* but she did not act or talk or think like
a woman. She would not know how to take care of a
man as a woman should, nor would she want to. Leaving off prying a great root from the parched earth, she
answered softly:

"Our men work hard much of the time, and their
work is dangerous. We are more than happy, *hen,* we
are honored to spare them the burden of our daily
chores also. It gives us much pride to work the earth
and grow food and supply clothing and make shelters
for our families."

Alexandra did not hide her skepticism. "Just what is
this work that your men do?"

"They protect us from our enemies," Lark said
coolly, "and they hunt. Do not all men hunt?"

"Then why are they not hunting?"

Lark was about to retort that they had little game to
hunt anymore when her brother and the Cougar galloped up on their horses. She was frightened, seeing the
anger in their dark eyes, and seeing that their faces and
bodies were painted for war.

Alexandra tossed down her hoe—the stupid thing
was useless on such big stones—and glared up at the
Cougar. "It's about time you've come to help. This
work is too hard for—"

"Silence!"

Alexandra stared at his smoldering eyes and the
ominous-looking black stripes painted on his face and

body. She obeyed. He seemed so fiercely savage, so alien, she scarcely recognized him. In a daze, she watched him alight, and then he grasped her about the waist, lifted her onto Anoki, and jumped up behind her, his arms encircling her to take the reins. It all happened so swiftly, she hadn't the time to protest. The other brave extended a hand to Lark who leaped up easily to sit before him, and then both mounts were carrying them into the deep woods.

Alexandra turned her head to stare at the angry black slashes on the Cougar's face. "Wh-where are we going, and why have you . . . painted yourself that way?"

"Be silent, Alexandra."

"Has this to do with my father?"

"Woman, you will be silent!"

She was shocked, for it was not the Cougar who had spoken to her in English, but the other brave. Alexandra trembled, seeing in his eyes that he could as easily slay her as look at her.

Chapter 6

❧⟨∽⟩❧

A dam spoke a low command into Alexandra's ear:
"Obey, and do not anger him further. He is the sachem."

"What's a-a sachem?" she whispered. The brave looked not unlike the Cougar except for his thick black brush of hair. He, too, was lean and tall, and on his arms, too, were tattoos and wide bands of silver. He wore an earring in one ear.

"He is the chieftain of this tribe."

It subdued Alexandra instantly. The other chieftain she had encountered had wanted to buy her, but the Cougar had saved her from that frightening fate. She thought grudgingly that he had also saved her from the Oneida called Mojag and from the puma. It seemed he was always there when she was in danger. But not because he cared about her. He did not. It was because she was the pawn he needed in his game against her father. And he had a cruel streak in him, having her do the slave labor the other poor women here were made to do—and tying her to him as he had.

The thought of it brought back vividly her dream and the tall, shadowy form of her savior. She felt a glow of pleasure remembering how his kisses had tasted and how his hands had moved over her. It had seemed so real. Oh, dear, if only he would come riding out of these woods this very instant and save her. Oh, she *was* a fool. She shivered as the Cougar's warm breath touched her ear and the side of her neck.

"Look at that," Adam whispered, pointing. "Fences everywhere. And those signs saying the property is private." He was fuming. It was just as his brethren had reported. There were more of the damned things now than when he'd been here last. The settlers had refused to take his warning seriously.

Toward the end of the council meeting, when a scout had brought word that white hunters were close by, Adam, as war chief, had made the decision then and there that it was time to strike the first blow.

Alexandra whispered, "What's wrong with fences? I don't understand."

"It is not the way of the People," Adam muttered.

Seeing that this subject mattered to him deeply, she decided it was a grand way to annoy him. She declared, "But it is the way of my people."

"Lower your voice!" he growled. God, how a woman's voice carried.

Alexandra's frightened gaze flew to the sachem, but he had not heard her. She turned her head to the Cougar, said softly, sweetly, "Do tell me if I'm mistaken, but doesn't this land belong to England? And if it does, can't she do with it as she pleases?"

"Woman, does your tongue never stop?" Adam laid a warning finger over her lips when Hawk abruptly halted his mount and held up a hand for silence. Drawing abreast of the sachem, he inquired softly in Mohawk: *"Do you hear them, raktsia?"*

Hawk's black eyes glittered. *"Hen.* Open your ears and you, too, will hear them. They move about like a herd of elk."

For long moments, the two listened to the familiar noises of the white man moving through the quiet of the woods. Adam grinned over at his friend, nodded. They had found their prey, and they were as loud and clumsy and stupid in the forest as all whites were. The two male voices were bellowing from deep within Indian hunting grounds. Land that was now fenced and posted.

Hawk raised his head and sniffed the wind. *"O ne kwen sa."*

Adam nodded. He smelled it, too, now. Blood. They were too late. The devils had made a kill—and Alexandra was here to see the carcass when they recovered it. He said low to her, "You will wait here with Lark. In silence."

Seeing the dark flush on the braves' faces and the deadly light in their eyes, Alexandra was frightened. "What's happening?"

Hawk growled softly in English, "No more talk, Gold Hair." Turning to Lark, he said in Mohawk, "We go to claim that which is rightfully ours. We will return soon. Guard this tongue-wagger for the Cougar and tell her nothing, pretty one." He saw the quickly hidden surprise in her eyes. It was good. She had seen and sensed in those two small, unexpected words that his feelings for her were now special. It was time she knew.

"We will proceed with this as we planned earlier," Adam whispered as he and Hawk swiftly and silently dismantled the split-rail fence blocking the trail.

"I say we kill them," Hawk muttered.

"Iah, raktsia. Your people agreed around an earlier council fire that killing would bring them down on us. We agreed only to frighten them." And to continue frightening them and pray they would come to see the danger of their ways. He leaped onto Anoki's back, drew an arrow from his quiver, and notched it. "Are you ready?"

Hawk's lips tightened as he mounted. He craved to shed white blood and taste revenge. It would give him tremendous satisfaction. But he valued too deeply the respect and friendship of the Cougar to go against his wishes. His was the wiser and cooler head in these matters. It was why Hawk had made Cougar his war chieftain. He sucked in a deep breath and exhaled it. "I am ready."

The horses, their hooves muffled by a thick blanket of pine needles, moved silently toward the clearing where the two men were examining the kill. Rage swam over Adam when he saw that they had taken two bucks. He met Hawk's angry eyes, saw his nod, and the two let loose a barrage of frenzied whoops, charged, and began circling the hunters. The whites stared, frozen by the noise and the sight of their black warpaint.

"Holy gawd, Mohawks! Where's m' damned musket? Gawd . . ."

"Wha' d' thee Injuns w-want?"

"This is Mohawk land," Hawk said when they finally brought their mounts to a halt. His voice was deadly in its quiet. "These are our bucks whose blood you have spilled."

"Thee's wrong, Injun. This kill be ourn, an' this be my land an' m' son's. S-see—" The settler pointed, his voice cracking in his fright. "It's f-f-fenced."

Hawk gave a harsh laugh. "You are squatters."

"Nay, n-not us. We was tole it w-was all proper an' legal t' live here. Thee's trespassin', Injun."

"Do you think I am ignorant?" Hawk raised his voice. "Your king has allowed our hunting grounds to remain in Indian hands. These signs and fences are not his doing but yours. You have until midday tomorrow to remove them. Leave your rail fencing. The wood, too, is ours."

Seeing the older of the men glance stealthily toward his musket, Adam took aim. The man gave a hoarse scream and jumped as the arrow sang through the air and landed in the earth at his feet. Adam swiftly notched a second.

"Go now, white man," he called. "Take your son, leave your weapons, and go. Do as my brother says. Remove the signs and fencing by midday tomorrow. Tell your neighbors to do the same or we will do it for them."

When the settler hesitated, uncertain, Adam warned him softly, "I will aim higher the next time, and I do not miss my mark."

"Nor do I," Hawk added, and let fly an arrow of his own at the feet of the younger man. He laughed as the two screamed and fled, cursing, but when he turned to Adam, his face was serious. Now it was time to give thanks to their brothers, the deer. They would also leave part of them here where they were slain so that they would not be offended and leave this land forever.

Alexandra had watched in silence as the braves entered the woods, for she had no wish to incur the further wrath of the sachem. Her skin crept as she thought of the hatred she had seen in his eyes. He, for certain, did not want to buy her. He wanted to bury her. She forced it from her mind to wonder and worry about what the two of them were doing. They had certainly looked frightening with those black stripes painted on them. It was almost as if—oh dear!—as if they were going on a raid or to war. But that was ridiculous. Surely they would not have brought her and Lark along if that were their intention. But what if they were about to fire some lone household and take captives? Blazes, now she really was frightened. She was trying to calm herself when an unearthly noise came from deep in the forest. She stared at Lark, felt the hair stir on her arms.

"What . . . was that?"

Lark looked toward the woods and back at Alexandra. In truth, she did not like this at all. She murmured, "It . . . was a scalp-yell."

"A scalp-yell!" Alexandra hugged herself, remembering the hideous shriek the Oneidas had made when they'd attacked Tiyanoga—and they had been painted, too. "Why would they give a scalp-yell? Wh-what are they doing?"

But she knew. She saw it all perfectly. They had attacked an isolated cabin, slain the man, and they would soon appear with his wife and children and all the loot they could carry. Oh, God, she mustn't allow her crazy imagination to run amok this way. She told herself she was being hysterical until she heard a man's hoarse scream ring out from the woods.

She cried, "Lark, they're killing my people! I must go to them."

Even as she started down the trail, she knew it was hopeless. What could she possibly do to forestall two Mohawk braves bent on slaughter? But she simply could not stand there doing nothing. Before she had gone ten steps, Lark stood before her, crouched, eyes intent, and a knife gleaming in her small brown hand.

"I am sorry, Alexandra. My brother said I was to guard you, and guard you I will." She moved closer. "You will remain here, and you will be silent." She hated this child-woman with her bold tongue and a beauty that dazzled her, but she would never harm her, and she would be kind to her. In truth, she felt a special sadness for her. Alexandra was stolen and alone and frightened.

Alexandra's eyes welled as another scream came from the deepening shadows. "They're slaying my people . . ." She had no doubt that Lark would use the knife glittering in her hand if she tried to go to them. Blazes, she felt so helpless . . .

"Your people are not harmed," Lark answered firmly. It was true that Silver Hawk craved to kill any who took Mohawk land for themselves, but more than one voice was required to make such a decision. And the Cougar was war chief. Even before that, his voice had taken on much importance. He had begun to speak on their behalf in the great halls of the white man, and with his own money he had helped to feed and clothe them. He was a force among them, and he would not scalp whites. She said again, "Your people are safe."

Alexandra did not believe her. "Then why do they scream?"

Lark murmured, "It is said that even a lone Mohawk strikes terror in the hearts of whites."

"Are you saying white men are cowards?"

"Iah," Lark replied softly. "A Mohawk strikes terror in the hearts of his Iroquois brethren also. Come, sit now and be silent." She pointed to where a log lay on the ground.

"I want to go to them."

"No one has been slain, Alexandra. Our braves have gone only to retrieve what is rightfully theirs. They will return soon."

When her captive obeyed sulkily, Lark was able to reflect finally on her brother's parting words. Pretty one, he had called her. Pretty one. How strange it sounded. Ever since the day he had won her from Akando, he had called her fox-kit or puppy tail—or tadpole or grasshopper. But never to hurt her, only to make her laugh. His brown eyes, usually so fierce, were always warm and gentle when he looked on her. He was good to her, her tall, stern chieftain brother, and she adored him. On that day when she gathered the courage to tell him and her mother and father of the man she had chosen, she was certain he would be pleased. Was not the Cougar his best friend?

As Alexandra waited, the silence of the forest closed in on her. Even the birds and insects seemed to have lost their voices as she sat on the log, afraid to move, straining to hear, with the Indian maid standing nearby with her knife in her hand. It seemed forever before the braves finally appeared. She saw that they bore the muskets and powder horns of their enemies in addition to their own weapons, and that their horses dragged behind them the carcasses of two deer. She turned her head, unable to look at their lifeless bodies.

So this was what they had gone to claim as rightfully theirs? These poor bloodied animals? But they were not theirs! she thought, seething. It was clear they had stolen them from those men, heaven help them, whose screams she had heard. She was outraged, and furious to see that Lark accepted it so meekly and without comment. Well, she herself could not. She confronted them.

"How honorable you are! How brave and sporting to have stolen someone else's game and weapons. Did you kill and scalp them first? Or perhaps you merely wounded them. Blazes, y-you disgust me, both of you!"

Seeing that terror was mixed with her anger, Adam kept his voice gentle. "We have not killed your white hunters, Gold Hair."

Alexandra's teeth chattered. "S-so you say."

Gazing down at her from his mount, he felt a huge regret that she was frightened so much of the time. He wanted only to show her the suffering of his friends. Now it seemed he was harming the Mohawks' cause in her eyes more than helping it. And he was angry with her far too much of the time—and impatient. Hell, he had to be more patient with her. Much more patient.

On their way back to the castle, he broke the icy silence between them. "We did not harm your people, Alexandra."

"I don't believe you," she choked. "I heard your scalp-yell. You sounded just like the O-Oneidas . . ."

As he felt her trembling, Adam's rage toward himself mounted. He tried always to think of the consequences before he said or did a thing. Why, then, had he not stopped to think that this would remind her of Tiyanoga?

"And they screamed," Alexandra persisted. "Why did they scream if you didn't harm them?"

Adam's mouth twitched at the memory. He said gravely, "It is true they squealed like women." When she twisted around and darted a furious look at his painted face, he added, "They were . . . merely frightened."

"No wonder, with you two looking and sounding like two demons from hell! Like the Oneidas."

"But we are not the Oneidas." He drew an easier breath, seeing that her fear was gone and the spitfire had returned. "We did not harm or steal anyone, and we took only what was ours. Perhaps those particular whites will not trespass on our land again."

Alexandra met his eyes, held them defiantly. "You, sir, were the trespassers."

"*Iah.*" Adam reminded himself that he was going to be patient. "The fences and signs of whites have no place on the sacred lands of the Mohawks."

She was so breathtakingly lovely in her fury, he could not take his eyes from her. And it had been so long since he had been close to a woman, he'd forgotten how it was. He had forgotten how fragile their bodies were and how satiny their skin was. He had forgotten how soft and tempting their lips were, and forgotten their sweet woman-smell, so tantalizing a fragrance that it needed no scent to enhance it. And the women he had known best, Eliza and Lark, possessed a courage equal to that of the bravest man. And now here was this fiery young Alexandra who would have slain him with one fierce look were it possible. Reluctantly, he forced his thoughts back to their talk.

"Listen well, Alexandra, for this is what you are going to hear again and again and what you will tell your father. This is the truth. We would gladly share our land with whites—there is plenty for all—but the whites refuse to share. Your people want to plunder and own."

"This is so boring! I'm sick of hearing it!"

Adam gritted his teeth. "But you are going to hear it."

"I won't listen!" She gave her head a wild shake and thought, incredibly, that she was once more on the verge of a tantrum.

"You will listen." Sweet Jesus, but she was infuriating.

"I won't!" Her heart was pounding, fluttering in her throat as she put her hands over her ears. "You're a tyrant!"

In truth, he was, Adam thought suddenly, and he was being as childish as she. He drew a deep, calming breath and gently pulled her hands away from her ears. Holding them captive under his own, he said quietly, "I will try not to be a tyrant, but it is for this I have kept you with me, Alexandra. To hear what I have to say and to see what I have to show you."

Shock radiated throughout Alexandra's body. The big dark hands imprisoning hers felt like those in her dream . . . like those of her savior . . . warm, strong, protecting. And she knew suddenly, beyond any doubt, that with his hard arms around her, she would never fall off Anoki, nor would the sachem dare harm her. The thought filled her with terror. She did not want to be grateful to this man! She hated him, and she refused to go all shaky at his touch merely because he was tall and had hard muscles and white teeth and a comely face. He was a savage. Her mother would be appalled, and her father would want to—

She closed her eyes. Papa was gone. The few childhood memories she had of him, sitting on his knee at the Larches, and his teaching her to ride, were all intertwined now with his terrible cry and the tomahawk in his side and his blood spilling on the ground. She swallowed, lifted her chin. She was strong. She was not Mayjay. She would recover from this, and nothing and no one would defeat her or tell her how to think or change the way she felt about him.

"I hate you, you know," she said dully. "All of you."

"I see that you do. I am sorry."

"And your Mohawks hate me."

"They hate what your people do." Adam's breath caught. He had not even been aware as they talked that his thumb was stroking, testing, exploring the silky skin of her hand and the fragile bones beneath it. How soft it was. How incredibly small . . .

Alexandra swallowed, felt her heart turn over. Blazes, she could not believe what was happening inside her. It was . . . wonderful. Little waves of heat, of excitement and pleasure rippling through her, and all because he was stroking her hand. It was as if she were melting, as if her body, her flesh, the very blood racing through her veins were on fire. And all because of her hand—and his.

She stiffened, wondering suddenly if he could tell what she was feeling. How absolutely hideous if he could. And what on earth had they been talking about? She cast about frantically through her thoughts, remembered finally, and murmured, "If your people feel all that dreadfully abused, they should take their grievances to court. Surely there are courts."

Adam held her hands less tightly, mindful of the bruises Mojag had left on her white skin. "There are courts, *hen,*" he replied gruffly, "but they are days away from our castles and villages and they favor the white man. Their judges do not know our tongue, nor do we know theirs."

"You know English, and Lark. Even *he* knows it." She nodded scornfully toward the sachem, riding ahead of them.

"We are but three out of many."

Alexandra was grateful to have something to think about other than her thumping heart and tingling skin. "I can't believe there's not one single white in this entire land who doesn't speak or can't learn Mohawk or whatever gibberish you speak and interpret for you."

Adam could not suppress a chuckle. She was a veritable marvel. An incredible mixture of intelligence, innocence, arrogance, and bravery—and beauty. He said, "Many have tried to learn our gibberish and failed, Alexandra."

"And I suppose that pleases you no end. I think the Mohawks *want* to be misunderstood. It gives them a grand excuse to make trouble and feel sorry for themselves."

"I think it is more likely that few whites can cope with words such as *oneharadesehoengtseragherie.*"

Alexandra turned. "That's . . . one word?"

"One." Her slow blink of amazement so delighted him that he was moved to add, "There *is* a white who has learned our tongue and who fights for us in the courts of the king. He is called Warraghiyagey. He Who Does Much."

The Cougar's big hands still held Alexandra's captive, and still sent waves of sensation throughout her body. She could neither make it disappear nor prevent its coming. She could only surrender to it—and enjoy it. And for a change, she was even enjoying talking with him. She liked his admitting that a white had learned their tongue. It was quite honorable of him. He could have remained silent.

She said in a small voice, "I shouldn't have called your language gibberish . . ."

Her apology pleased Adam. "I see well why it would sound so to your ears." His own learning of the tongue had been a nightmare. But for his determination and the patience of Hawk, he never would have learned as much as he had.

"That man you spoke of," Alexandra murmured, trying to forget the heat radiating through her. "The one called He Who Does Much. Is it William Johnson?"

Adam was surprised. "Do you know him?"

Heat. It was all through her now. Shimmering, flickering, pulsing heat. It was nerve-racking. She had never felt such a thing. She tried to draw her hands away from his, but it was hopeless. She could not free them without making a fuss. She clung desperately to the thought of William Johnson.

"I've heard of him. But Papa never called him Warra-whatever or the other. He called him William Johnson the bastard." She felt the Cougar's deep laughter resonating through her from her head to her toes. "He also called him that damned Irishman, a clod, a cheap title-seeker, a damned Mingo-lover, a squaw-man, and a traitor to the Crown." She could not stand it another instant. She turned her profile to him, said softly, "If you'll release my hands, I'll not hold my ears anymore. I promise." She was almost disappointed when he did her bidding without any comment.

As they neared the castle, the sachem's mount drew abreast of them. Lark, sitting behind her brother with her arms about his waist, called over, "You should know, Alexandra, there is a another besides War-raghiyagey who has learned our tongue and helped our people. He is called Lord Adam Rutledge."

Alexandra stared across at her. "What? Old Rhu-barb?" She simply could not believe it. A lecherous, self-important, overfed, titled old windbag of an En-glishman? Her laughter rang out. "You can't mean it . . ."

Lark replied stiffly, "It is so. Without his help, our people would have had to move from here several years ago."

"My goodness . . ."

Adam at first feared Lark had forgotten his warning, but her eyes meeting his said she had not. It was just that she had to speak up for him. She had to. But Al-exandra would never hear from her lips who Lord Adam Rutledge really was. Understanding that, Adam had relaxed and enjoyed the moment.

It had been over two winters since he had heard such laughter bubbling from the lips of a woman. It warmed his heart even as it brought back memories that tore at him. But it puzzled him also. Why had Lark's words amused Alexandra so, and why the devil did she call him Old Rhubarb? "Do you know Lord Adam then?" he asked.

Sensing his change in mood, Alexandra straightened her face. "I've only heard about him from my father. Like the other."

Hawk fastened his sharp gaze upon her. "If what you heard was like the other, it would seem your father mocked him."

Feeling safe with the Cougar's arms about her, Alexandra shot back, "My father certainly did not mock him." Rather, he had wanted to mop up the floorboards of Tiyanoga with Lord Adam Rutledge. She smiled, recalling Papa's magnificent rage.

"I would know what amuses you so," Hawk said quietly.

Finally realizing her danger, Alexandra murmured, "It's . . . nothing. Really."

"Let it pass, *raktsia*," Adam said low in Mohawk.

"*Iah*. She belittles you, and I will not have it." In English, he said, "Speak, woman, or I will slice your lying tongue down the middle so it will be as forked as the words you say."

Alexandra gave a small shriek as his long arm reached over and seized their mount's bridle. Unable to think quickly enough to lie, she cried, "My father wanted me to marry him, and I would not!"

Adam gave her shoulder an awkward pat and covered her hands with his again. "It is all right, Alexandra. It is all right." Marry him? In God's name, this was the damnedest thing he'd ever heard. Wade Chamberlain had never approached him about marriage. And stranger still, what was her objection? She could do a damned sight worse. "But we are curious, *onkiatshi*. Why would you not want to marry such a . . . very fine gentlemen as Lord Adam?" His black eyes, flickering with amusement, met those of Silver Hawk.

"It's none of your business, you know!" Tears of mortification filled Alexandra's eyes. When they slid down her cheeks, they shamed her further, but in truth, that dratted sachem had scared her half to death with his talk of slitting her tongue. "With him threatening me with bodily harm, I suppose I must tell you!" She glared at the chieftain, her wet eyes sparking fire. "The truth is, I'll not be given to anyone against my will, especially not some pompous, overstuffed, creaky old lord who wants a young wife to paw and to warm his bed!"

Alexandra held her breath as the sachem gazed at her in awful silence, and then, unexpectedly, he threw back his head and the woods rang with his laughter. When the Cougar joined in, relief swam over her. They laughed all the way back to the castle, but she had no idea why. She knew only that the sachem was not going to slice her tongue in half. At least not at the moment.

Chapter 7

$\diamond\!\!\!\!\diamond\!\!\!\!\sim\!\!\!\!\diamond\!\!\!\!\sim$

As Silver Hawk rode homeward through the misty green of the spring woodlands, he was content. Maples were showing their red flowers, birches were leafing, warblers were singing, and his body was filled with warmth—from laughter, from his satisfying encounter with the enemy, and not least, from having Lark close, her slim half-naked body spooned behind him and her arms about his waist. He had slowed his mount purposely, putting distance between him and the Cougar, for he wanted her to himself. He wanted no talk except with her, and no thoughts except those of her. His head was filled with her. She was beautiful, so beautiful. She was brave and gentle and clever—and she was beautiful. She made fine clothes and wove strong baskets—and she was beautiful. She cooked well and was respectful and charming and amusing—and she was beautiful. By the Great Creator, but she was beautiful.

Tell her now, he ordered himself. Tell her you want her to be your woman. Tell her now.

Again and again the words trembled on his lips, but each time he caught them back before he could give voice to them. *Iah,* he could not. His mother was right. Lark knew him only as a brother. She would be horrified if he told her how he felt. But he was not her brother, he thought resentfully. She was from a tribe far away, the Ojibwa, and there was no shared blood whatsover between them. She had been stolen from her

95

people as a twelve-year-old, and for one year had known slavery and misery until he came to the Seneca village and saw her and was moved by pity for her. He turned his head now, giving her his handsome profile. He asked quietly:

"Are you still happy with us, tadpole?"

"*Hen,* my brother." Lark was relieved to hear the familiar endearment once more. "Can you not tell?"

Silver Hawk nodded. She was a far cry from that pale, scruffy little fox-kit he had brought home for his mother to fatten and nurse back to health. He had wondered often, too often, if the Seneca Akando had robbed her of her innocence when she belonged to him. It pained him so to think of it that he realized he did not want to know. He could not bear to know.

"My brother . . ."

"*Hen,* little one?"

Lark laid her soft cheek against his strong, straight back. "You are troubled."

Silver Hawk chuckled. "Now, how would you know?"

"I know. I think it is about me."

In silence, he gathered his worried thoughts. Perhaps this was the time to tell her after all, or at least prepare the way. "I admit," he said slowly, "I have been considering your future and to whom you should be given."

"I have a family," Lark protested. "I need no one else."

"You need a husband to protect you and provide you with meat."

"I have you to protect me and provide me with meat. I am safe with you for a brother. You are sachem." Lark's heart had begun to thump. It was only right that she tell him about her beloved, but she could not. Not just yet. Not until the Cougar knew that she was for him and he was for her, and that might be many moons yet . . .

"Several braves are interested in you, my sister."

"I am not interested in them."

"Every woman needs a man to take care of her and give her children."

It was long moments before Lark said in a small voice, "It must be the right man . . ."

"It will be the right man, I promise you."

Silver Hawk's sense of well-being overflowed. So, there was no one yet who had claimed her heart, and he could take his time about this. There was no need to frighten her. It was good. For a certainty, she would be his, this woman whose happiness he had nurtured these many years. He sighed, much amazed by the singing of his heart. He had known many women in his thirty-one winters, but when had he ever cared as much for a woman as he did for this one? He wanted no one but her, and he wanted her forever. His only regret was that he had not realized it sooner.

Alexandra saw that the braves' spirits were still high as they returned to the castle. As the Mohawks gathered to rejoice over the bucks, Lark drew her to the same longhouse where she had earlier given her food. Then Alexandra had sat outside on a stump eating her corn-meal. Now she was taken inside where the women were cooking over fires spaced at intervals down the central corridor. Seeing Fox Woman sitting before one of them, Alexandra smiled. She received a grave nod before the old woman's attention returned to her cook pot.

"This is where my family sleeps," Lark said, showing Alexandra a curtained compartment containing furs and several neatly folded blankets. "You will sleep here also."

"Thank you." Looking about, Alexandra saw that it was one of many such compartments lining both sides of the long, rectangular dwelling. She knew instantly that sleeping there would not be pleasant. The air was thick with smoke, and the longhouse would be noisy and crowded when all the small private quarters were filled with families. And she abhorred the thought of sleeping with strangers. A new worry struck her suddenly. "Does ... your brother, the sachem, sleep here, too?" she asked. She could not imagine closing her eyes once during the night if that were the case.

"*Iah*. He lives in a wigwam on the edge of the woods. The Cougar stays with him when he visits us."

"I see." Thank you, God. Thank you, thank you that I would not have Silver Hawk or the Cougar close by in the night. As she gazed about, the smoke stung her eyes, the smell of the strange food filled her nostrils, and the Mohawk tongue buzzed in her ears. Without warning, she saw the Larches in her mind's eye—and Mama dressed for dinner in a silk burgundy gown. Overwhelmed with the need to weep, she clenched her hands into fists and felt the nails bite into her palms. She looked back to Lark. "I should be helping."

"*Iah*. You have already helped this day. Let your sore hands rest. Lie down and rest your body also if you wish before the evening food is ready."

Alexandra's heart warmed toward her. "You're very kind, but in truth, I'd rather get my writing things from the Cougar."

Lark said quietly, "You can write?"

"Aye. I've always kept a journal. A diary."

"Then you must certainly be left to your writing."

Alexandra was subdued as she sought the Cougar. She did not much like herself at this point. She hated the giddy romantic feelings she'd felt for him, and she hated it that she had almost wept in front of the three of them. In fact, she'd made quite a spectacle of herself over old Rhubarb. Now all she wanted was to find a quiet place where she could curl up and write—if the Cougar would part with her supplies. Seeing him leaning against a tree, sharpening his knife, she walked over to him.

Adam looked up. "Good evening, Gold Hair."

"Good evening." She would not, she told herself,

look at those long dark fingers curved about the flint and blade ... or notice how strong his hands were ... and how beautiful. Like the rest of him. *Damn.* She could not resist. She looked. Heart galloping, she said, "I would like very much to begin my journal, so if you will please give me my writing things ..."

"Of course." Adam studied her quietly as he continued to whet his blade. The little fox was all eyes and glorious pink skin and heaving breasts—as if she were frightened again. But then she'd had quite an ordeal this day. "Know, Gold Hair," he said, "that Silver Hawk will never harm you."

"What makes you so sure?" Silver Hawk had been far from her thoughts.

"I will not allow it."

"How that relieves me," she replied crisply.

Adam's eyes flickered, amusement in their black depths as he recalled her tirade against that ancient, overfed moneybags, Lord Adam Rutledge. Old Rhubarb. He hadn't laughed so hard in a long, long time.

"May I have my things now?" Alexandra asked, impatient.

"Hen. Come along." He slid his knife into its sheath and the flint into the small buckskin bag at his waist. As she trotted along after him, he brooded over what Alexandra had said about her father, and worried that Wade Chamberlain could offer her to a stranger so casually. It was unconscionable. The old boy hadn't the vaguest idea in hell what sort of man Lord Adam Rutledge was. He could be a brute like Mojag, or an insatiable womanizer like old Willie Johnson. But Adam doubted it would make any difference. He sensed it was a title the old buzzard was after. With his daughter as Lady Adam Rutledge, Chamberlain's chances for attaining a minor title of his own for his war efforts were greatly enhanced. Bet on it. He slowed his step so Alexandra could catch up.

"You will write of what you have seen today?" he

asked. "The fences and signs? The whites who slew our game?"

"Most definitely I will write of what I have seen today," Alexandra replied firmly. She would write of their trespassing on posted land, stealing the kills and the weapons of white settlers, and possibly wounding or even killing them. She had only the Cougar's word that they were not murderers.

"Good." The deceitful little wench. She was damned lucky Hawk was not here. Her face had turned three shades of red as she had told her lie.

Alexandra waited outside while he retrieved the buckskin bag from the wigwam. He removed from it several sheets of paper, the inkpot, and a quill, and handed them to her.

"You will return everything to me when you are through."

"Aye, master." Her green eyes burned through him.

Adam was unscathed, and determined to say what was on his mind. "I find it strange, Gold Hair, that your father would give you to a man you have never met and whom you despise." Seeing her blink, he added wryly, "I thought whites were . . . more civilized."

She was stung. "Not that it's any of your business, but Papa only wanted what he thought was best for me. He would never have forced me to marry anyone against my will." In truth, he might have tried, but he would not have succeeded.

"I am glad to hear that. You should know, Alexandra, no Indian would give his daughter to one she hated."

"My father lies dead, and I find this subject too tasteless to discuss."

"I have told you, your father breathes."

"Then prove it! Return me to him."

"Iah."

"Why not? You wanted me to see things—well, I've seen them!"

Adam saw that she was not going to change.

Whether he kept her one month or one year, she could not or would not understand the wrongs done to his Mohawks by the British. Her mind was set. It should have angered him, yet he understood. She had been cruelly abducted, she thought her father had been slain, and now he would not return her to her people. Such a one as Alexandra was not going to look kindly on those who did such deeds. Aye, he understood. Eliza would have behaved so under similar conditions.

"My mother will be frantic," Alexandra said. It was a feeling she herself was experiencing frequently now. "She will have me dead and buried along with Papa. It will kill her. I have told you and told you, but you just don't care!"

Deciding that her mother might well expire from her grief, Adam felt a twinge of alarm. He indicated the paper and quill. "Write to her. Tell her you are unharmed." It was a thing he should have thought of sooner.

"You . . . would actually send a message to her?"

"I will send it."

Her heart lifted. Now if only she had some idea of where she was and how far from Tiyanoga, she could perhaps indicate it in some way. Trying to hide her excitement, she asked, "How long will it take to get there? Will you send it by horseback or—or canoe?"

Adam crossed his arms and gazed down at her hopeful pink face. He shook his head. "Abandon it, Gold Hair. None will find you. Write quickly, here, now, and it will be taken to her." He pointed to a smooth, flat stone nearby. "Use that to write upon, and say only that you are unharmed, nothing more. Your mother should not be made to worry." Her devil-father was another matter. A man willing to give his daughter to the highest bidder did not deserve consideration. Nor did he deserve such a daughter as this one.

Alexandra's face burned. Damn him, and damn his always knowing what she was thinking. She did hate him, even if she sometimes felt silly about him. She fetched the stone, plumped herself down, uncorked the ink, and angrily scratched out a brief message: *Darling Mama, I'm the prisoner of a stupid, ugly savage called the Cougar. He has not harmed me, and he says he'll return me soon. I love you terribly. Alexandra.* She rose, eyes snapping, handed it to the brave, and watched as he calmly scanned it. He handed it back.

"Read it aloud," he ordered.

"Why should—"

"Read it," Adam growled.

Hiding her astonishment, Alexandra obeyed. "Dear Mother, I'm fine and you're not to worry. I'll be home very soon. Love, Alexandra."

Adam's eyes glinted. "Why do you not read what is written, Alexandra?"

"I—" She was speechless. She watched as a smile touched his mouth, but not his eyes. He waved his hand.

"It is a fine letter. Leave it as is."

Watching him take the foolscap in his long dark fingers and fold it, Alexandra wondered if he was bluffing. Did he really know how to read English, or did he only want her to think he did? He had not blinked an eye over her insulting description of him, but he was clever. He was so clever.

"I will send this on its way this eve," Adam said. "We will be on our way also."

Her head jerked up. "I thought we were to spend the night here. Lark showed me where I was to sleep."

"I have changed my plans."

She had not looked forward to a night in the longhouse, but now it seemed a paradise compared to another night on horseback. She asked dully, "Where are we going?"

"To other villages."

"But why? Can't I see all there is to see here in this castle?" She imagined being taken so far from

Tiyanoga, perhaps into Canada even, that all hope would be lost of ever seeing her mother or her own people again. And a new fear gripped her. As he had won her from the Oneida, could not some other brave win or steal her from him? Or what if he fell ill or was wounded? What if they were ambushed? "Please, can't I stay here with Lark until you return? I'll wait for you, I promise!" She crossed her fingers. She would promise him anything to remain here.

Adam felt himself wavering. He exposed her to danger every time he took her to a new place, and for what? He was not going to change her mind about anything. And yet those glimpses of tenderness and compassion he had seen in her, those breaches in the hard shell encasing her, made him hopeful. He could not give up on her. Not yet. And he had to admit, it gave him a good feeling to keep her out of Wade Chamberlain's clutches for at least a while longer.

Alexandra held her breath as the Cougar gazed at her long and intently. She could not imagine what he was thinking, but it was not good. She moistened her lips. "Please, may I stay?"

But he had made his decision—and there was another reason that he wanted her with him. He enjoyed it. He enjoyed the sight of her slender, softly curved body and golden hair, the faint fragrance that clung to her skin. Even when she was lashing out at him, the sound of her voice was sweet to his ears, and her rare smiles made the dark days seem brighter. And he liked the way she felt in his arms as they rode. Why not? She was female, and he was male. It was nature. He could admire her perfection as he might admire a sculpture or a painting that he felt no need to possess. He needed no woman, now or ever. Even were he tempted, he would never be so disloyal to his darling . . .

"Can't you answer a simple question?" Alexandra snapped when he made no reply.

"Do your journal writing now if you wish, Alexandra."

"That's no answer."

"We leave at sunset."

"But—"

"Iah."

"Damn you!" she cried after him. She fumed as she carried the stone writing surface to a quiet spot under a tree and settled herself against its trunk. She dipped her quill into the inkpot and, with trembling fingers, put the nub to the paper. Bastard! Every time he offered her some small kindness, he immediately canceled it with cruelty. She hated him. But she would have some small measure of revenge. She was going to write exactly what she saw and heard and felt, not what he wanted her to write. And if it was personal, she would write in French. It was another small stab at him.

For three weeks, they had traveled between villages, never staying more than one or two days in each. They had gone from the tender pastels of April to the greening of May. Maples were in leaf, buttercups were blooming, and mayflowers filled the woods with their elusive sweetness. Adam saw none of it. He cared only that his captive saw the hunger and desperation and anger of his brethren. In each village they visited, he led the raids to recover those kills that should have been theirs. Now he turned and gazed long at Alexandra riding behind him. She was on a mare roped to his, and she was listing dangerously to the right. Her eyes were closed. Hell, she was sound asleep! He brought Anoki to an abrupt halt.

"Alexandra!"

Alexandra jerked awake and blinked her sleepy green eyes at him. *"Hen?"* She had been dreaming. She could not close her eyes without dreaming . . .

Adam hid a smile. More and more she was using

simple Mohawk words, and he wondered if she was even aware of it. "Are you all right?"

She masked her eyes and her face as he so often did. "Of course." The words were no sooner spoken than she had to cough.

In truth, she was not all right, but she was not going to tell him. She was dying, slowly but surely, and it would serve him right when she fell dead at his feet one day. She ached all over—her head, her eyes, her stomach and back and shoulders—and her skin was raw from insect bites and scratches from brambles and thorns. Not least, her bottom was sore. Blazes, but her bottom was sore—and her thigh muscles.

She loved horses and she had a sweet mare back home, but if by some miracle she survived this journey, she did not ever want to see or smell or ride another horse as long as she lived. Nor would she eat pemmican or jerky. Ugh. She sat taller as the Cougar dismounted and strolled back to her. He stroked her mare's glossy neck and then held up his arms to her.

"You will ride with me now." Having sensed her distaste at the intimacy of two on a mount, he had bought this gentle Narragansett for her in one of the first villages they had visited. But he had not counted on her being so exhausted she could not hold her seat or keep her eyes open. Hell, he'd had her working too hard. In truth, she'd worked like a drudge without complaining—hauling water and firewood, hoeing fields, planting seed, pounding corn. Now he felt remorse. "Come," he said gruffly.

Alexandra looked down at him with deep suspicion. "Why?"

"You were asleep. You could have fallen off Dyani and hurt yourself."

"Don't!" she said sharply, and coughed again.

"Don't what?" He was shocked, seeing her closely for the first time in many days. Why had he not seen the changes in her? Purple shadows under her eyes, strain and fatigue etched on her face—and she had lost weight. Sweet Jesus, she was wasting away. He *had* let her work too hard.

"Don't pretend you care when you don't," Alexandra said stiffly.

Adam grew still, feeling the inner earthquake that was suddenly rocking him to his core. He did care. He cared far more than he had ever wanted or intended. He had thought, God's truth he had, he'd thought he was responding only to her being a female. She was young and soft and vulnerable, a beautiful woman at his mercy and under his protection. How could he not respond? But he saw now that there was more. He cared about her, not merely because she was a woman but because she was one special woman. Because she was brave and proud and bright and fearless—because she was Alexandra . . .

He pulled in a shaky breath. Nay, man, he would not have it. He had vowed before God there would never be another woman in his life to break his heart. He had not yet recovered from losing the first one. He scowled up at her, said brusquely:

"Do not annoy me further, Gold Hair. You are trouble enough as you are without breaking an arm or an ankle and making yourself totally unbearable."

Alexandra loosed a peal of laughter. What a joke. So she was trouble, was she, but not yet totally unbearable? She shook her head. "My goodness, and to think I've not even tried to be troublesome. I've just been me."

The sound of her laughter, even in sarcasm, was like the wind's song in the trees. Even as he reveled in it, Adam was exasperated with himself and with her. "Your tongue wags too much, woman. Come."

"Thank you, nay, I'll stay where I am." She simply could not go back to sitting close to him with his arms around her and those disgusting sensations sweeping through her.

Adam said sharply. "It is not open to debate." He grasped her, lifted her down, and removed from her mare the soft blanket on which she had been riding. He fastened it about the barrel of his stallion.

Alexandra crossed her arms and watched him in silent fury. He deserved a tongue-lashing, but it would be a waste of breath—and would probably make her cough more. When he cupped his hands to help her mount, she obeyed with icy dignity, putting her small moccasined foot into the stirrup they formed.

"Sit sideways, it will be more comfortable . . ."

"That I doubt," she snapped. But again she obeyed, and when she was settled, he vaulted up behind her and took the reins, his arms once more sealing her in place.

She waited anxiously for the familiar waves of fire and ice to begin assaulting her. When, after long moments, they did not appear, nor was she reduced to a disgusting puddle of helplessness, she drew a breath of relief. How wonderful. She felt completely normal. No chills or hot fingers of fire creeping over her. And he was right. This was far more comfortable—cradled against his chest and having him do the steering—than sitting astride her own mount and trying to stay awake. She felt safe and warm and strangely content. Through eyes misty with fatigue, she stole a glimpse at his face. Seeing that his own eyes were distant, she stared. He was a thousand miles away.

"Does my face not meet with your approval?"

Alexandra averted her eyes. "Actually, I was thinking that—maybe you hurt somewhere." She thought of her own bottom and how it had ached until now. "Do you?"

Adam chuckled. Her candor never ceased to amaze him. "*Iah*, Alexandra. I do not hurt." Except for his heart.

"I'm glad. I've wondered these past weeks—what if you did? What do your people do when they're sick?"

"In every village, we have those skilled in *o-non-kwa*. Medicine."

"Ah."

He was surprised and pleased she had even given it thought. For while she had worked side by side with the Mohawk women, she had been moody and withdrawn from them. And when her time was her own, she had spent it with her journal. He had not looked at it yet—he'd not had the time—but he would. He was damned curious to see what she had written, and he'd give it a thorough perusal before sending it off with her.

Lulled by the stallion's rhythmic swaying and her own feelings of comfort, Alexandra felt herself mellowing. He was actually treating her as a human being—not that it would last, it never did—but for the moment, she almost liked him. She said quietly, "I've been meaning to tell you, I *do* see that things aren't good for your people. I'm sorry . . ." She had been deeply troubled, in fact, that in each village there seemed to be insufficient food and clothing.

Her words electrified Adam. "I thought you had not noticed." Or cared.

"Of course I noticed." She hesitated. He was not going to like her next words, but they had to be said. "I noticed, too, that, just as in Lark's village, the women worked and the men were sleeping or playing games—or talking and smoking. Can this be why there's not enough food and their clothing is in shreds? Don't Indian men ever work until you come a-and get them off their rumps?" She held her breath. She'd been about to say "help them steal game," but lost her courage. The rump thing did not sound any better. Oh, dear.

Adam felt his jaw tighten. She would never see things the way he intended, and he was not going to explain again about fences and signs and lost hunting grounds. Not now. What the little wench needed was a lecture on the Indian male. On how the loss of his land and his freedom to move about humiliated and demoralized a man raised to be a hunter and warrior.

"Now you're angry . . ."

"I am not angry, but there is much you do not understand and much I would say to you. Later."

They rode in silence for some moments before Alexandra murmured, "Actually, there's ... something else I would say to you. Now."

"On how you would run the country?" Adam muttered.

She chuckled. *"Iah.* But it might help you to run it."

He didn't want to hear it. He was still mulling over her earlier pronouncement, and more than that, he was damned concerned about her. Those dark smudges beneath her eyes and her loss of weight—and that cough. When had it begun?

Alexandra slanted him a sidelong glance, watched him closely through lowered lids. "I wonder if you really can read. Because if you can't, and you can't write either, you really should learn."

Adam thought of his many years of schooling and replied gravely, "There is wisdom in what you say."

"Just think, you could be a liaison like Warra-Whatever—you know, Sir William. Or Old Rhubarb." She grinned. "Sorry. Habit." In all seriousness, he would be good at it. With his noble features and bearing and stoic manner, there was not an Englishman alive who would not be impressed by him. Even Papa, she thought sadly. And it had not escaped her notice that the Cougar seemed to be loved and respected, almost idolized, in every village they had visited. But she would not tell him that and give him a swelled head.

"I should think educating yourself so you could stand up for your people would solve their problem faster than hauling me about with you from place to place like a sack of potatoes. And when did one wrong ever right another wrong? Besides, whatever I might think about your Mohawks isn't going to affect any Englishman's attitude in the slightest, I assure you." When he remained silent, she turned to him. "Well? What do you think?" But he was miles away again.

Adam had scarcely heard her. He was remembering her every sniffle, every limp and scratch and ache. Now he recalled he had heard her muffled coughing as they rode through the night. Was it the throat sickness coming on? Good God. She had been fragile to begin with, and now she was tired and undernourished to boot. Wide open to all the ills that struck folk unaware in this wilderness. It filled him with such terror, he decided on the instant that he had pushed his luck far enough. He would not push it another inch. He was taking her to Windfall.

Chapter 8

Alexandra opened her eyes and immediately closed them. She was dreaming, a good dream for a change, and she preferred it to reality. Asleep, she was in a lovely bedchamber with sunshine streaming through the Irish lace curtains on the windows. Awake, she was goodness only knew where—in some smoky longhouse probably. Or probably she was still on horseback. She stretched, wiggled her toes, and moved her head from side to side, testing the pillow. It was lovely—soft and encased in the finest of linen. Sniffing it, detecting the faint aroma of roses, she felt her entire body go on the alert. This was no dream—this was real . . .

She opened her eyes again, cautiously this time, and gasped. She was back in England! But—how had she gotten here, and where was the Cougar? Looking down at herself, she saw that she still wore doeskins, but her moccasins had been removed. They sat neatly on the elegant rug that covered the floor. Beside them was the bag containing her belongings. A chill went through her. This was frightening. Had she, for some reason, been unconscious all the time it would have taken for her to be transported back to New York City, and onto a sailing ship, and across the Atlantic, and thence to this house, wherever it was? Surely such a thing was not possible. That left only one answer: She was still in the vast northern reaches of New York Colony. But that, too, seemed impossible. Only Indians and settlers lived here. To whom then did this house belong, and why had the Cougar brought her here—if indeed he had . . .

Heart pounding, Alexandra slid off the bed and moved quickly across the room to a window. Parting the lace curtains, she looked out upon a vast swath of green that swept majestically down to a blue, sun-glittered river. The Hudson? It was the only river she had seen in this land, nor did she know of any other. Lowering the curtain, she turned frightened eyes to the spacious bedchamber; the ornate canopied bed and beautifully carved washstand, a massive chest of drawers, a settee beside a large fireplace with an impressive-looking oil over it . . .

She put her hands to her temples. This was beyond belief. Who would have built such a grand place in the middle of nowhere? Some master criminal who had amassed a fortune and had nowhere to spend it? God . . . Wondering suddenly if she was being held captive, she flew to the door. Oh, thank God—it was unlocked. Thank God . . . With trembling hands, she opened it a crack, and then wider, wider, until she could slip through. Heart still racing, she looked about before she stole down the spacious hallway. She stopped frequently to hold her breath and listen for sounds, but she heard nothing. No one. She was tempted to call out the Cougar's name, but decided against it. She could be in the hands of someone truly wicked. Someone who had slain the brave or impris-oned him. Oh, God, maybe there was a dungeon be-neath all this beauty, and he was in it.

Fearing for him now more than for herself, Alexan-dra crept down the wide stairway. She stopped at the bottom and listened again. Nothing. Nothing but her own rapid breathing and the wild beating of her heart. Silently, eyes wide, her entire body alert, she slipped through the quiet rooms—the dining room, drawing room, library, kitchen. It was an English manor, one of the loveliest she had ever seen, but where was everyone? It should have been filled with servants going about their daily chores; instead it was empty, and dust and grime were everywhere. Seeing a teapot on the table, a strawberry cozy lying beside it, and two delicate china cups in their saucers, Alexandra sensed that the heartbeat of the house had stopped long ago. And now she was here. Alone.

The thought chilled her as she returned to the silent foyer and stood looking around. What should she do now? She could not stand here forever. Oh, if only the Cougar were here! She would give anything to see him walk through that door; give anything to be back in one of the smoky villages they had visited these past weeks. She yearned to be surrounded again by people and barking dogs and children shouting and playing. But the memory only made her feel worse. She was here, wherever *here* was, and that was that. She must make the best of it, just as she had tried to make the best of every new situation ever since she was stolen. And the first thing she must do was explore to see who and what was here and if she had any chance of escape. But as she moved toward the door, her legs stopped working. It was opening. She made a small strangled sound and fled blindly toward the kitchen. She remembered seeing another door there.

"Alexandra!"

Turning, seeing the Cougar there, a tall dark haven, she went weak with relief. "Oh, Cougar! Oh . . ."

Adam frowned, seeing her white face and her shaking. "It is all right, Gold Hair. I am here."

"Oh, God!" It was a whisper. "Oh, thank you, God . . ."

She flew into his arms. She needed to feel his warmth and strength flowing into her. She needed to feel safe. But when he closed his arms around her and held her tightly against him, she forgot all about feeling safe. Shock and pleasure were shooting through her, and when she became aware of the hardness of his shoulders beneath her fingertips and the texture of his bare skin, she snatched back her hands and drew away from him. How could she have done that? It was the second time now that she had thrown herself at him.

"Blazes, you make me s-so mad! Where were you, and why did you leave me here? I thought I was all alone."

"I would never do that to you."

"How was I to know? I-I thought something awful had happened to you. I thought you were in some dungeon . . ." How silly it sounded now that he was here all hale and hearty. She sounded like a hysterical female. She added faintly, "I guess I have too much imagination."

"So it would seem."

His heart was drumming. Holding her close even for that one moment had been sweet beyond belief. It had awakened again all those thoughts and feelings he had hoped to put behind him forever. How soft a woman was and how warm, how satisfying to comfort and protect her, how tantalizing that deep, flaming ocean of hunger into which he had been plunged. But he had not meant this to happen, and it was not going to happen again. He would not allow it. He would be kind to her, aye, and he would be courteous, but he could give her nothing more of himself than that. Nothing.

Alexandra watched as he crossed his arms and gazed at her. His face now wore the mask he donned so often. She hated it when he did that, when he made it absolutely impossible for her to know what he was thinking. And how hideous if he thought she had thrown herself at him for any reason other than fear.

"It was stupid of me to be frightened," she murmured. "It's just that it was weird waking up in a house like this with not a soul around. I . . . thought I was back in England somehow . . ." Feeling as if they were being watched, she looked back over her shoulder at the dim interior of the house. "It's so quiet. Where are we, and where is everybody?"

"The house is called Windfall—and we are alone here," Adam said.

"Do you mean—all alone?"

"Hen."

She had known it. No house that was loved and lived in had such a cold, sad, empty feel to it. And there was all that dust. Alexandra walked outside, sat on the top step of the portico, and gazed down on the sun-glittered river. "This is the craziest thing I've ever seen. A manor house in the middle of nowhere—" She shot him an accusing look as a thought occurred to her.

"You put me in that bed."

"Hen." And when he'd seen how dead to the world she was, he had locked her door, galloped downriver to Dover's store and brought back supplies. He had thanked God she was still sleeping when he'd returned to unlock her door or she would have clawed it down. He hadn't a doubt of it. "Was it not comfortable?"

"Certainly it was comfortable . . ." She had never noticed how thickly lashed his eyes were. Short, straight, thick black lashes . . . straight black brows over jet-black eyes. She had never seen eyes so black before . . .

"Well, then?"

She was imagining him carrying her up the stairs, placing her on the bed while she slept and . . . She blushed fiercely thinking of those strong dark hands moving over her body and his lips brushing hers, perhaps brushing her skin . . . She continued to gaze at the river, twisted a strand of hair about one finger. "It's . . . not important . . ."

Adam's mouth curved as he observed her pink face. So. She thought he had taken advantage of her, and to deny it would be a waste of breath. He said, "There is food. Are you hungry?"

"Nay." Food was the furthest thing from her mind. She rose, descended into tall grass filled with buttercups, and walked around the great red-brick dwelling with the Cougar by her side. Returning to the front, she studied its curved portico and pillars and the large lilac bushes that were about to open their purple blossoms. In truth, it was a beautiful place. Fit for a king. Turning to the brave, she asked. "Why did you bring me here?"

Deciding it was best not to tell her of his concern for her health, Adam replied, "I saw that you were tired. I thought you needed familiar surroundings for a while."

Alexandra laughed, which in turn made her cough. "You must think I live like royalty."

"You do not live in a Mohawk longhouse, Alexandra—or on the back of a Narragansett mare."

Seeing how grim his face had become, she said, "I guess it wouldn't be too good for your cause if you returned me to Tiyanoga all worn out and sickly."

"I admit, there is that." Adam's black eyes tracked over her; the spun-gold hair, her small perfect teeth showing between rosy lips, the watchfulness in those amazing green eyes. Within him, the glow of his caring swelled, filling him with its warmth—and with alarm. She must not know. She must not have the slightest hint of what was happening to him. Fighting for control, he said gruffly, "You will be blooming when I return you to your father, Gold Hair. Never fear."

The slow, deliberate way his eyes moved over her brought a fresh wash of pink to Alexandra's face. Worse, that deep twinge she had felt before speared her again to send its lovely warm ripples raying out into her limbs. She sighed. All he had to do was look at her and she turned to jelly. She quickly put her attention back to Windfall.

"Whose house is this?"

"It belongs to the Duke of Dover."

She raised her eyebrows. "The brother of—"

"—your enemy, Lord Adam."

"I never said he was my enemy!" she protested. "I simply don't care for that type of man, and I refuse to marry him—should he ever ask for me, that is." She swiftly changed the subject. "How is it that you have a key?"

"I oversee the house for Lord Adam. It was he who lived here."

Alexandra's hopes soared. "When?" Had he been there when her father had invited him to the party to meet her? Was Tiyanoga that close then?

Adam read her face as easily as he had ever read Eliza's. He saw that she was still hoping to escape from him. "It has been two years since he left," he replied.

"He never came back?"

"Iah."

Alexandra gazed thoughtfully at the empty house. "It's strange. It looks inside as if he left in a great hurry. As if life here just came to a standstill. I wonder what happened?"

Adam said crisply, "Perhaps you can ask him someday."

Alexandra gave her head a emphatic shake. "Thank you, nay."

"He is not a bad sort. You might even approve of him."

"Perish the thought I'll ever have to meet him. But on the other hand, I do hope he hasn't met some vile end."

"He has not met a vile end."

"How can you be so sure? Maybe not all your brethren like him as well as the Mohawks. In truth, why else would he abandon such a place as this for two years?"

Adam smiled. "He is alive and well, I promise you. I have seen him recently."

Alexandra blinked. "Is he . . . likely to return while we're here?"

When he saw her very evident distaste at the thought, his amusement turned to irritation. In God's name, what ailed this little wench that she hated him so? He had never abused a woman in his life, and he was damned tired of her intimating that he did. "You need food," he said. "Come."

Alexandra did not argue. She felt so hungry all of a sudden that she was light-headed. She tagged after him up the steps, through the open door, and back to the kitchen. Now she noticed the heavy rafters, the churn standing in a corner, and the great open hearth with copper pots and ladles hanging close to hand. Her eyes grew large as the Cougar strode to a corner table and emptied onto it the contents of the burlap bag that sat there. Potatoes and onions spilled out, and several smaller bags.

Alexandra moved closer and touched them in amazement. This was real food. Not jerky or pemmican. "Where did all of these things come from?"

"I kept the springhouse stocked," Adam lied. "And while you slept, I caught some fish."

Alexandra's mouth was already watering. "Will we have to fire up the hearth to cook?"

"I have a fire going outside." He watched with interest as she lifted the bags and sniffed them.

"Flour and sugar, I'll wager, but what's this?"

"Cornmeal. The other is salt, and this"—he unwrapped a small greasy packet—"is salt pork."

"Are there mixing bowls and spoons?"

He shrugged, looked about. "Somewhere."

In truth, he was at a loss. The kitchen had never been his domain. Eliza had ruled it, guiding firmly but gently the two young Palatine German girls they had hired as servants. Now he could not believe what he was seeing—this small, spoiled English city girl taking command of the Windfall kitchen, opening cupboard doors, exploring drawers, her beautiful face flushed with excitement. He had never seen her so animated, and he felt his earlier fears for her vanishing.

"Have we water handy?" Alexandra asked. "Is there a pump? If I'm to make bread I'll need it, and I should wipe up a bit, it's so dusty!" She blew a lock of silver-gold hair out of her eyes.

Adam was astonished. "Bread?"

"Not the real thing, of course, since I have no yeast, but I'll do my best. It would be grand if there's a griddle. If not, some flat stones will do. We can lay them on the coals ..." She had watched the Indian women cook cornmeal cakes that way.

Adam left in a daze of disbelief to fetch the water. When he returned with a bucketful, she had opened windows, vanquished the dust on the worktable, found a griddle, and was busily stirring together flour, corn-meal and salt in a large wooden bowl. She looked up with shining eyes as he entered.

"Oh, good, you got water." She ladled a bit into the flour mix, combined the two with a wooden spoon, and kneaded it briefly. "There. Now for the potatoes and onions ..."

"The coals are not yet hot enough to bake them." She was moving far too fast for him.

"I saw a frying pan. Why don't we slice and fry them—it won't take as long and I can make the bread at the same time."

They went outside. Adam carrying the long-handled frying pan and griddle and vegetables, Alexandra hugging the bowl of dough in her arms, and resting atop the bowl's rim, two paper-thin china plates and the necessary utensils. She carefully set the plates aside in a safe place and took the pans from his hands. After putting them on the hot coals, she turned to the Cougar.

"Have you ever sliced a potato or an onion?"

Adam crossed his arms. "It is woman's work," he said. It was the belief of the Indian male, and was what Hawk would have said. He would do well to remember it. Hawk had been his model on more than one occasion.

Alexandra grinned. "In that case, I'll not tell—but do get busy." She took a potato and a paring knife and put them firmly into his hands. With another knife, she sliced off two chunks of salt pork and tossed them into the pans. "I'll help you after I get the bread made." When he did not move but stood staring at her, she said gently, "It's not hard. This is all you do . . ." She took his potato, brushed off the dirt clinging to it, and sliced it deftly into the skillet, skin and all, to sizzle in the pork fat.

Adam silently did her bidding, his attention seemingly on the potatoes, but it was not. It was on her. He was intrigued by her complete change of mood and the brightness of her eyes, and baffled by how cleverly she shaped the dough into small symmetrical patties and laid them on the spitting griddle. In God's name, who was this pink-cheeked, happy young homebody, and what had she done with the sulky, arrogant little witch he had been hauling around the countryside?

Adam studied her openly as they sat in the grass eating off Dover's priceless Wedgwood dinner plates. He mopped up the succulent juices with the last of the bread, savored it, put the plate aside, and leaned back against a tree trunk, his hands behind his head. "You have amazed me . . ."

Alexandra, too, put her plate aside. "Why? Because I know how to mix flour and water?"

She had been all too aware of the Cougar's silent scrutiny while she ate. She was guilty of her own secret study of him. She had scarcely been able to keep her eyes off him as he'd obediently sliced the vegetables and then stirred them so they would not burn. She had noticed from the very beginning that he was different from the Mohawks . . . They were all dark-skinned and muscular and tall, aye, but he was taller, more leanly built. His skin was bronze rather than mahogany, and the play of the sun's rays upon it as they ate was enchanting—smooth, polished copper over rock-hard muscles that flexed and rippled as he refilled his plate or reached for more bread. And she liked it that he did not have that strange stiff brush of hair springing from his scalp as the others did. His hair was long and free and was kept from his eyes by a thin leather band with a feather in it. And he shaved. She had never seen the others shave. They plucked out each hair as it grew with what appeared to be a clam shell . . .

"It is not that you mixed flour and water, Alexandra," Adam replied softly to her question, "but that the two things became bread. Very good bread. I did not expect it of you."

Seeing her in the kitchen, flushed and bright-eyed and with flour on her nose, had brought back in a rush the way it had been in the early happy days with Eliza. He had crushed the memory instantly. It was not why had come to Windfall, to revive memories. Now that he was there, he could hardly wait to leave.

He continued to study Alexandra quietly. She had brightened while she was cooking, but now she had slumped again. Seeing that the dark smudges beneath her eyes were more prominent, he felt anger uncurl within him. Every extra day he kept her here with him was a gamble. There was danger everywhere—snakes, bears, pumas, disease, abduction. If he had any sense at all, and if he had anything remotely resembling a heart, he would return her to her father just as soon as she was ready to travel.

He was not prepared for the loneliness the thought stirred within him. He smothered it, as he did his memories. A woman was the last thing in the world he wanted or needed. No matter what his heart told him, his head reminded him that when he had left Windfall two years ago, he'd made a vow that he swore by still. He would have no woman again, and no child. He would have no laughter in this house to remind him of what he had lost. He did not need such things. The Mohawks were his life now. He was one of them. He was more Indian than white, and he knew now that the heart of an Indian had beat in his breast long before he had seen this land he now loved. He doubted he would ever return to his own people for more than a visit. He rose abruptly and bent to smother the fire.

Gazing on his suddenly grim face, Alexandra asked softly, "Who are you really?"

Only his iron discipline kept Adam from showing his shock. He forced himself to ask easily, "Who do you think I am?"

"I don't know—but you don't look like them. The Mohawks."

He released the breath he had been holding. "I am not Mohawk."

"And not Oneida?"

"Iah. My people are not of the Six Nations. They are from . . . a far place." God knew, it was the truth. As he watched her yawn and rub her eyes, concern nagged him again. What she needed was twenty-four hours of good, solid sleep, and a week's worth of meals like the one they'd just eaten to lighten her step and put the flesh back on her bones.

"I should wash these beautiful dishes and put them away," Alexandra murmured.

"Why?"

"Why? Because they're dirty and they're Wedgwood, that's why. Besides, we can't eat off them again until they're washed."

"There are others. There are fifty others where those came from." He had never quite understood why old Dover had bought so damned much crockery.

Alexandra's giggle at his evident disapproval turned into another yawn, and another and another. "I guess they won't run away at that." It was a good thing the servants at the Larches could not hear her.

Adam's face did not show the battle he was waging, the tug-of-war between his growing desire and his vow. He enjoyed looking at her far too much. Her softly rounded body, the winsome curve of cheeks and chin, the sweep of golden lashes over those sea-green eyes, sunlight trapped in her wild cloud of hair . . . Not trusting himself to look at her further, he continued to smother their cookfire. "I suggest you get more sleep."

"It's daylight."

"There are none here to say you cannot sleep in the daylight if you are tired."

"I guess you're right." When they rode at night, she had always tried to sleep a bit during the day, but she never quite got enough. And when she did sleep, there were always her dreams to plague her. Dreams of Mojag stealing her. Plain and simple, she was exhausted. She yawned again. "Maybe I will go up for a little. Shall I use the same bedchamber?"

"If you wish. And Alexandra, I have put your writing things and your journal in the bag with your belongings."

"Th-thank you . . ." It was a surprise. She was nearly to the kitchen door when she heard her name called. She turned. "Aye?"

"There is a lock on your door, Alexandra. Use it if you wish . . ."

"Thank you again." But she knew she would not. Not with the trust that was growing between them. She gave him a smile and a friendly wave. "I'll try not to sleep the day away . . ."

Chapter 9

When she returned to the bedchamber, Alexandra quickly removed the Indian clothing she had worn for so many days. After closing the draperies against the sunshine, she crawled between the sheets. The cotton was smooth and cool against her bare flesh, and for the first time, she felt gratitude toward the English lord who had lived there. How ironic it was that she, who cringed at the very thought of him, should be reaping the rewards of his luxurious taste. But she didn't want to think about Lord Adam and his neglect of Windfall now. She wanted to sleep. She badly needed to sleep.

She yawned, stretched, closed her eyes—and saw the Cougar. The memory of him overpowered her, driving every thought of sleep from her head. All she wanted was to think about him; the way he looked and moved and spoke, and the way his eyes moved over her. It caused a lovely, fiery little comet to streak through her body. And caused guilt to cloak her afterward. She felt so guilty. How could it be that so soon after Papa's death, she could feel this way? It was only four weeks ... But she did feel this way. She couldn't help it. She had gone from hating the Cougar to liking him. Liking him very much.

From the very first, he had been gentle with her. She couldn't deny it. And aside from tying her to him that one night and being a bit of a tyrant—but then what man wasn't?—he had been considerate and protective.

And although she pretended otherwise, she understood, she really did, why he had not returned her to Tiyanoga. But he would. She had doubted it for a while, but no more. He would return her to Tiyanoga. She shook her head. She dared not start thinking about Tiyanoga or she would never get to sleep.

She yawned again, closed her eyes, turned first on one side, then the other, and then onto her back between the rose-scented sheets, but sleep would not come. She saw in her mind's eye the Cougar lifting her onto Anoki or Dyani . . . She recalled his deep laughter . . . She saw him lying on the narrow bed next to hers, a rope linking them, and saw his veiled black eyes moving over her, brightening her cheeks, making her heart tremble.

What was he thinking when he looked at her that way? she wondered, her breathing quickening. Was he thinking the same thing that she was? That he liked what he saw? That he wanted to touch her? Kiss her? She sat up, her hands to her cheeks. What was this thing that was happening to her? She hated it, and the power he had over her. He could make her heart race and her knees turn to water just by looking at her, touching her, being near her. Aye, just by existing. No other man she had ever known in her life had done that to her or made those exciting glitters of stardust flicker through her bloodstream. Yet when she returned to England—and she knew now that she would—she would never see him again.

She threw back the sheet and sat up. This was hopeless. She was not going to sleep. She was as restless as the wind that had picked up and was now whipping the treetops and filling the sky with gray clouds so that her bedchamber was darkening. She slid out of bed onto the carpeted floor. She could not go downstairs, not yet. She could not face him. She wanted to prowl, to pace. Her eyes went to the dressing room. Perhaps there was something in the closet there, a man's shirt or dressing gown that she could throw on rather than donning her doeskins. Any old thing would suffice for the brief time she meant to wear it.

Entering the small dim room, Alexandra noticed again the faint scent of the bed linens. Roses. And when she swung open the double closet doors, the lovely aroma nigh enveloped her. She stared, seeing that the closet was filled with gowns. In the dwindling light, she saw that they were mostly day gowns, but she also counted two ball gowns and three riding gowns, and innumerable coats and jackets and capes. On the shelf above stood a row of shoes and gleaming boots.

Her curiosity now fully roused, she began opening drawers. Each was stuffed with a different item of dress—purses, muffs, gloves, underthings, jewelry— wonderful jewelry. She carried several pieces to a window in the bedchamber and grew wide-eyed examining them. My goodness, it was a fortune she held in her hands! A sapphire necklace, an emerald and diamond bracelet, a lovely chain-thin circlet of gold set with amethysts . . . No wonder Papa had been so eager for her to meet Lord Adam Rutledge! He was disgustingly wealthy, and remarkably well-prepared for female visitors. Or was he wed, and Papa had not known? She shook her head. Nay, it simply was not possible. Papa would have known.

As she returned the lovely things to their drawers, she contemplated the fact that she was a female visitor. Why should she not wear one of the gowns? Just for a bit, of course, and who was there to care? She remembered vividly the freedom she had felt when she'd first worn Mohawk garb. Now it would be just as wonderful to feel soft cotton against her skin again. In the fast-fading light, and to the accompaniment of thunder, she searched out a simple day dress and carried it into the bedchamber. It was lovely, a creamy lawn sprigged with violets and as light as a cloud. Not bothering with a camisole or petticoat, she quickly slipped it over her head. She sighed. How absolutely lovely it felt, as soft and weightless as a breeze, and it smelled wonderful. She had almost forgotten what civilization was like . . .

Spying a tall oval dressing glass in a corner, Alexandra approached it almost shyly—and stared in shock at the pale stranger gazing back at her. She gasped. This could not be she! It couldn't. Her hair was ghastly, all long and wild and tangled, and she was practically skin and bones. It was true she had not felt well, she ached and was tired much of the time, but she'd never dreamed she looked so dreadful. Touching trembling fingers to the dark shadows under her eyes and the hollows in her cheeks, she realized why the Cougar's black eyes had studied her so frequently. It was not because he had the same yearnings for her that she did for him. Nay. It was because he thought she was ill. That was why he had brought her here. He was worried about her.

She sank to the carpet and covered her face with her hands. Only once had she come close to crying during this entire ordeal, but she was alone now. And as the first crash of lightning cracked open the sky, she wept silently. For the father she had lost, for her mother, and for the Alexandra who had been lost somewhere between Tiyanoga and here, wherever *here* was.

Adam had hoped not to use the Windfall kitchen during their stay, but with the storm coming, they would be eating inside this night. As he put his attention on laying the kindling and logs and brought a candle from the table to light them, memories swarmed over him. He attempted to ignore them, but they would not be denied: his darling in that very rocker, sitting in the warmth and the fireglow with her sewing in her hands . . . the two of them entangled in each other's arms in the great tester bed upstairs . . . the oils she'd loved so and hung side by side over the mantelpiece in their bedchamber.

He shook his head, a ghost of a smile touching his

lips. She had so talked about those damned oils and yearned for them—family portraits of him and her—that old Dover had shipped them over as a Christmas surprise for her the first year. It was good of the old boy, and they'd given her pleasure before she had . . . He shook his head, overwhelmed by the terrible image forming in his mind.

After catching up the pail, he strode outside to the pump, filled it, strode back to the kitchen, and latched the door behind him just as the deluge began. He lit a second candle, and had just hung the kettle over the fire when the first lightning seared the sky. He wondered if the noise had awakened Alexandra and frightened her, and then remembered her earlier terror at being alone. He grabbed a candle and took the stairs two at a time. He knocked on the door of her bedchamber.

"Alexandra . . ." When another terrible crash shook the house, he knocked louder. "Alexandra?" The door opened.

"A-aye?" Alexandra tried to dash away her streaming tears, but it was hopeless. She was crying a river.

Adam was shocked to see how pale she was and that tears streaked her face. What was this about and how long had she been crying? He set the candle on a table and put his arms around her. He said quietly, as if to a child, "You are safe, Alexandra. I am here."

Alexandra's heartbeat doubled as the brave held her and gently, gently stroked back the hair from her damp face. She reminded herself that she was skinny and ugly and he was comforting her out of pity. He was sorry for her, and worried about her. Being kind to her was his way of protecting his Mohawks. Even so, it was lovely being warm and safe inside the hard circle of his arms, and feeling the heavy thudding of his heart.

Her breath caught, but it was not the lightning, crashing and filling the storm-dark room with flashes of silver, that had startled her. It was that she had received a sudden glimpse of the truth. The tall, shadowy figure in that unforgettable dream she'd had—the enemy from whom she had been fleeing but who had become her savior, her haven from danger—it was the Cougar! It was his kisses, his hands which had so electrified her that she remembered them and yearned for them still.

"Don't be afraid," Adam murmured. His lips sought the pale, soft cloud of her hair.

Alexandra nodded, too numb and confused to speak. She was torn between wanting, needing his warmth and strength, and realizing the danger such closeness could bring. He was Indian, a savage, and everybody knew that there was a limit to what even a gently bred Englishman could tolerate without snapping. She gulped back the near-hysterical laughter waiting to leap from her throat. Her dear old tutor had taught her well.

"You need not cry anymore, Gold Hair."

His deep voice vibrated through her body like an organ through a church.

"I-I know."

With every ounce of strength he had, Adam was battling his desire to gather her closer and kiss her tears away; kiss her wet mouth and swollen eyelids; kiss the sweet curves of her cheeks and the small dimple in the center of her chin. He gritted his teeth, tightened his muscles in resistance. *Iah,* he would not. It would frighten her, and in his heart, he was still wed to the only woman he would ever love. His role now was that of protector, not lover. He would never cross the line, nor would—

His thoughts shattered into a million fragments as he noticed for the first time what she was wearing. He released her, felt the blood draining from his face.

He asked harshly, "What is that you are wearing?"

But he knew full well what she was wearing. It was the gown Eliza had worn the first day he had met her. He wanted to roar at Alexandra, shake her, demand an explanation for this act of sacrilege. Eliza's clothing, her belongings, the room they had shared, all had been banished from his thoughts and his sight on that night she had died—until now. He stiffened his body to keep himself from trembling.

Alexandra was stunned by his blazing eyes and the rage on his face. And she was frightened. She had never seen him so angry. "I'm . . . so sorry."

What had angered him so when just moments ago he had been the very soul of tenderness and compassion? Would Lord Adam have disapproved all that fiercely because she had donned one simple day dress out of the many elaborate gowns he kept for his mistresses? Perhaps she had overstepped, but it was not such a serious crime as all that.

"I never intended t-to be seen like this." she murmured. "I just wanted to wear a-a nice dress again for a bit. It's been a while and they're all so lovely and—" Her face burned with embarrassment. She was whining like a servant caught doing a shoddy job. "Do please ignore my babbling. It was wrong of me and I apologize. If you'll excuse me, I'll take it off immediately." She turned toward the dressing room.

"Wait . . ." Adam was hit by remorse. Where was his head? He was blaming her for not knowing the very things he was keeping from her. And he saw suddenly that her dressing in Eliza's clothing was but part of the familiar surroundings he wanted for her. As his gaze moved over the soft lines and embroidered details of the achingly familiar dress, it was like a lance going into his heart. He drew a ragged breath. If it gave her comfort, he would pay the price. He said thickly, "I forgot for a moment that Lord Adam is a man of . . . exceeding generosity."

Alexandra gave him a wintry stare. "Indeed."

"He would want you to wear anything you wished while you were his guest. He would insist."

"Indeed." He was lying. He was positively choking on the words. What on earth was his worry? Did he think she would pop the seams or spill fish grease down her front? "Do thank His Lordship for me when you see him next but"—she cringed as lightning lit the room, crashed deafeningly—"but I prefer my Mohawk garb. It will just take me a moment to—"

"Do you like the dress?"

"Of course. It's beautiful, but—"

"Then wear it."

Alexandra studied his face, but it was unreadable. Once more he had surprised her. He was always surprising her. She shook her head. "You baffle me."

"I have also frightened you."

She raised her slender shoulders in a shrug. "Aye."

Adam regretted it more than she could ever imagine. He was a damned brute. "I'm sorry. Will you allow me to make amends?"

Alexandra was taken aback. "What sort of amends?"

"Come to the kitchen." He held out his hand. "Come, Gold Hair . . ."

Alexandra hesitated. She really should not. Not now when she knew he was the man in her dream, and not when his voice sounded so velvety and husky and his black eyes were masked, as though he did not want her to see what they held. But she wanted to . . . she wanted to. Shyly she laid her hand in his and felt his long fingers close around it. As they walked down the darkened hallway, lit by his candle, she was nervous. All of that dark gleaming skin—and he always seemed so much taller when she stood close to him. He towered over her. And having her hand held so firmly by his was sending a thrill burning through her. She swallowed, said carefully:

"Lord Adam has very elegant taste in artwork."

"The paintings belong to the Duke of Dover. Everything in this house does."

"Oh." Thunder, lightning, and the slashing of rain against the tall casement windows accompanied their descent to the first floor. "I hope we don't float away . . ."

"We are on a hill."

"Of course. Thank goodness . . ."

He did not tell her this was the damnedest storm he had encountered in the four years he had lived in this valley, and it seemed to be sitting right over Windfall. His worry was that lightning would strike one of the oaks towering above the house. But for now, the kitchen was a haven. It was warm and cheerful with the fire crackling and the water in the kettle just now beginning to bubble.

"Would you like tea?" he asked. He did not allow his gaze to linger on the vision she made in his darling's flower-sprigged gown.

Alexandra smiled. "Tea? Do you mean it?"

"It is in the pantry." Right where he had left it. Making it for Eliza and sharing it had been one of their treasured afternoon rituals.

"I'd love some tea. Shall I make it?" The paper-thin cups and saucers she had seen earlier had been washed and were draining on a snowy linen towel.

"The next time," Adam replied. Eliza had burned herself on her first attempt at wielding the heavy kettle, and he wanted no such accident with this maid.

Alexandra moved restlessly about the kitchen, admiring its brick floor and stone hearth, fingering the blue calico curtains, and listening to the rain and wind rattling the panes. She tried not to jump as lightning continued to crash over their heads. Blazes, what an awful row. She hated lightning, and storms like this terrified her, but with the Cougar radiating such calm, she could hardly do less. Her gaze kept returning to him. Why and how did an Indian brave who declared cooking was woman's work know so much about making tea in an English kitchen?

She watched, fascinated by the lithe grace with which he moved between hearth and table, his every movement measured and purposeful. When the tea was finally brewed and his big hands competently fit the strawberry cozy over the pot to keep it hot, Alexandra grinned up at him.

"I make bread, you make tea. Now it's my turn to be amazed." She raised her voice to be heard above the thunder rolling up and down the valley.

"I have seen it done many times."

It had been a mistake, telling her to wear the gown, Adam thought. Not for the reason he had expected, that it would bring back unbearable memories, but for one that was far worse. He did not see Eliza's face and shining brown hair adorning it; he saw only Alexandra's luminous green eyes and the firelight reflected in that amazing silver-gold mane of hers. He was betraying his darling . . . forgetting her. Had her skin been as white and soft and fragrant as Alexandra's . . . her breath as sweet . . . her breasts as full? He could not remember. All he could remember was how small and warm and wonderful she had felt in his arms. And how much she had loved him and he her. Aye, that he could remember.

Alexandra removed the cozy and poured his tea, but before she could give it to him, lightning split the sky. She jumped, glared at her shaking hand and the cup rattling in the saucer. "Blazes, I've gone and sloshed your tea all over. Oh, I do hate this stupid weather! When will it stop?"

"Soon . . ." Adam warned himself not to touch her again. But it was an order he could not obey, not when she looked so frightened. He put the cup and saucer on the table, took her hands and, his eyes distant, listened to the keening beyond the windows. Already it was farther away and less insistent. "It is moving on," he said, and hoped to God it was so.

Hearing the rumbling and crashing, Alexandra murmured, "It's still too close for me."

At the moment, she was more frightened by the fire racing through her veins than she was by the storm.

And she wondered, What would he do if he suspected how she felt? Surely he could see it on her face and feel it in her hands, feel the heat tingling through them. He had to feel it. Withdrawing them, she poured a second cup of tea and gave it to him.

"I'll take the sloshed one, I don't mind ..." She emptied the spilled brew into the cup, took a sip and sat in the rocker. "I love rockers beside a kitchen hearth. It gives me such a cozy feeling ... and you make good tea. Hot, and strong and not a bit bitter. It's very good ...." Listening to herself, she was horrified. She sounded just like Mama.

Adam lowered himself to the hearth where he sat cross-legged, drinking his tea and studying her thoughtfully. He had never heard her chatter so. His narrowed gaze did not miss the brightness of her eyes and the high color touching her cheekbones. He saw then that her face, her throat, even her breasts above the neckline of her gown were turning pink. He frowned. Either she was too close to the fire or she had a fever. But she had not coughed recently.

Seeing his dark eyes moving over her, Alexandra laid a hand on her heart. It was shaking her whole body. She returned her gaze to the flames and cast about frantically for something to talk about. Anything. "You say the duke has never lived here? Only Lord Adam?"

"That is so."

"What is he like? The duke, I mean. It's a pity he built this beautiful place and furnished it and then never lived here."

"It was not of his choosing. He was called back to England on business, and took ill there."

"What a pity. Not seriously ill, I hope."

"I am not informed." It was the truth. He did not know nearly as much as he wanted. Dover's infrequent letters promised that he was still doctoring and soon would be fit as a fiddle, but in his heart, Adam felt his brother was dying. He read between the lines, and saw the shakiness of his brother's hand, and worried. Dover had never been robust.

"Well, let's hope he gets better soon and comes back," Alexandra said. "Windfall needs him." She had kept her eyes everywhere but on the Cougar, but his image remained in her mind to taunt her. Firelight causing his skin and hair to gleam, shadows leaping over the long, sculptured, muscular length of his arms and legs. "I should think he'd be afraid someone would break in and carry off all his valuables." She thought of the many paintings and of the jewelry she had discovered upstairs.

"My people have no use for the treasures of the white man, Alexandra. Even if they did, they would not steal them."

"I meant the settlers."

"It is not a concern." She was his concern. Something was wrong. She could not sit quietly, nor could she look at him.

Alexandra rose, placed her cup on the table, and refilled it. "May I offer you more?"

Adam got to his feet. "I have had enough." And he'd had enough of worrying about her. "Alexandra, are you—"

Alexandra screamed as an ear-splitting crash sounded over their heads and Windfall shuddered. It was as if all the demons in hell had arrived and their shrieks and roarings were echoing up and down the valley. She wanted to fly to the Cougar, to be with him when the house fell down around them, but she forced herself to stay where she was. She could not run to him every time she was frightened. But when he came to her and pulled her into his arms, she wrapped her own arms about his waist and buried her head against his chest.

"Oh, Cougar . . ." She was shaking.

"Shhh. It is only noise now. The storm is dying. You are safe . . ."

For long moments they stood holding each other. She did not realize how cold she was until his warmth began to seep into her icy limbs. She stopped trembling finally, raised her head, whispered, "It's childish of me to be so frightened."

"*Iah,*" Adam murmured. "I have never seen such a storm."

"You didn't shriek."

He tilted her chin, smiled down at her. "I wanted to."

"Oh, aye." She grinned, imagining it.

"You are a brave woman, Alexandra. Never doubt it."

His words made her tremble all over again. Aware suddenly of the breadth of his back and the smoothness of his skin beneath her fingertips, Alexandra withdrew her hands, rested them on his forearms—and felt their hardness and the crisp black curls growing there. "I should drink my tea before it gets cold."

Adam fought the fire moving through him, fought his overwhelming desire to taste her and touch his lips to her hair, to her throat and her own soft lips. Let her go, he ordered himself. Let her go . . . let her go . . . but, sweet Jesus, he could not. He held her more tightly. "Stay," he said low.

Alexandra looked up at him, astonished. "You mean—like this?"

"Like this. In my arms." He smoothed back her tumbled, fire-kissed mane of hair. "Stay, Alexandra."

She whispered, her breathing quickening, "I thought lightning had hit the house. I thought the roof was going to fall on us. That's the only reason I'm . . . where I am . . ." She turned her head, listened to the distant thunder-muttering and the wild beating of her heart. "Maybe the storm's coming back . . ."

He heard the eagerness in her voice. "Do you want it to come back?"

Alexandra met his black gaze without blinking. "Aye," she said softly, "just . . . for a bit . . ." When he pulled her closer, she lifted her mouth, felt him gently, gently brushing it with his.

Chapter 10

As the Cougar's lips grazed Alexandra's, pleasure flamed through her, so hot and sweet that she gasped in surprise. She had never felt anything as delicious as his small tender kisses brushing the corners of her mouth, the peaks of her upper lip, the dimple in the center of her chin. She did not want him to stop, and she shivered as the flame within her seemed to turn to sun-dust and leave a shimmering, scorching trail of excitement in its wake.

Adam muffled a groan. He had seen instantly that she was untouched. He was the first to kiss her fresh mouth, perhaps even the first to hold her, and now he saw that she was hungry. Frightened but hungry. With gentle coaxing, he could have her for the taking—but she would hate him afterward, and he would hate himself. Nay, here it would end. He would hold her, aye, but only long enough to deaden the ache in his heart and the emptiness in his arms. And he would kiss her. What good was it to hold a woman close and feel her warmth and softness without tasting and kissing her? He touched his tongue gently to her lips, saw her eyes fly open. He said low, "I will not hurt you, Alexandra."

Alexandra's heart turned over and then resumed its racing. He had touched her with his tongue! No one, not even Justine and Sara, who had been wedded women when she left England, had ever said anything about tongues. "I . . . don't know how t-to do that."

Adam smiled. "I will teach you." As he ran his tongue lightly over his lips once more, he saw her eyes grow luminous.

"Is it . . . an Indian custom?" It shocked her even as it fascinated her.

"Many people have been known to do it," he answered gravely. "Even Englishmen."

"Am I . . . supposed to do it also?"

"Only if it gives you pleasure." Adam raised her small hands to his lips, kissed the pink tip of one finger, tasted it, tasted the pearly nail.

In turn, Alexandra shyly raised his hand to her own lips, shyly kissed one finger, shyly touched her tongue to it. She grinned up at him. "I've never tasted anyone before. You're salty—and smoky . . ." She laughed with the excitement of it. "Quite tasty, in fact."

Adam gathered her to him more closely. He had known he was as hollow and empty as a miser's heart, but he had not realized just how hollow and empty. Like this house, he mused, he was just a shell. There was no light or warmth in either Windfall or him anymore. And now, suddenly, here was this young Alexandra, as alive and warm and bright in his cold world as the fire on the hearth. Her flame would warm him briefly, but then it would be gone. He reminded himself it was as he wished it. Never again would he have another woman or child to lose to death.

He lifted Alexandra's chin, kissed her lips long and tenderly, and then tasted them once more. He felt a tremor ripple through her and then her own small pink tongue met his hesitantly, but willingly. He heard her quickly indrawn breath, felt the speeding of her heart and his own heart thundering.

"You taste like springtime," he said thickly.

Alexandra whispered, "How can that be?"

He laughed softly. "You are a woman . . ."

She was shaken. Shaken by the heat burning in his black eyes, by the pure enchantment of his words, by his closeness and the sleek, leashed, savage power of him—and by this strange way of kissing that she had never heard of before. It brought them so close, and was so exciting she wanted him to do it again . . . and again . . . and again.

"You are young, soft, tender, fresh, unspoiled . . ." He kissed her temples, traced the curve of her cheeks and chin with his lips, kissed her long golden lashes. "You are warm . . . and you have about you the scent of flowers . . . You not only taste like springtime, you *are* springtime, Gold Hair."

Heart pounding, Alexandra touched his face, felt the rough stubble of a day's beard on his jaw and throat, ran her fingers through his thick mane of black hair. The masculine texture of his skin and hair enchanted her. "And you're like no man I've ever seen before . . ."

Adam's eyes flickered with his hidden amusement. "Do the men of England look so different, then?"

"Aye. They wear ruffles and satins and wigs and ribbons and"—she shivered as he stroked her hair and kissed her ear, the side of her throat, his breath warm and moist on her newly awakened flesh—"and they're not as tall or as"—she gasped as he drew her gown off one shoulder and pressed his lips to her skin—"as strong as you . . . or a-as beautiful." Oh, nay, why had she said that? He would hate it!

Adam chuckled. "It is you who are beautiful, Gold Hair." The kisses and caresses he had given her had been small and teasing; intimacies that he had known would not frighten her. Now he wanted to taste and explore her further. His hungry body demanded it, and he saw in the way she had responded, the easy way she fit into his arms, that she was excited. "You are very beautiful . . ."

Embarrassed, Alexandra shook her head. She remembered too well her dreadful reflection in the dressing glass. "I was never beautiful—and especially not now. Now I-I'm skinny."

"Iah." Drawing her gown lower, Adam gently cupped one perfect naked breast in his hand, and with his thumb stroked her small upthrust nipple. "You are soft and round in all the right places."

Alexandra's breath caught as a golden burst of heat radiated throughout her body from that one small spot where he continued to touch and tantalize her. In a daze of delight, she marveled that Indians would know such things. A small moan escaped her lips, only to be stopped by the Cougar's deep kiss. It stirred her so intensely, she was scarcely aware that he was still caressing her bared breast until his mouth closed over it, electrifying her.

As Adam suckled the velvety hardness of her nipple, stroked the skin around it, musing that it was satin, pure satin, he was filled with such a rush of desire, it nearly staggered him. And when Alexandra cried out in pleasure and arched her body against his, hunger roared through him. His every sense was afire. He craved to taste and touch her everywhere, inhale the intoxicating freshness of her resilient young body and bury himself in her softness. But he could not. He was her protector, for the love of God, and now he wondered—Did he possess the strength to protect her from himself? Feeling desire pounding through him with every beat of his heart and every breath he drew, he feared he did not. He dragged in a deep breath and abruptly put her from him.

"You had best go to your bedchamber, Alexandra."

Alexandra stared in astonishment at the harsh lines of his face. "But . . . why?"

"Just go. Take the candle to light your way. I will fetch you when it is time to make dinner."

She was scarcely able to hide her confusion and disappointment. And she was hurt. Why was he so changeable? And what on earth had she done now to make him so stiff and grumpy? The truth dawned as she saw that his black eyes were shuttered, half-closed against the heat smoldering there, and that his breathing was uneven and rasping in and out of his lungs. He wanted to couple with her! Blazes! Without another word, she caught up the candle and left.

Adam's relief was mingled with regret. Bloody hell, that had been close. And it was all his fault. She was an innocent. He had had no business tempting her that way. If they had made love, she would have suffered the torment of the damned afterward. It was bad enough, a woman of her class and innocence sleeping with a man outside wedlock—but with one she thought was Indian? He shook his head. *Iah,* she was not ready for that. The guilt would have destroyed her. Now she would be upstairs pacing, furious, weeping perhaps, remembering that she hated him and why she hated him. He sighed. It was all right. In truth, it was best.

Still throbbing with need, he took up his quiver and bow case and went out into an early twilight. The storm was gone, and had left behind it a teeth-chattering chill and a bracing wind for which he was grateful. It cleared his head. He was grateful, too, for the tall wet grass that soothed his fire as he waded through it, tracking the rabbit that had exploded out of its burrow at his approach. He would snag it for their evening meal, fetch more potatoes from the springhouse, and wash the dinner dishes before Alexandra came back down. On second thought, he would not do any damned dishwashing. No Indian male would ever stoop to such a thing if a squaw was handy.

The soft folds of Alexandra's borrowed gown swirled about her moccasins as she paced the floor of the bedchamber. She'd been going back and forth endlessly, wringing her hands, holding her head, pounding her fists together, but it seemed the longer she walked, the more agitated she became. When her angry gaze fell on the writing table in the darkest part of the room, she took her candle to it, uncorked the inkpot, dipped the quill, and with a hand that shook, began to write rapidly in French:

May 15—Cher Journal, I hate myself. I really do. I feel so guilty and ashamed I could die. Today I allowed the Cougar to do so many things to me—all sorts of things!—that he sent me to my room so he would not mate with me. Once more he has saved me, this time from myself! I was too stupid and silly and wallowing in his arms kissing him even to see what it was doing to him. In truth, I could have just held and kissed him all day. Why, why, why do men have to go all passionate and want to couple right away when the other feels so wonderful?

Alexandra gripped the quill so tightly her fingers turned white.

*But there's more to this than his just making me feel wonderful. He's saved me again and again and guarded me and taken care of me, yet not until today did I realize he's the one from my dream! My savior-dream. And I've seen how he's fighting for his people and how much they love him—*she stared at the flame, twirled the quill slowly and thoughtfully—*and now I wonder, am I in love with him too . . .*

She rose, walked the room again, brooding, unseeing, wondering—How did one discover if it was love. What did love feel like? If only Sara and Justine were here to talk to. Oh, they would absolutely swoon over him. But how natural was it to feel fire shooting through one's body when a man just looked at one? Her friends had never once talked about such a thing, just as they'd never talked about tongues . . . Alexandra sighed, contemplating what it would have been like to couple with him. For one magical moment she imagined it, and then put it from her mind. It simply would never be. Even if she were in love with him, it would never be. They lived in two different worlds, and some day soon she would be back in England again, and he would be a memory . . . She dipped her quill, wrote firmly:

The truth, plain and simple, is that no one lives and breathes in England who is like the Cougar. And if he wants to kiss me, I'm going to kiss him back.—And I refuse to feel ashamed or guilty. It's a promise.

Hearing his knock, Alexandra quickly put away her writing things and called, "Come in."

She was dazzled. He had donned buckskins against the growing chill of the day, but he was still tall, still dark, and his black eyes, reflecting the flame from his candle, glittered. He reminded her of the wilderness itself, going from storm, to calm, so savage, yet so beautiful, and with the prospect of danger always present . . .

Adam had not known what to expect. He hid his surprise at the sweet smile she gave him and the look of serenity on her face. "You may come downstairs now, Alexandra."

"Very well."

Alexandra took her candle and followed him through the dark hall, its fine paintings blooming and fading into the shadows as they passed. He had said he would fetch her when it was time to cook supper. Well, maybe she would and maybe she wouldn't. He would have to ask her very nicely indeed. But when they reached the kitchen, the air was already filled with the mouthwatering aroma of roasting meat. She looked toward the hearth, unable to tell what was on the spit except that it looked crisp and brown and smelled wonderful.

"I thought I was to make supper."

"Have you ever skinned a rabbit?"

She paled. "I would starve first."

He had thought as much. "Now you will not have to starve. The meat is done. There are potatoes in the coals."

She drew a deep breath. Once more he had saved her.

"I'll wash the dishes afterward. And I haven't forgotten the ones from lunch."

"They await you still."

He felt a childish resentment that she was in such calm spirits whereas his nerve endings were still raw. He had a waterfall of worries cascading over him. For one, he could not eat in this kitchen. At least not on this night when Eliza's presence seemed to be everywhere. They had lived in this room in the wintertime—she had cooked, mended their clothing, knitted and dipped candles here. He had read by the fire, repaired his weapons, and consulted with the Mohawks who were free to come and go at will. His door was always open to them. And after all this time, he still believed another door would open and Eliza would be there.

"We will eat in the dining room," he said.

Thinking of the lovely walnut table she had seen there, Alexandra said, "I should put a tablecloth on it first." In the buffet, she found a fine damask cloth, and after she had covered one end of the table, they brought their plates in, seated themselves, and without preamble began to eat.

It was not at all like their earlier meal outside, she thought wistfully. Then they had talked, laughed even, and the sun had smiled down on them. But from what she had seen of this house, it had no sunlight within even when the day was bright outside. It was a house of loneliness and darkness and silence. A silence that was now so thick it was oppressive.

She stole a quick glimpse at the Cougar's impassive face. Was he still thinking, as she was, of what had happened between them? She doubted it. He would have put it from his mind the instant she left the room. He was probably thinking now of the silliness of the white man's ways—tablecloths, china, silver, ornate candlesticks. It wouldn't surprise her a bit if he felt out of place. He was a savage in the manor of an English lord, and this night he did indeed look savage—his mouth a flat grim line, black eyes masked beneath half-closed lids, his jet-black hair swinging long and free over his shoulders and back. He no more belonged here than she belonged in a Mohawk longhouse.

Alexandra sighed and cut a bite of meat. "I haven't inquired today yet—when can I see my mother again? I can't impress upon you too strongly how much she'll be suffering."

"So you said yesterday," Adam's voice was clipped. "My answer is the same as it was then, and the day before." And all the days before that. "Your parents have been—"

"I have only the one now," she said mildly, although the intensity of the look he gave her made her shiver.

"—have been informed that you are safe, and that you will be returned in good time. Your mother will have received your letter long ago."

Adam's nerves were stretched to bowstring tautness. More and more he saw that this plan of his had been a mistake. Keeping her with him would not help his Mohawks, it was harming her, and it was tearing him apart. He could not escape the memories here. This room had as many as the damned kitchen. He could almost hear his darling's voice . . .

Alexandra watched curiously as the Cougar lay down his fork, gazed at his plate for long moments. "Is something wrong with your food?"

"*Iah.*"

"Mine is delicious. I do thank you again for making it."

She frowned. He was looking at her, but he did not see her. His thoughts were miles away. As shadows danced on the papered walls and the wind keened beyond the tall casement windows, she ate quietly and then watched in amazement as he strode suddenly to the window and yanked the draperies shut. He then went to the other window and stared out into the darkness.

Alexandra went to his side. "What is it?" she whispered. "Is someone out there? Do you hear something?" She could not see a thing in the pitch-blackness, but her imagination provided a band of painted savages lurking there and watching them. Watching and waiting. "Cougar . . ." He did not answer. "Cougar, you're frightening me . . ."

"Go back to your dinner, Gold Hair. It is only the wind."

"Are you sure?"

"I am sure. Go. Eat."

Adam remained at the window, straining to hear, his hands tightly gripping the draperies. He had been about to close them against the rising wind, but his heart forbade it. It was as if she were out there weeping. He clenched his jaw, told himself this was insane. She was not out there weeping in the night; it was as he had told Alexandra. It was the wind in the trees.

Even so, he could not force movement into his muscles to shut the sound out, nor could he vanquish the memory he had smothered these two long years. It overpowered him. He saw again her white sweat-streaked face, the pain and misery in her eyes as he cradled her poor, worn, misshapen body in his arms. He bent low, his ear to her lips to catch her ragged whisper that had destroyed him and torn his heart, torn his very soul into pieces: She was so sorry . . . so very sorry . . . She was leaving him . . . Could he forgive her . . . She was so sorry . . .

It was long moments before Adam could thrust away the terrible image. He released the draperies, went to the other window, and reopened those he had closed. He was shaken. He stood looking out into the darkness, composing himself before he turned to Alexandra.

"Come, Gold Hair." His voice did not sound like his own. "Let us finish our food."

Alexandra could not pull her shocked gaze from his face. He seemed so drawn suddenly, and his eyes were damp—it was as if he had just lost his dearest treasure. And there she was, doing nothing to help him. Yearning to comfort him, she said, "Is anything wrong? Can I help in some way?" What had he seen out there to make him so sad?

"Nothing is wrong, *onkiatshi.*" He was touched by the tenderness and concern he saw on her face, but he would not accept it. "We will eat now, and not waste this food."

Seeing the familiar mask return to his face, Alexandra knew this was a thing she must never mention to him again, but she would never forget it. She was still pondering it, wondering what it was about when he said abruptly:

"Alexandra, I am taking you back."

Her eyes flew to his face. "I—beg your pardon?"

"I will return you to Tiyanoga." He watched her hungrily, saw her grow quiet, wondered what she was thinking. He half-hoped she would protest, but what would he do then? He could not keep her here.

"Thank you," Alexandra replied softly. She had thought she'd be filled with the wildest elation when she heard those magical words. Instead, she felt slightly dazed and not quite believing. But Mama, if she had not already died of a broken heart, would be overcome with joy. And in truth, the sooner she got away from this tall dark brave and the way he made her feel, the better off she would be. "Can we leave tomorrow?"

"*Iah.*" Every moment he was near her was one of torment, but she needed at least a week to gain weight and the strength for travel.

"Then when can we go?"

"Soon."

Her eagerness rankled him, but what else had he expected? Day in and day out she had begged to be returned. And now he would return her, and part of him would go with her. And it was his own damned fault for allowing himself to care for her. He was a fool. And double a bloody damned fool for dragging someone so delicately made through this wilderness for whatever reason.

His eyes moved reluctantly over her slight form still attired in Eliza's gown. He saw the tiredness that she tried to hide, the drooping of her head on that delicate neck, the sagging of her shoulders and the heaviness of her eyelids, those dark hollows under her eyes . . . They worried him still, as did her thinness. He shook the thought off. So she was thin and tired. It was not fatal, nor was the cough. She would sleep and he would stuff her for a week and she would be as good as new. He damned well was not going to continue coddling her. The next rabbit he took, she could jolly well skin herself.

He said crisply, "You can wash up now."

"I'd be happy to," Alexandra replied quietly. It was the truth. Dishwashing was nothing compared with skinning a poor bunny. In addition, she did not want to exacerbate his strange mood.

Adam was shamed by her mild reply. He was being a brute again. But if he was disgusted with himself, why was he taking it out on her? It was as if he wanted to hurt her. In silence he helped her to gather their plates and utensils and carry them into the kitchen. There he filled a small tub with boiling water from the kettle and carried it to a sideboard. He pointed to a long-handled sieve that lay there.

"I believe those are pieces of soap in the sieve."

Alexandra smiled. She knew it was soap and knew exactly how to stir up suds with it in the steaming water. "Thank you." She was warmed by his sudden show of gentleness. This was the Cougar she had come to know. "And thank you again for dinner. I loved it. I was so hungry."

"Be careful if you use more water," Adam muttered. "It is scalding and the kettle is heavy." He went out into the night, returned the fragile bones and pelt of the rabbit to the woodlands, and went back to the house.

The moon was high and bright and lit his way as he prowled around and around the house. Each time he passed the kitchen, he was tempted to gaze through the window to see what she was doing, but he did not, nor did he slow his step. Seeing the yellow candle-glow so warm and beckoning was wrenching enough without Alexandra's being there bustling about as Eliza had. His gaze drifted to the deep woods surrounding the house on three sides, moved to the fog wisps, eerie with moonlight as they wreathed the tree-tops, paused seeing the moon itself swimming in the river. He heard the distant cough of a big cat . . . the bark of a coyote . . . the hoot of an owl—but no weeping, no sighing.

He shuddered. Sweet Jesus, this place, this Windfall . . . He loved it, and loved far too much the way things had once been here. In truth, he could not bear a full week of being battered by memories—not with Alexandra flitting about in Eliza's gowns. His gaze returned to the window where her shadow moved to and fro across it. Pulled there by a force he could not resist, Adam looked in, his starving eyes devouring every small thing about her: firelight glinting like tiny flames caught in the pale net of her silver-gold hair, her small white teeth catching her lower lip as she furiously scoured the skillet, her slim arms, as white and flawless as ivory beneath her rolled-up sleeves, the adorable frown between her brows as she lugged the heavy kettle to the dish tub, added more hot water, and then returned it to the iron arm in the hearth.

Adam turned away, sick at heart. It was as he'd suspected this afternoon during the storm. Windfall and his memories were painful, aye, and he would find it difficult to bear them for a full week. But it was Alexandra who had left him totally without defenses and brought him to his knees. He wanted her. He ached with wanting her, and being in this house with her for seven entire days was out of the question. They would leave for Tiyanoga in three days, and doubtless she would be floating on air with her jubilation.

Chapter 11

The Cougar remained outside while Alexandra did the washing up, but as she neatened the kitchen afterward, he returned. She was vastly relieved to have him back, for she had not felt safe without him there. As she found a broom and began sweeping the brick floor, he lowered himself to the hearth and began examining his arrows carefully, one by one, in the firelight. Gazing at his strong profile, so dark and sharp against the flames, she felt a hollow where her stomach ought to have been. She was going to miss him dreadfully.

"Do you need my help, Alexandra?" Adam had felt her gaze upon him ever since he had come inside.

"Not at all." She quickly collected her wits and continued sweeping. "I was just curious, seeing you with your arrows—are they broken or something?"

Think of Mama, she told herself. Think of Mama and how happy she was going to be to see her. And how happy she herself was going to be to get back to civilization. The two of them would undoubtedly depart at once for New York City, and from there they would take the first boat sailing for London. It was a joyous prospect. She would make it joyous . . .

Adam's mouth curved. "They are not broken," he replied, thinking how very young she looked and acted at times. "On these four, the lashings have loosened and must be rewound. Those two"—he indicated the ones lying on the hearth—"must be fletched again. The feathers are worn. The others are bent."

Alexandra drew closer and peered down at them. It made her shiver to look at their sleek gleaming length and sharp points. "Are the feathers to make them pretty?"

His laughter rang out. *"Iah,* Gold Hair, the feathers are not to make them pretty." She had an amazing knack for lifting his spirits without even trying. "They are for slowing the arrow's butt end and making it fly straight."

She joined in his laughter. "How dumb I am." She could not pull herself away from him. She was trapped by the sound of his deep laughter, the sight of his white smile and black cape of hair, a sudden tantalizing glimpse of his dark throat.

Adam said gently, "I do not expect you to know about the construction of arrows."

She grinned. "I'm glad."

She finished sweeping, put the broom in the pantry, and returned to the dish tub. "I'll throw the water out if you'll please open the door." As she lifted it, he was by her side.

"Iah, Alexandra. I will throw out the water; you will open the door."

He did not see her smile as she yielded the heavy tub to him and unlatched the door. Watching him throw out a great arc of water into the darkness, she wondered, If she were his, if they were wed, would he still be as careful of her and gentle with her? Or would he be like all the other braves and lie about sleeping and playing games while she worked?

"Thank you," she murmured, watching him put the tub back on the sideboard. She had shocked herself. It had finally happened. Her brains *had* curdled. First wondering if she loved him and now this, imagining herself wed to him. Living in a longhouse, hauling wood and water, hoeing fields and pounding corn—and being with him forever. Being free to go into his arms whenever she chose, feeling no guilt when he kissed her because she would be his and he would be hers.

Adam returned to his arrows. Giving his full attention to one that was bent, he said, "Know, Gold Hair, that there are certain things you will do and certain things you will not do while we are here at Windfall."

Alexandra lowered herself to the hearth near him and tucked her legs and her gown neatly beneath her. She murmured, "I already know what I'm not to do." Dear God. She had wondered if she loved him and now she knew. She wanted to be wed to him. More than anything else in the world, she wanted to be wed to him. "I'm not to go down to the river alone because I might fall in and drown. I'm not to go into the forest alone because there are bears and snakes and pumas and men who might steal me . . ."

Adam's eyes twinkled over her briefly as he held the bent arrow high above the flames to heat it. "That is so."

"I suppose I'm not to be out of your sight at all when I'm outside."

"That is very good, Alexandra." He straightened the arrow carefully, sighted along it, straightened it some more.

Why, why, why was he who he was, she mourned, and why was she who she was? Why had she not been born Indian, or he white? Why?

Adam continued, "Also, you will not attempt to lift heavy tubs of water. You will not lift the kettle if it is filled to the top with boiling water."

Gloomy as she felt, Alexandra had to laugh. "You must think I'm dreadfully weak and fragile. But then I forgot—I must be tip-top for my return."

"I do not want you hurting yourself."

She sighed. "Is there anything I *can* do?"

He gave her a slow smile. "Cook. Wash the dishes." He began to heat another arrow.

"Lovely. What else?"

"Eat," Adam said. "Eat well and often."

She narrowed her eyes at him. "Then you do think I'm skinny!"

Her indignation amused him. "I do not think you are skinny. I have told you that." The image of her full white breast cupped in his hand, the soft nipple puckered by her excitement, burned behind his eyes. He forced it away, sighted down the arrow. "I want you strong and healthy for the journey to Tiyanoga. It is not an easy ride."

She crossed her arms. "What else am I allowed to do?"

"Sleep. You will go to bed early and get up late."

"And why is that?" she asked softly.

"Because I have been hard on you these past weeks. You have had little sleep."

"I don't need all that much sleep." His words of concern erased all the hardship she'd borne and all the resentment she'd felt toward him. Looking down, she traced the small flowers on her gown with a finger. "I want you to know that I'm glad I saw the things you showed me, and I really want to help. I'll do my best, but—"

"It is all I ever expected." When she rubbed her eyes and yawned, Adam said gently, "I think you are very tired now . . ."

"Maybe a bit. I guess I'll trundle up." She smiled, climbed to her feet. "Are you quite happy now? I've eaten a huge dinner, washed the dishes, and now I'm off for a good night's sleep."

"I am very happy. And just so you know—I will be sleeping outside this night."

She frowned. "Outside? But why?" Being alone here in the daytime would be bad enough, but at night . . . Blazes.

"I do not like to be closed in by walls," Adam said. Or by memories. He needed to see the sky and smell the air and the grass. And especially he needed to be away from this woman. The very thought of her in a bed, all silky and soft and naked, was more than he could take this night. "You will be safe. Lock your door, and I will be right under your window."

"In the wet grass and the wind?"

"There are bearskins stored here. I have used them before—and the wind does not matter." He studied her wide green eyes. "Do you fear sleeping in this house without me?"

"Of course not."

"Good." Adam got to his feet.

But she did fear it, she wanted to cry. She did! There were probably ghosts here. Yet in her heart, she knew she was more afraid of having him near her than she was of any ghost. She was afraid she would go to him, and if she went to him . . .

"If you are frightened during the night, call out the window and I will come." Searching her face, he realized she had not heard him. He took her shoulders. "Alexandra, tell me now, do you want me to sleep inside tonight?"

She blinked, pulled herself back from where she had been: lying in his arms, pressed close, their lips touching. "I'm sorry, I . . . didn't hear . . ."

"Shall I sleep in the house?"

Alexandra shook her head, heard herself laugh. "You must sleep where you want to—I'll be fine."

If only she hated him as she once had. If only they could have a hideous row over something. Over poor Papa. But she knew he would never argue with her. He would merely shutter his black eyes and continue with what he was doing, and she would go on loving him. And soon she would be back in the city and never hear his voice again or sit before him on his horse with his arms wrapped around her. She would never sit by the fire with him again or kiss him again. When she saw his black eyes moving over her, her heart flew into her

throat and fluttered so that she scarcely had the breath
to whisper, "Till tomorrow then."

"Until tomorrow."

Alexandra set her candle on the writing table. She
had said she was going to bed, but she knew she would
never get to sleep until she wrote down what was in her
heart—if then. For a long time she sat remembering,
staring at the flame, and then she took up her quill:

*Cher Journal—This is still the same day, but an eter-
nity has passed since I wrote the above. Everything has
changed. This afternoon I was a child all a-twitter over
a handsome brave who had given me my first kiss. I
wondered if I was in love, and now I know. I am. Oh,
Diary, I am. I love him! Of course, he has no idea, and
he certainly doesn't love me—except my body maybe.
But that's all right . . .*

She touched her fingers to her face, remembering,
marveling that he had said she was beautiful. She was
springtime. She sighed deeply, pushed back her hair,
and yearned for a ribbon, any kind of ribbon. She had
never worried before about being beautiful, but she
wanted to be beautiful for him.

*The other thing that's happened—I'm going back to
Tiyanoga! He told me tonight. Of course, I've longed
for this day. It's grand to know I'm going to see Mama
again and go home again and—*

She could not complete the sentence. She could think
only that she loved a man she would never have. Even
were such a thing possible, which it was not, he did not
want her. Oh, he wanted to bed her, aye, that was clear
enough, but he did not *want* her. Not for herself. He despised whites. He had made it very clear they were the
worst thing that could have happened to his people and
his land. And he had made it clear that her father had
been their most hated enemy.

She rose, carefully corked the ink, and carried her candle to the bedtable. Slowly, with wooden fingers, she un-

buttoned the borrowed gown, hung it in the closet,
snuffed the flame, and crawled into bed. She was so
tired—and she was without heart. Maybe she could sleep.
But when she closed her eyes, he was there, firelight
sending shadows dancing over his dark body and glinting
in his hair. And his voice was in her ears: *You are springtime* . . .

She sat up, put her hands to her temples, and tried
to quiet her thoughts. She could not. He was still there,
big and dark and strong and gentle and beautiful. Oh,
she did love him. She could not leave him. Not possibly. But if she stayed with him, it would kill poor
Mama. She shook her head, amazed by her naiveté.
Why was she even contemplating this thing? He was
certainly not going to ask her to stay! She could just
imagine the flicker of amusement in those black eyes,
see his mouth curling at the corners, if he even knew
what she was thinking. And, too, she would feel like a
traitor if she did not return home but remained here
with the Mohawks. She hugged herself, rocked back
and forth, shook her head. If only she had never come
to this land . . . If only she had never seen him.

Silver Hawk had armed himself and ridden out from
the Mohawk castle at an angry gallop as the sun began
its climb from beneath the earth. Now it was late afternoon and his thoughts still seethed. He was ready for
war. No white man alive, he fumed, save Adam
Rutledge and William Johnson, knew what dignity or
honor or courage was, nor did they want to learn. The
white devil cared only about getting money and collecting possessions. He was weak, pale, sickly, filthy in
body and spirit, he screeched when tortured, and he did
not keep his word. He was an abomination in the land,
and it was long past time that he was eliminated.

Silver Hawk was ready to let fly the arrow, but his
war chieftain had to be consulted first. And so he had
come here seeking him. He hoped that he would find

the Cougar at the trading post, or that the man Jared
would know where he was. As it was, he came upon
him unexpectedly near the great dwelling-place called
Windfall. Seeing his friend standing in the shallows
fishing, a willow holding-basket nearby, Hawk dismounted and called down to him softly:

"Sekon, rikena."

Adam looked up, frowning into the sun's slanting
rays. "Hawk!" Filled with sudden foreboding, he waded
to shore and strode uphill through the tall grass toward
the sachem. After the two had gripped each other in a
warm welcome, he asked low, "What is it, *ion
kiatenro?* What has happened?"

Forgoing the time-honored custom that dictated nothing be hurried, Silver Hawk said, "They have claimed
our land, *rikena.* We awakened this morn to find squatters on the fields which our women had cleared and
planted. One plot had just been planted yesterday with
corn. It is sacred land"—his throat, his very breath were
so constricted he could hardly speak—"land given us
by the Creator as a divine gift, and now it is fenced off,
leaving us with nothing. They say they have deeds . . ."

Adam's eyes glinted as he asked quietly, "What of
meat? Have you continued the raids to reclaim your
game?"

"Hen, but we are not always successful. The devils
have grown watchful." He spat furiously and then spat
again. How preposterous, how insane that this beautiful
land, their very world, should be overrun and defiled by
such a sorry repulsive object, such a low order of hu-
manity as the white man.

Adam said softly, "You want scalps . . ."

"I crave war. I crave to send messengers to my brethren in the Iroquois League and tell them to don their
war-paint."

"But you have not?"

"Our young men want war; our old men are grieving

and looking toward the west. All agreed we must lay it
before you. It is why I have come for you, *rikena.*"

Adam's brain raced. "I know little of farming,
raktsia. Is it possible to reclaim seed just planted?"
When Hawk looked doubtful, he asked, "Could the
children do it? But then the devils would hardly let
them into the fields . . ."

Silver Hawk gave a rasp of laughter. "I doubt they
will interfere with my armed and mounted men looking
on."

Adam grinned. Nothing struck terror into the heart of
the white man more than the sight of a mounted Mohawk, armed and silent, his dark eyes burning with
wrath. "Do it then. After you eat and rest, return to
your castle. Tear down the fences, save what seed you
can, and then come here. Bring your people to me until
this thing is resolved once and for all."

Silver Hawk's brown eyes glittered. "Here? All of
us?"

"*Hen.* All in your village." There was room aplenty
on Dover's ten thousand acres for them to live and
hunt, and any tenant who didn't like it could damned
well leave. In truth, he had long suspected Dover had
gotten his vast property on the cheap from someone
who had cheated the Mohawks to get it. This would in
some small way repay them.

"You lighten my heart, *rikena.*"

Adam waved if off. "You and your people took me
in and gave me back my life. Now it is my turn." He
wished he could take in the entire Mohawk Nation. In
fact, he wished he could give them back all their lost
land and their freedom to roam upon it where they
would. But he could not. He added, "I wish I could return with you to help with the move, but the Gold Hair
is here. I cannot leave her."

Hawk's eyes narrowed imperceptibly. "You have
joined with her, then?"

"That is not why she is here. I will not join again.

She has traveled with me and seen the hardship, and now I am about to return her to her father."

Silver Hawk's face remained impassive as he studied his friend's suddenly shuttered eyes and the heightened color that touched his broad cheekbones. So. He wanted her. Whether he knew it or not, whether he admitted it or not, he wanted her. Silver Hawk said nothing, nor did he ask about Adam's journey to the northern villages, for this morning's outrage against their own castle had changed everything. There *was* going to be war. He could feel the drums beating. He gave a soft whistle to his mare. The animal lifted its head from grazing and came to him, its ears pricked.

Adam was concerned, seeing that he meant to leave. "You must eat and rest before you go."

"I have not the luxury of time."

"Your mount is worn."

Silver Hawk smiled and stroked the gleaming damp arch of his mare's neck. "You know she is my treasure, my brother. I will not ride her hard on the return trip."

"Take Anoki," Adam said.

Silver Hawk was no longer surprised by anything this English nobleman said or did. He was the Cougar now. He was Indian. His natural temperament was Indian, and unlike Warraghiyagey, he had no squaw hunger. He was good on a horse, he had strong good looks like his animal-helper, the cougar, and he had responded to Indian ways as a bird takes to flying: speaking their tongue, catching a fish with his bare hands, treading the forest path that no white could penetrate, reading the bark of a tree and the bend of a twig as easily as a white man read a book . . . Silver Hawk swelled with pride, for it was he who had taught the Cougar all he knew of Mohawk ways. He nodded.

"As usual, you speak wisdom. I will take Anoki, and I will return soon. With my people." He patted the burlap bag strapped on his mare's back. "This is for you."

"What is it?"

"It is from Lark—squash, potatoes, nuts, apples."

"You surely cannot spare this."

Silver Hawk grinned, shrugged. "She thinks you will starve without a woman to feed you. She will be pleased to learn the Gold Hair is with you still."

Adam doubted it very much, but held his tongue. "Thank her for me, and I will thank her again when I see her. And *raktsia*, when all of you return, the Gold Hair is not to know who I am."

"None of our people will ever betray you."

It had been the middle of the night before Alexandra had finally fallen asleep. The next morn, blue skies and sunshine helped lift her gloomy spirits. It helped, too, that the Cougar was distant and polite. It was as if yesterday's kisses had never happened. As she made the bed and smoothed the flowered coverlet, she mused that he had liked the breakfast she had prepared. It was nothing but a porridge of cornmeal and water, but with brown sugar on it, and the berries and nuts he'd found in the woods, it was delicious. She had stuffed herself, and she was pleased that she had pleased him.

And now it was time to earn her keep. She was not going to be here much longer, and she wanted the place to be shining when she left. In fact, polishing furniture and washing floors and windows might even keep her mind off him, and he should be satisfied that it would keep her safely in the house. She was polishing the huge carved buffet in the dining room when she heard the kitchen door open and close. He had been outside. He was always outside. She could not imagine what he did out there when he was not hunting or fishing.

"Alexandra?"

"I'm in the dining room."

Looking in, smelling the beeswax, seeing her, warm and beautiful and alive with Eliza's apron about her waist and the sun in her hair, Adam was nearly pole-axed by a memory—a laughing Eliza on her knees polishing the same cherrywood buffet, sunlight streaming through the casement windows, glittering on the dining table and striking sparks off the silver candelabra and her own long brown hair.

He forced himself to return to the present, and told himself this had to stop. He was being drained, robbed of every joy of living. He could not drag this burden around on his shoulders any longer. He had to let it go, let the past go, let Eliza go. From this day forward, he had to let her rest, and let himself rest. He vowed it.

Looking up as the Cougar entered the room, Alexandra felt her heart tremble. It was always as if she were seeing him for the first time, feeling for the first time a sense of discovery, a heightened awareness of leashed lightning ... She said faintly, "Did you want something?"

Adam held up the burlap bag. "I have more food. A friend brought it by."

Alexandra stared. "A friend?" Was it the Englishman? Were they so close to the trading post, then?

"A Mohawk sachem," Adam replied. "The women of his village sent it."

"Oh." Alexandra followed him into the kitchen and watched as he lifted the bounty onto the sideboard. "My goodness, we can have a feast this evening." A going-away feast.

"Hen." He contemplated telling her that an entire Mohawk village would be arriving within the next few days. Whereupon she would make his life hideous with her questions. He would leave well enough alone, and deal with it when the time came. He moved toward the door.

"I'm polishing things a bit," Alexandra called after him. "I trust Lord Adam won't mind."

"I doubt he will notice." When he saw her face crumple, he gave himself a mental thrashing. Hell. Was he trying to hurt her because he felt guilty about wanting her? Was he angry with her because she was here and Eliza was not? Just moments ago he had vowed that from this day forward, he would let his darling go, let the past go. Eliza was gone, but Alexandra was here. She was a stranger in this wilderness through no fault of her own, and she needed every kindness he could give her. He said gently:

"I meant only that men do not notice such things. I will point out to Lord Adam what you have done. He will be pleased."

Alexandra watched from the window as he strode down the grassy slope stretching away to the river. How baffling he was. Ice one minute and warmth the next. Returning to the buffet with her rag and beeswax, she wondered if his mood change this time was due to relief. He was probably delighted she would soon be out of his hands. Or perhaps he was cheered by the prospect of all that wonderful food for dinner. It was one more thing she would never know, nor did she want to. Bending to her task, she decided she preferred iciness from him rather than sunshine these last days they would be together. It would make the parting easier.

Chapter 12

The next morn after breakfast, Alexandra spent hours working in the first-floor rooms of Windfall. In her wake, she left a trail of gleaming furniture—tables, large and small, the sideboard, straight chairs, armchairs, settees, bookcases, and cupboards. She had hoped, by staying busy, to keep from thinking about the Cougar, but it was not to be. Not only was his image in her thoughts, but she was consumed with curiosity by the change in him—his friendliness and kindness and sudden interest in her. Oh, aye, his interest.

During last night's delicious feast over which they had collaborated, he had actually questioned her about her likes and dislikes and asked if she had slept well. It was as if the wall between them had suddenly been knocked down, and with his turning so warm and helpful, Alexandra was left floating in a sea of freshly blossoming love. Now all that she had to do was hide the fact from him until she got back to Tiyanoga. But could she? She worried as she knelt and furiously polished the leg of a china cabinet. Sensing suddenly that he was there, she looked up. It was a thing she would never get used to, the silence and grace with which he moved. She smiled. "Hello. I . . . didn't hear you."

"Did I startle you?"

"*Iah.*"

Adam examined the gleaming Chippendale cabinet that held his brother's Wedgwood. "You are very good with beeswax, Gold Hair."

165

Alexandra laughed and felt a flush of pleasure. "It takes great talent and skill, as I'm sure you know." She pushed back a strand of hair clinging to her eyelashes. "I suppose it's time I made dinner."

"It is done." Her silvery laughter and the way she glanced up at him through her lashes had sent a swift dart of hunger through him.

Alexandra sat back on her heels and gazed up at him in astonishment. "You mean—dinner is cooked?"

"It is cooked."

"I don't understand."

"Just come." He reached out his hand.

As Alexandra took it and was drawn lightly to her feet, the familiar heat flickered through her. "I hardly know what to say. Except another thank you . . ."

"I will accept no thanks." Turning over her soft hand, he saw that dirt streaked it and was lodged thickly under the ovals of her small pink nails. He had never expected or intended for her to work like a scullion. She had to be dead on her feet after being at it all day, yet there was a brightness in her eyes.

"I'd best use some soap and hot water before I eat. I have quite a bit of grime on me."

After scrubbing her hands and face, Alexandra followed the Cougar outside into a red-gold May evening filled with the tantalizing aroma of cooking food and woodsmoke. After filling their plates, they sat down, the fire crackling between them, to eat pan-fried fish and vegetables that had been baked in the ashes. Alexandra speared a piece of fish, tasted it, and closed her eyes.

"It's grand. I didn't know how famished I was." She broke open the potato on her plate, saw its little white puff of steam escape, and forked into the fluffiness. She ate a bite and then shot him a grin. "This is amazing. I can see you being fierce in the woods—shooting deer and bear and enemy braves, but this I can scarcely believe—the Cougar bustling about making dinner."

Adam's mouth curved. "And I can see you dressed in fine gowns and jewels and waited on hand and foot by servants—but baking bread and peeling potatoes and washing dishes? And knowing what to do with beeswax?" He shook his head. "That I can scarcely believe."

"And now you think I'm madly domesticated," she said shyly.

"That also I can scarcely believe."

"Well, you're right. I hate the very thought."

Watching her gnaw greedily, childlike, on an apple, Adam felt the soft heat of contentment, a lightness in body and spirit he had not known for many moons. Even though he feared that war was approaching, now on this warm, sun-gilded evening, it was far from his thoughts. His darling was at rest, and he felt no guilt in talking with Alexandra, laughing with her, learning about her, and admiring her youthful perfection. He could not get enough of gazing at her: the sunset painting roses on her cheeks, turning her amazing cloud of hair to copper, tipping her long lashes with gold, making her soft lips redder and softer than ever. She was adorable, this child-woman he had won in battle—and she was mischievous and mysterious and seductive.

Did she know how seductive? he wondered, taking another potato out of the smoking ashes and breaking open its skin. He decided she did not. She was a complete innocent. She would be amazed to know she was a disturber of his peace and horrified to learn that he was intrigued and excited by the way she moistened her lips, pushed back her hair, rested her chin on one hand to gaze at him—one moment with wide childish eyes, the next with sultry lowered lids. He drew a deep breath and bit into the potato. She was the most seductive little fox he had ever seen, but he was not about to seduce her. She was safe with him.

"I would like to hear about your life in England." he said.

Alexandra raised her eyes from her plate. "You can't mean it."

"I have said it."

She shrugged. "There's naught to say except it was dreadfully dull." She had been enthralled, watching him eat, biting into the potato with his strong white teeth and chewing it. How beautifully shaped his mouth was and how square and masculine his jaw . . . She forced her eyes back to her plate. "I was born, I grew up—"

"Where?"

"At the Larches, my father's ancestral home back in Northamptonshire. I was born there, I grew up there, and now I'm here . . ." Suddenly she could not bear to think about returning to England. Not on this most perfect of nights. "That's it in a nutshell, I fear." She began carefully to lick off every delicious bit of apple juice from her fingers. It didn't matter a fig that her mother would have been horrified by her bad manners.

Adam gazed secretly, intently on the small scene being enacted so innocently before him. Lowered lashes sweeping her pink cheeks, her small plump tongue, so clean and rosy, lapping those slender white fingers. He looked away, seared unexpectedly by the fierceness of his need. It was some moments before he said quietly: "Someone taught you to write, and to speak French and German." And to do servant's work.

Another shrug. "I had a governess who spoke nothing but French to me, and Papa insisted I go to school. The classroom was on the top floor of the Larches, and my two friends and I went for seven years. We had a darling, stuffy old teacher called Piddington Pitts, a wonderful teacher actually, who managed to drill some of what he knew into me."

Adam cleaned his plate and put it aside, his black eyes dancing now. "The governess and the schoolteacher, I suppose they also taught you to bake bread and wash dishes and use beeswax?"

Alexandra giggled at the picture it made. "What a

thought! The truth is, Mama couldn't bear to scold the servants, and when Papa went to war, our meals grew more and more dreary, and the house collected absolutely heaps of cobwebs and dustballs. I was forced to use my whip on them."

Adam's laughter ran out before he said gravely, "I can picture it. I have seen your fierceness."

His laughter so warmed her that Alexandra blossomed, bubbling, chattering away about all the things she'd had to learn so the servants could not continue their cheating. "For that's what it was. They were taking Papa's money and doing the most shoddy work ever." She shook her head. "Poor Mama, she is really the most tenderhearted thing. I simply had to step in. I was fourteen when I began learning how to run a manor—more than I ever wanted to know, believe me. And wouldn't you know, housekeeping was all my two best friends could talk about. They were about to marry—nobility yet, ugh!—and were filled with visions of silver and china and servants and babes and—"

Suddenly hearing herself, Alexandra stopped, aghast. She blushed. This was an Indian warrior she was regaling with her stupid talk of crockery and cobwebs and greasy dishes. "Blazes, I'm boring you to death!"

"*Iah,* you are not."

"You're just too polite to say so." Oh, stupid, stupid, stupid! Except she'd felt so comfortable talking with him, so at home . . .

Adam said thickly, "In truth, your voice is as sweet to my ears as running water." He could not help himself, he had to say it. Her light, girlish voice and chatter of home things had filled him with the same sense of springtime he had felt with her before. She delighted his eyes and lightened his heart in a way he had thought he would never feel again. She had filled him with the sense of a new beginning, and he couldn't help but think—how wonderful if she could be here always . . .

Alexandra cocked an eyebrow at him. "Now you're

teasing me—and I deserve it." But he was not laughing. He was not even smiling. She saw in his steady dark gaze the same message she had seen when he had held her in his arms and kissed her. He wanted her, yet he had sent her away. And she had gone. But how she wished she had stayed to be held and kissed and comforted some more, for now such a thing was not possible. Now she loved him, and she dared not so much as touch him, or she would never want to leave him. And he must never know, for it would serve no purpose except to embarrass them both. She turned her head, overcome by the thought that soon she would be on the high seas and would never see him again.

"I have embarrassed you," Adam muttered.

"Nay, I was ... thinking of England."

It was some moments before he trusted himself to speak. "You will return to England one day, I promise you." And when she did, his springtime would go with her.

In silence he gazed at the dying flames and the soft approach of dusk and wondered why he tortured himself, feasting with his eyes on her fresh young beauty and reveling in her liveliness and her innocence, imagining how it might be were she to stay with him. For she absolutely could not. He had made a decision and there it stood. He would never wed again, nor was this any land for a woman. Beautiful as it was, it was a savage wilderness where death lurked everywhere, and where men could not stop hating and killing one another. Alexandra no more belonged here than Eliza had. She belonged in England where it was safe and civilized.

"Tell me about you now," Alexandra said shyly, breaking the silence. "About your boyhood and how you were raised." She'd been almost afraid to ask, for it seemed the warmth and magic that had touched the evening was slipping away with the coming of nightfall. And she had seen that distant look in his eyes again—just for a moment, but she had seen it—that glimmer of sadness.

Adam was caught off-guard by her question about his boyhood. Clearly he could not tell her that he had been raised in the centuries-old ancestral home of the dukes of Dover. He muttered, "I was raised as every other Indian buck is raised."

"I want to hear."

Taking up a piece of firewood, peeling off bits of it and feeding it to the flames, he racked his brain. He said finally, "You have seen our villages and long-houses and how we live and what we eat and wear."

"But what about you? I want to hear about you . . ."

God. After some moments, he said, "I was not unlike the young Mohawk bucks you have seen hunting and fishing—playing games."

"Like their fathers."

"It is so. Our way is not the way of the white man, Gold Hair. Indian males are spoiled. I was spoiled. My every wish was granted and every tantrum applauded." In reality his father's cane had connected all too regularly with the seat of his breeches back at Duke's Dover. He was a martinet, his old pater.

"Your tantrums were applauded?" She was wide-eyed. "But why?"

"Because my people believe in complete freedom. They believe that a man, from dawn to dusk and from childhood to old age, should not be restricted or told what to do."

Alexandra looked doubtful. "You'd let a babe touch fire?"

"That babe would never touch fire again. A boy must learn caution and discipline early if he is to grow into a man who lives by no rule but his own."

"And your girls and women?" she asked dryly. "I trust they're free to live by rules of their own also?"

"Our girls have freedom enough, and our women are well-satisfied—or were before the white man took our land for his own. They had meat to cook, furs to keep their families warm, the earth to till and plant and harvest . . ."

Up until now, he had felt only rage for this brothers' loss. Now he was filled with a deep sadness and nostalgia. No more was this world with its forests and rivers and game the Indians' alone for them to wander and hunt in at will. Adam knew that time was gone forever.

Seeing the shadow that crossed his face, Alexandra said softly, "I'm sorry I was so stubborn earlier. I didn't let myself see what was happening to the Indians because I knew it was what you wanted me to see. And I wanted to hurt you because you wouldn't free me. It was wrong and small and awful of me, for now I know how bad and how unfair things are for them."

She was so dear to him at that moment, Adam wanted to take her into his arms and hold her, just hold her. But he did not. He got to his feet. "It is unfair, *hen,* but it is also unfair that I have kept you with me against your will. I regret the grief I have caused you and your family."

Alexandra, too, rose. She held out her arms and smiled. "Look at me. I've recovered. I'm fine, and I'm certain now that Mama is, too. She's strong, and she knows that I'm strong, and she's gotten my letter. A-and good has come of this, Cougar, because I *will* make the commander at Tiyanoga see what's happening up here. I will." Perhaps it would be her grand moment, her chance to make this a better world for having lived in it.

She felt suddenly as if she were being swept along by a great river, as if what she said and felt and did were no longer under her control. She heard herself murmuring, "The other good thing to come of this is that . . . I met you . . ." She saw his black eyes widen.

She had poleaxed him. Adam said huskily, "Your being with me is a sun which has brightened my days, Gold Hair."

"R-really?"

"I have said it." He saw clearly that she had become attached to him, and it touched him deeply. He had not been easy on her. He wanted to kiss her sweet face and her mouth and her hair. He wanted to comfort her, hold her, make love to her ... make love to her ... make love to her ... It was a drum beating in his heart as he drew her into his arms. In the firelight, he saw her eyes glisten with sudden tears. He muttered, *"Iah,* Alexandra, you must not cry." He could not bear to see her cry.

"I'll ... so miss you," Alexandra whispered. She laid her head against his chest, heard the fast beating of his heart, and knew she would die if she could never see or hold him again. Quite simply, she would die of grief. She began to shiver.

Adam's arms tightened about her. "What is it, little fox?" When she made no answer, just shook her head, he tilted up her chin. "Come now, have I not comforted you before?"

Alexandra met his eyes, traced his beautiful grave features with her fingers. She wanted to imprint them on her mind so she would remember them forever.

Adam's breath caught as he saw the open adoration on her face. Sweet Jesus, the maid was as infatuated with him as he was with her. He had not known. He could no more put her from him now than he could stop the sun from rising or setting. He took her mouth, tenderly at first, and then more and more deeply as he felt her eager response.

"Oh, Cougar ..." It was a gasp between kisses. Alexandra wanted to weep, it was so wonderful, being crushed against him, his big, gentle hands exploring her face, her throat, and her breasts as she tasted his skin, his warm mouth and sleek, darting tongue. She saw his face transformed by passion.

She was home. The river she was riding had carried her home. She could not get enough of him, hold him closely enough, or feel or taste him enough or inhale the wonderful piney, smoky aroma of his hair and skin enough. She kissed his lips, his face, his shoulders, his hands, and then she was laughing, sheer joy, running her fingers through his black hair, smoothing them across the hard cords and muscles of his neck and shoulders and chest. How beautiful he was, and how she loved him, and how beautiful love was. So why were these stupid tears streaming down her cheeks?

Adam cupped her wet face between his hands. "Have I hurt you?"

Alexandra shook her head wildly. "*Iah*. You've made me happy. Oh, Cougar, I'm so happy. I'm flying ... soaring ..." She lifted her face to his again, lips parted, eager, hungry for more of his kisses. "Hold me closer. Oh, closer, closer, *please* ..."

Her evident joy and hunger kindled a fire in Adam that raced, burning, through his body. It was so sweet and hot and fierce a fire that he knew he must release her or bury himself deep within her. Tormented though he was by his need for her, he did not forget the decision he had made earlier. It would stand, it must stand. he would not take her; she was safe with him. She was a child despite her woman's body, and he alone was responsible for what had happened between them. He had tempted her, caused her to feel this way about him, and he was damned if he would take advantage of it. He gave her one last kiss and then put her at arm's length, his hands gripping her shoulders. He said huskily:

"Were I to hold you any closer, my Gold Hair, we would be one." He watched her blink those long-lashed, luminous green eyes.

Alexandra felt herself blush. She had done it yet again. She had not even considered the possibility of coupling in her excitement at kissing and holding him, feeling his body pressed against hers. It was a thing she did not understand or know about or need—oneness. Mating. Yet she knew it was a thing of such importance to a man, it could well cause him to forget everything and do violence in his eagerness to claim it. But never her gentle Cougar . . .

Adam gave her a little shake. "Do you understand what I said, Alexandra?" He saw, even in the twilight, the glorious color flooding her face, felt the hot wave of hunger cresting within him, threatening to overpower him.

"I'm . . . so stupid . . ."

"*Iah,* you are not." Adam traced her lips with his fingers.

"I am."

She was stupid and uncaring and unthinking, feasting on every new delight while he was in torment. Not until this moment had she even noticed the sweat glistening on his body and heard his ragged breathing. She knew suddenly what she had to do, aye, wanted to do. She would give him the same hot, wild, soaring pleasure he had awakened in her. She would mate with him.

The thought terrified her even as it tantalized her, but it was all right—he would not hurt her. He could be nothing but gentle. And no one, not Mama, not anyone, need ever know she was a fallen woman. And she would not get a babe from it for surely, surely it took more than one time to start a babe. Surely. Praying that it did, she raised his hands to her lips, kissed them, felt her heart beat faster.

"Teach me to make love, Cougar."

Adam concealed his shock. Feeling her lips and tongue exploring his hands, imagining the soft, naked curves of her breasts and hips, he felt ecstasy shivering over him, intensifying his arousal. He trembled, so great was his need to sheathe himself within her. Sweet Christ, help him. She was asking him to make love to her, begging him. But he had seen her fear and uncertainty. It had been one small flicker in her eyes, but he had seen. And he had seen her flying, soaring on his kisses and caresses alone. She was not ready for lovemaking with a starving man. It was for him she was doing it, not for herself, and he was not about to sacrifice her to his hunger. *Iah,* in this he would not yield. He pulled her back into his arms again, but only to cradle her.

"There will be no lovemaking, Alexandra. Now is not the time."

Alexandra leaned her head against his chest, whispered, "I wanted you to soar with me." But she was relieved.

"I will soar with you still . . ."

Gently he laid her back in the deep grass, and knelt beside her, unlaced the ties that held her shirt together, and slipped it off. He made a throttled sound looking on her nakedness for the first time: her silken skin rosy with desire . . . swelling upthrust breasts, taut buds of velvet crowning their tips. He cupped one, gently squeezing it, and touched his tongue-tip to her nipple. He heard her indrawn grasp of pleasure. He closed his eyes, tempted almost beyond endurance to take her. He saw himself wallowing in her, tasting, kissing, licking her sweetness. Devouring her. She was hungry and willing, eager to sheathe him within herself, so why not, in God's name? He was full, throbbing, shivering, near the end of his control, and she wanted him as much as he wanted her. Take her . . . take her . . .

Alexandra watched, her face fiery and her breath coming in small pants, as the Cougar's black gaze smoldering over her. What was he thinking, she wondered, and if they were not going to make love, what were they going to do? She did not understand. Suddenly remembering her shocking reflection in the dressing glass, she covered her breasts, said faintly, "I'm . . . not very pretty, I know . . ."

Her wistful words jarred Adam back to reality. God in heaven, forgive him for what he had been about to do. He was her protector. She trusted him, and he had almost betrayed that trust. It took no more than an instant for him to smother with steely anger the screaming primal urge that would have buried him deep within her. He stretched out beside her, pulled her into his arms, and gave her a slow, teasing smile.

"It is true you are not very pretty, Gold Hair. For the simple reason that you are very beautiful."

The huskiness of his voice made Alexandra shiver. And when he dipped his head to her breasts again, circling first one nipple then the other with his tongue before gently nipping and suckling her, she cried out softly and arched against him.

Adam felt a rush of heat filling and stiffening him. He could not wait much longer. His hands were demanding now, possessive, as his seeking mouth and tongue scorched over her body, knowing just where to kiss and touch her to light new flames—the back of her neck, the base of her throat, her wrists, her navel. And then his lips and his warm breath were brushing her ear.

"Hold me, little fox, just hold me . . ." Taking her hands, he drew them beneath his breechclout.

Alexandra was electrified to feel the warmth and the hardness of his manhood resting suddenly within her curved fingers. It was a living, pulsing thing she held in her hands, and the thought of its seeking and probing her secret place, breaching it and then hungrily thrusting inside her, sent a cascade of almost unbearable excitement coursing through her. Excitement and tenderness. Shyly, she brushed her fingertips over him, fearful that she might hurt him.

Adam groaned. "Little flower . . . beautiful little kitten—you are so soft . . ." He fought to control the savage hunger, the wildness growing within him as she began shyly to fondle him. He took her mouth again and again and again, suckled her hard little nipples, rained kisses on her face, her hair, her breasts, the soft flesh of her throat and shoulders, inhaled the tantalizing fragrance of her skin. He yearned to touch the velvety crease between her thighs, part the soft lips, gaze on her, press his hungry mouth to her—aye, take her maidenhood, but he held himself under tight rein. "Adorable little fox . . ."

So this was what she had heard about, Alexandra mused through a bewildering daze of heat and excitement and pleasure. This was why men sometimes did violence to feel this way. She was afire, her heart careening out of control as she returned his wildly hungry kisses. She was aching for him, yearning for him to be in that empty, throbbing, white-hot place within her that was waiting just for him. She had learned in the space of a heartbeat what oneness was all about and why men and women mated. It was a madness during which nothing else mattered but getting closer and closer. And giving pleasure. Above all else, she wanted to give him pleasure. She began to stroke his arousal, to cup with fluttering fingers the tautly drawn skin of the twin globes resting in her hands.

Adam forced out a quivering breath, groaned, crushed her to him, felt his pulses throbbing, growing hotter, close to exploding. Ah, God . . . Instinctively he slipped a seeking hand inside her leggings, sought the warm, wet softness between her legs, and finding the small erect bud of her desire, stroked it with gentle fingers. He heard her glad cry, felt the hot spurt of her love juices as his own wild pleasure peaked. His tongue found her hungry mouth and plunged, plunged, until his spasms ended and he lay drained in her arms. His last thought before he fell into a deep sleep was that she was untouched. She was safe. It was all that mattered. Alexandra was safe.

Chapter 13

It had taken the Mohawks two days to pack up their belongings, and to reclaim the seed from the newly planted field. They then began their trek, half of them moving westward, the other half, one hundred all told, turning their faces toward Windfall. Their horses and the largest of the dogs were loaded high with great bundles and sacks of equipment—cooking utensils, guns, axes, skins, everything they owned. Those things that did not fit onto the backs of the animals were borne on the backs of the women while the braves strode unencumbered and the children and smaller dogs frolicked about in excitement at this unaccustomed event.

Silver Hawk gazed on his people with a certain sadness as their journey began. He had told them the move was a temporary one—just until the problems with the white squatters was resolved—but he sensed in their bleak eyes, in the way none had turned to look back, that they knew the truth. They had slept and eaten for the last time in this castle in which they had spent the past two winters.

Lark felt no sadness at the unexpected move. As she plodded along the forest's soft, leafy floor with the other women, her soul sang. He was going to her man. For many moons, she wondered if the Cougar would ever be hers, and then the sign she had prayed for had come—the three dreams in which they were wed.

That was not all. Gathering wood in the forest, she had been startled almost out of her skin to find a handsome male puma watching her. She did not scream, but dropped her burden and turned to flee—and then she heard its low rumbling purring. Her breath caught as she realized this was yet another sign, for this was a cougar—her beloved's animal-helper. As she had stared at it, enthralled, it blinked its sleepy golden eyes at her, yawned, and, still purring, returned to the woods. And then two days ago, her brother had brought word that the Cougar had bidden them all come to Windfall. Now she raised her eyes to the skies and gave thanks to the Creator for a prayer answered. No signs could be clearer. She and the Cougar were going to join.

All of that day as they marched, Silver Hawk's dark eyes had yearned secretly toward Lark. He and the other braves, ever scouting for danger, were always fore or aft or far afield of the slow-moving caravan, but now they had stopped for the day, for the women were weary. Lean-tos had been raised, food eaten, and now all sat before their fires, the men smoking and talking low, the mothers tending their babes. Hawk watched as Lark drifted off by herself and stood staring at the moon and the star-glittered sky. He strolled over to her.

"What are you thinking, little one?"

Lark looked up into her brother's solemn dark face and smiled. "*Okarasneha,* my brother. I am thinking how beautiful the night is."

Hawk felt a flare of irritation at her greeting. My brother . . . But then how could he expect her to know how he felt about her unless he told her? He had waited long enough. Glancing about, and seeing that they were completely alone, he said low, "There is something I would discuss with you."

Lark smiled. "Of course—and afterward I would speak with you, my brother." She had gathered the courage finally to tell him of her choice. With the three signs she had received, there was no doubt in her heart that he would give her to the Cougar or that the Cougar would ask for her.

"Speak now," Hawk said gruffly. He did not want her attention wandering while he spoke of important matters.

Lark was suddenly uneasy. Why as he looking at her so strangely? "It is not my place to speak before you do, my—"

"Speak!" Hawk growled. If she said "my brother" one more time, he would carry her into the woods and show her that he was not her brother.

Subdued, Lark bowed her shining head. He was angry. She had chosen a bad time to tell him, but now if she did not, she feared he would grow angrier still. She said quietly, "You have told me that . . . I should choose a mate."

"That is so, and you said you needed no one but me to take care of you."

"I said, too, that if ever I did choose someone, it must be . . . the right man."

Seeing her shining eyes, Hawk stood very still and felt the sudden heavy beating of his heart. He asked brusquely, "You have found him, then?"

Lark nodded. "Four winters ago." She caught his hand between hers and held it tightly. "Oh, my brother, it is the Cougar. I love him. I . . . have always loved him."

It was as if she had tomahawked him. Hawk's eyes glinted as he thought of Adam, his white brother whom he loved above all men, and Lark, the woman he had chosen for his own. He muttered, "He has asked for you, then?" Suddenly he remembered the Gold Hair, the look on Adam's face when he spoke of her.

Lark blushed. *"Iah.* But I am certain he will. I have received three signs . . ."

Silver Hawk put an arm across her slim shoulders and drew her farther away from their encampment. "I would hear more about this thing," he said. After listening patiently to her tale of dreams, the purring puma, and Adam's summoning them to Windfall, he scowled. "That is all? There is no more than that?" His spirits had risen somewhat.

Lark was crushed. She had looked on the signs as direct word from the Great Sustainer. "The rest is . . . personal."

Ignoring the pleading he saw in her eyes, he said, "I would hear it."

She bowed her head. All of her days, she had known nothing but obedience, and she could not disobey now. Especially she could not disobey this beloved brother of hers to whom she owed her life, her happiness, and whom she treasured above all others—except the Cougar. Blushing again, she replied softly, "He said I was . . . beautiful a-and giving. He said my heart was tender . . ."

Hawk's gaze moved over the soft curves of her cheeks and chin and her liquid eyes, black pools of reflected moonlight. She was the most beautiful woman he had ever seen, and there was none whose heart was more tender. He said gravely, "I would agree with the Cougar."

Tortured by shyness, Lark murmured, "He said if he weds again, it is I he . . . will ask for." She did not add that he had said he would never take another wife, for she did not believe it. Not now.

"I cannot blame him for wanting you." Hawk said low, but it was a waste of breath. She had not heard him, and now his anger smoldered as he thought of the two of them, hungry and in each other's arms. And what did she mean, *if* he wed again? She of all people knew he planned never to wed again. Suddenly he had to know if it was as he suspected. He asked thickly. "Has he bedded you?"

Lark gazed at him with stricken eyes. The Cougar had not bedded her. Their sharing of each other's bodies that one night long ago had not been for passion alone. He had been cold and without heart or hope, and she had wanted to breathe life and warmth into him. The passion had come, *hen*—she would never forget how the fire had coursed between their bodies—but it had been a pure and sweet thing.

"Why do you not answer, Lark?" Hawk now had his voice and himself under tight control. She would never know how much she had hurt him.

"I was but gathering my thoughts, my brother. We . . . have mated, *hen*. And now with our people going to Windfall to live, I would join with him if he will have me."

Hawk was stunned. His heart felt as if a great hand were squeezing it. They had coupled . . . And she could be lost to him within days. He braced his feet more firmly on the earth, feeling it tilt beneath him.

"My brother . . ."

Looking down, he saw that she had knelt at his feet, her glossy head bowed. She wrapped her arms about his legs. "Rise, woman," he growled. "You are not a slave."

Lark did not move. "I beg you, my brother, give me to him if he asks."

Hawk grasped her arms, lifted her up. "I will give it thought and we will talk of it again—but you must not fall at my feet like that."

Watching her return to where the women were preparing the children for the night, Silver Hawk could not quiet his fury or his despair. He thought again of that young, terrified maid he had won from Akando the Seneca. She deserved only happiness, and he would do anything to give it to her—even if it meant giving her to another. But did Adam truly want her? Or had he flattered her and given her the hope that they might join just to have his will with her?

His resentment soared, but then he caught himself. *Iah!* Such a thing could not be. Not with the Cougar. Hawk would trust him with his life. But in truth, he

knew nothing of his white brother's dealings with
women since his wife had died. Nothing. As he walked
back to where his kin and friends sat about the fires, he
was sure of only one thing: If Adam had seduced Lark
into lovemaking with promises he never meant to keep;
if he had destroyed her and broken her heart, he, Hawk,
would kill him. But the knife would sink into his own
heart as well, for he loved this white brother of his as
he had never loved his own blood brothers . . .

Lark tossed on her bed of pine boughs and felt the
hot pain that gnawed at her everywhere—her back, her
legs and feet and shoulders. She ached all over, for
never before had she borne on her back such a great
burden for so many hours on end. Now she yearned for
sleep to end her discomfort, but sleep eluded her. All
she could think of was her talk with Silver Hawk.

What had happened, she wondered, her wide eyes on
the flames of a nearby watch fire. Why had it not gone
as she had hoped? She had been so sure he would be
happy for her, but instead he had scoffed at her sacred
signs, and had been stiff and distant and filled with icy
anger from the very beginning.

Was it because Adam was a white? But surely that
could not be. Hawk considered the Cougar his equal;
the two were closer than brothers. Was it because she
herself was of no importance, whereas Adam Rutledge
walked with the king in his own land? Did Hawk marvel at her stupidity, at how one who had been the slave
of a Seneca could think herself fine enough to join with
such a one?

Lark felt her eyes sting as tears gathered behind
them. *Iah.* Hawk was not such a man. It was he who
had made her stand tall and proud and taught her that
she was a woman of worth. He had taught her to ride
a horse and use a knife to defend herself so that never
again would she be in the power of such a one as
Akando. Thinking of the Seneca, she shivered. It was

the one thing Hawk had not been able to do for her—erase her memories and her fear of the man.

Quietly she rose from the pine boughs, removed her dreamcatcher from her small bundle of belongings, and hung it from the tree limb over her head. She then returned to the fragrant greens and closed her eyes. Now perhaps she would sleep more easily.

When Alexandra awakened, her first thoughts were of the Cougar. Hearing the ringing sound of metal on wood, she ran to the window. Seeing that he was splitting logs, she sank onto the window bench to watch. What a treat, seeing his tall, near-naked body in action. Long legs braced in an easy stance, his long arms upraised, the swift downward swing of the sledgehammer, wood flying, the next log set, the wedge placed, once more the graceful, powerful backward swing of the great mallet and then another crash and another and another as more logs were split asunder.

As her own life had been split asunder . . .

She loved him. Loved him. It was wonderful and it was awful, and as she pondered it, she grew aware of the silence. He had seen her . . . He was looking at her . . . and what could she possibly say to him and how should she act with him after last night? The way they had touched each other . . . the places they had touched each other . . . She could not believe it had happened. Her entire body grew hot with embarrassment at the memory.

"*Oronkene,* Alexandra," Adam called. When she responded with a small, nervous wave, he gave her an easy smile and a salute. Even from where he stood, he could see that her face was red, and he knew exactly what her thoughts were. She was ashamed of what had happened between them as he had known she would be. He raised his voice. "There is food for you in the kitchen. Bring it out here to eat and keep me company."

Alexandra made her way down to the kitchen and

found the food he had put out for her, but she didn't
feel at all hungry. Her stomach was as small and hard
as a walnut. In truth, she felt ill. With humiliation, aye,
but it was more than that. She was sick with loss, with
emptiness, with wanting him. She wanted to hold him
again, play with his hair, taste his warm mouth, feel his
sleek skin, run her hands over his smooth, hard body,
but as she walked outside to face him, she knew she
could not do any of those things ever again. Nothing
was going to change the fact that he was Indian and she
was white and they lived in two different worlds.

Adam rested on his sledgehammer as she drew near.
He frowned. "You have no food with you."

"I'm not hungry. I'll eat later."

She had gone from embarrassment to yearning and
now she was embarrassed again. How could she have
behaved that way? Teach her to make love, indeed.
What had happened to her modesty and self-respect? If
he had not been a gentleman to his very core, she
would be worrying and wondering this very instant if
he had started a babe within her. She had ignored the
danger last night, but now that she was in command of
her senses, she knew the possibility was very real. A
babe. It would have been a catastrophe, yet her heart
gave a little flip. What would it have been, a boy or a
girl . . .?

"Alexandra . . ."

She blinked. "I'm sorry—what did you say?"

Adam felt a bond of sympathy for her. He himself
had not slept last night, and his every thought this morn
had been of her. He had a continuing fierce hunger for
her, and gratitude that he had not taken her, but he felt
no shame over their near-lovemaking—only every other
damned emotion known to man. And now he had a new
concern. He had decided that she must know about the
arrival of the Mohawks, and that it would affect their
return to Tiyanoga. It was only fair that she know. He

took up his sledgehammer and split another log before he said matter-of-factly:

"My Mohawk brethren are going to be coming here to live for a while, Alexandra." He positioned the wedge on another log, swung, heard the clean, crisp crack of the separation. "They will arrive shortly."

Alexandra's eyes widened. "Really?"

"Hen." Seeing the delight on her face, he decided he would never understand women.

Alexandra was jubilant. She was saved! Now she did not have to struggle for something to say to him when all she could think of was what had happened last night. She asked, "Will they live in the manor?"

"There are too many for that." Looking on her heightened color and suddenly bright eyes, he remembered for the hundredth time her willingness to please him last night. She would have sacrificed her maidenhood to him. It was a thing he would never forget.

"How many will there be?" She could actually look at him and meet his eyes without feeling all hot and flustered.

"As many as two hundred," Adam muttered, and thought of her small pink tongue meeting his greedily, brushing over his skin and his hair, tasting his lips . . .

"Two hundred? This is no small thing, then." She watched him place the wedge, swing; felt a small curl of fire unwind deep inside as muscles rippled beneath his dark skin. She put her attention carefully on the logs and his tools. "Where will they live? Will they build longhouses?" Looking about, she was unable to imagine such an undertaking—not unless they meant to stay for a long time.

"They will erect wigwams," Adam said.

She nodded. "That's reasonable. You say they'll arrive shortly. Do you mean today?"

"Today, tomorrow, soon." He wished suddenly that she would go and leave him in peace.

"When did you learn they were coming? How did you learn?"

Adam curbed his rising temper. "Not now, Alexandra. You will hear of it all at a later time."

Seeing his annoyance, she realized she had rambled on far too long, but it was in self-defense. If she stopped talking, she would start thinking about him, and she could not bear to think about him, for then she would think of losing him. She put her foot atop one of the logs he had split. A large pile of them stood there. "May I help you in some way? Maybe start stacking these?"

Adam's gaze flickered over her. The only way she could help him was to remove her clothing and open her legs and let him take her. Let him bury himself in her and feel the ecstasy he knew awaited him. He shook off the need that was always there, always threatening to overpower him, and leaned on his mallet.

"You can help me by being patient."

Alexandra shaded her eyes from the sun and frowned up at him. "I don't understand."

Adam looked away from her soft mouth and creamy throat. Hell, he was becoming as bad as Willie Johnson. He had a Mohawk war brewing on his doorstep, and all he could think about was making love to this little fox. Her whispered words filled his ears and sounded with every beat of his heart. He could not forget them. *Teach me to make love, Cougar ... Teach me to make love ...* He thrust them away, said abruptly:

"Our trip to Tiyanoga is postponed for the present."

"Oh?"

It was some moments before Alexandra understood the full impact of his news. She would not be leaving him! They would be together, at least for a while. Not the way they had been last night, of course—she must never never do that again—but she could still see him and talk to him, and for now that was miracle enough. And it was a miracle. She could almost hear bells ringing and feel wings sprouting and lifting her in lovely, dizzying circles. For a certainty, the sun felt warmer, the air smelled sweeter, and the birds were suddenly singing their hearts out. She was filled with glory—and with guilt.

She nipped it swiftly. It was all right. Mama knew she was well and would be returning soon. And the new commander at Tiyanoga would still be there when she finally got back. Things had waited this long, they could wait awhile longer. And if it was selfish of her to want to be with him just a few more days, so be it. She was selfish.

"I am sorry," Adam said. "I know you are disappointed, but I must remain here until my brethren arrive and are settled."

"I understand. It's all right." She did not look at him, only at the wood. "Are you sure I can't help stack this?"

"There is no need. The women will take care of it when they arrive."

"Well, then, I'd best get back to the house. There's work still to be done . . ."

Adam took up his sledgehammer once more. He smiled at her. "As I told you, Lord Adam will know of your efforts, Alexandra, I promise you."

She shrugged. "It hardly matters. I'm doing it because I enjoy it."

As she mounted to the second floor to begin cleaning there, Alexandra thought wistfully that Windfall deserved a happier fate than the one that had befallen it. It deserved fires dancing on the hearths, rooms filled with laughter, and good smells coming from the kitchen. It deserved to be somebody's home. She hoped the Duke of Dover would return someday and claim it, but even Lord Adam would be better than nothing . . .

Her plan to work on the chamber next to her own was thwarted by a locked door. Good. It was probably used for storage and meant less work for her. She would start with the hall tables and the picture frames instead. But before she ever began, she heard men's voices and knew that the Mohawks had arrived.

Hurrying to the large window at the end of the hall, she saw the braves and youths emerging from the woods to the east, followed by the children who were laughing and leaping about excitedly. But she saw no women. It was some minutes before they came into sight, they and the horses. Both were plodding heavily, slowly under the huge burdens strapped onto their backs. Blazes! And the men and boys were as free and unfettered as any buck in the forest!

Indignation simmering, Alexandra watched as the women moved slowly to the field before the house, where they stood, silent, patient, and seemingly numb with fatigue. Where was the Cougar? she wondered. He had been there just a short time ago. Why was he not there now to tell everyone what to do and where to go? As she contemplated looking for him, a brave appeared and took command. Her heart sank when she saw that it was Silver Hawk, the sachem who had threatened to slit her tongue. But if Silver Hawk were here, it meant Lark was, too. She was one of those poor things loaded down like the horses.

Alexandra ran down the stairs and out into the May sunshine, but she saw instantly that she had made a mistake. When she had last seen these people, she had hated them all and had not hesitated to show it. Now few of them met her eyes, and those who did looked right through her. It was as though she did not exist. She told herself to turn around and go back into the house, but it was too late. Lark had seen her. Alexandra saw her eyes widen and then grow veiled.

Alexandra walked toward her and put a welcoming smile on her face. "Hello, my friend, it's good to see you again."

Lark said quietly, *"Sekon,* Gold Hair."

Lark was shocked. She had thought this maid was

long gone back to her people, but here she was at Windfall and looking more beautiful than ever. Why had Hawk not told her? Why had he allowed her to chatter on about love and signs and wanting to join with the Cougar when he had surely known she was here? And surely known Adam would want her for his woman even though he said he would never wed again. Perhaps they were joined already . . .

She murmured, "My brother was here several days ago to talk with the Cougar. He did not mention seeing you."

Seeing that Lark's black eyes burned with a strange light, Alexandra felt uncomfortable. "I . . . didn't see him, either. But I'm glad you're here Lark. Truly."

Lark yearned to slay her. With great effort, she made her mouth smile. "*Niawen*. But I cannot speak with you now, Alexandra. There is much work to be done."

"Please, let me help."

Lark shook her head. "Thank you, but there is no need."

Alexandra heard it for what it was—a dismissal. As she watched Lark slide the tumpline off her forehead and lower her burden to the ground, she sensed her hostility. What had happened? Lark had once offered her friendship, but now it was clear they were enemies. As she returned to the manor, Alexandra felt useless and out of place amid the noise and bustle. And she felt hated.

Chapter 14

A lexandra calmly made her way back to the manor through a noisy maze of animals and people and equipment. Only after she had locked the front door of Windfall, gone up to her bedchamber, and locked that door behind her did she realize how frightened she was. They hated her. It would not surprise her a bit if they wanted to scalp her. She was watching them from her window, remembering the outright hostility in Lark's black eyes when she heard the Cougar's voice outside her door.

"Gold Hair?"

"Just a moment!" As she unlocked it, she was tempted to tell him her fears—but how silly she would look. The Mohawks had only arrived and already she was complaining about them.

"Did you see that they have come?" Adam asked.

"Aye."

"Come down with me, then. It is important that you greet them." He had decided they must know immediately that she was no longer an enemy but a friend.

"I've ... been down already," Alexandra replied. "I've seen Lark. I wondered where you were."

"I was in the east woods cutting more deadwood." He had already spoken with Hawk and the earliest arrivals, but he had not yet greeted the others. His gaze narrowed as he marked the wide dark centers of her eyes and the tightness about her mouth. It was fear. "What did Lark say?" he asked carefully.

"The women all looked so tired, I offered to help. She said it wasn't necessary." Alexandra shrugged. "It doesn't matter. I was in the way, so I came back to the manor."

Adam saw that it mattered very much. She was hurt, and something or someone had frightened her enough so that she had locked the doors of the house and her bedchamber. This he would end before it went any further, he thought angrily. In his brief conversation with Hawk, he had learned that many of the braves, himself included, would be leaving soon, perhaps in the morn, to summon their Iroquois brethren to a war council. The sooner Alexandra and the Mohawks were easy with each other, the better. He took her hand. "Come down now, you will not be in the way."

"I can't!" Alexandra planted her feet. "I hated them when I saw them last, and they remember it. Now they hate me."

So it had happened already—the earlier animosity between them that he had hoped to avoid. He said easily, "They will not hate you when I tell them you are no longer an enemy but a friend." He drew her toward the door.

"It will take a miracle."

"Then we will make a miracle. Come."

"Cougar!" She clutched the doorjamb with her fingers, but he pried them loose and tossed her over one wide shoulder. "Cougar! *Iah!*"

"Greet them standing on your own two feet or from my shoulder," he said, striding down the hall.

"Neither!" It was a shriek smothered by her sudden laughter.

"Choose, Gold Hair."

"Please . . ." Alexandra could not stop laughing as she pounded his back with her fists. "Tyrant!"

"So you have told me before." He wanted to run his hands up and down her long legs and caress her sweet little bottom, but he kept himself under tight control.

He had saved her once from his hunger; he doubted he would be that strong a second time. "Choose," he said, carrying her down the stairs.

"Oh, heavens, do put me down! I-I'll go out with you if you insist." For if she did not, he would carry her out, backside first, and she would absolutely die of humiliation.

At the foot of the stairs, Adam set her ever so gently on her feet and grinned down at her flushed face. *"Niawen, onkiatshi."*

"What does that mean?"

His eyes danced over her. "It means 'thank you, my friend.' "

"Beast!" She punched his shoulder so hard it jolted her clear up to her collarbone, but he only smiled his white smile.

"All will be well with you and the People, Alexandra, I promise you." And if he could not make peace between them he would stay behind when the other braves left.

"If you say so." His smile had melted her. "I hope you know—I'm not really angry with you. And I shouldn't have socked you like that . . ."

Adam rubbed his shoulder. "The pain is great but it will pass . . ."

She grinned. "I'm sure it will."

"Are you ready?"

"I guess." She was not. She doubted she would ever be ready. She stalled. "I've just been wondering"—she gazed about at Windfall's elegant foyer and quiet rooms and imagined Mohawks going in and out and all over— "what would the Duke of Dover think of all this? Would he approve?"

"His brother approves," Adam replied crisply. "It is all that matters."

"Lord Adam knows?"

"It was he who told them to come. Whites have

claimed their cropland as well as their hunting grounds. This tribe has nothing left."

"Their cropland!" Alexandra's indignation. exploded as she thought of how hard the women worked to prepare and plant their fields. She knew. She had worked beside them. "Blazes, I can't believe anyone would do such a cruel and stupid thing. Just wait until I return to Tiyanoga. Changes will be made, I promise. Just wait!"

"It will be appreciated." Seeing her pink face and her fury, Adam remembered that not so very long ago, that same fury had been directed toward him and his Mohawks. Now she had more heart, more compassion for them than he had ever dreamed possible. It was a pity it would be wasted on Wade Chamberlain. "Come, Gold Hair, it is time to greet them."

Alexandra squared her shoulders. "I am ready." But she was trembling as she followed him across the portico, down the steps, and into the light mist that was swirling softly about them.

A sudden ominous quiet pressed against her ears as she sensed the Mohawks' dark eyes upon her and felt their hatred and anger reaching out and almost touching her. Yet how could she blame them? They had every right to feel as they did, having just been driven from their castle by those stupid, greedy whites. Her people. But when she gathered her courage finally and raised her head to face them, she found that no one was even looking at her. Every eye was on the Cougar as he moved among them, lifting and hugging children, greeting men and women with equal warmth, stroking the heads of dogs and the necks of weary horses.

Alexandra stood back and watched in fascination. She had seen the respect shown him in the many castles and villages they had visited, aye, but this was different. This was a far deeper and stronger thing than mere respect or even love. She was reflecting on it as he greeted Lark, smiled, spoke in her ear, and then tugged the shining black braid that hung down her back. And then his gaze was searching over the throng and Alexandra flushed, wondering if he were seeking her. He was! Her breath caught as their eyes met, and then he was calling to her, holding out his hand.

"Gold Hair, come."

Walking toward him, Alexandra had the strangest feeling that all this had happened before. It was so very familiar. And then she realized that it was her dream. Her dream! The mist . . . her fear . . . moving toward that strong, dark, outstretched hand . . . leaving her enemy behind her. Her heart was suddenly so full she could not look at him. And when he raised his voice and began to speak, she had to gaze down at her moccasins. Listening to the strangely beautiful but impossible-sounding words rolling from his lips, she wondered what was he saying about her—and wondered if he would be able to save her yet one more time.

When she finally dared look up, several women met her eyes and smiled at her shyly. She quickly smiled back. The braves did not deign to look at her, but she detected their barely perceptible nods as the Cougar continued to speak. Blazes, he was making a miracle for her, just as he had said he would. But why was she surprised when it was clear that they worshipped him? Aye, that was the word she had been looking for. It was more than respect, more than love. It was almost as if he were a god to them. She was studying their intent faces, puzzling over how such a thing could be, when his speech came to an end. As men and women alike gathered around him, talking, pointing, asking questions, she moved aside.

"Alexandra . . ."

Alexandra turned. It was Lark. Seeing that the maid's face revealed nothing except weariness, she smiled. "Hello, my friend."

"Sekon, onkiatshi." Lark's peace had been greatly disturbed by her own behavior. Why was she treating

this poor captive maid as a threat? It was almost as if she doubted the Great Sustainer who had thrice assured her that the Cougar would be hers. But she did not doubt Him, and she must stop this discourtesy. She must stop it now. She said gently, "I am sorry that I dismissed you so sharply. I have feared I crushed your spirit."

Alexandra looked at her in amazement. No one had ever been concerned about crushing her spirit before. She shook her head. "You haven't," she whispered, sensing this was a private thing between them. "I saw that . . . you were very tired."

Lark nodded. "It is so."

She could not keep her envious gaze from moving over Alexandra's face and hair—her soft white skin, apple blossoms blooming on her cheeks, the mist glittering like gems in that cloud of golden hair. Her heart trembled at such fairness, and she had seen well the adoring way the maid looked upon the Cougar as he spoke. What remained to be seen was how the Cougar felt about her.

"I am still tired," she said, "and after our wigwam is in place, my mother and I would be grateful for your help. She, too, is much wearied from our journey, and we have many things to put in order."

Alexandra nearly threw her arms around her, but she restrained herself. "My goodness, of course I'll help! Nothing would please me more . . ."

"*Niawen.* It will be appreciated."

And so it was that after the poles were driven into the earth in a large circle and fastened at the top, and sheets of bark were secured over the resulting conical framework, Alexandra helped Lark and Fox Woman place the bedshelves against the walls of the large, airy wigwam, and helped unpack their goods. When dusk fell and the cookfires were lit, she was still there, for she had seen that their weariness was great. She fetched wood and water, helped prepare the evening meal, and in turn was asked to share it with them.

Afterward, she sat before the fire and gazed sleepily at the transformation of the land around Windfall. There were wigwams everywhere, and cookfires and people and dogs. The horses had been tethered in a field of deep grass. Alexandra wondered what had become of the Cougar. She had not seen him since he had spoken on her behalf, nor had she seen Lark's brother, the scowling sachem, except for that one brief glimpse of him from the window when the Mohawks had first arrived. She was glad. She had feared he would come and eat with them as Old Father had. But now the father was gone again. All the men were gone, doubtless to the same place that had claimed the Cougar. She missed him. And she wanted to ask him what he'd said about her that had made the women smile at her and the men nod.

"You are tired," Lark said, seeing her yawn.

"A bit. But if I get busy, it will go away. What else can I do for you?"

"For now, all is done." Alexandra's willingness to help to do any chore asked of her, had taken Lark by surprise. She had thought white women knew only how to lie abed and nag their men to work. And she remembered well how Alexandra herself had hated to work. But it was as the Cougar had told them. This was not the same Alexandra they had known earlier. "Tomorrow," she said, "I will help you. In any way you choose."

Alexandra murmured, "You could help me now . . ."

"I will do my best."

Alexandra looked from Lark's curious eyes back to the cookfire. "I've been wondering . . . what the Cougar said about me."

The Cougar. That she still did not know his true identity made Lark feel easier. It was but one more sign. If he meant to keep this woman for his own, would he not be eager for her to know who he was? But he was not keeping her. He had revealed in his talk to them that he was returning her to her people. The thought had warmed her throughout the afternoon even as Alexandra's golden loveliness dismayed her.

"He said," she answered softly, "that you are not the same woman he brought to our village earlier. He said your eyes are open now and your heart is torn by what you have seen. He said your anger burns like a great fire at what your people are doing to the Mohawks and their brethren. He said soon he will take you back to your father and that you will—"

Alexandra looked up. "Did you say . . . my father?" She had never ceased grieving for him, but the ache had become muted as her thoughts were consumed more and more by the Cougar.

"Hen. He said the Gold Hair yearns now to turn around the old Grayhead's heart so he will make things right with the Mohawks . . ." Seeing the confusion in Alexandra's green eyes, Lark realized that the maid still thought the Grayhead had been slain. It did not seem right in her mind that she had not been told the truth. Or perhaps she had been told and could not believe it. Whatever the reason, Lark was certain the maid's nights were restless, and she knew she could make them easier. She slipped into the wigwam.

Alexandra never saw her go. She sat staring into the flames of the cookfires, dazed, almost giddy. Papa was alive. Oh, Papa! It was as if the sun had been under a cloud these past weeks and was shining down on her suddenly, bright and hot and beautiful and chasing away all the shadows. Papa was alive! Of course he was. She knew it now.

Always before when the Cougar had tried to tell her that he had only been wounded, she would not believe him. She could not. He was the enemy, and she had been furiously, stubbornly set in her belief that he was lying to mellow her. But he was not her enemy now, nor had he ever been. He never would have said her father was alive if he were not. He would never hurt her that way. But she would ask him one more time to make absolutely sure. She was deep in her thoughts as Lark emerged from her wigwam with a small, gaily decorated wooden hoop.

"For you," Lark said, placing it in Alexandra's hands.

Alexandra took the gift gratefully. "It's beautiful . . . thank you so much." She added shyly, *"Niawen, onkiatshi."* She stroked its satiny feathers and brightly colored beads and asked, "Did you make it?"

Lark glowed. *"Hen."* She felt compassion for this girl-woman, but it did not mean she liked her. Even though she was attempting to speak their tongue, Lark would never like her.

Alexandra continued to examine the hoop and stroke the feathers. "I've seen one of these before, but I didn't know what it was." It had hung over the Cougar's bed that night in the trading post.

"My people call it a dreamcatcher."

Alexandra held it up by its cord and watched as it spun in the breeze, it's feathers dancing. "I love it. And does it really catch dreams?"

"Hen. It catches bad ones." Lark's quick eyes saw that she had captured the maid's interest. "Hang it over your bed, and it will trap them in the net of grasses before they can reach you. The good dreams can then slip through the center hole and into your sleep."

Alexandra observed Lark's placid face for some moments before she asked quietly, "How did you know I had bad dreams?"

"All who are stolen have bad dreams. I . . . still have them."

"You . . . were stolen?"

"From my family. *Hen."* The memory would be with her forever. Her gentle mother and strong father, her small sister and handsome young brother, all lying choking in the blood gushing from their own scalps.

"Lark, I'm so sorry . . ." Why had she thought only whites were stolen? "When did this happen?"

"I was twelve winters."

"Oh, Lark . . ." It shattered Alexandra to think of it, the beautiful child Lark must have been, carried off by braves such as her own Oneida captors. She said with feeling, "But you were returned, thank God! There was a happy ending." Just as there was a happy ending for her. Papa was alive . . .

Lark did not reply. She had never meant to say as much as she had. She never spoke to anyone of those days. And now if she spoke or thought of it further, even her dreamcatcher would not save her from the terror that would come to her in the night.

Alexandra saw that it was growing late, and the time for confidences was ended. She rose. "Again—*niawen, onkiatshi,* for my dreamcatcher. I love it and I'll treasure it. And thank your mother for the food." Turning to Fox Woman, she nodded, dropped her a curtsy. *"Niawen,* Old Mother. I'm grateful." She felt their eyes upon her as she departed, carrying a blazing knot to light her way to Windfall.

In her bedchamber, she locked the door, closed the draperies, and lit several candles before adding more kindling and the flaming knot to the embers in the fireplace. She then went to the writing table, uncorked the inkpot, and began eagerly to write:

Cher Journal—So much has happened since I wrote last! Papa is alive, I'm quite certain of it, and the Mohawks have come to Windfall to live for a while. At first I was sure I'd be scalped in the night, the way they glared at me, but my darling savior saved me once again. Another thing, it was Old Rhubarb who invited the Mohawks here! I still can't imagine why such a man would care enough about Indians to help them so. I'm wondering if I have a completely wrong idea of him . . .

Alexandra ceased writing and stared at the door. Was that a knock she'd heard, or was it the fire popping and crackling on the hearth? Straining to hear, she moved silently across the carpet, put her lips to the crack. "Is anyone there?" Fearing suddenly that some brave had broken in and was seeking her, she covered her mouth. Oh, why had she spoken?

"Alexandra, it is the Cougar."

Of course it was the Cougar! What was the matter with her? She threw open the door, and when his black eyes searched over her, she forgot to breathe—or speak.

Adam smiled. "May I come in?"

"Of course."

She had been so happy, so excited about so many things when she was writing in her journal, but now she wilted. What on earth was she going to do about this predicament she was in? Thinking of the Cougar was as painful as not thinking about him. And when she was with him, it gave her no joy, for she could think only of that time soon to come when they would part and she would never seen him again. She had tried to tell herself that she was a woman now, not a spoiled child who had to have everything her heart desired. She had tried to assure herself that she would be fine after they said goodbye, and that she could grow used to anything. But she knew it was not so. She would never be fine again. Quite simply, she so loved this man; she could not live or breathe or exist without him.

Chapter 15

When Alexandra gazed up at him, her green eyes as wide as those of a lost child, Adam almost held out his arms. He caught himself. It was becoming a damned dangerous habit even though it was only to comfort her. Oh, aye, as if he did not enjoy the way her small, soft body felt when it was molded against his . . .

"I'm happy you came . . ." Her heart was still flying so that she was breathless. "I wondered where you were, and where all the men were."

"My brethren and I have been in council. They had much to tell me. I am glad you are still awake—I wanted to make sure all was well with you." But her eyes and her face told him that it was not, and his anger stirred. "You are still upset. Who has troubled you? Is it the women?"

Alexandra said quickly, "I'm not upset, and the women are friendly. Everything is fine." She bore his quiet scrutiny for some moments then murmured, "Lark told me what you said to the People about me, and I do thank you. It's made a big difference."

Adam scarcely heard her. If the women were not troubling her, what was? It was certainly not the men. They had more important things to think about than one small female. "Lark was friendly also?"

"Lark is wonderful. I like her. And Fox Woman is nice. I helped them put away things in their wigwam, and then we cooked dinner, and afterward we talked. And Lark gave me a dreamcatcher. See?" She pointed

to where she had hung it atop the bedpost. Meeting his
dark eyes, she told herself not to think about the future.
She would think only about now—and not about him.
"And Cougar, did you know Lark had been stolen?"

"Hen." He had not seen her this jumpy since the afternoon of the storm when she had sat by the fire and
babbled about rockers and tea.

"It must have been dreadful. She was just a little
girl—and how Fox Woman must have suffered."

Hearing that, Adam realized she had not heard the
full tale, nor would he be the one to tell her. He said,
"It ended well. Her life is good now." It was not Lark
he was concerned about, it was Alexandra. What in
damnation was the matter with her? If she refused to
tell him, he could not help her. Nor would he leave with
the others tomorrow. He could not risk it. "I will let
you get to sleep now. It is late."

"Cougar, wait!" She had just remembered her father.
Blazes, she could not believe she was so caught up in
her own affairs that she had forgotten him completely.
What kind of daughter was she?

Adam turned, waited as the fire danced and cast its
shadows about the room. "What is it, Gold Hair?" He
had known something was wrong.

Alexandra crossed her fingers. "I'm sorry, but I have
to ask you one more time—" Once more her hopes
were high, and his next words could dash them forever.
"My father . . . is he alive? I know you've said he is,
but I did see how he looked when he fell . . ."

A sigh slipped past Adam's lips. So that was all that
was troubling her—her devil father. He said patiently,
"It is as I have told you, Alexandra. Your father
breathes. He is in strong command of his garrison once
more."

She believed him. She truly, finally believed him, but
she was not prepared for the huge wave of relief sweeping over her. She put her hands to her lips so he would
not see their trembling. "I've been so stupid."

Amusement glinted in Adam's dark eyes. "You are not stupid. It is that once I was your enemy, and now I am not."

"You've never been my enemy . . ."

"I am glad you understand that."

"I understand a lot now. You tried to tell me how things were, but I was too bullheaded and know-it-all to accept it."

To think, if only she had returned to Tiyanoga sooner, maybe she could have changed things. Oh aye, and never gotten to know him . . . never kissed him or held him or felt her body awakening . . . never fallen in love with him . . . Was that really what she wanted? God knew it was not. She would not give up this part of her life for any treasure the world had to offer. But the Mohawks were suffering because of it.

"I promise you, Cougar"—her eyes were a green glitter in the half-light—"I *will* help your people when I return to Tiyanoga. You said we'd be leaving after they were settled in, and they seem well-settled to me already."

"This is a thing we must talk about. I do not know now when we will be leaving."

A small shiver of fear ran over her. "Why? What's happening?"

"There is great unrest."

"Do you mean war?"

"There is talk of it. All afternoon and evening we have talked of it, and tomorrow we ride to summon our Iroquois brethren here for more talk."

Alexandra put her hands to her cheeks. "Now I do feel guilty."

Adam could not contain his exasperation. He grasped her shoulders. "Alexandra, this has nothing to do with you. I will hear no more of this talk."

"I can't help it. I feel guilty just being white and being who I am—Wade Chamberlain's daughter!" Not only did she feel guilty, she was sick to death of hiding her feelings for him. Even his being annoyed and gripping her shoulders made her love blossom more wildly inside her, all hot and sweet and shimmering so that she was going to fly into a million pieces if she could not touch him and tell him about it.

Adam said gruffly, "I will not have you bearing this burden on your shoulders."

More than that, he regretted ever putting it there. And he feared now that it would be several weeks before he could finally return her to the parents she yearned for and the civilization where she belonged. As for himself, he faced torment in the days ahead. He could not stop the terrible fire of his need from blazing to life every time he looked at her or was near her. It was hell, and he damned well deserved every second of it. Seeing that she had bowed her head and covered her eyes, he muttered:

"Come, Alexandra, I will not have this." He released his grip on her and once more put his arms around her. Damnation, he could not let the maid stand there all forlorn and not do something about it, now could he? He said more quietly, "In no way are you to blame for what is happening—the trouble is all over the colony. Do not weep. You will see your parents soon, I promise you."

His arms enfolding her . . . his warmth . . . his caring and comforting . . . She could not live with this torment another moment. She had to tell him the truth, or at least part of the truth. There was no other way. She raised her head, said quietly, "I'm not weeping, Cougar—and it's not my parents I'm thinking about."

Adam gazed at her shining eyes and quickened breathing, the rapid rise and fall of her breasts. He felt his own breathing quicken. Sweet Jesus, how could he keep his hands off her when she looked at him like that?

"It's selfish of me, I-I know"—she twisted a coil of hair about one finger—"but I'm glad there's unrest and that ... you can't take me back to Tiyanoga. Cougar, I-I want to be with you." God help her, she had done it. She had said it. She had actually gotten it out.

Adam stood very still and asked quietly, "Why do you want to be with me, Alexandra?"

"Because I feel safe with you ..." She found a strand of hair to twist again. "I ... like to be near you. I like to watch you work, and I like the way you look and th-the way you feel and ... the way you hold me and kiss me ..." She tried to smile, but her mouth refused. It quivered instead. "I just want to be with you. Just for a little while longer."

Overcome, Adam lifted her into his arms and for long moments held her against his racing heart. He said finally, "And I want to be with you ..."

He touched his mouth tenderly to her lips and to the soft curve of cheek and chin, trailed small kisses down the side of her white throat, inhaled the intoxicating lavender scent of her flesh. He wanted far more than to be with her just for a little while longer. He wanted more than just one night, or one moon, or one winter. As her small, warm tongue hungrily greeted his, he saw suddenly and clearly what he had not allowed himself to see before. He wanted to be with her forever. And it was not just to satisfy his need that he wanted her. He loved her. He loved her innocence and beauty, her bravery and compassion. He loved her fiercely indomitable spirit—and her boldness. Without her boldness, he never would have known she wanted to be with him.

"Little snowflower ..." He carried her to the bed.

Alexandra felt suddenly shy. A moment ago she had been bearing her soul to him, and now he was lowering her to the bed and his black eyes were burning over her. Excitement shivered through her as he stretched out beside her.

"Do you want to be with me like this, Gold Hair?"

Alexandra nodded. If her life depended on it, no words could have slipped past her heart, which was quivering wildly in her throat. It beat harder still as he slid an arm under her, cradling her within it, and pulled her to his side. He murmured into her hair:

"Is this what you want, little fox?" He tenderly explored the delicate shell-like convolutions of her ears, traced the outline of her face and mouth with his fingers, savored the silken texture of her flesh.

"Aye . . ." Alexandra trembled, feeling his voice rumbling through her. This was what she wanted. But thinking beyond this moment frightened her, for what if this was all she wanted? To be held tightly against him and to feel safe, to be locked away with him so that in all the world, only the two of them existed in this quiet, flame-flickered room. But then she remembered how he had stirred her body to an awareness she had never known before. Wordlessly, she lifted her lips.

Adam took them hungrily. That she wanted to be with him aroused him as much as did the kiss she offered. He reveled in the softness of her lips, her small eager tongue meeting his, her sharp little teeth closing gently on his own probing tongue. He chuckled. "I think this, too, is what you wanted . . ."

"Aye . . ." It slipped out, as soft as a sigh. She wanted him to kiss not only her mouth, she wanted him to kiss her everywhere. Shyly, she touched his face with her fingertips, savored the masculine roughness of his skin and the soft warmth of his mouth and his silky lashes. She kneaded the hard muscles of his back and shoulders, speared her fingers through his thick black hair.

Adam caught her hand, raised it to his mouth, kissed the pad of each pink fingertip before touching the tip of his tongue to them. "How good you taste . . ."

Alexandra laughed, took one of his own fingers into her mouth, sucked it gently. "And how good you taste." Her breath caught as his other hand sought her breasts. As he gently squeezed and caressed them, heat raced through her body. She arched against him. If she had any doubts as to the path she trod, they had all vanished. She wanted more than just to be held by him. She wanted him to make love to her——more than she had ever wanted anything in her life . . .

Slipping her hands up under his buckskin shirt, she traced the lines of his broad chest—his muscles and bones and ribs. He was oak-hard, but his flesh was wonderfully resilient beneath her searching fingers. Finding his nipples, she withdrew hastily, embarrassed. He would surely be affronted if she touched him there. But he gave a low growl of pleasure and slid his hand beneath her shirt. Feeling warm flesh against flesh, Alexandra was electrified. As his fingers circled her nipples and gently caught them to tease and tantalize her, she gasped his name. Moved now by a passion beyond her control, her body stiffened, thrust against him as she felt a deep, delicious pulsing in her breasts.

Fire shot through him as Adam drew up her shirt. Sweet Jesus, he could not believe how beautiful she was. A vision . . . Her skin was white satin in the flickering half-light, and her swollen breasts were the most perfect orbs, their lush nipples puckered into silky buds that awaited his hungry mouth. The hot cords of his need were drawing him closer and closer to taking her, yet he was still bound tightly by his fear for her safety. How could he loose his fierce hunger on her, and yet, ah, God . . . Looking at her half-closed eyes and parted lips, feeling the warmth and sweetness of her small ragged breaths, feeling her softness pressed against him, he knew he would have no peace until he was buried inside her—nor would she.

He lowered his head to her breasts, touched one nipple with the tip of his tongue, circled it, and when she whimpered, took it deeply into his mouth, sucking and then gently nipping the taut little ruby with his teeth. When she shuddered, he moved to her other nipple, licking, sucking, nipping, his hands moving over her body slowly, caressing, teasing, building a fire within her that could only be quenched when he claimed her.

His voice was husky as he took her mouth again. "You are the most beautiful thing, Gold Hair . . ."

Alexandra was shaking with her need for him. The fire blazing within her was so hot and filled her so completely, it frightened her. Would she feel this way forever if they did not couple—all hot and swollen and throbbing inside and feeling as if part of her were missing? She wanted it to go away even as she wanted the sweet torment to go on and on tantalizing her. And when the Cougar harshly sealed her mouth with his and then lowered his lips to her throat to gently bite the soft flesh there, she moaned with the pleasure of it. He made things happen to her body and her senses for which she had no words. He had had only to touch her that first time to send her hurtling into the sun. She wanted that again. She wanted all he had to give. Wrapping her arms and legs about him, she clung to him like a wild thing, pressing, thrusting her body against his hardness in hungry desperation.

"Please." It was a soft gasp. "Teach me, Cougar. Teach me to make love."

Wordlessly, Adam unlaced her shirt, slipped her out of it, and pressed her back onto the mattress. Slipping an arm beneath her hips and raising them, he quickly drew off her leggings. He caught his breath, seeing her completely naked for the first time; her skin a sheen of creamy satin . . . those long, slim, rounded limbs . . . the beautiful curve of hips and belly . . . her slender throat flowing into elegantly carved shoulders and the full globes of her breasts . . . that pale cloud of down between her white thighs. She was glorious.

Seeing his black eyes feasting on her, Alexandra turned pink. "I . . . didn't mean for you t-to *look* at me!" She covered her eyes, unable to bear his scrutiny and what was sure to be his disappointment.

Gently, Adam took her hands, whispered against her

lips. "You delight my eyes, my Gold Hair. You are very beautiful."

"Nay."

"I have said it."

Alexandra grew pinker still. She smiled then. "So are you. Beautiful." When he gave a low laugh and shook his head, she added, "I have said it." She watched hungrily, the heat of her desire glowing, flaming through her, as he pulled off his shirt, revealing the broad shoulders and hard muscles and dark, polished skin that made her weak every time she thought of them. She watched as he tossed his moccasins to the floor and rose to tug off his leggings, raising one long dark leg at a time. And then he was naked . . .

Alexandra stared, seeing for the first time a male in the full-blown heat of arousal. She could scarcely believe it. When she had touched him there before, he had not been nearly so—so large. She quickly looked away, but uncertainty had gripped her. How did men and women ever couple if this was the way of it? Why, he would tear her asunder. But even though it frightened her, some primitive part of her thrilled to the thought of his wanting her and driving into her.

Adam had seen the widening of her eyes, and as he returned to the bed, he steeled himself to patience. As he lay down and slid his arm under her, he reminded himself again that she was a virgin. She had not even kissed a man until he had kissed her. He said softly, "I will not hurt you, Alexandra. I am going to love you."

"I-I know. Oh, Cougar, I do know." How rude of her, how childish to stare like that.

She sucked in a breath as he pulled her so close her nipples grazed the crisp dark curls on his chest. And then his body was touching hers from head to toe, his nakedness scorching her flesh and the heat of him spreading, glowing beneath her skin to pulse between her thighs. She sighed, feeling excitement rippling through her and sending a trumpet call to her brain, to

her heart, that she wanted him. In truth she did, even if
it hurt a bit. She certainly had never heard of coupling
killing a woman who was willing and eager for it. She
slid her arms around his waist, shyly touched the tip of
her tongue to the rough skin around his mouth and then
to his lips, tasting, savoring, inhaling the wonderful familiar woodsmoke and pine aroma of his skin and hair.

Adam was suspended in a bittersweet limbo between
heaven and hell. As he caressed the silken flesh of her
breasts and throat, he could not forget the fear he had
seen in her eyes. If she had told him to leave then, he
would have. Then and there. But not now. Not when he
had her naked in his arms, all warm and soft and satiny.
Iah. He was going to have her this night, by God he
was, but he hated it that he would have to hurt her. She
would be tight and small and frightened despite her
passion, and his desire for her was growing hotter and
wilder and more uncontrollable by the moment. When
she slid her arms about his waist and touched her
tongue to his lips, his restraint vanished. He rolled over
onto her, caged her beneath him, and caught her mouth
in a savage, thrusting kiss, filling her with it as he
would soon fill her with himself.

Alexandra's body quivered under his suddenly unre-
strained passion. The weight of him drove the breath
from her lungs and his savage kisses sucked it from her
throat, leaving her gasping. Seared by her own scorching desire, she wrapped her legs about his hips again,
twined her fingers in his hair, and drew his face closer,
covering it with kisses, pressing her body against his to
get closer, closer. She was dying for want of him, per-
ishing . . .

Alexandra's breath caught as he slid his hand between her thighs and touched her . . . there . . . stroking,
gently rubbing, teasing, his fingers fluttering over her
most secret of places. Feeling herself opening to him
like the petals of a flower to the sun, she wept softly—
with the ecstasy of it, with seeing his face glistening

with sweat and hearing his tortured breathing, with knowing he was putting her pleasure, her well-being before his own hunger.

Seeing her tears, Adam frowned. "Am I hurting you?"

"*Iah!* Please don't stop." She pressed his fingers to her more firmly and then felt them slide easily, deeply within her. It made her gasp. He was in her! His fingers were inside her, still teasing, rubbing, caressing her in such a way that her body bore down, wanting to trap and hold them there. And then suddenly it was not his fingers stroking her there but the head of his manhood.

"I will be gentle, Gold Hair . . ."

Parting her legs, kneeling between them, Adam prayed to God it was so. He stifled a groan of impatience, seeing how moist and pink and glistening she was—how beautiful, and how ready for him. It was agony, merely to touch himself to that small honeyed pool when he craved to thrust into her, again and again and again until the violence of his hunger was spent. He swallowed, dragged in a steadying breath, told himself for the hundredth time that he could not do with her as he wished. He would not harm her. He was her first . . .

"I'm not afraid," Alexandra murmured, seeing the grimness of his eyes and mouth, and knowing he was afraid for her. She laughed softly, lifted up her hands to cradle his face. "I want you, Cougar . . ." Never, never, never would she have arrived at so embarrassing a state otherwise. Naked . . . her legs spread in so ungraceful a fashion . . . an equally naked brave, his black eyes dilated with passion, straddling her. Just looking at him sent flames licking over her. She pulled down his head to her breasts, and as he kissed them, she shyly touched his erect manhood, felt it leap under her hand. "I'm not afraid," she whispered again, drawing his swollen shaft to that part of her which lay open and waiting for him.

Adam's love for her nearly overwhelmed him as she tried to guide him into herself. He chuckled at her sweet innocence, said huskily, "What you seek is farther back, little fox."

"Thank you . . ." What a pity when the other felt so wonderful. But when he guided her hands beyond where the flames licked at her so hungrily, she discovered they burned there also. They were everywhere. She uttered a small moan of pleasure, whispered, "Oh, Cougar, what you do to me . . ."

Adam was beyond words. His entire body was a driving, shuddering, sweat-drenched shaft of sensation, blood racing, heart pounding, hunger pulsing. His control close to slipping, he eased gently, gently into the hot, wet, sleek smoothness of Alexandra's body, gauging her face and her huge eyes, darkened with passion, for pain—for God help her, he could not stop now. Slowly, carefully, he moved into her, retreated, slid in, retreated, slipping in more deeply still . . . careful . . . careful . . . He held his breath as he connected with the thin, protecting wall of her maidenhead, felt her shudder, saw her bite her lip.

"Alexandra . . . ?"

"Don't stop . . ." she whispered. She twined her arms tightly about his neck, and once more wrapped her legs around his torso, instinctively lifting her hips to arch against him.

Adam's last control dissolved in a rush of fire. He drove into her deeply, felt the rending of that fragile veil, heard a gasp followed by her smothered cry. For long moments, he lay still within her, allowing her to adjust to his throbbing presence.

Alexandra forgot her pain as the Cougar began to move inside her again, slowly at first, and then more and more rapidly and powerfully. Wave after wave of sensation was burning over her, peaking, exploding, shimmering . . . Oh, God, oh, God, how she loved him. And to think, they would have this, and have each other forever, for she knew now that she was never going to let him go. Not ever. She was home, and she could only cling to him, trembling, weeping, laughing with the wonder and the joy of it. She had thought before that she had known ecstasy, that she had soared, but she had scarcely even beaten her wings. Now she was gliding, winging closer and closer to the sun, so close that in another moment she was going to be caught up in its fierce and wonderful fire and be consumed, but she didn't care—he was with her . . .

Chapter 16

Alexandra yawned and opened her eyes. Remembering the night before, she smiled and stretched languidly. It had been amazing and wonderful and unbelievable. And glorious. She still felt glorious. They had made love. She and the Cougar had actually made love, and it was the most perfect thing that had ever happened to her. Not only that, they had made love all night long in her dreams. Seeing her dreamcatcher hanging from her bedpost, Alexandra blew it a kiss. It had done well its job of filtering her dreams and allowing only the good ones to slip through into her sleep. She hugged herself recalling them. But why was she lying abed thinking of dreams when the living, breathing man who had filled them was outside waiting for her? Or was he? He had said he and the others were going this day to fetch their brethren for more talk. She so hoped they had not already left.

Hurrying to the window, she opened the draperies and looked down onto the scene that was still strange to her eyes; wigwams, cookfires, naked children, dogs wandering about. But she saw no men. Yet she had rarely seen them yesterday, either, she thought, quickly donning her doeskins and moccasins. Perhaps they were sitting around their council fire talking some more. But as she stole into a thick clump of bushes to tend her needs, she saw that the braves and the horses were indeed gone. Only the old men and the women and children remained. Walking back toward the new small village, Alexandra told herself not to be frightened. The Cougar's words alone would protect her—and she had Lark.

As she threaded her way self-consciously through playing children and barking dogs, she smiled at the women and exchanged grave nods with the men. Relieved to find Lark in front of her wigwam pounding corn, she thought how very lovely she was—like some soft, gentle, dark-eyed forest creature. She greeted her with a smile. "Good morning, *onkiatshi.*"

"*Oronkene,* Alexandra. A good day to you." The glow on the maid's face was a pain in Lark's heart. From the first moment she had laid eyes on her, she had thought Alexandra the most beautiful thing she had ever seen, but this morn she as so pink and white, so bathed in a golden radiance that Lark could only stare. And wonder what had caused it. Finally remembering her manners, she said, "Will you share food with us?" She and her parents had already eaten, but there was still a bit of cornmeal in the pot.

Certain they could not spare it, Alexandra shook her head. "*Niawen,* I've eaten." Actually, she was far too excited to eat, feasting as she had been on last night's memories. "I've come to help again—if you need me."

Remembering the sullen, sharp-tongued maid Alexandra had once been, Lark mused that it was a strange thing indeed, this change that had come over her. She replied quietly, "We have not yet collected enough firewood for the day, and there is always water to be brought from the river. And there is corn to be pounded and skins to scrape."

Alexandra laughed. "That certainly narrows it down. What would you have me do first?"

Lark rose, stretched her bent back, and flexed her tired shoulders. "If you would pound the corn for a bit, I will collect more firewood."

"Whatever you say."

As Lark fetched her tumpline and walked toward the

woods, she worried that it had not been a kind thing she had done, asking Alexandra to pound corn. The maid would not be able to lift the heavy pestle in its tall log mortar for more than ten heartbeats with those slim, soft arms of hers. But it was just what Lark wished. She wanted her to fail. It shamed her that she should feel such a way, but she could not help it. Suspicion had returned to gnaw her about Alexandra's sudden willingness to help. It was not the goodness of her heart that was behind it, she decided angrily; it was that she wanted to please the Cougar. She wanted him to think she was as docile and pliant as any Indian maid— because she herself wanted him.

But as Lark moved more deeply into the woods, its peace touched her, the peace of birdsong and sunlight on leaves and the fragrance of damp growing things. It caused her to wonder why she fretted so. It was wrong of her, and wrong to punish Alexandra for her own foolish imaginings. The Cougar was going to be hers, and if she did not believe in the signs she had received, then she might as well deny all she had ever believed for her entire life—that the Creator, the Lord of the Universe, was watching over her and guiding and guarding her.

Comforted by the thought, Lark looked about, her experienced eye seeking out the firewood she was there to collect. But as she reached for the first branch, she hesitated. Whose were those voices she heard? Straightening, she peered into the deeper woods where the morning mist had not yet lifted. She frowned. It sounded like women or children, yet she knew that no one else from the village was there at this hour. When the sound came again, Lark identified the voices. They belonged to one woman and a child.

Soft as a whisper, she stole forward on her moccasined feet until she could see them, a white woman and a little one of two winters or so. The were walking among the trees, chattering softly as they stopped to look at leaves and point at birds. Lark rubbed her eyes. It was so misty, it was difficult to see them clearly, but then it mattered little. Doubtless they were some of the tenants who lived on this land, and she would not disturb them. But then she saw how the woman's long glossy brown hair swung about her hips as she walked, and saw that the child was a little buck . . .

Lark froze, the hair stirring on her arms and the back of her neck as she recognized that sweet laughter and the familiar walk. It was her friend. It was! It was her dear friend and her darling buck-babe. As she started after the two, the mist swallowed them, leaving her with a thundering heart and a soul that was suddenly singing. They were not lying in the cold ground. The two had but stepped into that other world that awaited them all. It was what she had always been taught. And for the space of an eyeblink, for some reason she would never understand, she had seen that which she was never meant to see—their return to this world.

Her heart and eyes overflowing, Lark stumbled back down the hill, blindly grasping at any wood that appeared before her so that by the time she returned to Windfall, she had a great mountain of it fastened onto her back by her tumpline.

When Alexandra had finished pounding the corn, she returned to her chores at the manor. Her arms ached as she commenced scrubbing the upstairs hall floor on her hands and knees, but she soon forgot the pain. She had forgotten everything but the Cougar. They belonged to each other, and wherever he went and whatever he did, she wanted to be with him. She would still return to Tiyanoga, aye, for she yearned to see her mother and father again. And she was going to make Papa see these folk as she now saw them. But after that was done, she was going to return to the Cougar and stay with him forever. It was a promise. She was reflecting on it with quiet rapture when she heard the front door open.

"Alexandra, are you there?"

Alexandra hurried to the head of the stairs. "Aye, Lark, come up. I'm washing floors."

Lark mounted the steps cautiously, holding tightly to the polished banister and remembering that she had trod this path once before. It was when her friend had shown her two pictures newly arrived from England, likenesses of herself and Adam that were mounted in great gilded frames and hung above the mantelpiece in their bedchamber. Thinking of that happy day magnified the joyous sight she had seen earlier. But then had it really been her friend and her little buck, or had she imagined it? Lark sighed. She did not know. She simply did not know.

"I'm ready for your next chore," Alexandra said, wiping her hands on the small apron tied about her waist. Seeing Lark suddenly falter, she went quickly to her side and drew her safely to the second floor. "Are you all right?"

"I am not too clever on stairs. They are . . . so high." Lark tried to smile. "I came to thank you for pounding the corn. I did not expect you to do so much."

Alexandra grinned. "I didn't expect to, either. I thought my arms would fall off. But tell me, did you gather enough firewood, or do you want me to go out for more?"

Lark was torn between admiration and hatred for the maid. But then it was not hatred, it was hurt—and envy and resentment and jealousy. The hatred was for herself for having such unkind thoughts. She replied quietly, "I have gathered firewood enough for the day. Now I have come to help you."

Alexandra gave her head an emphatic shake. "Nay, my friend, there's no need." She would never heap extra work on a woman whose daily chores stretched from sun to sun. But when Lark placed a hand on her heart, Alexandra saw that it was important. Her honor and pride were at stake. "So be it. I'll fetch you a rag."

As they scrubbed the floors in companionable silence, Lark's mind walked in circles. Thinking of the dead was forbidden, but she could think of nothing but her friend now and remember that it was the room at the end of the hall in which she had breathed her last. She shivered, wondering if her peace had been stolen by Adam's terrible grief. Was that why she walked still? Except she and her small buck had seemed so content. But if she were indeed torn by Adam's grief, would her soul be eased to see Lark's love for him? To know that when they joined, she would make him happy?

She sighed. How very foolish she was, and how melodramatic. She had not seen "her" walking in the woods. Such things did not happen. She had imagined it. And she must not be thinking of the dead. Not ever again. Sinking back on her heels, she stared blankly at the floor.

Alexandra had been watching her friend with concern. It was clear Lark worked dreadfully hard, but was she growing ill in addition? Knowing she would never admit to it, Alexandra murmured, "I'm a bit tired. Come and rest with me for a little."

Lark followed Alexandra into her bedchamber, and seating herself in a strange soft chair that nearly swallowed her, she gazed about at the room's foreignness and rich furnishings. Had the Cougar ever been here? she brooded. Had he lain in that great ugly bed with Alexandra and made love to her? She looked away, sickened by the thought and certain now that although she would love him unto death, he would never love her. Not with this beautiful Alexandra here and not when she herself was no one of any importance. She wanted to flee, to run from the room and from this maid who was destroying her heart, her soul, her very life.

"Would you like some tea?" Alexandra ventured, fully concerned now. Lark had swayed on the stairs, and now her face looked chalky. "It won't take but a minute."

"*Iah*. No tea. I will just . . . rest a bit with you."

As she closed her eyes, the handsome face of her brother hovered in Lark's thoughts. Her mouth curved in a tender smile. How amazing it was that Silver Hawk was always there for her when she needed him, either in the flesh or in the spirit. It came to her mind then the first time she had seen him, how he had come to her, a slave of Akando, and told her that he would help her. By one means or another he would help her. And he had. He had taken her away from the Seneca to the safety of his people, and taught her that she was of great value. He had told her that for a Mohawk woman's life, atonement was double a man's, and he had told her to be proud always, to stand tall and hold up her head, for she was Ojibwa. Seeing his beloved face, hearing his deep voice saying the words, she was comforted. Silver Hawk believed in her, and she would not disappoint him. She filled her lungs, opened her eyes, and gazed over at Alexandra.

"I am refreshed," she said and smiled.

Alexandra was relieved to see that Lark's eyes were bright again and her cheeks were pink. She laughed. "My goodness, you really are—and so am I. I'll get back to my scrubbing, but please, don't feel you have to."

Lark climbed out of the deep, soft chair, grateful to be rid of it. "We will work together, *onkiatshi*, but I am curious—why do you clean a place that is not yours?"

Alexandra shrugged. "It's been a lovely port in a storm, and I guess it makes me sad, seeing it so neglected."

Lark was puzzled as she knelt beside Alexandra. "What is . . . a port in a storm?"

"It means a place that's safe. A-a haven . . ." Except it was not the house that was her haven, it was the Cougar. He was her haven, but she could hardy say that. She sloshed her rag in the bucket, wrung it out, and attacked a new part of the floorboards. "I guess I just want to leave Windfall better than I found it—and of course I do owe Old Rhubarb. Not only for the roof over my head, but for the pleasure of wearing one of the gowns he keeps here for his"—her voice trailed to a whisper—"his, uh, ladies . . ."

Alexandra bit her lip. Why on earth had she said that? It was only a guess on her part except it had seemed so likely at first that she'd come to believe it. Now she was not so sure, and she'd shocked Lark. For certain, Lark had a soft spot in her heart for Old Rhubarb.

Lark pondered Alexandra's words in silence. She now understood "port in a storm." She understood also that the words "Old Rhubarb" were an insult which had enraged her brother. And had the maid actually been so bold as to wear one of "her" gowns? She whose name was unsayable and whose sweet face she must not remember? She could scarcely believe the Cougar would allow it. And as for the final insult and the greatest of all—to hint that Adam Rutledge had brought women here, "Ladies." Lark began to tremble. It was not in her to raise her voice in anger to any, especially not to a stranger dwelling among them, but this could not go unanswered.

"What ladies are those?" she asked, the mildness of her voice veiling her outrage.

Alexandra's face turned red. "I really shouldn't have said that."

"That is so, you should not have." As Alexandra gazed at her in astonishment, Lark threw down her rag and got to her feet. She said stiffly, "I am ashamed of you, Alexandra. Lord Adam is the most honorable man I know. He has fought for my people in the white man's halls and in his villages and strongholds. With his own money, he has bought our food and clothing when we could not find game and when our traplines were empty—which is most of the time now. And he has brought us here. How can you speak so of the man when you do not know him?"

Alexandra was mortified. Her face grew pinker still. "I—I didn't know . . ."

"As for 'ladies' "—Lark simply could not hold her tongue—"Lord Adam does not consort with women. He is not Warraghiyagey!"

Alexandra climbed to her feet, the rag still clutched in her hands. "I'm . . . so ashamed. I'm stupid and judgmental a-and awful. I'm an awful person . . ." The more she heard about Lord Adam, the more she was convinced she was wrong about him. She had taken a childish dislike to him because he was a nobleman, and because her father had wanted to give her to him—and because the noblemen she knew were all made from the same mold. But now she knew, oh, how well she knew that Lord Adam was different. She murmured, "When I see him, I'll certainly apologize. Most humbly."

Seeing Alexandra's very real remorse, Lark felt her blood cool. She said quietly, "It sorrows me that my tongue was fiery. I should not have spoken so."

"Oh, Lark, you should! I deserved it. What I said was wrong, and I'm glad you told me so. Please, always tell me when I'm doing something dumb. Please do."

Lark felt her heart warming. As much as she wished it, she could not hate this maid. She was coming to like and respect her far too much for that—but she was still uneasy about her feelings for the Cougar. If only she could discover in some subtle way how the wind blew . . .

She recoiled sharply from the thought. *Iah.* She would not resort to trickery with such an open maid as Alexandra. Yet if she did not, she would have no peace. And if she did, she told herself, she deserved no peace. But she had no choice. Hating herself for what she was about to do, she said, "I must leave now, *onkiatshi*, but I will return tomorrow to help in any way I can."

"Thank you. It's much nicer working with someone."

"I will leave my sharp tongue behind." Steeling herself she added, "I am not myself today. I have been separated from my man for too long, and now he is gone again."

"I'm sorry." Alexandra was surprised and pleased that Lark would share such a thing with her—and it certainly explained her unusual behavior. "I'd hate that, too. Was he with the braves who left this morn?"

Lark nodded. *"Hen.* He is the Cougar."

"I see." The world opened beneath Alexandra's feet, but even as she felt herself falling into a black hole that had no beginning and no end, she clung to her composure. She would not break Lark's heart. Her new friend would never knew that the Cougar, that miserable tomcat of a Cougar, had betrayed her. She managed to smile and to look attentive. "Are you wed to him, then?"

"We will join soon." Lark's spirits lifted, seeing Alexandra's warm interest and the calm on her face. It was clear she wanted to hear more, and equally clear that she did not want the Cougar for herself. How foolish Lark had been to doubt the Creator. She continued eagerly, "He has said that when the right time comes, he will ask for me." It was such a very small untruth . . .

Once again Alexandra forced her stiff lips into a smile. "I see." Indeed she did. She saw that she had made the most awful mistake of her life last night, giving herself to a man out of wedlock, trusting her future and her happiness to a savage she had known for just a short time because she had been overwhelmed by his appearance and by her passion for him. What a fool . . .

"I knew from the first moment I saw him that he was my man," Lark said. "Since then I have had signs."

"I'm . . . so happy for you . . ."

"You gladden my heart, *onkiatshi.*" For four years, she had not allowed herself to speak to anyone of her love, and now she could not stop. "He says my heart is tender," she murmured, "and he thinks I am beautiful . . ."

Alexandra stared at her. Remembering that the Cougar had said that she, too, was beautiful, she felt the beginnings of hysterical laughter stirring within her. She swallowed, told herself she dared not so much as smile, for it would turn to tears and then what would she do? What would Lark think? She caught her tongue between her teeth, bit down, and balled her fists so the nails gouged her palms. She hated him! She'd been blind and mad and gullible, all three, for thinking she would actually come back here and wed him herself. Oh, God, how she hated him—but she hated herself even more.

"Do you have a man, Alexandra?" Lark asked shyly.

Seeing the other's radiant face and star-filled eyes, Alexandra told herself numbly that she had only herself to blame. It was no one's fault but her own that she had behaved so stupidly and irresponsibly. Certainly it was not Lark's fault. She whispered, "Nay. I have no man. I doubt I ever will."

Now Lark stared, seeing that the maid's eyes had grown damp. "My friend, wh-what is it?"

Alexandra laughed, shook her head. "It's nothing at all."

Lark was stricken. "I have hurt you . . ." And she saw now what it must be. Alexandra had a man across the sea whom she feared never to see again—and here Lark, stupid woman that she was, was chattering on and on about the Cougar. "My heart lies on the ground . . ."

Alexandra was moved to put her arms about her. "You've done nothing, and I'm grateful—oh, Lark, I'm so grateful to have you for a friend." Her heart was aching, more for Lark than for herself. Lark's life had

not been an easy one, and naught but unhappiness lay
ahead for her with a man such as the Cougar.

Adam returned to Windfall the night of the fourth
day and found that Silver Hawk had arrived ahead of
him. The brave was stretched out upon his bedshelf in
the wigwam they now shared, and as Adam lay down,
he rose on one elbow.

"Will many be coming, *rikena?*" he asked.

"*Hen,*" Adam replied. "Every sachem with whom I
spoke is coming and will bring his sub-chieftains." He
was drained, having thought and talked of nothing but
the conflict these past several days. Now he wanted
only to put it from his mind and sleep, but he saw that
Hawk was eager for talk. "What of you? Were you successful?"

"*Hen.* The Cayugas and Senecas will come. Those of
our brothers who have returned from the Onondagas
and Oneidas say they, too, will come."

Silver Hawk resented it that he no longer felt at ease
with the Cougar, and he resented bitterly that he did not
know the truth of what had happened between him and
Lark. He could not believe his brother would betray
her. He was an honorable man. But neither could he believe that Lark would say he wanted to wed her if it
were not so. She was completely without guile or de-
ceit. Torn first one way and then the other, and having
too much pride to put the question directly, Hawk thrust
the matter from his thoughts. It concerned merely a
woman, after all, and he must think only of the coming
gathering.

"Getting our brethren here is but the first step," he
said. "I fear many of them will be of little use to us unless we can sway them. They have lost heart and are
ready to leave their land and move westward without
even a fight."

Adam nodded. "I have seen it."

His thoughts were on Alexandra. He had not allowed

himself to think of her while he was gone, but the sight of her bedchamber window had stirred his memories— and his regrets. How did she feel about giving herself to him fully now that she had had time to think about it? Were her regrets as deep as his own? It was not that their lovemaking had been anything less than glorious, but he had not wanted to feel this way about a woman ever again. And he could not stop fearing for her or thinking he had harmed her.

Silver Hawk was as restless as the Cougar, but the Cougar slept finally. Not so Hawk. Faces and forms so crowded into his head that he could not lie still—Lark, the Cougar, the Gold Hair, Lark, the Iroquois, Lark . . . He sighed heavily, rose from his bedshelf, and silently went out into the night, where he paced at the forest's edge until the women began to stir.

Alexandra had been collecting firewood with Lark since sunup. Now, as the two talked quietly about the coming gathering, she saw Lark's face grow pink. Turning to see the cause, Alexandra spied the Cougar, his bow and quiver slung over his back, walking toward them. She looked away quickly, but it was too late. His image was branded in her mind—his height, those long limbs, his hair and eyes and skin startlingly dark against his pale buckskins. It simply was not fair that he should look so wonderful.

While he was gone, she had promised herself she would never speak to him again. But then she had convinced herself he was not worth ruffling one hair of her head over. It would be far better if she acted as if nothing had happened between them, absolutely nothing. And if it hurt his male pride, good. He deserved it. But now here he was and she still did not know which path to follow.

Adam smiled at the maids and greeted them. *"Oronkene,* Lark . . . Alexandra . . ."

"Oronkene, Cougar." Lark lowered her eyes. "I am glad for your safe return."

"Niawen." His gaze, divided between the two, did not miss Lark's quickly hidden adoration or Alexandra's anger. Hell. It was just as he'd feared. She hated him for taking her. He put his attention on Lark alone. "Have you been told our Iroquois brethren will begin arriving today?"

"Hen. We have been gathering firewood all morning, Alexandra and I, and we will continue."

"Good. I'm going now to see if I can take a buck or two and a bear."

Alexandra's blood was simmering as she watched him vanish into the woods. The man was amazing. Quite the smoothest thing she had ever seen. He had seduced her in such a way that she hadn't even known it was seduction. And the way he'd behaved with Lark just now, all respectful and reserved with never a hint of what was between them—it was a remarkable feat. He hadn't shown even a speck of guilt. Probably because he felt none . . .

Chapter 17

For three days, the Iroquois sachems and their sub-chieftains had arrived at Windfall. Now it was night, and in the meadow behind the great manor house, the council fire of the Six Nations burned. The braves sat about it in a large circle, and one by one, the sachems rose to speak of the fear that gripped them all: fear that the Six Nations were dying.

Adam, sitting at the right hand of Silver Hawk, studied their grim faces and felt their fear. There was no doubt in his mind that what they said was true. The Iroquois League was being destroyed. He had seen it happening ever since his arrival in this land four winters ago, and it had begun long before that. He watched an old Cayuga sachem finish speaking, and saw Silver Hawk climb to his feet. His talk would have to be a damned good one, he mused, but in truth, the young Mohawk sachem was an impressive sight in the firelight.

Hawk's bare torso and arms and face were painted for war, and the dried deerhoof rattles strung about his wrists and ankles hissed menacingly as he strode to the center of the circle. A drum began to beat. For long moments, he stood in silence before he began to thump his bare feet to its rhythm. He threw back his head then and uttered a single cry. The war cry that always preceded slaughter in this northern wilderness.

"My brothers of the Iroquois"—his glittering brown eyes searched the circle of braves—"I call for war.

Hear me, brethren. I call for war. But it is not an army we face now. It is stealth and trickery and the broken promises of the ones we fought for and thought were our friends.

"We believed Warraghiyagey when he said his mighty king across the sea would take care of us. But the king has not. Instead his English come in the night and are squatting upon our land when we awaken in the morning. Those who do not come by stealth come boldly in the day with deeds they say we have signed, but we have not. My brothers, this cannot go on. I call for war!" He sank his tomahawk into the black post he'd had erected there, and another war cry rang from his throat.

As Hawk returned to his place beside him, Adam said low, "Well done, *raktsia.*"

What Hawk had said was short and simple, and his cry had set Adam's blood coursing through his veins. He was observing the reactions of the others when a newly arrived brave stepped into the circle. Adam frowned, seeing that he looked familiar. The man was old, he wore a red blanket wrapped about his sturdy frame, and his long silver hair had a split feather in it—a sign that its wearer had been wounded in battle. As Adam tried to grasp an elusive memory, the brave raised his arms and said in a ringing voice:

"*Sekon,* my brothers of the Six Nations."

Adam's heart gave a thump. He had heard that voice only once and he would never forget it. It was William Johnson—Warraghiyagey himself. The man who had brought the Mohawks to England's side in her war against the French. He felt a welling of relief. With old Willie Johnson here, surely wisdom and caution would prevail. God knew, he himself had neither at this point. He felt the Indians' pain and rage so deeply, he was almost as ready for war as Hawk was.

Alexandra had not been satisfied to look down on the gathering from the window in her bedchamber. Not even Lark's wigwam was close enough for her to see all there was to see, and so they had stolen into the black woods. From its edge, hidden by bushes and trees, they knelt and gazed out onto the meadow where the council fire burned. When Silver Hawk strode to the center of the circle in his paint and rattles and let loose a cry to wake the dead, Alexandra jumped.

"What is it? What's happening?"

"He is calling for war," Lark murmured.

She could not help but notice how tall and strong and fierce her brother looked that night and admire the way his magnificent body gleamed in the fireglow. But what he said worried her. War . . . She sighed, thinking that men were never as happy as when they were going to battle—or planning one. For them, war was the greatest sport of all. How different women were. She wanted peace and quiet and a field to plant and harvest. She wanted babies—and she wanted her man.

From the beginning of the meeting, Alexandra had had eyes only for the Cougar. As hurt and angry as she was with him, she nonetheless had wanted to be close enough to see and hear him. Now she could not even look at him. It was too painful. Putting her attention instead on a dignified silver-haired brave in a red blanket, she decided he must be a chieftain of great importance. And as he spoke on and on and grew more excited, her worries about the possibility of war mounted. Did her father and the other commanders have any idea of what grave trouble was afoot? She doubted it, and at the thought, her head began to pound.

She whispered, "Lark, I've seen enough. I'm going back to the house."

Lark gripped her arm, spoke low in her ear. "There is danger. We will leave together. Come." She got swiftly to her feet.

Alexandra rose, prepared to flee, but it was too late. She was seized roughly from behind. Her attacker clamped one big hand over her mouth, and the other around her throat. She heard Lark gasp, saw her leap backward, heard a man's raspy breathing.

"If you scream or draw your knife," the brave whispered to Lark in her own tongue, "I will break her neck." To Alexandra he growled, "No make sound. I kill."

Lark stood frozen, trembling in her terrible fear for Alexandra. She saw dimly that the tall brave had a face that was comely, but there was cruelty in his eyes. And he reeked of alcohol. Seeing him sway, she felt a flicker of hope. She said as calmly as she was able:

"My brother, what is this thing you do? The Gold Hair is not our enemy, but a valued friend of the Mohawk."

"Then the Mohawks should guard her more carefully—and you, pretty one." He spoke slowly, for his tongue was clumsy. "Women of the Oneida do not prowl about in the darkness unless they are hungry for something." Removing his hand from Alexandra's throat, he cruelly squeezed her right breast and then grasped the softness between her legs.

Lark had never in her life raised her voice to a brave, but now she hissed, "Release her! We hunger for nothing. We are here only to watch the meeting and hear the speeches." She was horrified when he began to drag Alexandra deeper into the woods. She cried after him softly, *"Iah!* You must not!"

"Go in silence, woman," he said thickly. He clamped his hand around Alexandra's throat again. "This squaw was mine and I will have her now."

His words stunned Lark. Lord of heaven, it was Mojag, who had stolen Alexandra from her people! She darted ahead of him and stood between him and the deep woods, her arms outstretched. "You will not! I am the sister of Silver Hawk of the Schoharie Mohawks and I warn you—if you steal this maid or harm her, nothing will save you. My brother and the Cougar will track you to the ends of the earth. You cannot hide from them."

The Cougar. Dimmed as his brain was with crazy-water, the brave remembered well his battle with the Cougar. But it was said the devil had never taken the white squaw for his own. Why then would he care who claimed her? But—what if he did care? He was confused.

Seeing him sway again, Lark said low, "You are drunk and you have made a mistake." When he seemed to war inwardly over her words, she urged softly, "Release her! Otherwise you are dead." As suddenly as he had seized her, the brave threw Alexandra to the ground and vanished into the woods. Lark helped her to her feet. "Come! Quickly!"

Still hidden, the two slipped along the woods' edge, past where the braves sat in their somber circle, and across the meadow to the house. After they reached the safety of the kitchen, Alexandra closed the door behind them and latched it. She sank to the hearth where a small fire flickered and sat trembling, hugging herself.

"It was M-M-Mojag." Her teeth chattered. "I recognized h-his voice." And the brutal way he had squeezed her breast and forced his hand between her legs. "Oh, Lark . . ."

Lark sat down beside her. "You are safe now, Alexandra," she said, soothing, but in her heart she feared for her.

"What did he s-say?" Alexandra could not stop shaking.

Lark stroked back the maid's pale gold mane of hair from her white face. "He said you had belonged to him . . ."

"Oh, God." Alexandra rocked back and forth, still hugging herself and feeling the painful throbbing in her breast. "Oh, God . . ." She was going to be black and blue, but at least she was whole. She had thought he was going to rape her. She looked at Lark and tried to smile. "You're so brave."

Lark shook her head. *"Iah."*

"You are. You frightened him away. Wh-what did you say to him?"

"I said my brother and the Cougar would track him to the ends of the earth and slay him if he harmed you."

"And would they?" she asked faintly.

"They would."

Seeing Alexandra's frightened gaze darting about the room, Lark knew she was seeing Mojag in every shadow and behind every window. She went to them and quickly drew shut the curtains.

"I . . . want to go upstairs," Alexandra whispered.

"Then we will go upstairs," Lark said calmly. She lit two candles, gave one to Alexandra, and after determining that all the windows and the two doors were locked, they went up to the bedchamber. Lark locked the door behind them. "You are safe," she said again, "and when the council meeting ends this night, I will tell my brother and the Cougar of this thing."

"Niawen." Her teeth were still chattering.

Lark coaxed Alexandra to the cushioned window bench where they sat and watched the braves speak. She told her small stories that made her smile, and yearned to tell her that a great white chieftain was there who surely would let no further harm come to her. But she could not. The Cougar might not wish Alexandra to know about him, or want Warraghiyagey to know she was there. She sighed, thinking that nothing was simple. She thought, too, of Akando. Mojag had been drunk and cowardly. Akando, if he ever came for her, would not be drunk, nor did anyone consider him a coward. He would not be driven off so easily. Oh Great Sustainer, she dared not begin thinking of him. Not when she had Alexandra to comfort.

The council fire burned dimly when the braves finally disbanded for the night. Lark rose. She said, "I will go now to tell my brother and the Cougar of this thing. Sleep, Alexandra, for they will protect you from this man."

"I know." Alexandra caught her friend's hand. "Thank you again, Lark. Thank you for everything."

As the braves stood making talk and Warraghiyagey moved among them greeting each one personally, Lark stole to Silver Hawk's side. "Forgive me, *raktsia* . . ."

Hawk frowned, seeing her there. She should have been sleeping these many hours. "What is it?"

Lark whispered, "The Oneida who stole Alexandra is here. Mojag. He came upon us in the woods and—"

Hawk gazed at her in disbelief. "What were you doing in the woods?" he growled.

Lark grew pink. "We . . . wanted to see and hear better."

Master of the Universe. Here was their village filled with braves coming and going, many of them strangers, some with alcohol, and those two had been in the woods unprotected. It chilled him to think of it. "Continue," he rasped. "What about the Oneida?"

Seeing his great anger, Lark realized how foolish they had been. *Iah,* how foolish she had been, giving in to Alexandra's whim to steal closer. She stared at her moccasins. "I am sorry. It is my fault. I—"

"Woman, speak! What of the Oneida?" He wanted to shake her, spank her. In truth, he wanted to wrap her long gleaming hair about his hands, crush her to him, and kiss her sweet mouth until she whimpered with pleasure.

Lark swallowed. "He . . . was drunk. He caught her and covered her mouth and said if I moved or screamed, he would break her neck. He would have carried her into the deep woods but I-I shamed him. I threatened him with you and the Cougar, my brother." She heard a noise like a growl come from deep in his throat.

"From this moment forward, you will be on guard. You will not gather wood alone until these men leave, or go into the forest alone for any reason. Do you understand?" When she nodded, wide-eyed, he muttered, "Now go to bed. I will tell the Cougar and we will deal with this." As she moved off, he caught her arm, his eyes suddenly gentle. "Are you all right?"

"Hen, my brother." She was shocked and confused by the thrill that shot through her.

"And the Gold Hair?"

"She is frightened. She is in her bedchamber with the door locked." It was just his hand on her arm, she told herself. She had felt it hundreds of times. The difference was within herself. This night she had seen him with new eyes. This night he had been the fierce sachem of the Schoharie Mohawks, a warrior chieftain fighting for his people.

Hawk nodded, said brusquely, "You may go."

Lark bowed her head and stole away, but the memory of his strong, warm hand on her arm stayed with her. Even as she entered her wigwam and lay down upon her bedshelf, it glowed in her thoughts.

Seeing the urgency with which Lark had sought Silver Hawk, Adam went to him after she left. "Is anything wrong?"

"It is not good. The Oneida from whom you won your woman is here. He tried to carry her off." Seeing that a deadly light had appeared in the Cougar's eyes, Hawk knew it was as he suspected. The Gold Hair had stolen his heart away from Lark, and Lark did not even know it. What manner of man was he not to correct such a matter? His blood simmered, yet uncertainty still warred with his anger. The deed did not fit the man.

Fury exploded inside Adam's head, but he kept his voice low. "Was she harmed?"

"Iah, but she is frightened. I will post two braves at the doors of the house the remainder of this night to assure her safety. Tomorrow I will deal with the Oneida."

Adam said sharply, "Know, *raktsia*, she is not my woman, but she is my responsibility until I return her to her father. I will attend to the Oneida now. And I myself will guard her. I will sleep outside her bedchamber the remainder of the night."

Unless she invited him to sleep within, thought Hawk angrily. Say it. Confront him with it. Get it in the open once and for all—*she was his woman.* He felt disgusted with himself then. This was no time to be brawling with his war chieftain over such an unimportant thing as a woman. Not when he needed the Cougar's strong right arm and his keen brain to guide him. He gave a curt nod. "So be it, *rikena.*"

Alone in his wigwam, Hawk turned over and over in his mind his other smoldering worries. He resented greatly that Warraghiyagey had come unannounced and filled the ears of the sachems with his strange talk. For the man had promised, in his endless oratory, that if the Iroquois could be patient for yet a while longer, the whites would leave this land of theirs and the brethren would be left in peace.

At the thought, a bitter smile curved Silver Hawk's lips. He did not believe a word of it. The Irishman had lied before. The only way the People would be left in peace was for the white eyes to be laid in the ground. Every last one of them.

As Adam bridled Anoki by torchlight and led him toward the Oneida encampment, there was murder in his heart. And rage for himself. Why had he not seen the danger to Alexandra with these many strangers here? Stopping a passing brave, he said, "I seek the Oneida called Mojag. Have you see him?"

"Hen. He arrived during the evening and made camp over there." He pointed.

Adam approached the lean-to, tethered his mount, and thrust his torch into the soft earth. In its flickering light, he saw Mojag's supine form. He smelled the alcohol as he bent over him. "Mojag, awaken." When the brave did not move, Adam kicked him in the ribs. "Get up, man."

Mojag struggled against his stupor. Opening his eyes a crack, he saw the terror he had hoped never to see again: the Cougar bending over him, his eyes awful in the torch glow. He tried to stand, fell, and finally gained his feet. He shook his head to clear it, but could not. It seemed stuffed with cat-tail down. He straightened then and told himself he was every bit as good as this devil. It was just that the Cougar got him at a disadvantage every time.

"You surprise me, Mojag," Adam said softly.

"I did not know she was still yours," Mojag muttered.

"But she is," he lied. "She is still mine. She will always be mine." He wished to God it were so.

The alcohol in his blood, and the mildness of the Cougar's manner gave Mojag the courage to say, "I would buy her from you. I have much—" A fist crashed sickeningly into his mouth, and as he fell, he tasted blood and knew that he had lost teeth. He had not the time to discover how many. He was raised up roughly and once more his head snapped back with the terrible impact of the Cougar's fist. Again and again he was stood on his feet only to be knocked down again. He was as weak and helpless as a woman against such fury, and he was shamed. He prayed that no one was near to see his complete humiliation.

"Gather your things and get on your horse," Adam ordered. "You are going. Your weapons you will leave here."

Sagging, blood pouring, his ears ringing, and his heart roaring, Mojag had no choice but to obey. With his mount tethered to the Cougar's, he was led westward by torchlight for what seemed an endless time before his reins were slapped into his own hands.

Adam's anger had cooled, and as he looked at

Mojag's battered face and body, he was shocked. He had half-killed the devil. His face masked, he said, "Go home, Mojag. And if you are lucky, you will stop an arrow before you see me or my woman again."

Returning to Windfall, Adam unlocked the front door and took the stairs two at a time. The crack beneath Alexandra's door showed him that her candle was still lit. He was about to knock but hesitated. She had been angry with him that morning . . . But this might be a good time to talk about it. He did not want any anger between them. He tapped on her door, placed his lips to the crack.

"Gold Hair, it's Cougar."

For long moments, there was no reply, and then he heard her murmur, "Go away."

"Alexandra, I am sorry you were frightened, and that I was not there to prevent it. It will not happen again. Now we must talk."

Hearing his voice, Alexandra closed her eyes. How could he sound exactly the same, gentle and caring and loving, when nothing was the same at all? Everything had changed. Her world had been torn apart.

"Open the door, Alexandra."

"I don't see why."

"Gold Hair!"

His voice held such menace, she feared he would break down the door. She unlocked it and retreated in dignified silence to the window bench. She did not look at him as he entered and closed the door behind him.

For long moments Adam stood gazing down on her before he said, "I have dealt with Mojag. He is gone. You will not see him again."

"Thank you." She still did not look at him. She pushed back her hair and stared down at the meadow. It was empty now, but the fire still burned with a soft glow.

He was baffled. He had expected she might be skittish, or shy, or pink-faced with embarrassment for having given herself to him, but he had not expected this blast of wintry silence. It was not like her. He said quietly, "Even though Mojag is gone, you will stay in this house until the council fire is extinguished."

Alexandra's gaze remained on the fire. "Even in daylight?"

"Even in daylight."

She wished she could feel relief that the Oneida was gone, and gratitude to the Cougar for having driven him away, but she could not. The only thought filling her stupid head was that she loved him. Oh, why did she love him still? Why could she not hate him? She made herself remember the love and pride on Lark's face when she had spoken of her man—and to think he had betrayed her. She looked up at him, her eyes frosty.

"When will you take me back to Tiyanoga?"

"It is still uncertain." He added softly, "Alexandra, what is it?" When she did not answer but stared out into the darkness, he said, "I would not hurt you for the world, but I see now I have done that very thing."

"You flatter yourself, Cougar. You've not hurt me."

"Gold Hair, let us talk about this."

"There's absolutely nothing to talk about."

Little liar. She was dying inside. He saw the misery on her face and in her eyes, in the way her small white teeth had sunk into her lower lip to keep it from trembling. Damn it to hell. Was it the loss of her maidenhood that she was mourning—or was it that she had lost it to a man she thought was a savage? Yet if he told her the truth, that he was an Englishman by the name of Adam Rutledge ... He expelled a long breath. Sweet Jesus, that would be even worse. For both their sakes, she must never know. He could only attempt to ease what had happened.

"Know that I cherished our night together. I will always cherish it. And I meant every word I said. You are beautiful, Gold Hair. You are springtime . . . ."

Alexandra turned away. She did not want to hear such words from him. Not now and not ever. "Please—go. And please lock the front door when you leave."

"I am not leaving the house." When she turned startled eyes toward him, he said, "I will sleep outside this door tonight and every night as long as the council fire burns."

"But—"

"I have said it."

Chapter 18

Alexandra's thoughts went instantly to the Cougar when she awakened the next morn. Wondering if he was still outside her door, she stole over to it and pressed her lips to the crack.

"Hello?" There was silence. "Cougar? Are you there?"

She turned the key and cautiously opened the door. She'd half-expected to see him deep in sleep, but the hallway was empty. Looking out the window, she saw that the braves were already seated in their circle and the sachem wrapped in the red blanket was speaking again. She heard Lark calling to her from below.

"Alexandra, I have breakfast for you."

Alexandra leaned over the sill and threw her a wave. "Thank you, I'll be right down. Meet me at the back door."

As Lark watched her friend slicing the cornbread, she said, "I have good news for you."

Alexandra smiled. "I need some good news. What is it?"

"My brother says the Cougar dealt with Mojag last night. He is gone."

"That's wonderful . . ." She dared not tell her the Cougar had brought her the same news last night and slept outside her door. She murmured, "What happened, do you know?"

Lark sat down. "I know only that he is gone. My brother says he will never harm you again."

Alexandra joined her at the table and ate the food without tasting it. She was numb. Her close call with Mojag was still very much in her thoughts . . . war was coming . . . she was hopelessly in love with the wrong man—and Lark was going to be hurt by him just as she herself had been. In fact, looking at her friend's solemn face, she wondered if it had happened already. She said carefully, "You're very quiet."

"I am tired." But it was not tiredness that was overpowering Lark. It was fresh dread that Akando would someday come, win her in another game, and carry her back to his village again. The confrontation with Mojag last night had brought it all back to her in a rush, and if she did not speak of it to someone, she would surely go mad. Someone like Alexandra, who would understand her fears. In fact, she was the only one who could understand. She said, "I confess, *onkiatshi,* I am not tired. I am afraid."

Alexandra stared at her. "Afraid? But Mojag is gone."

"It is another I fear."

"The one who stole you?" Alexandra asked quietly. Lark nodded. "Akando."

Seeing that she was shivering, Alexandra touched her hand. "I've seen your bravery, my friend." She would never forget Lark's facing the Oneida and defending her. A kitten spitting at a mountain lion. "You're the bravest woman I know."

Lark shook her head. "I am not brave when I think of Akando. I have not told you, Alexandra, that when he and his Senecas raided my village, he . . . slew my family." Seeing the shock and confusion in her friend's eyes, she said, "I am not Mohawk. I am Ojibwa, and none of my blanket are left. They are all in the ground."

"Oh, Lark . . . ."

"When I was twelve winters, Akando and his Senecas came, and from that day on, I belonged to him and

his family. I belonged to his mother, and to Yellow
Tooth, his father, and . . . to his three brothers."

Alexandra knew well from the look in Lark's eyes
what fate had befallen her. It filled her with such rage,
she would have slain Akando on the spot had he appeared just then. Lark had been a child. Just a little girl.
She said huskily, "It's over and you're here and you're
safe. Your brother will never let him harm you again,
nor will y-your man." The words stuck in her throat.
The Cougar would never allow anyone to harm Lark
bodily, nay, but it seemed he thought nothing of breaking her heart himself.

"I have made you sad," Lark murmured, seeing tears
glisten in Alexandra's eyes. She shook her head. "My
need was for talk, *onkiatshi,* not your sorrow. I should
not have spoken." Nor had the telling made her feel any
better or less afraid.

"I'm a friend," Alexandra replied, "and that's what
friends are for." She touched shy fingers to the gleaming black plait of hair hanging down Lark's back. "And
I'm sad for what was in the past, aye, but this is now.
Now I'm happy for the wonderful life you have and for
what's to come. You have a kind family who loves you,
and a . . . good man you will wed soon. Oh, Lark"—she
put an arm about her and hugged her—"you're one of
the lucky ones . . ."

Lark laughed and returned the unexpected embrace,
her cheeks brightening with pleasure. "Your tongue has
no fork in it? You really think I am lucky?" At that moment, she could almost believe she would wed the Cougar and never see Akando again.

Alexandra grinned. "My tongue has no fork that I
know of. See?" She stuck it out.

And she vowed that if she did nothing else that day,
she would tell the Cougar what a lucky man he was, having such a superb woman as Lark to love him and, aye,
to put up with him! He should be ashamed of himself,
and she would certainly tell him so. What better way to

prepare herself for that time when she would leave here and never see him again?

Adam was restless. The speeches had gone on all day, and after the evening meal, there would be more talk and argument. The sachems were further from agreeing than when the council fire was first lit three nights ago.

"What do you think, *rikena?*" Hawk asked as they ate the venison and squash and potatoes the women had prepared. "I do not trust this thing which Warraghiyagey proposes—this selling great tracts of our land to England. He promises the king will forbid white settlement on it, thus protecting us completely from further white encroachment." He laughed, but there was bitterness in the sound. "Does he actually believe that?"

"Perhaps he intends to profit personally and buy more land for himself." Already William Johnson possessed vast tracts in the northern wilderness.

"It is likely." Hawk's thoughts drifted as he imagined Lark in the Cougar's arms, imagined them kissing, caressing, coupling. It pained him so, he caught his breath. "And what of this other talk of his—extending the English boundary farther west so whites can move there? I admit to some liking for the idea."

"Your brethren are out there," Adam said. "Would you inflict on them what your own people have suffered?"

Hawk grinned. "The white devils will get an ugly surprise when they learn how many of the People there are beyond the mountains and how fierce they are." His brown gaze flickered over the Cougar as he studied him. "Why not make it easy for them to go? It would free us of them."

"Believe me, my friend," Adam said, "it will not free you of them, and it will crush your brethren."

Hawk drew a deep breath. The Cougar's counsel was

as straight as an arrow. These very things he had concluded for himself. The white horde would indeed crush his brethren in the West. Whites were as grains of sand in the sea, as drops of rain and flakes of snow in the air. They were without end.

He muttered, "You are right. I say deal with the devils here and now. I call for war."

"I am of a mind to join you . . ." Adam's words were so soft even his own ears did not hear them. He rose, stretched. "I suppose we will parley into the night again . . ."

"*Hen.* We begin at sundown."

Adam clapped Hawk's shoulder. "Till then." For now, he had other matters to attend to.

As shadows stretched across the gold-drenched meadow, Alexandra resigned herself to the fact that the Cougar was not coming. She had been primed for hours to tell him exactly what she thought of him, and of how wonderful and brave and beautiful Lark was, and of how fortunate he was to have her. But she had been indignant for so long, she had lost all momentum—and now she was bored to death. She was bored with house-cleaning, bored with her journal, bored with nothing to read or study . . . In fact, it was strange that a house such as this did not have books in the bookcases. She had not even thought about it before. She started as she suddenly saw the tall figure standing in the doorway. Blazes, how long had *he* been there?

"Good evening, Gold Hair . . ."

She was beautiful, Adam thought. He would never get used to how beautiful she was. Gazing at her silhouetted in the window, her slender body and silken halo of hair etched against the red-orange glow of the dying sun, he knew he had never seen a more breathtaking sight. Thinking of her in Mojag's brutal embrace made his knees go weak.

"Good evening," Alexandra replied crisply.

She would be stern and cool and incredibly polite and proper, she told herself. She would not look at his mouth or his hands, nor would she look at his dark eyes to see if there was concern in them. But she did. She looked—and there was concern in them. A thing like that could not be hidden. He had been concerned for her last night, and he was still. Her heart stopped, thumped and began to race as she felt her love for him brimming over. She could no more stop loving him than she could stop breathing, and she yearned to feel again those glorious flying-into-the-sun sensations that only he could arouse in her.

She gritted her teeth. He was Lark's, and she would not hurt Lark—or let anyone else hurt her. She gave him as polite and stony a gaze as she could muster.

"I must thank you again for dealing with Mojag. I might not have shown it, but I'm very grateful."

"You are my responsibility." It angered him that she should still be hurt and embarrassed and that he was still powerless to do anything about it. If only she would talk to him . . .

"I trust I can go outside again now that Mojag is gone."

"*Iah.*"

"*Iah?*" Alexandra got to her feet. "Why on earth not?"

"There are too many strangers here."

"But they're in a circle talking all day! And I'll be in the village with Lark." When he made no answer, she asked softly, "Please? This place is so frightfully gloomy, and I've scrubbed floors and polished furniture and written in my journal till I'm sick of the lot of it."

"The parleying will not last much longer."

Alexandra's eyes took on a wicked glitter. "I suppose you're right to be concerned. I suppose Indian men *are* more savage than white men."

Adam stepped inside the room. "Know, Alexandra, it is not the custom of Indian men to mistreat women, but those like Mojag are always among us. I will not risk endangering you further. You will remain here until the council fire is extinguished."

She sighed, returned to the window bench, and muttered, "The eleventh commandment carved in stone." She added, "Will you . . . come tonight again?"

"I will sleep outside your door as I did last night."

And she wanted to be with him there, or with him in her big, comfortable bed with its rose-scented sheets. She wanted him closer than close, kissing her in his strange, exciting way, wrapping his long dark legs and arms around her and holding her so she could not escape. Not ever. She looked away quickly. She was awful—and wicked. And so was he. Her anger kindled all over again as she thought how he had started this whole impossible thing when he'd asked her to stay in his arms and kissed her and told her she was beautiful. And all the while he belonged to Lark and was telling her *she* was beautiful. The snake! Except she should not demean snakes.

And now was the perfect time to tell him what she'd planned all day long to tell him. Do it, she told herself. Do it! She swallowed, moistened her lips. "I've been talking with Lark."

Adam was wrenched, seeing her turmoil. "I have seen that you are friends now. It is good."

"She . . . told me about Akando and what he did to her family and . . . the rest of it . . ." She saw the shuttering of his eyes.

"She is very strong, very brave," Adam muttered. He could not talk to any woman of what he thought of Akando and what he wanted to do to him. Even the devil's own clan hated him.

"She may be strong and brave," Alexandra said, "but she's also very frightened."

"Of Akando?"

Her outrage leaped. "You of all people should know that."

Adam frowned. "I do not understand."

Alexandra was breathing hard. She raised her voice. "And I don't understand you. Lark is a wonderful woman. She's beautiful and giving and loving . . ."

Adam was baffled. "She is all of that."

Alexandra got to her feet. "Then why did you come to me to make love when you had her?" She had feared she would begin to weep at that point, but she was too angry to cry. She had only to think of Lark's hopeful face to give her the strength she needed. She faced the Cougar, hands on her hips and her eyes blazing green fire. "Well?"

It was so ridiculous, Adam nearly laughed aloud. "I made love to you, Gold Hair, because it was you I wanted. Not Lark." He reached out to touch her hair, the satin of her cheek; nothing more than to touch her, but she slapped his hand away.

"You miserable beast, you! Hasn't she been hurt enough without having her man put her aside for another?" Alexandra shook her head pityingly. "In truth, Cougar, you disgust me. Had I but known . . ."

Adam was flabbergasted. Him? Lark's man? What in God's name was this? Lark knew he would never marry again, so how had this mix-up come about? Or was it a mix-up? He wondered suddenly if she had concocted this whole thing to keep Alexandra away from him— and decided it was probably exactly what the little vixen had done.

From the very first moment he'd seen Lark, her beautiful black eyes had followed him. And then he had fallen ill and she had nursed him through his sickness. And not to forget, never to forget, they had made love. He had not a doubt she had saved his life that day and kept him alive all of the other days. He had admitted it to her and had admitted he cared for her deeply. But he was not her man. He was not going to wed her, and he would set this matter straight with her the first thing in the morning.

Seeing the Cougar's grim face, Alexandra was glad. She said sharply, "I hope you're ashamed of yourself, and I hope you think twice before you betray Lark again. She deserves your loyalty. A-and all your love . . ." Something in those fathomless black eyes gave her a twinge of uncertainty.

"Every woman deserves that of her man," Adam replied quietly.

"How admirable of you to think so."

Sweet Jesus, he was going to put Lark over his knee and tan her backside when he saw her. But right now, all he felt was relief. Alexandra was not angry with him because they had made love, or because she had demeaned herself with an Indian. It was all this confounded game Lark was playing.

"I would have you speak to Lark of this thing again. More carefully." After he himself had seen her.

"Are you saying that what she said isn't so? Or that I didn't hear it correctly?"

He had not betrayed Lark, but he couldn't help but feel a bloody bounder. This was going to hurt and embarrass her. "I am saying only that you should speak to her of it again, Gold Hair."

Alexandra had no chance to respond. He was gone. As she watched him take his place beside Silver Hawk in the circle of braves, she knew she was not going to do as he asked. Not if she could help it. She had no intention of hearing again Lark's recitation of how beautiful the Cougar thought she was or how tender her heart was or how she had received her signs. She had heard all she was going to hear! All she wanted was to wallow in self-pity for a few minutes, and then make herself a pot of tea and get to work on her journal. She was behind on it. She had drunk two cups and filled two pages with writing when Lark called to her from beneath her open window.

"Alexandra, can we talk?"

Alexandra looked down at her friend's small upturned flower face, pale and beautiful as a pond lily in the thickening twilight. "Of course, I'll be right there." But as she took a candle and ran down to unlock the door, she wondered what was amiss. Lark had sounded frightened.

Chapter 19

Alexandra unlocked the door to admit Lark and locked it after her. "Welcome. I was having tea upstairs. I'll get another cup if you'd like some."

"I would like it very much."

As they lit their way up the dim stairway to Alexandra's bedchamber, Lark was in an agony of worry. She had been listening to the parleying, and within the past hour, the other Mohawk sachems had begun arguing with the Cougar and the Schoharie Mohawks over Alexandra. Why return the Gold Hair to her father, they asked, when it was the old Grayhead and men like him who were the source of their many ills? Why should he be allowed to see her again if he did not enforce the laws? Rather they should send him her scalp. And even if the Grayhead agreed to keep the laws in exchange for her return, one could never trust any white devil to keep his word for long. They should keep her as a hostage.

"You seem upset." Alexandra set her candle on the writing table. "Is it . . . Akando again?"

"Iah."

Alexandra was her friend. This concerned her, and she deserved to know about it. But if she told her, Lark felt certain it would terrify Alexandra as much as she herself was terrified. *Iah,* she could not. She would leave it to the Cougar. Just thinking of him calmed her and lifted her spirits, for she knew he would never allow any harm to come to the maid.

"How are the talks going?" Alexandra removed the strawberry cozy from the pot, poured Lark's tea, and handed the cup to her on its dainty saucer. She refilled her own cup.

"There is ... much arguing," Lark said. She sat on the window bench and gazed down on the great circle of braves sitting cross-legged about the leaping flames.

Alexandra joined her. "Are we closer to war?" Her stomach turned over every time she thought of Silver Hawk's war cry and his sinking his hatchet into the black post that still stood there.

"I am not sure. The Schoharie Mohawks want it ..."

Alexandra cradled her cup and stared gloomily into its amber depths. Sometimes, such as now, she thought that talking with her father could have made a difference. Other times, she knew she would only have enraged him. What she needed was to bypass him completely and go directly to the king. Oh, aye, as if she knew the king.

"I have made you sad again ..." Lark saw that her friend's beautiful green eyes had grown distant.

"Nay, you have not."

"I made you sad earlier when I bragged to you about the Cougar ...."

Alexandra felt a small leap of panic. She could not bear to hear about him again. "You didn't, Lark, I promise you."

Lark did not believe her. She saw well that Alexandra had been wounded by someone. The wound was still raw, and she herself had rubbed salt in it with her big talk of her and the Cougar. It shamed her that she could have spoken with such a forked tongue about the two of them, and now there were amends to make. She said gently:

"I would say one more thing about the Cougar."

Alexandra could only stare at her. Why was she doing this? Why could she not just let it go? "I'm sure it's private," she said faintly. "I . . . really don't need to hear . . ."

"My friend, I need to say it."

Alexandra yielded to the pleading in her eyes. "Then of course you must."

Lark kept her eyes on the distant fire. "I spoke with a crooked tongue about us, and it shames me. I told you he would ask for me someday."

Alexandra's heart beat harder. "Aye. That's what you said."

"His own words were, if ever he wed, he would ask for me. I did not tell you that he vows he will never wed . . ."

The silence stretched out endlessly before Alexandra found the voice to say, "Then . . . you're not promised to each other."

"Iah. But we will be." Lark smiled. "I am a patient woman." She was at peace. It had been the right thing to do, telling Alexandra the truth, and as soon as this gathering was ended, she would tell Silver Hawk also.

Alexandra hoped her happiness was not shining over her face. The Cougar had not betrayed Lark, and it made all the difference in the world. But why would he vow never to wed? Unless his people did not believe in matrimony. She said carefully, "I know very little about your Cougar although we've traveled many miles together. I've gathered he's not Mohawk."

"That is so. His tribe is from very far away."

"How did you meet him then?" She had a hundred questions, but she feared sounding too eager.

"He was . . . passing through our village when he grew very ill." Great Creator, would she never escape telling these untruths? Yet it was the Cougar's own wish that this maid not know who he was or anything about him. "My brother said he should remain with us until he recovered. He was with us four moons."

"Four moons!" Alexandra was shocked. He was so strong and vital, so needed by them all that never once had she considered that he might take sick. Or die. "What illness did he have?" And would it ever return?

"He had fever and delirium and waking dreams . . ." Lark grew very still seeing the color drain from Alexandra's face. She continued quietly, "Night and day he had dreams which he could not tell from reality, so night and day I stayed with him so he could not harm himself."

"He was . . . so ill he wanted to die?"

"I know only that he did not want to live."

"Oh, Lark . . ."

Alexandra loved him, Lark thought, despairing. Lark had sensed it, feared it all along, and now there was no doubt—the look in her eyes, the anguish on her face. She loved him. Even thinking he was Indian, she loved him. Hurt blazed within her, and anger, as Lark thought that two times now her man had been taken away by others. She felt fresh despair as she imagined Alexandra's learning the truth—that the Cougar was not Indian at all, but a white man.

Let her be gone before then, she prayed. And let her be gone before the Cougar learned that she loved him. He could never keep his vow not to wed if a woman as beautiful as Alexandra desired him. But then why did she not tell Alexandra that the two of them were lovers? Why not? Alexandra would not want him then, and in truth, they had been. The words trembled on her lips.

"When did you know you loved him?" Alexandra asked softly.

"From the first moment I saw him."

Alexandra nodded. "I recall now your saying that before . . ." It made it quite final somehow, like the last nail in the coffin. "I'm sure it was your love as well as your care that healed him." She managed a warm smile. "He'll be your man one day, Lark, I know he will."

Lark bowed her head. With each passing moment,

she was seeing more clearly Alexandra's love for him. She saw her kindness and her dignity and her willing yielding of the Cougar to her own undeserving self, and heard her praise and encouragement. And then she thought of the untruths she had told and was still willing to tell. Oh, Great Sustainer, she was shamed. She got to her feet.

"I must go now," she said dully. "The hour is late, and I am tired."

As they descended the stairs, the feeling was growing in her heart that the Cougar must surely love Alexandra. How could he not, being with her day in and day out for so many weeks and seeing her kindness and tenderness—and her beauty. And if he had not yet seen the kind of woman Alexandra was, he soon would. He was not blind. And if Alexandra could return the light to his eyes, she, Lark, would gladly put away her own dreams. For him she would do anything, and she would do it now, cleanly and swiftly before she could change her mind.

"*Onkiatshi—*"

"Aye?" Why was Lark staring at her so strangely?

Lark tried to speak, but it was as if a hand were closing about her throat to stifle her next words. She pushed them past her lips. "Know, Alexandra, I will never be the Cougar's woman."

Alexandra blinked. "What? Have you . . . had some new sign just now?"

Lark could not help but smile. "*Hen.*"

"I don't understand." Lark loved the Cougar as much as she herself did. The very way she said his name spoke of her love for him. "Lark, what's happened? How could—"

Lark laid a finger across her friend's lips. "Just know that it is so, Alexandra."

"Lark, wait!" Alexandra followed her outside, but Lark had slipped into the night.

* * *

Adam threw down his fur robe before Alexandra's
door, sank onto it, stretched out, and gave a muffled
groan. He was bone-tired and worried as hell. The
conference was ended, and the Mohawk brethren had
reached an agreement: Alexandra should not be returned to her father. Not now, perhaps not ever. He
shook his head, rubbed his eyes, felt fear seeping into
him. The subject had arisen so unexpectedly, he'd
been unprepared for it. Even if he had been, he could
not have changed the collective minds of the Mohawks. They were in an ugly mood. Aware suddenly
that Alexandra's door was opening slowly, he rose on
one elbow.

"Okarasneha, Cougar." Alexandra met his eyes,
knew instantly that she was losing herself in their hot,
black depths. It always happened, whether an hour had
passed or a week.

Adam scowled up at her. He was staring and he
didn't care. The candle she was holding illuminated her
face from beneath, and she looked like a young angel
even in her doeskins. Her golden hair hung halfway to
her waist now, and her face was pink and white and
glowing. Softly rounded. He saw with relief that she
was well on her way to regaining the weight she had
lost.

"Why are you still awake, Alexandra?"

"I need to talk to you. Will you please come in?" She
opened the door wide and watched as he rose to his feet
in one easy movement.

Adam followed her inside, crossed his arms, and
waited in silence. He wondered what was to come,
whether she was still furious with him. He had not yet
had a chance to speak to Lark. He watched with interest
as she composed herself, straightening her shoulders,
moistening her soft pink lips.

"It seems I . . . have an apology to make . . ." When

he remained silent, Alexandra felt her cheeks growing warm. "I've talked to Lark and—" Blazes, she hadn't thought this through carefully enough. She certainly did not want to embarrass Lark or betray her confidence. "And it seems I misunderstood something she said. Somehow I thought you and she ... were affianced."

Adam's face and eyes did not reveal the weight that was lifted from his shoulders. So. Lark had told the truth with no prompting from him, and now Alexandra was protecting her. Their generosity toward each other warmed him beyond words, and now he would go along with the game. He had no wish to embarrass either of them. He asked, frowning, "What is affianced?" It was a word no Indian, no matter how educated, would know.

Alexandra's face felt warmer still. "It means to be promised to each other. I thought you and Lark intended to wed someday, and I was angry because I thought you had ... treated her badly. But then—" She could not continue. Not with his black eyes moving over her as though he were starving.

"But then?" Adam asked softly.

"Lark said you would never marry ..."

God in Heaven, that wide, watchful, hungry look in her eyes ... Why wait any longer to tell her that he loved her and tell her who he was? She had already said she wanted to be with him, they had made wonderful love together—now was the time. And if she cared for him as he knew she did, it would not matter. Tell her ... tell her ... But then his wiser self warned him that he must choose the moment carefully, and the moment was not now. She hated Adam Rutledge, and the shock would be too great. He set her candle on a table, gently took her shoulders.

"When I told Lark I would never marry, I spoke the truth, Alexandra. I never intended to join with any woman"—he saw her beautiful eyes widen—"but then I met you."

Alexandra felt light-headed suddenly. "What are you saying?"

Adam gave a soft laugh and pulled her into his arms. The sweet familiar fire raced through him as her breasts grazed his chest and then were molded against it. "Be my woman, Gold Hair . . ."

Alexandra's eyes widened as his words took on reality. "Are you saying . . . you want to wed me?"

"Aye." He smoothed back her hair, stroked her face, traced the fine edge of her lips with his fingers. "Join with me. Marry me. Be my wife, Alexandra."

Alexandra laughed. "I'm dreaming."

Adam took her mouth in a hungry kiss. She tasted so sweet, and her lips were so yielding, it was torture to stop. He said thickly, "Did that feel like a dream?"

"One of my very favorites . . ." The dream in which her savior had come. She felt the fire moving through her, and suddenly there was no one else in the whole world but the two of them.

Adam held her so close, so tightly he heard her soft whimper. Dear God, how he loved her, the way she looked, the way she fit into his arms, the way she tasted, the way she talked and laughed and walked, the way she blinked her beautiful green eyes at him . . . He loved her, even though he'd thought he could never love another woman again. Nor had he wanted to. But this sweet Alexandra—he wanted to share air and food and water with her, he wanted to protect her and grant her every wish, he wanted to tread the earth she trod, hold her, kiss her, fill her with himself . . .

He brushed his lips over her eyelids and golden lashes, the tip of her small nose, her cheeks and forehead, her sweetly curved chin and slender throat; he felt the soft cascade of her hair brushing his face; silky, fragrant, a fragrance that was hers alone. He held her then, just held her and felt tears steal behind his eyes. He said low, "I love you, Gold Hair. I cannot walk this earth without you beside me. I love you."

Alexandra stared at his grave face and damp eyes and was almost too overcome to whisper, "I'm so glad, because I've loved you for ever so long . . ."

She would have told him of the exact moment she first knew it, but she was without breath as her lips were sealed by another of his hungry kisses. She felt herself lifted as if she were a feather, carried to the bed, lowered to it gently, and then he was beside her, pulling her to him, his hands and mouth already moving over her eager flesh and stirring those fires within her that only he could stir. It was her dream all over again. She was home . . . in his arms . . . safe from every danger . . . yet she was soaring far from the earth, spiraling, hurtling out of darkness into the delicious white-hot brilliance of the sun. Of the Cougar.

She loved him, Adam thought, scarcely able to imagine it, to believe his good fortune. She had loved him for ever so long . . . As his passion mounted, he yearned to pour himself and his own love into her even as he poured out a torrent of silent thanks for her. This woman was his, and he adored her, treasured her beyond all this earth had to offer. He drew off her doeskins and caressed her breasts, took her small hard nipples into his mouth, kissed them, brushed her burning skin, felt her hungry softness arching against him . . . And then she was slipping his breechclout free of the band securing it, stroking, cupping his swollen shaft between her hands, opening her legs, drawing him toward her center, guiding him, her eyes shining, eager.

Adam groaned as he slid into the hot, sweet fire of her sheath, felt her clinging to him and their pulses throbbing, drumming together . . . drumming . . . drumming as his thrusts within her body grew deeper and wilder and harder. He heard her husky cry of pleasure, her soft whisper against his mouth,

"Oh, Cougar, I do love you so. I never thought you'd be mine . . ."

He wanted to answer, to tell her he loved her beyond what words could tell, but only her name sighed, shivering, from his lips. "My Gold Hair . . ."

Chapter 20

As Adam lay in the great canopy bed with Alexandra sleeping in his arms, he felt completely drained, and completely content. When had he ever been so content? A smile filled with tenderness touched his lips as he remembered. He had been content with Eliza. He would never forget that. She had been sweet and wonderful and his heart's dearest love, but now the past must sleep. Eliza was gone, and it was Alexandra who had journeyed with him to paradise three times this night. He looked down at her beautiful, peaceful face and brushed his mouth lightly over her lips and hair. Ah, God, his little Alexandra . . . his Gold Hair . . . his woman. Aye. She was his. Of that there was no doubt. But how could he keep her here in safety, the way things had fallen out with the other Mohawks? As he gazed on her, worrying about it, she stirred and opened her eyes.

"Hello, beloved . . ." Alexandra slipped her arms around his hard waist, snuggled closer, and murmured against his chest, "It was wonderful. Each time . . ."

Adam's eyes danced over her. "It was . . . very satisfactory."

Alexandra lifted her head, gave him a mocking look. "Satisfactory!"

He chuckled and ran his hands over her silky skin. "Know, my Alexandra, you are my sun and my moon and the rainbow that arches over the four corners of my sky. From this night forward, I leave a piece of my heart with you . . ."

She gave him a grin. "Only a piece? You have all of mine." She kissed his mouth, slid her hand down his chest and over his hard abdomen to where his manhood already stood erect. It was amazing—he was hungry again and so was she. But his hand closed over hers. He drew it to his lips and pressed a kiss on it.

"We must talk, Alexandra, and then I must leave."

Alexandra sat up, instantly alert. "For where?"

"Tiyanoga."

"Am I to go?" Even as she said it, she knew he was going without her.

"Not this time," Adam replied. "Only the sachem and I will go." He had put the whole ugly situation from his mind, but now it loomed, and she had to know about it. At least part of it. He pulled her back down into his arms. "Our Mohawk brethren in the east have decided you should stay here at Windfall awhile longer."

"I'm willing," Alexandra replied promptly. She was savoring the strong masculine lines of his face and his black mane of hair spread gleaming over her pillow. He was her own sun, her moon, her rainbow that arched over the four corners of the earth. Hers. He had said he loved her and wanted to wed her. She simply could not fret anymore that he was Lark's man she was stealing. He was her man.

"They have decided that if your father wants to see you again, he must enforce the Crown's laws."

Alexandra listened to the slow, heavy beating of his heart beneath her ear. She murmured, not raising her head, "It would only seem fair." Adam's pride in her and love for her was so huge, so overpowering at that moment, he could have gone to the window and shouted it to everyone. He said only, "You are in no danger now, for your father will agree."

"I know." She snuggled close.

"And know, too, that my Mohawks will guard you

well while I am gone." It was so. Unlike the rest of their Mohawk brethren, the Schoharie Mohawks cared about what happened to her. But it was the future Adam feared, not the present.

"Will I . . . go back to Tiyanoga soon, do you think? I do want Mama and Papa to see that I'm all right."

"As soon as an agreement is reached with your father, I will return you." How could he tell her that no one trusted her father, that the man would agree to anything to get her back and would then renege, and that the Mohawks in his jurisdiction would crave revenge. Trying not to think of their fury and the threat they had made against her, Adam thought of it. Sweet Jesus . . . Great Creator . . . *Be with her and protect her, and guide me in protecting her.*

Sensing his change in mood, Alexandra felt suddenly shy. "Do you still want to join with me?"

"Do I want to breathe?" Adam replied huskily. "I would be as one dead without you, Gold Hair." It left him numb, thinking of life without her when he had just found her.

Alexandra hugged him so tightly, her arms ached. "I'll come back to you, you know I will, but first I mean to do battle for your Mohawks. I can't bear to see such injustice." To think she'd once viewed them only as savages. Now they were the Cougar and Lark and Silver Hawk and Fox Woman. Day by day she was attaching more names to more faces, and there was not one among them that she did not like and admire.

"It will be appreciated," Adam murmured, touched by her fierce new protectiveness. But he knew that her anger and her brave words would be but a small dam against the white torrent sweeping over them. No one could help except perhaps the king himself.

"Will you carry a letter to my parents when you go?" Alexandra asked. "I want to tell them again that I'm all right."

"*Hen.* Write it now, for we will leave soon." They

dressed quickly, and as she began to write her message, his gaze drifted over her bedchamber, so familiar and yet so strange. There in that far dark corner a cradle had once stood waiting, and a German nursemaid would have slept in the bed in which he and Alexandra had just made love. His eye caught the dreamcatcher hanging on the bedpost, and his heart lurched. But it was not Eliza's. He had hers. It was the only thing of hers he'd retained. The rest of her possessions he had wanted never to look on again.

"Here's my letter," Alexandra said softly, seeing the distance in his eyes. "I've said I'm well and happy and they're not to worry." She put her arms around his waist and laid her head on his chest. Suddenly it came sweeping over her again, the icy thought that he'd once been so ill he had not wanted to live. And he had that strange look in his eyes again—the way he'd looked that night. She hated it, and it frightened her. She whispered, "I'm afraid for you, Cougar . . ."

Adam kissed the top of her head. "Your worry is wasted."

"You'll . . . come back, won't you?"

"I will come back. I promise." But her words turned his blood to ice. He asked carefully, "Why do you think I would not?"

Alexandra shook her head. "It's silly, I know, it's just that . . . I'm so happy I fear it can't last. Oh, Cougar, I love you so! In truth, I do." She stood on tiptoe, cradled his face, kissed him almost in a frenzy; his mouth and cheeks, his jaw with the black stubble on it. "Please be careful. Please . . ."

As he rode toward Tiyanoga with Adam, Silver Hawk's rage smoldered. He could not remember ever having been so angry for so long over so many things. There was Warraghiyagey, who talked of naught but the future; his Iroquois brethren, who had ignored his call for war; and most especially, there was his brother, the Cougar, who had stolen his woman and who rode by his side in a silence as deep as his own. All day long they had ridden, and now as night walked its way across the sky, he could not keep his own silence another moment. He was about to speak when the Cougar said:

"Shall we make camp here for the night, *raktsia?*"

"*Hen.* It is as good a place as any." It was protected, and there was a stream close by. After they had eaten a handful of pemmican and stretched out on their bedrolls under the stars, Hawk muttered, "I would talk with you, *rikena.*"

Adam sighed. He had seen well Hawk's black mood from the moment Warraghiyagey had appeared at the gathering. Hell. War and old Willie Johnson were the last things on this earth he wanted to talk about tonight. His own thoughts were heavy with Alexandra's last words, words so similar to those Eliza had spoken on their wedding night, they clung to him like a shroud. He could not shake free of them. Was it a sign? He had become Indian enough so that he was a believer. He had seen too many signs come to pass to laugh them off.

"*Rikena . . .*" It was a growl.

"I am here, *ion kiatenro,* and my ears are open. Speak."

Now that he was faced with it, Hawk's tongue refused to move. He resented hugely that this misery had come upon him, and resented the two perpetrators of it, his adopted brother and his adopted sister. If only he could hate them both, it would cleanse his spirit—and this night he was drawing close to the possibility. In fact, if he learned the Cougar had had both women, the Gold Hair and Lark, he would indeed hate him. He would be tempted to slay him . . .

Adam gave him an impatient look. "Why do you not talk? Must I stay awake waiting?"

It was some moments before Hawk could loosen his tongue. He said finally, hoarsely, "The words . . . are choking me." He had decided to tell him everything. Everything. Shameful as it was, there was no other way.

Adam was taken aback. There was no time in his memory when he and Hawk could not talk. Sensing the brave's struggle, he kept his eyes straight ahead and said low, "I would hear these words which choke you, *raktsia.*"

Silver Hawk nodded. He would not drag this out. He would say what had to be said and be done with it. He drew in a deep breath and muttered, "There is a woman I would have."

Adam darted him a swift glance, but Hawk was staring at the moon, his face like a thunderhead.

"Know, *ion kiatenro,*" Hawk continued, "I am unlike my brothers in the matter of women. While they are content to move from squaw to squaw, I have found the one woman I would join with forever. But there is a problem." His heart drummed and roared against his rib cage and his throat clamped shut. When he forced his voice through it, it rasped. "She . . . says she is yours."

It took Adam several moments to realize he had heard him correctly. He sat up, and slowly uncoiling his body, rose to his feet. He stood watchful, slightly crouched, his narrowed gaze never leaving the sachem; a puma ready to spring. Alexandra? He wanted Alexandra? He said quietly:

"She speaks the truth, my brother. She is all mine. Know well I would die for you in battle, but I will not give you my woman."

Silver Hawk, too, climbed to his feet, his hand resting on the hilt of his knife. It was not a comfortable sight, seeing the Cougar angry. He said carefully, "I am surprised you crave two squaws, *rikena;* it is unlike you. Have you changed so much, then?"

"What do you mean, two?" Adam growled. "What nonsense is this? There is only one woman I crave. The Gold Hair."

Hawk's eyes glittered. So. He had abandoned Lark

for the white squaw. It was good news for Hawk, *hen*, but the little tadpole's heart would be broken. "What of Lark?" he muttered.

"Lark? Man, is it Lark you want?"

"It is Lark I want," Hawk declared, "but she is expecting you to ask for her. She says she loves you. She has loved you for four winters."

Lark. He wanted Lark. Adam almost laughed aloud in his relief, but the dangerous look on Silver Hawk's dark aquiline face made him think better of it. But it was clear what had happened. Lark had untangled the matter with Alexandra, aye, but she had not yet told Hawk the truth. And this thing had to be settled now. He could not lose Hawk's friendship over it.

"I owe Lark my life," he said, "and I care for her deeply. I thought she should know it. I told her if ever I were to wed again, I would ask for her. But I told her it would never happen. I meant never to share my life with another woman. But then I met the Gold Hair and—"

Silver Hawk shook his head, held up his hand. It was enough. It rang true. The Cougar spoke the truth as he always spoke the truth. He said gruffly, "It shames me that I doubted you."

And he regretted deeply that Lark would be hurt. But unlike the other terrible hurt she had suffered at the hands of Akando, he saw that this misfortune was of her own making. But he would be there for her again. He would help her as he had before, and this time it would not be as a brother. This time it would be as the one who loved her above all else in the world. But as he lowered himself to his bedroll, the one thing that had remained unsaid clawed him mercilessly. He could not speak of it. Not now when he had already shamed himself once with his suspicions. For an eternity, he lay agonizing, staring at the sky, and then the Cougar's voice came.

"Raktsia—"

"Hen?"

Adam had sensed the sachem's worry. Hawk was a proud man and one who was powerful with the women. Now he was wondering just how powerful Adam himself had been with Lark. If he were Hawk, it was a thing he, too, would be brooding over. He said:

"When she found me at Windfall, the Land of Death was so near I could see the blue sky and smell the grass. I wanted to go, I was not afraid, but she held me, your Lark, and she warmed me and coaxed me back. She made me want to live again. It was the only time, my brother. The one and only time."

Hawk could not help but reach out and catch the Cougar's outstretched hand in his powerful grip. The two clung in silence and then Hawk muttered, *"Niawen."* The thing was dead and gone now. It was buried. It would never cross his thoughts again. But to think, he could have slain his brother in his anger. To think. And then he surely would have turned the knife on himself.

It had been five days since the Iroquois had departed from Windfall and Alexandra's freedom had been returned to her. She was like a child at Christmas upon leaving the gloom of the manor house and returning to the sun and the wind and the sky. She followed Lark about from one chore to another, curious, watching, studying how the women punched holes in the deer hides they had brought with them, and then stretched and softened and smoked them. She watched how they made thread and twine and mats and baskets from roots and bark, and all the while she held close to her heart the thought that someday she would be one of them. For when she wed the Cougar, she would live and dress and eat and work as they did. He would want it that way, and what he wanted, she was going to give him. She would do absolutely anything in this world to make him happy. But her own happiness was dampened by her concern for Lark.

Alexandra still had no idea why her friend had given up the Cougar. Certainly Lark did not know, nor did anyone, how things stood between Alexandra and the brave. The maid had to be crying inside, dying even, but only rarely did it show in her calm dark gaze and serene face. That morning, for instance, as Lark patiently showed her how to prepare venison for pemmican, Alexandra had seen the sadness in her eyes. She bit her tongue to keep from comforting her. She loved the maid, and so wanted her to be happy it was an ache inside her. If only Lark could talk about the Cougar and about how she felt and why she had done what she had—but it was a subject Alexandra did not dare mention.

"After we have sliced the venison," said Lark, cutting the meat into inch-thick strips, "we must score it. Crosswise, like this." Dextrously wielding the knife, she demonstrated, and Alexandra imitated her as best she could.

Hours later, when the sun stood overhead and the strips hung smoking on poles high above the fire, Lark said, "You have learned that lesson well, Alexandra. Now all that remains is to guard the meat against dogs and wolves. And vermin."

"For how long?" Alexandra asked faintly. She was remembering suddenly how she had once thrown pemmican away in disgust.

"Not long. Only three days. It should be ready for the mortar then." She wiped her hands on the grass. "And now I must go for firewood."

Alexandra tried not to show her dismay. Since dawn, she had been pounding corn, carrying water, and slicing up the poor deer. She was ready to drop, but she murmured, "I'll go with you."

Lark frowned. "*Iah.* You are tired." She had seen the dark shadows of fatigue beneath Alexandra's eyes. "The Cougar will not take it kindly if we work you too hard and you grow ill."

Lark felt empty, thinking of Alexandra in his arms. She had surrendered him, *hen,* but the memory of his face and the sound of his voice filled her every waking thought. She tortured herself wondering if Alexandra loved him as deeply as she herself did, wondering if she could somehow discover the answer without asking the question. And she wondered, too, did the Cougar love Alexandra? Had she done the right thing in giving him up, or had she been foolish? Oh, if only she could fight free of her unhappiness and confusion, but they clung to her brain like cobwebs.

"I'm not tired and I won't grow ill," Alexandra said. "I'm going with you."

Lark had to smile. *"Niawen, onkiatshi."* As they entered the soft light and stillness of the great woods, she said, "You have relieved me of many burdens since we came here." It pained her to admit it, but perhaps the Cougar would be a lucky man to get such a one.

"And you've taught me many things," Alexandra replied. "I hope I can remember them all." Her thoughts raced. It was so quiet here, and so peaceful—perhaps Lark would be moved to talk about her unhappiness. But there seemed no way to bring up the subject. She murmured, "You must have used a great deal of wood during the gathering ..."

"Hen, our men cut much in preparation. What remains is here waiting to be carried out."

"They're good men, your braves. I didn't understand them at first, but now that you've come to Windfall, I've gotten to know them better." Her pulse quickened as she realized how innocently she had drawn near the forbidden subject of the Cougar. But did she dare mention his name? As she continued to collect the wood, she told herself to do it. Do it. Say something. Anything! She murmured finally, "I even know your brother and the Cougar somewhat better now."

Lark stared, seeing on Alexandra's beautiful face the look she had seen once before. Eyes glowing and filled with tenderness, her skin luminous, as if a flame had just been lit within her. She sighed, knowing she had the answer to one of her questions. The maid adored him. She loved him beyond telling, and Lark did not know whether she was sad or glad. She was too numb to feel anything. She asked softly, "And what do you think, now that you know the Cougar somewhat better?"

He is my beloved, Alexandra wanted to cry. He is my savior, my warrior, my lover, my protector. He is my happiness and my heart. He is my breath, my very life. She said only, "I . . . think he's quite special. I admire him. But then I admire all of you, and as you know, Papa's going to hear it and a whole lot more."

"It is kind of you, *onkiatshi*. Look, there is one of the stockpiles they left for us." She moved toward it.

Alexandra could not believe it. Lark was the one who was supposed to talk, and instead it was she who had talked, and now the moment was over and they were right back where they had begun. Talking about wood. Blazes. She absolutely could not stand it. She had to say something. "Lark . . ."

"Hen, onkiatshi?"

Alexandra bit her lip. She was forever leaping before she looked, yet now she had looked, seen the risk, and she was still about to leap. She said, "If you should ever want to talk about . . . anything, or if I can ever do anything for you, will you please come to me? Please . . . ?" She crossed her fingers as Lark blinked her black eyes and looked at her in surprise.

"Niawen, Alexandra. I will certainly do that. *Niawen."*

Lark felt a sweet warmth moving through her. The warmth of a growing friendship. Alexandra had sensed her turmoil, and just by being herself, by being Alexandra, she had eased Lark's soul. The Cougar would be in good hands with her. She would be a strong woman for him, and she would love him like no other—but Lark was not pleased that he was deceiving her. The maid had no idea she was to remain a captive even after her father agreed to the Mohawks' terms. It was not right.

She was brooding over it when a faint movement caught her eye, a movement among the trees ahead of them. Her blood turned icy as she recognized the familiar slender figure, her long brown hair swinging, and the tiny buck clinging to her skirts. She stopped, rooted. Was that weeping she heard?

"Lark, what is it?" Alexandra whispered. Her first fear was that Akando had come, or that it was a strange brave bent on harm, but looking toward where Lark stared, she saw nothing. "Lark?"

"I thought I heard a . . . strange sound." Lark pointed to where her friend still walked, the chubby legs of her toddler running to keep pace. "It came from over there . . ."

Aktsia, she cried to her silently, why are you here? How can I help you? Please, can you not be happy and lie at rest? Oh, Great Sustainer, why does she walk in these woods? Help her.

Alexandra put an arm about Lark's shoulders and felt that she was trembling. She did not show her concern, but said firmly, "It's all right, no one is there. Perhaps you heard the wind. I sometimes hear it. See—it's making the treetops sway."

Lark glanced briefly at the trees, and then back to where her friend had been, but she and the little buck were gone. It was as if they had never been there at all, and in truth, perhaps they never had. Alexandra had not seen them. Lark tightened her mouth. *Iah.* She had seen them. And if she denied it, she was only deceiving herself. She had seen her friend and her boy babe twice now, but it was a private thing and not to be talked about. She straightened her shoulders. "I have been foolish. I hope I did not frighten you."

"You didn't. I'm sure it was the wind."

"*Hen,* it was the wind . . ."

Chapter 21

On his way back from Tiyanoga, a cloud hung over Adam's head. It was the same black cloud that had accompanied him there—his fears for Alexandra. All the days of their journey, he had tried to reach a decision regarding her and finally he had made it.

"What are you thinking about, my friend?" Silver Hawk asked.

It was some moments before Adam replied. "My woman. I fear for her."

"You do not think the Grayhead will begin to enforce the Crown laws with all possible speed?"

"I am sure he will."

"Then what is your worry? We will have our hunting grounds and cropland and you will still have your woman." And he would have his. He was going to begin a gentle pursuit of Lark very soon now.

Adam made no answer. He was remembering their meeting with Wade Chamberlain in Chamberlain's sparse quarters in the Tiyanoga blockhouse. The colonel had been pleased to see that Lord Adam Rutledge was taking part in the negotiations, and by Adam's belated apology for missing his party. But his mood had changed to rage when Adam had delivered the Mohawks' ultimatum in the Cougar's name. Who was this Cougar bastard, he'd roared, and how dared he keep his daughter to bargain with?

Seeing that his white brother's thoughts were far away, Hawk prodded him. "That is what was decided, *rikena.* We will keep the Gold Hair even after the laws are enforced."

"It is not that simple," Adam muttered.

The entire journey, he had been tormented by Alexandra's words, so like Eliza's that they seemed an omen, a sign that she would never be his. The thought was ice down his spine and an arrow in his heart. How could he bear it if anything happened to her, if for the rest of his life he could not see or hold her again? It was the very reason he had vowed never to join with another woman, and now it was too late. Heart, soul, mind, and body, they were already one. But unlike Eliza, Alexandra lived. She breathed. And the most important thing was not his own happiness but keeping her safe. Keeping her alive. And to do that, he had decided finally that he must return her to civilization as quickly as possible.

"Why is it not simple?" Hawk persisted. "If we keep her with us, the old Grayhead will be forced to keep order. If he does not—"

"Enough!" Adam growled.

Hawk watched his brother with narrowed eyes as he rode by his side. He said quietly, "You had best tell me the rest of your thinking, *ion kiatenro.*"

Adam allowed his blood to cool before he replied. "I fear the eastern Mohawks will be too ready for revenge if the laws are not enforced quickly enough. They will expect instant results."

"You fear for your woman even in our safekeeping?"

"My brother, I would fear for my woman even if she were in a cage with ten men guarding her. Keeping her will force her father to obey the Crown, but it will take time for the word to reach the other garrisons." He shook his head. "Can you promise me, *raktsia,* that no one of our brethren will seize or harm her tomorrow or next week if he feels the Grayhead has betrayed him?"

Hawk looked at him steadily. "You know I cannot. Nor can we guard her every instant of the day. We must hunt when we return, and our women and our old men cannot guard her . . ."

"*Iah*, they cannot." And so his world was going to end, Adam thought. Alexandra was right, just as Eliza had been. There was some happiness that was too great to last.

Silver Hawk was deeply troubled by the Cougar's pain. In his mind, he knew it was wrong for a man to care about the loss of a woman, but in his heart, he knew he and his brother were not like other braves. He said low, "You will return the maid to her father, then?"

"As soon as possible. And he must be warned of her danger and return her to New York City immediately."

"This will anger our eastern brethren."

"I have no choice."

"Nor do I, then. I will not turn my back on you. As long as the sun shines and the rivers flow with water, I will be here for you. I will go with you."

Adam could not speak for some moments. He nodded. *"Niawen."* Hawk was more brother to him than his own blood brother had ever been. It caused him to think of Dover and to wonder how the old boy was. It had been a long while since he had heard from him.

It was late afternoon of the following day when Adam eagerly mounted the staircase of Windfall and followed the shadowy hallway to Alexandra's bedchamber. He found her working diligently on her journal and stood in the doorway silent and smiling, watching her. He said finally, *"Okarasneha*, Gold Hair."

Alexandra gave a small shriek and nearly jumped out of her chair. "Cougar! You scared me half to death!"

Adam laughed. "Then I must comfort you." He was by her side in two long steps, and the small catch in her breathing and the glow in her eyes told him all he needed to know. As he lifted her in his arms and covered her soft parted lips with his, he did not allow himself to think beyond this moment—to that time when she would be gone. "I have missed you, Alexandra."

Her warm, sweet breath against his face and her hot little tongue greeting his sent chills flickering up Adam's spine. As his mouth and hands sought her hungrily, Alexandra slid her arms about his neck to press him closer and kiss him more deeply. As he carried her to the bed and began undressing her, she knew that this was not going to be a time for exploration and the leisurely flowering of their passions. He was parched for her, starving, dying for her, just as she was for him. Heat shimmered through her, flames that pulsed and licked at her, searing her flesh, her breasts, her lips, her very core, as he drew off the last of her clothing.

Alexandra's breathing was as ragged as his as she helped him to undress, and then she was embracing him, giving herself to his tender ravishment, feeling his hot, seeking mouth on her breasts, holding his shaking body close, pulling his head down to hers, biting, kissing him, feeling his warm hands stroking, molding, caressing her.

When she pressed her body against his like a drawn bow, Adam took her—hard and deep and thrusting savagely. Wrenched by need and beyond self-control, he wanted nothing more than to sink into her again and again, to see her passion burn as hotly and fiercely as his own. When he heard her cry out in pleasure, felt her tighten about him to sheathe him in silky fire, he sealed her mouth with his, and then murmuring his love against her lips, carried her with him into paradise . . .

This was the last time, Adam thought, holding a sleeping Alexandra in his arms. Tomorrow night they would leave for Tiyanoga. But he promised himself they would be together again when this turmoil was all over. The thought trailed into oblivion. The turmoil would never be over. England was growing more and more impatient with these far-off colonies of hers and with subjects who refused to subject themselves to her. The Indians hated them both—the English and the settlers. When war came, and it would, he would be in the middle, and how could he ask Alexandra to wait for him? Yet how could he not?

If they wed, he thought, suddenly hopeful, she could live in New York City and he could see her when he was able to get away. But then he thought of himself dead or mutilated and knew he could not ask her to pay such a price. She was young and beautiful and she deserved better. She would forget him. She would deny it now, but she would forget him. Seeing that she had awakened, he brushed his lips across her forehead.

"You are beautiful when you sleep, beloved."

Alexandra smiled, murmured, "You're beautiful always . . ." She gazed up at his face sleepily, and thought how wonderfully brave and handsome he looked in the dancing half-light. "You have to be a dream." She touched wondering fingers to his mouth and jaw. "You're too magnificent to be real . . . too wonderfully Indian . . . too wonderfully, savagely Indian. Ummm."

Adam chuckled, tasted her soft lips, said low, "Are you interested in hearing of your father?"

Her eyes flew open. "My father! Oh, Cougar, how awful I am. Of course I want to hear about him. Is he all right? Did he look well? And did you see Mama?" She felt ashamed. A good daughter would have asked about them the very first thing. Oh, dear . . .

"I did not see your parents," Adam replied, "but I understand they are both well. They were happy for your letter."

Alexandra raised herself on one elbow, frowning. "What do you mean, you didn't see them? Isn't that why you went—to talk to Papa?"

"The commander of Tiyanoga would hardly deal amicably with the man who is holding his daughter captive, little fox." He could not prevent his fingers from moving over her as he spoke, caressing her skin, smoothing her hair, tracing her mouth. "We thought it best, the sachem and I, that Lord Adam take my place, and he was willing."

He hated the lies needed for his pretense, but the moment was never right for the truth. Even if by some miracle she did not resent his subterfuge, he could not ask her to bear the burden of such a lie now that she was returning. The risk of her inadvertently letting it slip out was too great. But he would confess one day. The time would come.

Alexandra frowned. "Lord Adam? My goodness, I never even thought of such a thing, but I can see that you're right. I'm sure Papa dealt quite amicably with him." She was no longer surprised by Lord Adam's continual popping in and out of the Mohawks' lives.

Adam grinned. "I hear he was not all that amicable."

"Papa seldom is." She added anxiously, "But he will start doing his job finally, won't he?"

"An agreement was signed," Adam said. "He will forbid his men to trespass on Indian land within his jurisdiction, and he will send them to remove the settlers' fences and signs and read them the law." It would serve no purpose to tell her that once she was in Wade Chamberlain's hands, he would tear the damned agreement to shreds.

"I'm glad." Alexandra took a deep breath and stroked his arm, which lay across her breasts. She loved to see its dark hardness pressed against her white skin, and loved the way the crisp black curls felt beneath her fingers. She said quietly, "I suppose this means I'll be going back soon."

"Tomorrow night."

She nodded. "Aye. Tomorrow night. I'll be ready." It was a lie. She would never be ready to leave him. She tilted her head, gazed up at his face, and thought how very quiet he was. Was he missing her already as she was already missing him? Struggling to keep her voice even, she said, "I worked on the Indian portions of my journal while you were gone but it's still not quite finished. I'll add the remainder tomorrow before we go." She gave him a shy sidelong glance. "I suppose you'll want to read it."

Adam smiled. "Every word. Do you mind?"

"All this while, I wasn't sure you could . . ."

"And now?"

Alexandra laughed. "I haven't a doubt of it." He probably read better than she did. "Oh, before I forget, I'm running out of paper. Is there any here in the house that you know of?"

"Alexandra, let us not talk of paper."

Her eyes widened. "All right. What should we talk about?"

"You," he said. "You will not be coming back here to Windfall."

Alexandra sat up. "I never expected to. This is the duke's manor, and Lord Adam's. It's you I want to be with—in whatever village or castle you'll be living in." She felt frightened suddenly, seeing the closed look on his face. "I . . . *will* be returning to you, won't I? Cougar?"

"Not for some time," Adam said quietly.

"Wh-why not? I don't understand. You asked me to wed you—or have you changed your mind?" It felt as if her heart were shaking her entire body.

Adam pulled her back down beside him. "I have not changed my mind. I want you with me wherever I am, and I want us wed, but it will not be soon."

Alexandra lay as stiff as a lodgepole and stared up at the canopy arching over her head. She crossed her arms, felt the sickish stirrings of fear and fury. Something was wrong. Something was terribly wrong. "I don't understand this at all. I thought I was to go to Tiyanoga and talk to my father and mother, and after a reasonable length of time, I thought I would come back to you. I thought it was what you wanted."

"Alexandra, look at me."

"I'm not sure I want to!"

Adam took her chin, turned her face to his. "There is one reason only why you must not come back to me for a while. It is too dangerous. I fear for you."

Alexandra's eyes were like green saucers. "You can't tell me your Mohawks would hurt me, for I won't believe it!"

"The Schoharie Mohawks would never harm you, but there are others who will. If your father does not produce change swiftly enough, they will seek revenge. They will come for you, Alexandra, and I cannot risk that."

"Come for me to do what? Steal me? From under the eyes of all these braves?" She laughed, but it had a hysterical edge.

"They would not come to steal you."

"Then what? I want to know." When he made no answer, but tightened his arms to hold her naked body closer, the truth dawned on her. She gasped. "They'd . . . slay me?"

Adam did not allow himself to think of the abomination that was planned for her. He said gruffly, "You will be in no danger if we leave right away."

Alexandra struggled free of his arms and sat up again. "Will they merely slay me, or . . . will they scalp me first?" She heard her shallow breathing, the pounding of her heart, the crackling of the fire on the hearth in the sudden stillness. "Cougar, I . . . want to know . . ."

Adam, too, sat up and, cradling her against his chest, gently rocked her back and forth, brushed his mouth tenderly over her lips, her chin and cheeks. "We will take you to safety, Hawk and I," he said. "You will not worry."

"Oh, Cougar . . ." It was a wail. "What makes you think I'd be any safer at Tiyanoga than here? I was st-stolen from Tiyanoga!"

"It is but the first step of your journey," he said calmly. "You must return to New York City, Alexandra."

It was as if he had told her she must go to some far-flung reaches of the Empire. "I won't leave you!"

"You must."

"Iah!" She wrapped her arms around his neck and covered his face with frantic kisses. "I love you! I can't go that far away from you. I-I'd rather be scalped!" She buried her face in his neck, felt tears gathering.

Torn to see her suffer so, Adam muttered, "Gold Hair, don't cry."

"I-I need to cry . . ."

He knew it was so. If anyone needed to cry, it was Alexandra. In silence he held her and listened to her quiet sobs. He kissed her hair, her teary face, and her wet mouth as she wept, and when her tears subsided, he lay back on the bed, pulled her down into his arms, and kissed her again. "I love you," he whispered.

"Does that mean you'll . . . come for me in New York City?" Her voice was still thick with tears.

"I will come for you."

She muttered, "I suppose they'll drag me on the boat kicking and screaming and take me back to England." She scrubbed her eyes, pushed her damp hair behind her ears. "Will you come for me there?"

"I will come for you there. Wherever you are on this earth, I will come for you."

Alexandra shook her head. "This is impossible. It's all quite impossible. Once we say goodbye, we'll never see each other again."

"I will come for you," Adam said. "Never doubt it. You are mine and we will wed." Nothing had ever seemed so real to him or so right, and nothing, not even war, could come between them. "And before we wed, we will talk, you and I, for I have many things to tell you, Alexandra."

"Tell me now," Alexandra murmured. His deep voice soothed her, and his words had driven away all her worries. He would come for her and they would wed. He had said it. She pulled his hands down to cup her breasts, and kept her own atop them. She loved their warmth and their bigness and loved the tender way he caressed her, loved the rough texture of his skin against her own flesh.

"Now is not the time for talk," Adam said huskily. Holding her naked breasts in his hands was sending fire searing through him again.

"What is it time for?" She gazed up at him through lowered lashes, offered him her parted lips.

"Little flower . . ." Alexandra heard the catch in his breath as she slid her hands down over his taut thighs and back up over the heavy muscles of his chest and shoulders. She teased the black swirls of hair around his nipples and, drawing them to hard nubs, touched her lips to them, trailed kisses over his chest and abdomen.

A gasp tore from Adam's throat. What a sweet, shameless little wanton she was. He had never intended to have her again this day, but she could not escape him now. She was booty. He slid an arm under her and was gathering her closer when he heard Hawk shouting suddenly from within the house.

"Rikena! Are you there?"

"I'm upstairs!" Adam shouted and put Alexandra from him. He had left the front door unlatched, but Hawk would never intrude unless it was urgent. Swiftly donning his leggings and moccasins, Adam strode to the top of the staircase. "What is it?"

"My brother, I need you . . ."

"I will come." Seeing Alexandra had dressed quickly and followed him, Adam said sharply, "Remain in your room and lock the door."

"What is it?"

"I do not know. I will return." As he joined Hawk, he said, "Have they come for her so soon, then?"

"It is not the Mohawks, it is Akando. The devil has come for Lark."

Adam looked at him, scowling. "What do you mean, he has come for Lark?"

"He has challenged me to another game of hand. It is his right to try and win her back."

God in heaven, had they not troubles enough already? "Just how long is she to be tossed back and forth between the two of you? Forever?"

"We each have one challenge," Hawk muttered. "I had thought he was not interested . . ."

Seeing the torment in his brother's eyes, Adam said as easily as he could, "You won her once, you can win her again."

"It is my thinking," Hawk said as they moved to the meadow behind the house. "But know, *rikena,* if I do not win her this time, I will not let that devil take her back into slavery again. I will kill him."

Chapter 22

∼◦◦∼

Fox Woman looked up from her work as Lark burst
into their wigwam.

"My mother . . ."

Seeing the terror in the maid's face and voice, she
threw down the moccasin she was making and climbed
to her feet. "What is it, my daughter?"

"He has come . . ."

"Who has come?"

"Akando," Lark gasped.

Fox Woman stared at her, gaping, and felt her old
heart shudder. Akando. For seven winters she had not
allowed herself to think that this day might someday
come. Now she put her arms about her daughter's trembling body. "Have you seen him?"

"From a-a distance."

"Where is your brother?"

"He has gone for the Cougar."

Fox Woman closed her eyes and gave thanks to the
Creator. If the Seneca had arrived last night or this
morning even, Silver Hawk and the Cougar would not
yet have returned from Tiyanoga, and what would have
happened then? But it had not fallen out so. The two
were here, and all would be well. She lifted Lark's chin,
met her frightened eyes.

"No harm will come to you, my daughter. Your
brother will not allow it." But her heart was in her
stomach.

Lark spun as the wigwam flap was lifted, but it was

not Akando. It was Silver Hawk. He came in, accompanied by the Cougar. "We are taking you to the house," he said. "You will remain with the Gold Hair until this is settled. Come." He held out his hand to her.

Lark felt the blood draining from her face. She looked from Hawk to the Cougar, fear giving her tongue unaccustomed boldness. "What is there to settle? Drive him away. Please." Her teeth began to chatter, "Just d-drive him away."

"We cannot. You know we cannot."

She bowed her head. "I . . . know." She felt his strong arm around her as he drew her through the opening and into the twilight. The Cougar was close by her side, she was surrounded by Mohawks, but even so, she stopped, frozen, when she saw Akando. He sat astride his horse a short distance away, and she saw that he had not changed. His face was still the one she saw in her nightmares—broad through the cheeks and divided by a nose like a hatchet, and his mouth . . . She shuddered in disgust, remembering his full lips moving over her endlessly.

Akando gave her an icy glance before moving his gaze to Silver Hawk. He raised his voice. "I have not all the time in the world, Mohawk. I would play this small game of yours this night so my woman and I can be on our way."

Hearing a soft moan, Lark realized it had come from her own lips. It was happening. After being accustomed to having a home and a family and to holding her head high, she knew it was happening. It was not a dream. She was as she had been before Silver Hawk saved her—a squaw to be won or lost in a game of chance. A squaw who had risen so high above herself, she had thought to wed an English lord. Perhaps this was no more than she deserved, to be returned to Akando and his family. But having known freedom, she knew death was preferable . . .

"You are not to fear, little one," Hawk said low.

The smile she gave him was tender. He had been kinder to her than any blood brother, yet she had never told him how very much she loved him. She would do it before Akando took her from here. "I am ... at peace, my brother."

Hawk gave a brusque nod. "Come then, we will take you to the house. Swiftly now."

Akando urged his mount forward, scattering those on foot. "Where are you taking her, Mohawk?" he growled. "I would see her."

Seething, wanting to slay the devil, Adam grasped the black stallion's bridle. "Ride to the meadow and wait there!" he ordered.

Akando laughed, swept him with an insolent gaze. "Who are you that I should obey you?"

"I am called the Cougar."

Akando hesitated, seeing that the Cougar's black eyes spoke of murder. He shrugged, smiled thinly. "It matters little where I wait, but do not make me wait too long." He looked at Lark's bare shapely breasts, gleaming hair, and soft mouth, and ran his tongue over his lips. "You have grown into a very fair woman. I look forward to having you back in my lodge."

Watching him canter toward the meadow behind the house, Lark felt herself wrapped in a strange calm. The worst had happened. She need no longer fear it and wonder where and when he would appear. And she had no illusions about what was going to happen now. He would win her in the game which he and her brother were about to play, and he would carry her off with him. But she would never return to the grim life she had lived before in his stockaded village. Never. For certain, she feared death far less. Only as they neared the house did she grow aware of the low talk between Silver Hawk and the Cougar.

"Where the devil did he come from?" Adam exploded.

Hawk's angry eyes met Adam's over Lark's head.

"He learned of our whereabouts from one of his Nation who attended the gathering. But have no fear, *rikena*, I will make him sorry he ever found me."

"What is this damned game he has challenged you to?" Long ago he had heard the story from Hawk, but not in detail.

"It is the game of hand. I learned it at a pow-wow on the frontier the same year I won Lark with it."

Adam was worried. "What kind of game is it? Is skill involved?"

"I have told you, have no fear. She will be mine, one way or the other."

"Will you play the game tonight?"

"*Iah.* He would like that, for by firelight he could use trickery—but I will play him only in the daylight. When the sun climbs the sky, we will play."

Reaching the manor house, Adam unlocked the door and shouted, "Alexandra!"

Hearing the Cougar's voice, Alexandra took up her candle and ran to the head of the stairs. "I'm here." Seeing the grim faces of the three, she feared the worst. She whispered, "What is it?"

"Lark will spend the night with you," Adam said.

"Of course." Her eyes were wide. "She can sleep in my bed with me."

Hawk laid his arm across Lark's shoulders as they walked back to the bedchamber. He murmured in their tongue, "You are not to worry, tadpole. You will not go with him."

Lark smiled up at him. "I know." She must confess her lies now, for she might not have another chance. She took his hand. "I must speak with you, my brother . . ."

"*Hen?*" Hawk's heart turned over. She was so fair and so brave—and so terrified. He hungered to embrace her, kiss her there before the others as a man kisses his beloved, but he reined himself. He was not one to show his feelings or wear his heart where all could see it.

Lark drew him apart from the others. "I have told you an untruth," she whispered. "Forgive me. I meant to correct it before you left for Tiyanoga, but you were gone when I awakened. My brother, my tongue burns with the lies I told you. The Cougar never said he would wed me. I made myself believe he would. And when I said we had mated, it was not as it sounded. It was but one time, for we are not lovers. Never were we lovers, my . . . dearest friend . . ." She felt her cheeks flame as the endearment slipped out unbidden. Never again would she look on him as her brother. He knew it and she knew it. In truth, these past weeks she had been looking on his strong body and handsome face in a way that was strange and shocking for a sister.

Hawk held himself stiff so he would not pull her close and hold her against his pounding heart. She had called him her friend. Her dearest friend. And she had opened her heart to him about the very thing that had so crushed him. It was some moments before he could make his tongue work. "This . . . is good news," he muttered. Unable to contain himself, he raised her hand to his lips, pressed a kiss on it, and saw the widening of her black eyes. "I have much to say to you after this is over, little one. Be waiting for me . . ." He felt the Cougar touch his arm then.

"We must go, *raktsia.*"

Hawk nodded, but his thoughts and his eyes were on his beloved. It was a new beginning, but now he had to deal with the devil waiting in the meadow. He said sharply, "Lark, you will stay here with the Gold Hair until I return for you."

"Will it be tonight?"

"Iah. Tomorrow. Sometime tomorrow."

Lark craved to throw herself at his feet and wrap her arms about his legs in thanks, but she dared not. It would anger him. She lifted her chin, met his eyes, and said simply, *"Niawen."* Only after they were gone did she realize she had not thanked the Cougar or even bidden him goodnight.

After the men left, Alexandra looked at her friend's subdued face and knew that something awful had happened—or was about to happen. "Have . . . the Mohawks come for me?" she asked in a small voice.

"*Iah.*" Lark beckoned her to the window, pointed to the Seneca sitting astride his stallion. "That . . . is Akando."

"Oh, Lark . . ." As she looked at him, Alexandra's skin crawled. This was the man who had slain Lark's entire family, enslaved her, and hurt her in a way no child should ever be hurt. She said quietly, "Maybe you should sit where you can't see him."

"No matter where I sit, I see him in my mind," Lark murmured.

Alexandra nodded, and thought of Mojag. "I understand." She studied the brave resentfully in the fading light. He was big and powerfully built and sat his frightening-looking black mount like an angry statue. But his face had about it the puffy look of dissipation. "He's fat," she said.

"I fear it is muscle."

"He still looks fat." When Lark did not smile, Alexandra said gently, "Please . . . you mustn't worry. Your brother and the Cougar are here, and all these braves. They'll not let anything bad happen to you."

"You are kind, Alexandra, but it is not so simple. There is to be a game played. I . . . am to go to the winner."

Alexandra looked at her in disbelief. "What?"

"It is the game of hand—a silly thing men play to win knives or rings or beads . . ."

"You're not a knife or a ring or a string of beads!" Alexandra protested. "You're a woman! Blazes, this isn't civilized!" She remembered then how not too long ago she and her friends had been the prize in the deadly battle Mojag and the Cougar had fought. She sucked in a shaky breath. A battle was bad enough, but a game? "How can such a thing be allowed?"

"It is the way of it," Lark murmured. "Silver Hawk won me from Akando. Now it is Akando's right to . . . win me back if he can."

"Then it's a way that should be changed," Alexandra replied angrily. "Will there be a third challenge after this, and a fourth?"

"*Iah.* Only the two. There it will end." Her mouth curved wistfully. "Now it is you who must not worry, Alexandra. This will fall out as it is meant to." Dusk was moving heavily over the meadow now, and she could barely see the three figures—one mounted, the other two on foot. She said, "If you will forgive me, I am very tired . . ."

"Then do come to bed." Alexandra turned back the bedcovers and plumped a pillow for her. "Can I make you some tea? Are you hungry?"

"I am just very tired. If I could only sleep a bit . . ." But when she closed her eyes, she saw Akando and his brother, and she saw Yellow Tooth, his father, and the Seneca castle with its tall stockades, from which there was no escape.

It was the middle of the night, and Adam had yet to sleep. He heard Hawk's uneven breathing and knew he was awake also. And suffering. Adam, too, suffered thinking of Akando's cruelty and the life Lark would be returning to should he win her. It gave him no comfort that Hawk had sworn to kill the devil should that happen. For Hawk would then feel honor-bound to offer himself to Akando's old mother to replace him. But, Adam would never let that happen. He would not. He sat up, too agitated to lie abed another instant. Damn that ugly bastard Akando to undying hellfire.

"It is not a good night for sleeping," Hawk muttered.

"I will kill him for you if the need comes," Adam said.

Now Hawk sat up. "It is not your fight, my brother."

"Your fight is my fight. What happens to you affects my life, and if you slay him, we will lose you."

Hawk muttered, "It will be well worth it."

"You would take Lark there with you?"

Hawk thought for some moments. "I do not know."

"I know. You would not subject her to the ones who slew her people and abused her."

Hawk lay back down, his head resting on his crossed arms. He could not bear the thought of a life without her, yet he knew he would never take her to the Seneca castle. He filled his lungs, said finally, "You are right, *rikena*. She must stay here."

Adam, too, lay back down. "It is settled, then. Your place is with her. If the devil wins, *I* will kill him." God knew, it would not be for the pleasure of it, but out of necessity.

"And after that?" Hawk asked. "Is it you we will lose to the old Seneca mother?"

Adam laughed, gazed up at the smoke-hole and beyond to where a star was shining. "I am not as Indian as all that, my brother—Nor have I your honor."

Hawk smiled. "I accept that you are lacking in Indian blood, *rikena*, but not honor. But then this all matters little. Neither of us will have to kill the devil, for tomorrow I win. Sleep assured of that."

It seemed to Alexandra that she had just fallen asleep when she awoke again. Opening her eyes, she thought immediately of Lark and the game of hand, and how awful it would be if she were won by a man she feared and could not stand. She saw Lark standing quietly by the window in the pearl-gray darkness of dawn. She was gazing down onto the mist-filled meadow.

"Lark?"

Lark turned. *"Oronkene,* Alexandra."

Alexandra climbed out of bed and padded over to her. "I spent most of the night thinking about this thing, and I've been wondering—if you took ill, would Akando want you? I mean contagious-ill. We can cover you with spots—I have some berryjuice—or we could even hide you somewhere, and then when the Cougar takes me to Tiyanoga, you could come, too. You'll be safe there."

Lark smiled. She was deeply touched. "You are a good friend."

"And you're the sister I never had . . ."

Lark steeled herself to calm. She would not weep. She was an Ojibwa woman and she was strong. She said, "And you are my sister. You will replace the little one I lost to the Senecas."

Alexandra pressed her lips into a thin line. She would not bawl and disgrace herself. She would be every bit as calm and dignified as Lark. "You honor me, but now, my sister—"

"*Aktsia,*" Lark said. "*Aktsia* is the older sister; you are *khekena,* the younger."

Alexandra was growing more and more nervous. "Yes, well—*aktsia,* let's talk about my ideas. What do you think? Can they work?"

"They are very fine . . ." Lark's eyes had returned to the meadow. Soon the men would be coming. She was grateful that this time she would not be forced to sit beside them upon a blanket, the object of everyone's eyes while the game was played.

"We don't have too much time," Alexandra fretted, "and in truth, I think we'd best try to come up with something else. I rather doubt Akando would believe the red spots, and I'm not quite sure where we could hide you." Alexandra frowned, seeing Lark's eyes were distant. "*Aktsia?*"

Lark did not hear. She was with Akando, stumbling behind his great ugly horse, tethered to it, her hands bound. If they returned to his faraway village by the same path Silver Hawk had used when he brought her back to his family, they would pass through a steep gorge with a narrow ribbon of river rushing below. At the time, she had thought how very beautiful it was. Now she thought only of what a very long fall it would be. Straight down . . .

"Lark! We have to talk about this."

Lark turned. Seeing Alexandra's concern, she shook her head. "You must not worry, *khekena*. I will not be with Akando for long."

Alexandra did not like the look on her face. She was too calm, too resigned. "Have you thought of some way of escaping then?"

"*Hen*. I have a way . . ."

"What is it?" Alexandra asked quietly. She knew what she herself would have been driven to do had Mojag taken her and had there been no hope of escape. "Lark, you . . . worry me."

"It is all right, *khekena*. Let us not talk of it now."

Lark felt almost faint, seeing Akando swagger to the center of the meadow. Great Preserver, if it frightened her so just to look at him from this distance, how could she ever accomplish what she intended? And how could she free herself from the tether if she had no knife? He would never let her have her knife . . .

Alexandra stood beside Lark as the sachem himself strode onto the green toward Akando. She almost forgot to breathe as the men sat on the ground and faced each other in silence. "Your brother will win," she said firmly. "Never fear, he'll win." He had to. He simply had to.

Lark nodded. She felt numb as she thought back over her life with Silver Hawk, the fierce yet gentle chieftain who had taught her to be her own woman. She knew now that he loved her. She knew also that this brother she adored had been her man all along. The Great Sustainer, in his wisdom, had sent him to her in the very beginning, and she, stupid woman that she was, had been too smitten with the Cougar to see it. A silent cry tore through her as she thought of the years wasted.

And the possibility that they would be parted just as they had found each other.

Silver Hawk had sent out the order that the People were to go about their daily chores as the game was played. This thing was private, between him and the Seneca. He would not turn it into a spectacle such as the one in which he had first won Lark. He had agreed, however, that his brother the Cougar should be concealed in the woods nearby.

Leaning against a tree, his arms crossed, Adam waited as, hour after hour, the two played their damned game. Seeing Lark watching from the window, he suffered for her, knowing she waited in terror. And he tortured himself thinking of Alexandra in a like situation or one that was worse. It could happen. Until she was safely back in New York City, anything could happen.

He yawned again and again and felt sweat streaming down his body, for the day was a hot one. It was difficult to stay awake as first Hawk and then Akando hid two small cylinders of bone, one marked and the other unmarked, one in each hand, while the other tried to guess which hand held the unmarked bone. His head began to throb as the twelve sticks each of them kept to mark their wins moved back and forth endlessly between them, Hawk gaining the edge, and then Akando, and then Hawk.

Finally, toward late afternoon, Hawk had in his possession all but one of Akando's twelve sticks in addition to his own twelve. Adam held his breath as Akando rattled the bones, palmed them, and went through a series of gyrations to befuddle his opponent before he finally held out his fists. Sweet Jesus, let Hawk win, Adam prayed. Let this torture end. Sweet Jesus ... Even as his words winged skyward, Hawk pointed to Akando's right hand. Seeing that it held the unmarked bone, he let out a wild whoop of victory, and shouted:

"She is mine!" Looking up to the window where Lark waited, he called to her, "You are mine, little beloved!" He was laughing, transformed, no more the intent, brooding, grim-faced chieftain who had played the game. "I have won you again!"

Adam's own spirits soared as he saw Lark laughing and weeping and Alexandra hugging her. But within one beat of his heart, it was all changed. He heard Akando's growl of rage, saw his arm go back, saw the flash of the knife in his hand.

"Hawk! Behind you!"

Hawk whirled, crouching, but it was too late. The Seneca's blade, already airborne, tore into his chest. That same instant, a scalp-yell burst from Adam's throat and an arrow from his bow found Akando's heart. He raced to Hawk then and knelt by his side. "My brother . . ." As carefully as he could, he removed the knife and saw the sachem's blood flow, glistening, from the wound.

"Did you slay him?" Hawk's voice was already fading.

"Hen." Adam saw that the Mohawks had begun to gather around their fallen chieftain.

"Then she is safe," Hawk said, smiling.

Tears stung Adam's eyes. "She is safe for all time, *raktsia.* You will have a long, happy life together." Seeing Lark and Fox Woman running across the green, he waved the others away. Lark was dry-eyed, but her face was drained of all color as she knelt by Hawk's side. Fox Woman knelt at his feet and beat her breast.

"Neka is bringing medicines and a dressing for your wound," Lark murmured, soothing. But when she examined the gash, her fingers trembled, for there was much blood.

Hawk caught her hand and raised it to his lips. "Before I leave," he murmured against its softness, "I would tell you . . . what I could not tell you . . . before."

"You will not leave!" Lark whispered.

"In my heart"—his voice grew fainter—"you have . . . been my woman . . . since the first day I saw you . . . What a pretty little fox-kit . . . you were . . ."

"You will not leave me, Silver Hawk!" Lark's voice grew higher in panic.

"Why did I . . . not tell you then? We could have . . . had these years together."

As his hand sought her face and hair, Lark caught and kissed it. She kissed each long dark finger and his palm before cupping it to her cheek. "Hawk!" Her voice thick with the tears streaming from her eyes, she kissed his mouth, smoothed his hair, cradled his face in her hands. "I love you. I want you. Please, please do not leave me. Live, beloved. I will not let you go. Live! Hawk! I will stay by your side . . ." She bent over him, wrapped her arms about him, and laid her head on his chest. "I will breathe life into you and take care of you as you have taken care of me. Oh, Silver Hawk, stay with me . . ."

Silver Hawk did not hear. His eyes had closed, and he was singing his death song.

Chapter 23

Alexandra had followed Lark's frantic flight to the meadow, but when she knelt by Silver Hawk's side and began crying his name, Alexandra could not watch. She moved off by herself, closed her eyes, and began to pray. Within moments, she felt a reassuring hand on her shoulder.

"Are you all right, Alexandra?" Adam asked.

Unable to speak, Alexandra nodded, hands still clasped in prayer. Steeling herself, she looked back to where Lark was bent over the sachem, weeping, kissing his face, calling to him. She shut her eyes and prayed more fiercely.

"She has realized this day that he is her man," Adam said quietly.

Alexandria could not hide her dismay as the terrible impact of his words sank in. Oh, nay! Oh, poor Lark. After four years of believing the Cougar was the man she loved, she now realized it was Silver Hawk? Now, when he was dying?

She shook her head. "That's the saddest thing I've ever heard. How did—"

"I know nothing," Adam muttered. "Only what I am hearing." He himself was shaken to his depths.

As Alexandra returned to her prayers, she heard Silver Hawk begin to chant in a high voice. She listened for some moments and then said excitedly, "Cougar, he's singing! He must be feeling better! Oh, please, God, let him feel better."

Adam tightened his lips. It was not for him to tell her Hawk's chanting was the death howl of a Mohawk warrior warning destruction to any who got in his way. Seeing Neka, the medicine woman, hastening to Hawk's side, he said, "I must go to Lark now. Stand with the others, Gold Hair. I will not have you off by yourself like this and unguarded."

Adam went to Lark then, raised her to her feet, and put his arm around her as Neka knelt over Silver Hawk. He watched as, carefully and swiftly, she cleansed his wound and examined it. She said:

"Have the men carry him—"

"Will he live?" Fox Woman cried.

"I do not know," Neka answered. "If he lasts the hour, his chances will be better."

Fox Woman gave a wail and tore at her hair. "He is gone! My son is gone! I feel it in my heart and in my bones. I have lost my firstborn son!"

Adam felt the shudder that convulsed Lark's body, but she did not cling to him weeping. She stepped away from him, and he saw her black eyes glitter.

"My mother," she said sharply, "Silver Hawk still breathes, and he will continue to breathe." To Neka, she said, "Where would you have the men carry him, Old Mother?"

"To your wigwam," said the medicine woman, rising unsteadily to her feet. "He will need constant care."

"Then he will get it." She called to the braves in a ringing voice, "Carry my man to my wigwam!" Going to where the women beat their breasts, she said, "Do not grieve! Your sachem will live." She crossed her arms and lifted her head. "I have said it!"

Everything had changed in the blink of an eye, Alexandra thought as she pounded corn in the log mortar. Akando was dead . . . Lark loved Silver Hawk . . . and Silver Hawk had lain gravely wounded for three days.

Because of it, the journey to Tiyanoga had been postponed yet again.

Seeing the Cougar enter Lark's wigwam, she waited eagerly for him to reappear. Without Lark to talk to as they worked together, she knew little of what was going on—only what she saw with her own eyes or learned from the Cougar. Seeing him walking toward her at last, she called out anxiously:

"How is Silver Hawk?" In truth, she was almost afraid to know.

"During the night, the heat left his wound," Adam replied.

Alexandra stopped her corn pounding. "Does that mean he's going to be all right?"

"*Hen*. Many prayers have been answered." Adam thought how warm and pink and luscious she looked, and that too many days had passed since he had held her in his arms.

Alexandra closed her eyes and felt a warm rush of relief flowing over her. "That's wonderful news. Lark is going to be very happy, and I so wanted this for her."

Adam nodded. "She is the reason for my brother's recovery. He knows he has much to live for. He has his woman now."

"And Lark has found her man." She was so happy for the two of them that her own life suddenly seemed dim in comparison. Thinking about the journeys that lay ahead of her, she said, "I wish I didn't have to leave. At least not for New York City or—or England."

Adam's black gaze was admonishing. "Just remember that I will come for you. Wherever you are, I will come for you."

Alexandra looked down at the corn in the mortar and sifted it through her fingers. "I don't think you realize how big the sea is, or how far away England is. I don't think it will be all that easy for you to find me."

Adam chuckled, allowed his fingers to rest briefly on her smooth cheek. "I will find you."

"Oh, aye." She could just see him galloping half-naked on Anoki through London and the English countryside, looking for her. He would cause a riot.

Adam took her chin, made her look at him. "Gold Hair, I will come for you. I have said it, and I will hear no more of this. Now that my brother is out of danger, we will leave for Tiyanoga tonight."

She shrugged. "Whatever you say." It would be useless to argue anyway.

Seeing his brethren gathering down by the river, Adam said, "We are off to hunt now. The old men are here, but I cannot ask them to watch you every second. You will remain in the house while I am gone."

"But I'm needed here! With Lark and Fox Woman tending to the sachem, there's not—"

Adam felt a burst of impatience. "Go, Alexandra. Now. I have not the time to argue with you." With all that had gone wrong these past few days, he was not about to return from the hunt to find her slain or stolen. He lifted the heavy pestle from her hands and pointed her toward the manor. "The corn is unimportant. Leave it to someone else."

She wanted to lash back at him, but she knew he was right. If she had been stolen from a garrison town full of soldiers, she could certainly be taken from Windfall with only old men about—and he had said that this time she would not be only stolen. The thought made her hasten her steps. But as she closed and locked the door behind her, she realized that being ordered to stay inside was not all bad. The past three days since Silver Hawk had been wounded, she had been so busy with extra work, she had fallen into bed at night without adding one word to her journal. What she had come to think of as her Indian report was still unfinished, and in addition, there was the tale of Akando and Lark and Silver Hawk to be told.

Blast! She had forgotten completely to ask the Cougar about writing paper before he left. When she'd asked before, they had gotten off the subject completely, and now she would have to write in the tiniest scrawl imaginable to get everything down. Unless there was paper in that locked storage room—and unless one of those keys she had seen hanging in the pantry would open it.

Filled with hope, she carried all five keys upstairs with her and began trying them. When the first four did not fit, she crossed her fingers before slipping the fifth into the lock and was thrilled when it turned. Lucky, lucky, lucky! Pushing open the door and stepping cautiously inside, she detected the faint scent of roses.

"H-hello . . . ?" she murmured, and immediately felt foolish.

In the dimness, she discerned that the room was a bedchamber, and as she crossed to the windows to open the draperies, she could not shake the impression that she was trespassing. And so she was—but not for long. Just as soon as she looked for paper, she would leave. No one need know she had even been there.

Going to the writing table, Alexandra smiled at the fat stack of paper in one of the drawers. Her luck was holding. As she removed several sheets, her curiosity was stirred by the faint handwriting on an envelope. She frowned, carried it to better light, and saw that it did indeed say what she thought it did. It was addressed to Lady Adam Rutledge. A strange sensation moved up her spine. Lady Adam Rutledge? Old Rhubarb had a wife? Blazes, Papa had been completely addled if he'd dragged her and Mama all the way up to Tiyanoga to meet a man with a wife. What a shock. Lady Adam Rutledge. It was strange that Lark had not mentioned it.

Filled now with curiosity, Alexandra gazed about the mysterious bedchamber and saw that it was furnished in beautiful taste—a high-backed mahogany settee and several chairs covered with petit point, a canopied four-poster and a matching draped dressing table, an ornate silver gilt looking glass, a handsome washstand still holding a ewer and basin, two large bookcases ... so this was where all the books were! Spying two gilt-framed portraits mounted above the handsome fireplace at the far end of the room, she forgot all else. Were they of the elusive Lord Adam and his lady?

Disciplining herself, Alexandra studied Lady Adam first. She was very young, with warm brown eyes and long, straight brown hair. She was a beauty. In truth, Alexandra would not have expected less. It was the standard thing for an aging nobleman to wed a young, beautiful woman to display and to warm his bed. She looked eagerly to Old Rhubarb himself then—and felt a stab of disbelief as a pair of dangerous-looking black eyes gazed back at her from a familiar darkly handsome face.

She gripped the mantelpiece and stared more closely. Was this a prank someone was playing on her? This could not be Lord Adam Rutledge. This was the Cougar. He had the same eyes, the same thick webbing of lashes about them, the same black brows above the same dominant triangle of a nose, except in the portrait it was powdered and curled and tied back with a ribbon. He even had the same lean, powerful frame and wide shoulders beneath the ruffles and lace and satin in which he was garbed.

Alexandra's eyes ached, she was staring so hard. It couldn't be Lord Adam, she thought as panic clutched her. It was an impossibility. A trick. A silly, stupid trick of some sort. But even as she stood on tiptoe to read the small brass plaque fastened to the gilded wood, she knew it was not a trick. She knew it would say Adam Rutledge. And it did.

The remainder of the day was a nightmare as she walked the floor of her bedchamber raging, weeping, and then raging some more. It was sunset when she heard shouts and saw from her window that the braves had returned from their hunt with several deer. And when she saw the Cougar who was not the Cougar at all dismounting from Anoki, she felt a fresh burst of rage. No wonder he had laughed so heartily, he and the sachem, when she had called Adam Rutledge Old Rhubarb and said Papa had wanted her to wed him. And to think how she had worried over his making love with her and betraying Lark when he was already wed to another. Wed!! Her Cougar, who just this morning had said yet again that wherever she was on this earth, he would come for her. How poignant and heroic. Hah! She could never believe another word the man said now that he'd lied to her about such a monumental thing as this from the very beginning. And Lark—did Lark know? Of course she did. They all knew ...

Remembering his wife's beautiful face and soft brown eyes and long, silky brown hair, Alexandra wanted to scream. She had always admired brown hair and brown eyes. They were so much more beautiful and elegant than her own stupid pale coloring. Lady Adam. Eliza Rutledge. Where was she now? Had she gone back to England and was she awaiting him there? Or did she travel back and forth?

Alexandra shook her head. She was sickened for both Lady Adam and herself, for of course he would never tell his wife about her. He probably thought neither of them would ever find out about the other. Well, she had found out, and she was going to tell him a thing or two. He was not going to get away with this scot-free. Yet the very thought of admitting to him that she knew of his treachery made her shrivel inside. How humiliating and mortifying to have been so taken in. Hearing a knock and his low voice, she glared toward the door.

"Alexandra, we are back." When there was no answer, Adam knocked again. "The women have made our evening food. You may want to eat before we leave." He frowned at the countinuing silence. "Alexandra?"

"I'm . . . not hungry," she answered finally. She could not face him. Not any of them. They all knew his secret. Lark, Fox Woman, Silver Hawk, Neka, all the Mohawks. The whole Iroquois Confederacy, most likely. She was the only one who did not know . . .

Hearing the huskiness in her voice, Adam suspected she had been weeping. He was not surprised. He had known her tender heart would be broken by their departure. He said gently, "It makes little difference if you eat now—we will have food along for our journey. But we leave at dusk, Gold Hair. Come down soon."

The moon was rising and the night insects were buzzing and singing as Alexandra closed the door of Windfall behind her for the last time. As she walked through the wigwam village toward the field where the horses were kept, she wished she could slip away with as little fuss as possible. She did not want anyone to see her red eyes. But then it seemed they were all too busy to say goodbye to her anyway. There was not a soul in sight. She was disappointed that Lark was not about. She had wanted to say goodbye to her at least and tell her how happy she was for her. Perhaps the Cougar would fetch her from the sachem's bedside, just for a moment.

"Khekena . . ."

Alexandra turned, her eyes lighting. "Lark!"

"We have come to say goodbye."

Alexandra's breath caught, seeing Fox Woman was there, and Old Father, and Neka. The whole tribe was there, following behind her on silent feet. Her heart turned over. She had resented their deceiving her, not telling her about the Cougar, but she saw suddenly that they could not have. They had only followed the orders of Adam Rutledge, for how could they have defied or denied the English lord who was their savior?

She looked on them smiling, her eyes blurring with tears. Men, women, children, even the dogs were there to say goodbye. "I'm so glad you came, all of you. Lark, how is Silver Hawk? I hope he's better."

Lark beamed. "He is thriving. Even now he wants to be up and about, but we will not allow it, my mother and I."

"I'm so happy for you. For you both. I'm just so happy."

"*Niawen*. I am sure your own happiness lies just ahead."

Alexandra smiled her brightest smile. "I know it does. It's waiting for me in Tiyanoga."

"I am glad." Lark did not believe her. Alexandra still loved the Cougar, of that she was sure, but whether he loved her was not clear. It puzzled and saddened her.

"It will be wonderful to see my folks again," Alexandra bubbled, "and then of course Mama and I will be off to England just as soon as possible. I'm dreadfully eager to see my home and my friends again—it's been absolutely ages ..." Seeing how quiet Lark had become, she put an arm around her, and the two hugged as they walked. "But I'm going to miss you," she whispered. "So much."

"And I you, *khekena*. I had ... thought you might come back here to stay."

Alexandra replied quickly, "It was never a possibility." As they arrived at the horse field, she was surprised to see that a small band of armed braves was there talking to the Cougar. "Are they going, too?"

"*Hen*. The Cougar says he needs six men to replace Silver Hawk." She shyly held out a rawhide bag for Alexandra. "For your journey, *onkiatshi*. It is the pemmican we made together."

Alexandra remembered well the many hours of hard work that had gone into it. It was as precious as gold. She swallowed. "*Niawen*."

"And my mother—" Lark pushed Fox Woman forward. "My mother has a gift for you."

Alexandra's heart was full as Fox Woman, her wrinkled face wreathed in smiles, handed her a pair of beautiful doeskin moccasins decorated with beads and porcupine quills. Alexandra had seen her making them but had no idea they were for her.

"Niawen, onkiatshi. I am grateful." Unthinking, she dropped her a curtsy and heard the chuckles, saw the smiles.

"My man sends you this," Lark said, pointing to the luxuriant sheepskin lying in the arms of Old Father.

"Niawen," Alexandra whispered, smiling at Old Father and overwhelmed that Silver Hawk, who had once threatened to slit her tongue, would give her such a beautiful gift. To Lark she said, "Give him my thanks."

Adam took it from her arms. "I will put it on Dyani, and then it is time we left, Alexandra."

She did not look at him. "I'm ready."

Alexandra put the bag of pemmican and her new moccasins into the cloth bag that held her journal and writing things and dreamcatcher. But her thoughts were back in the locked bedchamber where the scent of long-dead roses hung in the air and secrets lay in the shadows—where Lord Adam and his lady had made love and slept in each other's arms.

"Khekena," Lark said faintly, "my heart is bigger because I have known you."

Alexandra, who had vowed not to let her emotions overcome her, could not speak. She could only wrap her arms about Lark and embrace her fiercely. She said finally, "Because of you, and all of your people, I've seen things I never saw before and learned things I never knew. My heart, too, is bigger because I've known you."

Adam said to Lark in Mohawk, "I have seen your concern, *khekena,* and you should know, Alexandra is my woman. We will wed."

Lark's eyes lit. She touched her heart. "Cougar, I . . . feel such gladness for you. And for her . . ."

Adam's dark eyes spoke his thanks. "I knew you would."

"What are you saying?" Alexandra asked. "Speak English."

Adam laughed. "I will tell you later." Making a stirrup of his hands, he helped her mount the Narragansett. When she was settled comfortably on the thick sheepskin, he leaped onto Anoki. "Are you ready, Gold Hair?"

"Hen." She could not believe it. She was actually leaving here and returning to Tiyanoga . . . and from there to New York City . . . and from there to England. She was never going to see these people again.

Lark caught Alexandra's hand as Dyani, surrounded by the armed braves on their mounts, started forward. *"Onen, khekena,"* she cried after her. *"Onen . . . onen . . . seknen wasatenkionhe."*

"She says goodbye," Adam said, "and safe journey."

"Onen," Alexandra called back. *"Onen . . ."* She watched Lark's small waving figure until she could see her no more, and then they were in the deep woods and riding directly into the moon. It was huge and golden, but Alexandra scarcely saw its beauty through her blurred eyes. Lark had been weeping as they left, and Fox Woman, and if Alexandra dared start, she would be weeping not only over losing Lark, but over losing her love, her very life. She kept her gaze on the moon as the Cougar drew beside her.

"Old Uncle is giving us much light for our journey. It is a good sign, Alexandra."

"It's very beautiful," she answered shortly. She ordered herself to think of the journeys ahead and of her mother and father and Sara and Justine—and old Piddy Pitts. How grand it would be to see them all again. "When will we get to Tiyanoga, do you think?"

"The day after tomorrow before dawn." Seeing that she was struggling for composure, Adam kept his eyes straight ahead. He knew the parting had been hard on her.

Alexandra seethed in silence as they rode. She yearned to hurl at him all that she knew, and to demand answers to the hundreds of questions flying through her head. But if she did it now, she would turn into a sodden, red-eyed object of scorn before these braves instead of the righteous pillar of wrath the occasion demanded. Nay, she would not say a word now. She would wait until she was in command of herself, and then ... then ... She said crisply, not looking at him:

"I assume you still don't want my father to see you, but what if he does? Accidents do happen."

As far as she could tell, he was in a terrible pickle. He was the Cougar to her, while Papa knew him only as Lord Adam Rutledge. She began to wish fervently for some hideous encounter among the three of them so that this whole miserable mockery would come unraveled. It would bloody well serve him right! But why had he ever played such a dastardly trick on her to begin with? Pretending to be Indian, pretending to be unwed, pretending, pretending, pretending ...

"Your father will not see me or these men," Adam replied. "I have sent word ahead to my friend from the trading post. He will meet us west of Tiyanoga, and it is he who will place you safely in the commander's hands." A hard ride would compensate for Jared's delay in starting.

Alexandra made herself count to five slowly before she even dared look at him. "The same friend," she asked icily, "who refused to help me?" She saw the flash of his white smile, saw the moonglow strike glints off his long black hair as he nodded.

"He is the one."

"I really don't appreciate being subjected to him again."

"It will not be for long."

As his black gaze moved over her in a slow, intimate

caress, Alexandra felt the heating of her skin and the quickening of her breathing—as if she were already in his arms. She looked away. Furious as she was with him, she still felt as weak as a kitten when he made love to her with his eyes that way. It was disgusting. She yearned to hate him, needed to hate him, but she could not. God help her, she still loved him. But she hated what he had done to her. It was low and sneaky and despicable of him, and she could never forgive him.

Adam studied her quietly. Head held high; quick, angry breathing; sharp tongue; flashing eyes. The old Alexandra. The spitfire. He understood that she was crushed by leaving Lark and by the prospect of their own parting, but this was not grief. This was fury. And he was surprised by her anger toward Jared. She knew as well as he that if Jared had done her bidding, they would not have found each other. Hell, it was a mystery. Even so, he kept his voice easy.

"If you wish," he said, "we can talk of this when we make camp tomorrow morning, Gold Hair. But until then, we ride in silence."

Chapter 24

The following morning, the Mohawks made camp in a small clearing by a stream. As the braves pitched a lean-to for Alexandra and tethered the horses, Adam came to her.

"We must talk before you sleep, Alexandra."

"Very well." She almost laughed aloud. Sleep. As if she could sleep with the memory of those portraits in her thoughts.

"I have told you that you will not be safe in Tiyanoga. I want to make absolutely certain you are aware of that."

"I'm aware of it."

"You will tell your father as soon as you arrive that he is to take you to New York City immediately. My friend will tell him also. It is imperative." She looked at him so stonily, he felt a swift welling of anger. "Why do you look at me that way?"

"What way?"

He waved it off. What in damnation was going on with her? This was not the Alexandra he knew. This was the sulky, silent little wench she had been in the beginning. He told himself to remain calm, be patient with her. "I need to know that you understand what I am saying."

"I understand."

He was tempted to shake the pout off her face. "Repeat what I told you."

She looked at him resentfully. "This is ridiculous.

312

You said I'll not be safe at Tiyanoga and I should leave for the city immediately." She understood perfectly. She understood, too, that there could be another reason that he did not want her anywhere in the northland. If Lady Rutledge were about to arrive, for instance, Alexandra Chamberlain could be quite an embarrassment to him. Oh, God, she could not think it of him. Surely he wouldn't . . .

"If you should need me for any reason before you leave for the city," Adam said, watching her closely, "there is a man in Tiyanoga called John Stargazer. He lives in the Lower Town, and he always knows where to find me."

"I've seen him." She remembered the distant figure Mayjay had pointed out as the only Indian in town.

"Good. Those are the things I wanted to say to you. And now . . ." Hell, he could no more stay angry with her than he could spank a kitten. And he had to find out what the matter was. He took her hand and drew her into the woods away from the bucks who were grinning at them. He pulled her into his arms, looked down at her beautiful, mutinous face. "Why are you angry, Gold Hair?" And why was she trembling so?

Alexandra shook her head. She was fighting desperately the shower of fire and ice radiating throughout her body, trying desperately to see in him the man in the portrait—the man with the curled and powdered hair, satin waistcoat, and ruffled cambric shirt. That man she could hate. But she saw only the Cougar in his pale buckskins, his black eyes filled with concern. But you're not the Cougar! she wanted to scream at him. You're Adam Rutledge! And he was married.

"Alexandra, talk to me . . ." Adam smoothed back her hair, cradled her face, and bent his head to her soft lips. They, too, were trembling.

"Have you . . . nothing else to say to me?" Alexandra asked. If only she did not love him so, it would be easy to strike out at him—or if he were short and fat and

bald and wrinkled. But he was not. He was beautiful.
He was tall and lean and smooth and his black hair was
long and thick and shining.

"I have said what is important for your safety."
Adam continued to soothe her, stroking her hair, brushing soft kisses over her face and lips. But there would
be no lovemaking. He would not risk embarrassing her
with these bucks close by.

"You said you had much to tell me . . ." The lovely
face of Eliza Rutledge hung in the back of Alexandra's
mind.

Adam lifted her hands to his lips, breathed in the
faint scent that was hers alone. "I have four winters of
my life to tell you about, Gold Hair, but the time is not
now. Now you must sleep."

She knew that no amount of begging would move
him. "But you will tell me one day?"

"It is a promise. It stands beside my promise to come
for you." Measuring her mood and seeing that she was
still troubled, he cupped her face, frowned down at her.
"You are unhappy with me, Gold Hair. What have I
done?"

Her heart was going so fast, she could scarcely catch
her breath. "It's just this heavy feeling—this worry
that—"

He kissed her fingers one at a time, slowly, lovingly.
"It is all right, beloved, tell me."

"I . . . fear you have someone else that . . . you
love . . ."

Someone else? Sweet Jesus. Women. There was no
telling what they could come up with. Gently he pulled
her against him, held her, felt her hearts's frantic beating. "Why would you think such a thing?"

"I-I don't know." She yearned to tell him the truth,
that she had seen the pictures and knew he was wed,
but she didn't dare. She could not imagine what he
would do. "You're so handsome," she murmured, "and
I see how the women look at you." It was true. There

was no woman among the Mohawks, in all the villages they had visited, who did not look on him with adoring eyes. "It's just ... a heavy feeling. It frightens me."

Adam could not help but chuckle. "Put your feeling away, Gold Hair, I have no one else whom I love. Believe me, I do not." Something made him add softly, "But once I did ..."

Alexandra blinked, looked up at his grave face. "You ... loved someone?"

He could not imagine why he had said it, except he had known for some time now that he could think of Eliza and say her name without being destroyed. He said quietly, *"Hen.* I loved someone very much."

"Was it Lark?"

Adam shook his head, ran his hands through the silken veil of her hair. "Lark I love in a special way, but not the way I love you."

"The ... someone you loved very much ..." Her heart was pounding so, she would have fallen in a heap without his arms around her. "Don't you ... love her anymore?" She sighed. What subtlety. And why would he even answer such a question? But he did.

"She is gone, Alexandra."

Gone? Alexandra was shocked. Stunned. Lady Adam was ... dead? That young, beautiful, brown-haired Eliza was dead? It hit her like an arrow in the heart as she saw suddenly how it must have been. How he would have wanted to die in his grief, and how Lark had kept him alive. And the sadness she had seen in his eyes, the way he had stared out into the night. And no wonder he had been so white-faced and filled with rage when he saw her in Eliza's gown. No wonder. Oh, God, if only she had known. If only someone had told her.

"Oh, Cougar ... oh, I'm so sorry." She slid her arms around his waist, laid her head on his chest. She wanted to weep for him, take away his pain. "I'm so very sorry ..."

"It is all right, Gold Hair. I have put it to rest. The past is sleeping, and now I have you."

"And I have you." Thank God she had said something . . . Thank God she had not allowed this to come between them. As for his telling her who he was, she could wait. Sooner or later, she would hear it. He had promised. And she believed him. She believed him.

"Your heavy feeling . . ." Adam spoke softly against her temple. "Is it gone now, Gold Hair?"

"It's gone. It will never come back." She brought his head down, kissed, tasted him while the forest watched.

"You wondered what Lark and I spoke of?" he murmured against her mouth.

"Hen."

"I told her you were my woman, and that we would wed. It made her happy."

Alexandra laughed. "And it makes me happy."

She felt a wonderful warmth blossoming inside her—relief and love and trust and hope—everything she had been afraid to feel since she had stumbled so unwittingly into that shadowy, rose-scented bedchamber. And now everything was going to be all right. They were going to have a life together. She didn't know how or when—she knew only that they would. He had said it.

The horizon was turning silver-gray as Jared Pennburton neared Tiyanoga with the little Narragansett roped to his stallion. He grinned, thinking back on his rendezvous with Adam. The way those two, Adam and Alexandra, had looked at each other when they'd kissed and said goodbye, he would face all the devils in hell to make things work for them. As it was, he had only the one to face—Wade Chamberlain. Looking over at Alexandra, he saw that her green eyes were huge. She was scared spitless. He asked gently:

"Excited about seeing your folks?"

"Aye, and a bit nervous."

He marveled that she took his breath away every

time he looked at her. That rippling mantle of golden hair and her ivory skin—and not to forget the rest of her. "Nervous, eh? Why would that be?"

Alexandra grinned. "I've changed."

"Ah." Damn, but she was adorable. Old Adam had really gotten hold of something special. He could not have been happier for him. He smiled at her. "I don't think you have to worry, Alexandra. I think your mother and father will be overjoyed to see you just the way you are, changes and all."

"I hope so."

"I know so."

As the words left his lips, Alexandra heard shouts, and then uniformed men with long muskets came galloping out from the town and escorted her back to Tiyanoga as if she were royalty. Folks she did not even know came out of houses and buildings to smile and wave at her and follow along as if it were a parade. She saw Mayjay waving and crying, and she thought in amazement that she'd practically forgotten all about them. It was as if they were part of a dream. And then her mother was running out of the house and down the walk to the street, weeping, waving her handkerchief, calling:

"Alexandra! Oh, Alexandra! Oh, my baby, my precious! Oh, Alexandra!"

"Mama!" Alexandra slid off Dyani and flew into her arms and was smothered in a lovely soft cloud of bosom and silk and rosewater. "Oh, Mama! Oh, I've missed you! And how I love you!" Only then did she realize that the whole town was crowded around looking on, smiling and clapping.

Lydia Chamberlain wiped her eyes and kept her arm tightly about Alexandra's waist as she said, "I do thank all of you so very much for your warm welcome for our daughter—but I suspect she is very tired now and should rest."

Alexandra added, smiling, "And I thank you all. I'm

glad to be back. Mayjay"—the two were gaping at her—"will you come back tomorrow and visit?"

"Aye, tomorrow," Mary said. Jane added, "We can hardly wait."

"Come along, darling." Lydia drew her up the hill and into the house.

"Is Papa all right?"

"Perfectly. He's at the fort. His office is there, you know, and I'm sure he'll come as soon as he hears." She caught Alexandra, kissed her fiercely, and then held her at arm's length. "Do let me look at you, darling." Her eager eyes devoured her child's long, wild, flyaway golden hair; the pink in her cheeks; the smudges on her face; and the outlandish garb she wore—skins decorated with beads and quills and fringes. She shook her head. "Oh, my dear, we really should—" She jumped as the door opened.

Alexandra cried, "Father!" She broke down then. He really was alive! She had known he was, of course, but yet . . . She went to him, felt his hard arms go around her, smelled the faint familiar aroma of cedar and to-bacco on his uniform, felt the stiff bristles of his gray beard scratching her face. "Oh, Papa!" Stern and crabby though he was, she did love him. She tried to gulp back her tears. He hated tears. "I thought for the longest time you were d-dead!"

"Now, now, girl." He held her close, kissed the top of her head, and then held her away from him. His eyes swept her, head to toe, and lingered on her leggings and tunic. He had a hundred questions, but first things first. He asked gruffly, "Were you harmed, Alexandra?"

"*Iah,*" Alexandra blurted, and felt her cheeks grow hot at her mistake. She added quietly, "Nay, Papa."

Wade Chamberlain said tautly to his wife, "Explain to her what I mean."

Now Lydia's pretty face turned pink. She stroked Alexandra's hair, and her cheek, and thought how lovely she was, how very beautiful. In truth, she had never seen her look so beautiful. She asked softly, "We are concerned, dear, Papa and I. We cannot help but wonder, did any Indian man . . . touch you? The way a-a husband would?"

An Indian man? Alexandra replied gravely, in all truthfulness, "Nay, Mama, no Indian man touched me. Not that way." Only Lord Adam Rutledge had touched her as a husband would. And God willing, he would be her husband someday. The thought was a hot, steady flame burning within her.

Lydia's heart stopped, when she saw the look in those incredibly green eyes. Dear Father in heaven, she was lying. No wonder she looked so pink and dewy and glowing. She was in love. Oh, dear God, dear God . . .

Wade demanded, "The Oneida who stole you did not harm you?"

Alexandra shook her head. "Nay, Papa. He wanted t-to join with me"—she heard her mother gasp—"but the Cougar won me and—"

"Won you!" Lydia cried.

"He never harmed me—"

"My darling child, my sweet precious!" She enfolded her lamb and covered Alexandra's face with kisses. "Won you! I simply cannot believe such a thing."

"He kept me only so Papa would listen to him. He wants you to know about his people, Papa, and the way they're being treated."

Wade Chamberlain was breathing through his nose. "Get her out of those damned heathen skins," he ordered his wife, "but first answer the door." He returned his cool gray gaze to his daughter. "Alexandra, never doubt I am grateful for your return, but I will not hear another word about those damned Mingoes, do you understand? I have more to think about than coddling savages."

"Wade . . ."

"What is it?" He turned, glared at the tall blond man who stood behind one of his own men. Gentry, he thought instantly. They had a certain look about them even in the wilderness.

Jared stepped forward. "I'm Jared Pennburton, Colonel Chamberlain. "I brought your daughter."

Wade drew himself to his full six feet, clasped his hands behind his back, and walked around the stranger slowly, inspecting him as if he were a new recruit. He asked finally, "Just how did my daughter come to be in your hands, sir?"

"Alexandra, darling," Lydia whispered, "do come along with me and—"

"Stay, Alexandra"—Wade interrupted his wife—"and sit. Both of you. Sit." After they had obeyed, he turned to the aristocratic newcomer. "Now. As I was saying, I want to know exactly how my daughter came to be in your hands, sir."

He was a bloody tiger, this old boy, Jared thought, but then Jared had been around a real tiger in his boyhood. Adam's pater, the old Duke of Dover. Now there was a tiger. He gave the colonel a genial smile, said easily, "The Cougar's a . . . sort of friend, sir. He sent a message asking if I'd be kind enough to drop off your daughter and I said all-righty-ho, and here we are."

Wade glared at him. "Where might I find this Cougar now?" He knew the question was bootless.

"I can't rightly say, sir," Jared answered with all honesty. "He moves about. He's not Mohawk, you see. His tribe's not from around here, and he just passes through from time to time. I see him whenever he's in the area. Which isn't too often," he added quickly.

"Where and how did you get my daughter from him?" He would kill the bastard when he got hold of him. There were no two ways about it. He would kill him.

"It was west of here, sir. Three leagues or thereabouts. As to the how—he just handed her over, her and her mare. A lovely little Narragansett, and—"

The bloody idiot. Wade snapped, "What is your work and where are you situated?"

"On the Duke of Dover's spread on the Schoharie, sir. Northwest of here, don't ya know. I collect rent from His Grace's tenants and tend his trading post. It's how I met the Cougar. He stops in the store from time to time."

Wade narrowed his gray eyes to slits. Dover's land was a good stiff ride from Tiyanoga. "Did you know my daughter was stolen, Pennburton?"

"Aye, sir. It was rumored Oneidas took her." No use in lying and getting tripped up, Jared decided. This was tricky business.

"And when you got this message, sir, did you not think to alert us before the Cougar arrived so we could seize him?"

Jared met his angry gaze without a blink. "Nay, sir, I did not. The Cougar's not an Oneida, and he said he was returning her to your hands. I assumed he was a rescuer, not an abductor. Was I wrong, sir?"

Wade ground his teeth. "Where, pray is Lord Rutledge? I had thought somehow he might have the courtesy to see this thing through to the end since he became involved in the negotiations."

Jared donned an air of polite mystification. "I never know where he is, sir. I rarely see him. He could be in Albany or in any one of thirty villages I can think of. As I'm sure you know, he's very interested in Indian—"

"Alexandra!" Wade turned to his daughter.

"Hen?" Alexandra gasped. Seeing her father's face turn scarlet, she put her fingers to her lips. She did not even try to correct herself.

"Have you any idea where the Cougar took you? Can you think of any landmarks that might identify the place?" He snatched his riding crop from the mantelpiece and slapped it impatiently against one tall black boot. "Come, girl, surely there's something."

Alexandra told herself it was his frustration that was making him so curt. He was not angry with her, only

with the situation and with himself for not being able to
confront and punish her abductor. At least she hoped
that was so. And then she'd had to go and answer him
in Mohawk. Blazes. But her lips were sealed to his
questions. She was never going to tell him she had
stayed at a house called Windfall, a fantasy house in the
wilderness, or tell him that the Cougar was a pretender.
Her beloved pretender . . .

"Can you not answer a simple question, Alexandra?
In what direction was this place?"

"In the north somewhere," she murmured, "a-and
maybe west. There was a-a river and longhouses and
some wigwams a-and trees . . ." When he rolled his
eyes, she cried, "Papa, I was in lots of villages and they
all looked the same. They all had empty traplines and
hungry children and settlers squatting on the land
and—"

"Lydia, take her," Wade said sharply. "Get her out of
those damned stinking skins and give her a scrubbing
and put a dress on her."

Alexandra's temper flared. "Why do you act as if I'm
not here, Papa? Speak to *me* if you want me to take off
these damned stinking skins and give myself a scrubbing and put a dress on! And in truth, I don't think I
will. My clothes don't stink, and I like them. I like
them better than a—"

"Alexandra!" Lydia cried. "Darling, please—do not
talk to your father so!" And then, "Wade, the child is
not herself. Do go easy on—"

"I'm completely myself, Mama, and I'm not a child,
I'm a woman! You both had better realize that right
now."

Realizing that a major squabble was brewing, Jared
saw that he had best get Adam's message delivered.
"Sir," he said low, "I'm to tell you—your daughter is in
grave danger."

"What? What sort of danger?"

"The Cougar says the Mohawks in this area might turn nasty soon, and he fears they may harm her."

"In God's name, why?"

Jared met his eyes squarely. "He said you would know, sir. He said to send her down to New York City just as soon as possible. Get her away from here."

Wade felt his eyes popping and his heart pounding. He had thought he could not possibly be more aggravated than he already was—until now. The Cougar, the bastard, was one step ahead of him. He knew. He had known all along that Wade had never meant to honor their agreement once Alexandra was safely returned. Damn the devil. But why then had he returned her? Unless he hoped for leniency when he was caught. And he would be caught, sooner or later. He said stiffly:

"I will certainly send her to the city. I scarcely need the Cougar to tell me that."

Lydia cried, "The Treasure left for New York yesterday! There will not be another ship for a week. Oh, Wade!"

Wade shot her a scathing look. "It's a to-do over nothing, woman. Control yourself. She's perfectly safe in the house and on the grounds. Perfectly safe." He looked over to where Alexandra stood in the middle of the floor gazing at them, her green eyes huge in her small white face. He tried to recapture the image of the sweet golden-haired child she had been, so obedient to him and so adoring, but he could not. She seemed a stranger in her heathen garb; defiant; her lips defiled by that disgusting language; talking in that whining way about the Mingoes. And he was afraid to think what might have happened to her during her captivity even though she denied it. He gave Jared Pennburton a wintry look. "Sir, tell your friend his days are numbered. I thank you for escorting my daughter on the last part of her journey." Thank him? Hell, he wished he could jail him except he hadn't reason enough.

Alexandra went to Jared as he moved to the door. "Are you going back to your store now?"

"Nay, lass, I thought I'd stay on until tomorrow."

She saw in his eyes that he was worried about her, and it touched her. "Will you come and see me before you leave?"

"Alexandra . . ." Wade cast her a warning look.

"If I'm to be a prisoner here, Papa, put me in jail and be done with it." She crossed her arms and waited, and as she did, the strangest dizzy feeling came over her—as if the room were tilting. She swayed, felt Jared's steadying hands grip her shoulders, saw deeper concern in his blue eyes.

"Are you all right, little lady?"

"Hen, ion kiatenro. Niawen." Her breath caught as she realized she had done it again, answered in Mohawk. But it made the Cougar closer somehow. "Will you come back?" she asked again, and added in a whisper, "Please, Jared?"

Jared smiled, bowed over her hand. *"Hen, onkiatshi.* I'll certainly come back."

Chapter 25

"So," Wade said after Jared's departure. "What was that all about?"

Alexandra was so tired suddenly that she sank into a chair, yawning. "It wasn't about anything, Papa. Jared was kind to me and I like him. I told him to stop and say goodbye before he left."

"He'd better watch his step, m'gel. It's not looked on kindly, an Englishman's being too friendly with an Indian who's stirring up trouble."

An Indian who was stirring up trouble. What if he knew it was an Englishman who was stirring up trouble! Oh, Papa . . . Her exasperation was close to the surface. He had forbidden her to speak of the Mohawks, but she had vowed a hundred times he would know of their plight, and it was a promise she meant to keep. She said firmly:

"The Cougar's not trying to stir up trouble, Papa. He's trying to right the wrong that's being done."

"Darling," her mother said, "do come and rest now. I know you're tired. You're yawning and shaky—and I'm sure you're hungry. Let me get you a bite, and then we'll pop you into your nice clean bed. It's waiting for you . . ."

"Not now, mama." Alexandra did not take her eyes from her father. He stood before the hearth, gazing at the fire and smacking the palm of one hand with his riding crop. "I need to talk to Papa."

"Go with your mother, Alexandra," Wade said. "Get some sleep. Perhaps it will clear your thinking."

"My thinking is clear, Papa." Their eyes met and held, and Alexandra's did not waver.

Wade shook his head. "I wish to God I knew what those devils had done to you to change you. You're not the same Alexandra I knew. You used to be a sweet, docile child, and now look at you!"

Alexandra laughed. "Docile? Papa, I haven't been docile since I was four years old, if then."

"You were a pliant and respectful daughter. Now you're argumentative and rude."

"I was always argumentative and rude!" Alexandra shot back. "Ask Mama and Piddy Pitts. They're the ones who raised me!" Seeing his face growing redder still and her mother wringing her hands, she said, "Oh, Papa, I do love you, in truth I do. But I don't know you—and you don't know me. When I was little, you were always at your club—and then you went to war . . . But none of that matters now." She stood up. "The only thing that matters is what's happening out there in those woods. Do you know what's happening, Papa?"

Wade slapped the crop against his palm. "Nay, I do not, nor do I want to know—especially not from you. The sooner you put your unfortunate time among the heathen behind you, the better."

"I'll never put it behind me. Papa, a war council was called. Chieftains from the Six Nations were there, and they were all angry. Some of them are ready to go to war because settlers are taking their land and their game. And the soldiers who are supposed to prevent it are as bad as the settlers." She watched as he returned his crop to the mantel, poured a brandy, and sat down before the fire.

"Are you finished?" Wade asked.

"I have bushels more. I kept a journal so you could read about everything that's happening. I'll get it."

"I think not." He swirled his brandy, inhaled the vapors, and took a swallow.

"But I wrote it especially for you to see! Their land is being stolen, Papa, and they haven't enough food, some of them, or enough skins to make clothes or to barter with!"

"Then let them move on." Wade raised his snifter, took another swallow, and gazed at her steadily over the rim.

"Why should they? This is *their* land."

"Correction. This is English land, and it's not big enough for us to share with savages."

"Papa—"

He rose. "The king either doesn't know or doesn't care that we're crowded in here with them. All he wants is to keep us under his greedy thumb so he can grab all the tax money he can get. And so here we sit, squeezed into a strip of land no wider than a musket barrel while the Indians you feel so sorry for are free to go where they choose. I say if we can't leave, they have to. We'll force them out if need be. This land is England's."

Alexandra was astonished. She'd had no idea he was angry with the king as well as the Indians. She looked at her mother's white face, back at her father's red one, and said quietly, "Of course the land is England's, Papa, but the king has said the Indians can keep their hunting grounds. They're not greedy. They're willing to share . . ."

"I'm not willing to share."

"The land is . . . sacred to them."

"Sacred? Bah! It's no more sacred than my big toe!"

"They've been here forever . . ."

"Then it's high time they left. Plenty of land out west!"

She asked faintly, "Don't you care that they're suffering?"

"It's their own choice. In fact, I'd be happy if they

all died off, and happier still if I could help it along. Send them someone with the pox ..."

Lydia gasped, "Wade Chamberlain, I cannot believe you said that!"

"And I cannot believe I've been discussing this with women. I must be out of my mind."

Alexandra gazed at him blankly. He had said she was not the Alexandra he knew—well, he was not the father she knew. It seemed the Cougar understood him much better than she did. She murmured, "Then you don't intend to keep your end of the agreement. I suppose you never did."

Wade glared at the two of them. They were looking at him as if he'd just strangled a litter of kittens. "They blackmailed me, damn it!" He turned to Alexandra. "They had you; what else could I do but agree? I couldn't leave you there."

"You could do now what you promised you would. The Cougar trusted you, papa."

Wade made no answer but finished his brandy. He knew immediately he should not have drunk it. He was sick to his stomach as it was, seeing the hurt on her face when she talked about the damned Cougar. It could mean only one thing, and while he didn't want to know about the two of them, he had to. Best to come right out with it. He asked stiffly:

"Alexandra, are you ... that bastard's squaw?" He could not even look her in the eye, he was so afraid for her. "The truth, now."

Alexandra answered calmly, "Nay, Papa." It came out easily, for she was not that bastard's squaw. Not yet.

Wade was not at all sure he believed her. But he so wanted to, he muttered, "Good girl." He caught her, held her to him, and was ashamed to feel tears behind his eyes. But then she was his little girl, no matter what. He put her from him then and said crisply, "We'll say no more about any of this, Alexandra. Run along now and do as your mother says. Get some rest. You look tired." He patted her pale cheek.

"I'll rest for now." She wished she could catch his hand and give it a kiss as she had when she was small. "And if you won't read my journal, I'll have to tell you what it says. I made a promise—to the Cougar, to the Mohawks, and to myself."

"Alexandra!" His voice was threatening.

"I promised, Papa," she replied softly. He used to frighten her when he looked at her that way, but no more.

It was the day after Alexandra's homecoming. She had had long visits with her mother and with Mayjay, and now all she could think of was her father's treachery. When Jared arrived to say goodbye, she had already decided that he was her only hope. She had to tell him everything. Well, almost everything. Certainly not about the Cougar's being Adam Rutledge. She could not divulge such a monumental secret. Only the Cougar could do that.

"So—" Jared smiled down at her as they walked on the neatly clipped grounds of her father's house in the June sunshine. "You're dressed like a proper English girl today. Upon my soul."

Alexandra said glumly, "It makes my folks happy."

"Well, now, you look quite fetching. Surely wearing a gown and satin slippers isn't as bad as all that."

Alexandra caught his arm. "It's not the gown I'm unhappy about," she whispered. "It's what I learned yesterday. I'm being a traitor telling you this, but I have to. Jared, it's Papa—he's not going to keep the agreement he made with the Mohawks. He never intended to. I'm so ashamed for him, yet I feel so guilty for tattling."

Jared drew her behind an oak that shielded them from any watching eyes. "Don't, lass," He lowered his voice. "Don't feel ashamed, and don't feel guilty. The Cougar already knows about your pater."

"He knows?"

"Aye. Why do you think he insisted you leave for the city as soon as possible?"

"He feared I'd be scalped . . ."

"Aye. And he feared it because he knows the workings of your father's mind, as do his Mohawk brethren. They forbade him to return you, lass. He was supposed to keep you hostage so your father wouldn't renege, but he feared for you."

"I . . . didn't know." She closed her eyes, saw him striding toward her, saw him holding his arms out to her, always caring for her, guarding her, helping her. He was so wonderful, and she missed him so—but now it seemed she could never go back to him. She held her head, shook it in frustration. "Why is Papa this way? I can't fathom it. He didn't used to be." She met her new friend's gentle blue eyes and saw the concern in them. "He said he'd just as soon they all died. He talked about the pox . . ." She thought of Lark and Silver Hawk and how they had just found happiness.

"We'd heard. It's been rumored for some time."

"I'm worried about him, and so is Mama."

"It sounds as if he's been fighting too long." Jared tapped his head. "He needs a long rest. No Indians to think about."

"He won't even look at the journal I kept. It's all there—the fences and signs and squatters and fur-stealing. The rotting carcasses. The land theft. He just doesn't care." She gave Jared a rueful smile. "I once thought that the person who really needs to see it is—"

Jared grinned. "The king."

"I'm not teasing. I mean it."

"So do I."

"Really?"

"Aye. Let's do it, b'God."

She stared at him, realizing he was serious. "Are you saying you know someone who knows the king?"

"I know tons of people who know the king. In fact,

I've met the old boy myself although I doubt he re-
members."

"You! My goodness, this is so amazing I-I can't even
think. How on earth do we—"

Jared took her shoulders. "Will you leave it to me?"

Alexandra was laughing, hardly able to believe this
was happening. "I'd love to leave it to you. I wouldn't
have the faintest idea of how to begin."

Jared was serious suddenly. "I know exactly how to
begin." His gaze went to the house. "Is your pater
home?"

"He's at the fort, but Mama's there, of course."

"Mama I can handle." He took her arm. "Come, Alexandra, lead me to your writing table. I have a letter
to write while you fetch your journal."

He did not have to handle Mama. Blessedly, she was
napping. He was able to begin immediately to compose
a letter to Charles Jefferson Hamilton, Esquire, a long-
time friend of the Pennburton family, and a banker who
enjoyed the friendship of the king and had his ear. After
Alexandra had read and approved his effort, Jared
swiftly made up a packet of the journal and letter;
wrapped, addressed, and sealed it; and tucked it inside
his waistband.

"The old boy's at his New York bank this time of
year," he said. "He'll either carry it to His Majesty personally or send it ahead."

Alexandra murmured, "I still can't believe this is
happening. Do you think it will help?"

"Do you?" Jared asked softly as they walked toward
the front door.

Alexandra looked thoughtful. "I don't know. We're
so far away from England, and I'm not really sure the
king cares. Papa says—" She shook her head. "I guess
it doesn't really matter what Papa says, does it? What
matters is that we're trying. The Cougar will know
we're trying, and he'll tell the others."

"Aye. We'll give it a jolly good try. I mean to ride

downriver like a bat out of hell till I catch up with the *Treasure*," He tapped the packet. "This will reach Charles Hamilton, I promise you. If I don't return by tomorrow night, you'll know the old clipper outsailed me and I had to ride farther than I intended."

Alexandra walked with him to his mount, and looked on him with admiring eyes. "You're something, Jared Pennburton. You're really something. The Cougar's lucky to have a friend like you." She threw her arms around him, kissed his bearded cheek, felt his arms tighten about her.

"Do as your folks say, Alexandra," Jared muttered, his emotions suddenly overcoming him. But then it wouldn't do to think of what might become of Adam if anything were to happen to this maid. "Stay near the house, just to be safe. You never know. I'll stop on my way back to see how things are." He kissed the top of her head, leaped onto his mount, and was gone. He never looked back.

That same afternoon, one of his lieutenants entered Wade's office, saluted, and said, "Sir, there is an Indian to see you. He says it's important."

"You don't say? Important in what way?"

"He has news, sir."

"Does he now?" Wade leaned back in his chair, crossed his hands over his abdomen. "Mingo?"

"I'm not an expert, sir, and I didn't ask. If he's Oneida, I didn't want to scare him off, considering."

Wade nodded. "Wisely done, Thomas. Send the devil in. And, Thomas, this will be private, but I want four guards outside the door."

"Aye, sir."

Wade wiped a speck of dust off one boot, got to his feet, and tugged down his jacket. He stood tall as the Mingo entered, but the bastard still topped him by two inches. The fellow looked crafty, dangerous, and treacherous all rolled into one, and Wade disliked him instantly. He crossed his arms, looked stern, and said, "Name?"

Mojag's face was impassive. "No name."

Wade's eyes crackled. "Tribe?"

"I walk alone."

Striding to the mantelpiece, Wade took down his crop, began slapping his palm with it. He asked slowly, "Why are you here?"

Mojag crossed his arms. "I know Cougar."

Wade kept his silence but he felt a surge of excitement. Either he was rolling in luck or this was some Mingo trick.

"I know Cougar," Mojag said again. In truth, he knew many things about the devil. He knew of his lust for the Grayhead's daughter, and knew that he was the white lord who was a savior to the Mohawks. But the man was no savior to him. His body still had not recovered from the beating he had received from the Cougar, and his honor and respect were gone forever. He craved vengeance. Looking at the Grayhead, he said softly, "I can give you Cougar."

Wade lifted the crystal decanter on his desk, poured a brandy, pushed it toward the brave, and poured one for himself. "Drink," he said.

Mojag sat, drank the firewater, and masked a smile. He would never have the Gold Hair, the most beautiful squaw he had ever seen, but neither would the Cougar have her. Instead he would be hanged. And this Grayhead would learn that his only daughter had been spoiled. For some reason, that mattered much to the English.

Wade waited until the brave had swallowed half of his drink and then said, "How can you give me the Cougar?"

"Give me hair," Mojag said. "From the Gold Hair's head." With his dark fingers, he showed the length and the width.

The Gold Hair? Wade did not allow his mouth to fall

open. The bastard meant Alexandra—and he wanted her hair? He shrank inside at the very thought of even a strand of her beautiful hair in the devil's hands. And that he knew about her made Wade's heart turn over.

He cleared his throat. "Tell me more."

"I wrap hair around Mohawk arrow ... shoot ... Cougar find. She his squaw. He come if fears Mohawks scalp her."

Squaw? Wade's knees would have buckled had he not been sitting. Squaw. It was his worst dream come true. But, nay, the thought of her being scalped was far worse. Would they actually go that far to avenge themselves on him? He took a swallow of brandy, gripped the glass so his hands would not shake, and saw that his knuckles were white. He drew a deep breath. First things first. She would be safe here at Tiyanoga until the next sailing. He would keep her in the house under guard, but for now he would deal with the Cougar. He poured more brandy into the Mingo's glass.

"After you send the ... hair," he muttered, "how long before the Cougar comes?"

Mojag shrugged. "Not know. But he come. Cougar come, I promise."

Wade walked to the fireplace and held his hands to the flames, but their iciness was a thing that would not leave. Not until this business was concluded. He turned to the savage. "How much?" he asked, rubbing his fingers together. "What do you want for this? Sending hair to the Cougar?" Thinking of himself stealing into Alexandra's bedchamber in the darkness with a pair of scissors appalled him. But he would do it. To be rid of the Cougar, he would do anything.

Mojag said nothing. He drew an imaginary knife across his throat.

Wade's eyes narrowed. "You want him dead? You want nothing more?"

"Is all I want. Cougar dead."

Wade took a deep breath. "Come in the morning. I will have the hair."

Mojag nodded. "I come." He tilted back his head and quaffed the remainder of the brandy as if it were water. His eyes glinted. "You know about Cougar, old man?"

Wade was affronted by such disrespect, but helpless to punish it. He scowled. "Know what?"

"Cougar is lord." Seeing that the Old Grayhead did not understand, Mojag grinned. It was as he had suspected. He did not know of this amazing thing. That a white was war chief of the Schoharie Mohawks. None of these so-smart white devils knew. "Long time Iroquois know," he said. "Long time. Cougar is lord."

"Indeed." It didn't make a damned bit of difference to him what the devil called himself. Chieftain, king, sachem, lord—the Cougar was a heathen and a savage and he had despoiled Alexandra. He looked forward to the day when he was dead and every bloody heathen was gone from the land. "If you'll excuse me," he said stiffly, "I have other business to attend to."

Chapter 26

Adam was on tenterhooks. He had left Alexandra in Jared's hands three days ago, and a hard ride should have had him back home yesterday. But he hadn't shown. Adam could only pace and worry. Prowling about Dover's store his first day of waiting, he'd learned from the German tending it that Jared was going to tie the knot soon. Four years ago, he'd vowed to bed the first plump wench he found in the northland, and she had turned out to be the pastor's daughter. But that maid had more in mind than bed, and she'd finally reeled him in. Adam chuckled thinking of it. But she was a good girl, and a pretty one. She would make him happy.

Now he had been at Windfall two days and all he could do was wander helplessly through the village, patting the heads of dogs and children and suffering silently. Silver Hawk had taken pity on him, and drawn him into his wigwam, where they sat pondering the problem and sharing a pipe.

"What is your plan if you do not get word today?" Hawk asked.

"I will leave for Tiyanoga tonight," Adam replied, "for it will surely mean something is wrong."

Hawk nodded. "I will go with you."

"*Iah*. You are not yet ready for the hard ride I mean to make." Hawk was recovering well, but Adam saw that he was still weak.

"Then take one of my men," Hawk said. "Take many

men if you wish. They are yours, *rikena*. As you know, they have been on a hunt, but I expect them back to-day." He looked up as Lark lifted the flap.

"My husband, may I come in?"

Hawk frowned, seeing that her face was pale and she was out of breath. She had been running. He got quickly to his feet. "What is it?"

Lark held out an arrow. "It was standing in the field we are clearing." Her hand shook as she gave it to the Cougar.

Adam took it and stepped outside to examine it in the light of day. His heart fell to the ground when he saw the silky pale gold strand of hair twined around it like a vine about a branch. Ah, God, nay . . . Holy Creator, *iah!*

Hawk took the arrow from the Cougar's hands and examined it grimly. "It is Mohawk. And this—" he touched the gleaming tendril wrapped about it—"is this from the Gold Hair, *rikena?*"

"Hen." No one else in the world, Adam thought numbly, had hair as fine and lustrous and of such a color. He uncoiled the pale gold strand from the arrow, raised it to his nostrils, and caught the faint flower scent that always clung to Alexandra. His heart crashed against the wall of his chest as he wondered what in God's name it meant. Were they holding her captive? Had they already slain her? He tore it from his thoughts. *Iah.* They would have sent her entire scalp, not just a strand of her hair. And they would have sent it to her father. So what in God's name was this? He was too numb to think it through.

Hawk said quietly, "I will assemble a war party as soon as my men return from the hunt."

"To go where?" Adam asked dully. "Where would we begin to look?" He must think, think, but his thoughts held only fear. He said finally, "I cannot wait for your men, *raktsia*. I will leave for Tiyanoga now. Only there can I learn what has happened." Unless she had never reached the garrison town . . . But he would not think of such madness. Jared was a good man; he would have gotten her there. There was no reason to doubt it. Calm replaced his fear. "When your men return, send them to the Place of the Clearing—where we always make camp. I will come to them there as soon as I have news."

"It will be done," Hawk said.

"Have you your other clothes?" Lark asked, her worried eyes on his buckskins.

Adam nodded. "I always have my other clothes. I will change when I near Tiyanoga."

"Let me give you food. It will take but a moment."

Adam caught her hand. *"Iah, khekena,* I could not eat, and I am leaving now. This instant."

Hawk followed him outside. "Know that I ride by your side, *rikena."*

"Niawen. If I do not come back, or if I cannot, I will send John Stargazer in my place. Or he will send someone." There was no time for more talk. Adam leaped onto Anoki's back and they headed south.

Alexandra envied her mother. When life became too difficult for Lydia Chamberlain, she always had her drop of laudanum to carry her off to sleep for a few hours. Alexandra had worries aplenty that she wished she could forget, but never with laudanum. As her mother slept, she went outside, walked aimlessly around the house, and thought about the Cougar. His Lordship, Adam Rutledge. It was still difficult to believe that he was who he was. He would always be the Cougar to her. But she had begun to wonder, and the thought terrified her. Would she ever see him again?

When they had been together, she had known she would. When she could see him and hear him and touch him, she had trusted him with her life. But now that they were parted, she was becoming more and more uncertain. Not of her love for him; she still loved him with all her heart. But she was uncertain of his love for her, and if he would come for her as he had promised he would. She hoped so. She surely hoped so. Everything was so confusing and complicated now— even more than it had been three days ago. Then she had merely suspected she was pregnant. Now she knew she was. She had tried to tell herself she could be mistaken, but she had been so queasy and dizzy these past few days—and her woman's time had not come . . .

"Alexandraaa! Hoo hoo!"

Seeing Mayjay hastening up the path, Alexandra felt a huge leap of impatience. Mary and Jane Hatch were the last people on this earth that she wanted to be with right now. She wished she could be rude, but doubtless Papa would be here long after she departed, and their father was his friend. She put a smile on her face.

"Hello, there. I was just going in to"—she cast about for an excuse—"to start dinner for Mama."

"This news simply can't wait!" Mary said.

"Oh?"

"It's about the Cougar," Jane continued, "and it's a secret. Raise your right hand and promise not to breathe a word."

Alexandra raised her right hand. "I promise not to breathe a word." Seeing their beaming faces, she felt as if a dark cloud was suddenly hanging over her head. "What is it? What's the secret?"

Mary said in a hushed voice, "Your pater just had a meeting with our pater and—you *do* promise not to tell? Papa would hide us, absolutely."

"For goodness sake, I said I promised, now tell me!" Her heart had begun to thud. Any meeting having to do with the Cougar could only be bad news. "Do tell me, I'm on pins and needles."

"Your pater said they were going to catch him!" Jane breathed.

"It's to be a trap!" Mary said. "Doesn't it sound intriguing?"

"My goodness." Alexandra kept her face placid, but inside she was screaming. "How are they going to do it, did they say?" Her hand stole to her belly under her apron.

"Papa said a savage came to the fort with news of his whereabouts—"

"—and a damned clever way to lure the devil here. Those were his exact words!"

Alexandra gave a tight smile. "I doubt very much the Cougar could be lured anywhere by anyone—but let's hope it works."

"Oh, it will work, never fear. Your pater says that even the Cougar, sly as he is, will fall into this trap like a moth into a flame."

"And our pater says the beast deserves to be hanged for all the agony he put you through and your poor mater."

"Not to mention the colonel."

"But I did think he was quite handsome though, didn't you, Alexandra?"

Alexandra felt sick to her stomach. "I really didn't notice—but I do hope they get him, of course. What sort of . . . trap are they talking about?"

"We couldn't hear too well through the door, but it has something to do with an arrow."

"An arrow? You mean, to shoot him?" If only Jared would return, he could ride to warn him . . .

"We've told you, silly, he's to be hanged. The arrow is to lure him here somehow, and soldiers will be waiting for him west of here. A long line of men strung out, hidden, of course, so that when he rides past, they'll nab him! Oh, how I wish I could see it! Handsome or not, it was dreadful of him to keep you so long."

"It was cruel," Jane said. "Your poor mater slept a lot. Our mama said it was . . . unnatural . . ."

Damn their stupid mama, Alexandra thought, and struggled to sound calm as she asked, "When is this all to happen?"

"Soon, I'm sure. The message has been sent. What a shock for him!"

"Aye, what a shock." She simply could not wait for Jared to come. She had to handle this herself. She would go to John Stargazer and—dear God, was the man still here? She murmured, "It's lucky we have no Indians in town who'll make a fuss over it. But I recall there *was* one, wasn't there? But then maybe he's left."

"John Stargazer? Oh, aye, he's still here all right—down in the Lower Town."

"He stands there like a statue, but they say he sees and hears everything everyone does."

"Queer old duck."

"I agree. He's a queer old bird."

She was hugely sick, Alexandra thought suddenly. She was going to vomit. God, please, make them go. Please. She managed a smile. "I'd best go in now and get the potatoes started for Mama, but do keep me posted . . ."

"Right-ho."

She strolled in the front door and raced through the house and out the back door, her hand clamped to her mouth. She made it to a clump of bushes with time only to drop to her knees before she began retching. When her stomach was finally emptied, she found her mother watching her with wide, frightened eyes.

"H-hello, Mama." She pushed back her hair and climbed weakly to her feet.

Lydia Chamberlain said quietly, "Come into the kitchen, Alexandra. I'll get you a damp cloth."

Alexandra followed, as docile as a lamb and quite willing to be mothered. She sat down on a bench in the inglenook, mopped her face with the cloth, and kept her eyes on the fire flickering on the hearth. "Thank you, Mama."

Lydia sat on the opposite bench and gazed at her daughter's white face. "Look at me, Alexandra." When

Alexandra obeyed, she studied her for long moments and then said, "You're with child, aren't you?"

Knowing there was nothing for it but the truth, Alexandra said softly, "Aye."

Just a short time ago, she had been filled with confusion; worrying about the Cougar's love for her, wondering if she would ever see him again, certain that the unwelcome babe growing within her was the world's worst catastrophe. Now none of it mattered. Now all she could think of was finding John Stargazer and getting a message to the Cougar. She had to find John Stargazer.

She asked, "Where's Papa?"

"At the fort. He'll be home soon, and we must get you cleaned up before then. He cannot hear of this, Alexandra. He will"—she shook her head—"well, I just cannot imagine what he will do—or what we are going to do with you!" She sat down on the bench beside Alexandra and took her hands. "Was it the Cougar? Did he force you?"

"Mama, I love him. I'm going back to him."

"Alexandra!"

"Please. I am. Trust me, Mama."

"Trust you!" Lydia wrung her hands. "How can I trust you when you've allowed a savage to make y-you pregnant! He must have forced you. Don't try to protect him!"

"Mama, you raised me to know right from wrong. I know a good man when I see one. He's kind and gentle—"

"He's Indian!" Lydia choked and pressed a handkerchief to her lips. "Your father will kill him!"

"Not when he knows him," Alexandra said quietly.

"Alexandra, you simply cannot be with an Indian. You are returning to England with me."

"Mama, I haven't the time to talk. I must find someone."

"Find someone? Where?"

"In the town." She started for the door.

"Papa forbids you to leave the grounds, you know that! It's far too dangerous. Mr. Pennburton said those awful Mohawks could be watching and waiting for you. Alexandra, come back here! Darling, please . . ." She gasped, seeing her husband looming suddenly in Alexandra's path.

"What's all this?" Wade asked. "Are you going somewhere, Alexandra?"

"Papa, I . . . do so hate being cooped up. I just want to take a little walk in town." She felt young and trembly and helpless.

Wade shook his head. "Not by yourself, you won't. This is precisely why I've ordered a detail to look after you when I'm not about. They'll be on the job first thing tomorrow."

"Oh, Papa . . ."

"It's that or nothing, Alexandra. I'll not risk your being taken again—or worse. Now, what will it be?"

Alexandra shook her head. "It's suddenly lost its appeal." It was hopeless. She went to the door, looked toward the town, and nibbled on her thumbnail. Blazes, she could just see herself talking to John Stargazer with a detail of Papa's men surrounding her. But if it were the only way, so be it. She would do it. In the meantime, she would hope and pray that the Cougar had not yet received the message and was not on his way. It was quite possible. She must not lose all hope yet.

Wade studied his girl narrowly. She was as jumpy as a jackrabbit, and his wife looked as if she'd just swallowed a raw oyster. Green around the gills. What was all this? He looked from one to the other. "All right, ladies, I want to hear it. What's going on here? Lydia? Alexandra?"

He laid his riding crop on the mantelpiece, turned to Alexandra, and crossed his arms. Did she know? Had she somehow heard about his plans? But then he could not imagine how such a thing could have happened.

Nay, it was just that she wanted her head and was champing at the bit. He should give her a hug, comfort her in some way, but it went against his grain when she had betrayed them so. The squaw of some bloody Indian, he hadn't a doubt of it, and he'd had so many grand plans for her. Young Rutledge would have been smitten if he'd ever managed to be in the same room with her, and now this—what a bloody, rotten shame. He was sick at heart, and it was only right that she know how she'd disappointed him. He said grimly:

"Alexandra, I talked yesterday with a brave who told me you're the Cougar's squaw. What have you to say?" He expected her to flinch or weep, but she did not. She lifted her chin and met his anger head on with a defiant glow in her eyes.

"I've already told you, Papa, but it seems you'd rather believe someone else."

"In this case, I do. It rang damned true."

"Indeed? And who is this paragon, pray?" She was too angry to be frightened.

"It makes no difference who."

"Is it the same person who told you how to trap him?"

So. She did know. He felt a leap of annoyance. "Who told you that?"

"It makes no difference who," she shot back. "What I want to know is why? I'm home, I'm safe, and the Cougar allowed no harm to come to me—why do you want to trap him?"

"He's a damned troublemaker, that's why. Giving orders and ultimatums to His Majesty's commanders, leading raids, holding you hostage—" He added gruffly, "Taking you from your mother and me . . ."

Alexandra was surprised to see tears in his eyes. And she must never forget that he had nearly died trying to defend her. She whispered, "I swear before God, I'm not his squaw."

In truth, Wade did not know whom to believe. But he

would know soon. If the devil showed up to rescue her, he would know. He said crisply, "Then it shouldn't matter to you if we take him into custody."

"It matters very much!" Her voice rose.

"This is bootless, Alexandra. The discussion is ended. I'm weary, and I'm hungry. Help your mother get dinner on the table."

She felt her anger swelling, filling her until she seemed ten feet tall and invincible. "The discussion is not ended," she said quietly. "I love you, Papa, know that, but if you do this thing, I'll never call you Father again. In fact, you'll never see me again."

"By all that's holy. Lydia, do you hear the maid?"

"I mean it!" When he suddenly gripped her arms, she gasped, "Papa, that hurts!"

"I mean it to hurt." Wade gave her a shake. "Now you listen to me, my girl. You're my daughter, you belong to me, no one else, and you'll bloody well do as I say. You are returning to New York, you're sailing for England on the first ship out, and furthermore, there will be no more shilly-shallying regarding marriage. You will be wed before the year is out and you will wed the man I choose for you."

"I-I won't, you know." Her magnificent calm and fury had all but vanished.

"You have nothing to say about it. That ends it."

Seeing her mother huddled on the settee and weeping softly, Alexandra murmured, "Mama, it's all right—please don't . . ." She returned an icy gaze to her father. "You're still hurting me." He released her, and as she watched him pour a brandy and lower himself into his chair by the fire, she was not sure if she hated him. For certain she grieved for him, and she was hugely angry with him. She shook her head. "You're not civilized. Not even the Indians you disdain give their daughters to men they don't love."

Wade's wintry eyes remained on the fire. "Don't expect from me what you'd expect from a savage, Alexandra."

It was almost midnight, and Wade could not sleep. He sat on the porch in the dark, smoking, brooding, thinking over the angry words that had passed between him and Alexandra. He shook his head, sighed. Those Mohawk devils had turned her all around in her thinking. She was wrong and he was right. Most assuredly he was right in his dealings with them, and right to seize the Cougar. With him not there to agitate them, they would eventually give up hope and move on. He would make sure they did. His own people came first, and what the Crown did not know wouldn't hurt it. Most folk thought as he did. As for Alexandra, she didn't know what was good for her. No woman did. But he would have no trouble finding a powerful, highly placed husband for her. Hearing muffled hoofbeats, he rose and saw a horse and rider approaching in the starlight.

"Colonel Chamberlain, sir . . ."

"Aye, Lieutenant?" He knocked his pipe out and got to his feet. His heart beat harder. A visit from Chester Hatch at midnight could mean only one thing. "Do you have him?"

"Aye, sir. He's in a holding cell."

Wade breathed through his nose. "Excellent. I'll be right over."

"Aye, Lieutenant!" he called after him sharply. "I want this affair kept quiet. I have reason to believe your daughters overheard our conversation in your home and told Alexandra."

"Sir!"

"There's no way she could have known of our plan other than from those two eavesdroppers. Speak to them, Lieutenant, and discipline them, or I will do it for you."

"Sir!"

Wade hastened to the small stable behind his house, tacked up, and in stealth rode through the dark town to the garrison. He looked with fondness on the large irregular square huddled on the knoll—palisades surrounding the two-story stone blockhouse—and he thought with anticipation of what awaited him. The mighty Cougar, chained and helpless in a holding cell. Riding into the enclosure that now teemed with lathered horses, he dismounted and entered the blockhouse. He heard laughter, revelry, and in the light of the wall torches, he saw that his men were flushed with their victory. Seeing him enter, they grew quiet.

Wade gave a crisp nod. "Well done, men. Go home now and sleep. And continue to keep this matter quiet. It wouldn't do for the Mohawks to get word of it."

As they filed out, his anticipation grew. He turned to his men on duty. "You two, come. You others, remain here." Taking a wall torch, he strode through a narrow passageway to the back of the blockhouse where the cells were. Stopping before one, he snapped, "Unbolt the door."

When it was opened, he stayed without, his torch revealing the small, pitch-black, windowless hole for the horror it was: a wet earthen floor, rivulets of water streaming down the stone walls, foul air—and the devil chained to the wall. Wade blinked, felt a twinge of grudging admiration. The bastard showed no fear at all. He stood as tall as if he were on some mountaintop somewhere instead of in this stinking cell.

Adam had been sitting in the blackness cursing his stupidity, but he rose as the door opened. He shuttered his eyes against the blaze of light and said nothing.

"Well, well, well, well, the Cougar, I presume." Wade stroked his gray beard and studied his captive. Six-four, lean, fit, half-naked, his long arms bearing tattoos and a narrow silver band on each, a wild mane of black hair, a murderous gleam in his eyes ... God, what a specimen, and savage-looking as they came. He hadn't a doubt the devil could rip the chain right out of the wall and throttle someone with it if he'd a mind to. Well, he'd not have the chance for he'd not be here that long. He crossed his arms, asked low, "What brings you here?"

Adam had agonized over Alexandra's safety all the way from Windfall. But when he was seized, he had realized immediately that her hair wrapped around the arrow was nothing but a trick to draw him here. It meant she was safe. Sweet Christ, that was the most important thing—she was safe. Whoever betrayed him had known he would be so obsessed with finding her that he'd give no thought to himself and would come instantly. And so he had. And now there was nothing for it but the truth. Hell, this old devil knew him—or soon would.

"Well?" Wade growled. "Cat got your tongue? Not so cocky now, I should think." He frowned, thinking there was something familiar about the fellow. But then all of these red devils looked alike to him. He could not tell one from the other. "I've asked you a question, and I want—"

"I have come for Alexandra," Adam said in a clear, clipped voice.

Wade grew very still. This was not the voice of any Indian he had ever heard. This was a voice from home, from England—and he had heard it before. He entered the cell, thrust his torch closer to the brave's face, stared, and was hit by a thunderbolt of recall. Good God. The Mingo had said it—he'd said the Cougar was lord. And now Wade saw that it was so. The Cougar and Lord Adam Rutledge were one and the same. Good God.

Chapter 27

Alexandra got no sleep. She paced about her bed-chamber all night long, trying to think of a way she could contact John Stargazer. And while her father ate breakfast, she pondered it. Nothing would work. Even if Mayjay brought him to her, they were sure to blab to their father, who would blab to *her* father. And if she sought the man out, accompanied by the detail, they would surely report it to Papa. And if she sent John Stargazer a note through Mayjay, she had no assurance that they would deliver it—or that he could read it. There was just no way to accomplish her mission. After the detail had arrived and her father had departed, she threw up her hands.

"Mama, this is an absolute outrage! I'm a prisoner here."

"Darling, I know. I feel so badly, but Papa is only thinking of your safety."

"So he can marry me off!" Alexandra said bitterly. "But just how many Englishmen do you think will want me when they discover I've got a-a papoose growing inside me!" She was horrified when her mother sank onto the settee and burst into tears. And she was amazed that she had not thought sooner of the idea that was thrilling through her now. Mama. Mama would take the message. Surely she would.

Lydia shook her head again and again. "It's dreadful, just dreadful," She wept. "It's so unfair!"

Alexandra went to her and knelt beside her. She

349

would have comforted her, except she hadn't the time to spare. "Mama, do hush and listen to me. I told you yesterday, there is someone in town I must see." She took hold of Lydia Chamberlain's plump shoulder and gave it a little shake. "Mama! I need you!"

Hearing the urgency in Alexandra's voice, Lydia raised her drenched green eyes to her daughter's. "I'm sorry, darling, I know you need me. Now of all times. I'm just a-a dreadful mother, wailing away when you're the one who needs comforting." She sniffed, felt the tears welling again.

"I don't need comforting, Mama, I need for you to go to Lower Town. I can't leave here, but you can."

Lydia blinked and dabbed her eyes with her sodden handkerchief. "Lower Town?"

"Aye." Alexandra tucked a stray wisp back into her mother's carefully coiffed hair. "Yesterday I learned from Mayjay that Papa has set a trap for the Cougar. I need your help to get word to him."

"You'll get no help from me," Lydia cried. "The man *should* be trapped! He kept you from us and—"

"Mama, he's a wonderful man. I love him, and you would love him, too, if you knew him."

"Indeed I would not! He's a heathen Indian, and just look what he's done to you!"

"I'm going to have a wonderful babe," Alexandra said softly. The thought of it was suddenly almost as exciting as soaring into the sun with the Cougar. "And you're going to have your first grandchild, Mama."

"Oh, God!"

Seeing that she was about to weep again, Alexandra said firmly, "Mama, trust me. The Cougar is like no man you've ever seen in your life. He's a savior to his people. He's loved and admired and respected, and Mama, believe me, if anything happens to him"—now her own eyes glistened—"if Papa should trap him a-and harm him, I'll want to die, too. I will, Mama."

"Oh, Alexandra . . ."

"Mama, don't bawl. You have to go to Lower Town and find the Indian who lives there."

"The Indian!"

"Aye." Ignoring the pleading in her eyes, Alexandra pulled her to her feet. "Dry your eyes. There's no time to waste. The Cougar could be on his way this very minute." She considered telling her that it was Adam Rutledge she would be helping, but she feared to. He might elude capture, and she knew how important it was for him to be able to function as the Cougar.

"Darling, I could not! An Indian! I've seen him, and it frightens me to look at him!"

"Then don't look at him. I just want you to talk to him and give him a message." Her mouth twitched when she saw her mother was pulling down her corset and patting her hair.

"Wade will slay me . . ."

"He won't, you know."

Lydia dabbed her eyes again. Very well. If this was what Alexandra wanted, she would do it. She had done little enough for anyone in her life except play cards and order servants about—and she had not even been very good at that. Too, she had always hoped this darling child of hers would find a man she loved dreadfully to wed, and now it seemed she had. But an Indian . . . Oh, dear. But it was all right. It was all right. She would manage Wade somehow—or die trying. She patted her hair.

"Do I need a hat?"

"Nay, Mama, no hat. Just hurry. Tell John Stargazer that the Cougar is not to come to Tiyanoga under any circumstances. Tell him an arrow will be used somehow to trap him. Hurry, Mama, do." Alexandra stared at her mother's face as Lydia kissed her goodbye and hurried out the door. She had never seen Lydia look so pretty. Her cheeks were pink and her eyes were bright and— blazes, she looked twenty . . .

Alexandra watched as she hurried down the hill, nodded to the detail posted there, turned right, and then disappeared behind the trees that screened the road. Alexandra could not sit still. She weeded the small flower garden her mother had planted and walked around the house fifteen times. She counted. The sixteenth time around, she saw her mother hurrying back and ran down the hill to meet her. Seeing her face, Alexandra felt her heart begin to pound.

"Couldn't you find him?"

"I found him!" Lydia was breathless. She put a hand on her heart. "He says—oh, darling, he says your Cougar was taken last night!"

Alexandra looked at her numbly. It was as if a fist had hit her in the stomach. "Nay . . ." The small, unrecognizable voice she heard was her own.

"He said the Cougar was trapped by a-a strand of golden hair. It was wrapped around an arrow and shot into a field near where he was staying."

"Golden hair!" Alexandra touched her own, a sudden terrible suspicion dawning. "Mama, see if my hair has been cut! Look in the back!"

Lydia went behind her, ran her hands through the mass of silvery-gold ripples and thought that even if a bushel had been cut off, it would never be noticed. What a mane. But then she saw it. A piece had been whacked off right on the outside where anyone with eyes in his head could see it. She gasped, "It's cut!"

"Papa did it!" Alexandra cried, scarcely able to believe he would do such a diabolical thing. Her own father! "The Cougar thought the Mohawks took me and he was coming here to find out what had happened . . . so he would know where to look for me. Oh, Mama . . ." She felt a huge rage building inside her.

"Darling, I-I feel dreadful about this."

"I'm going to him!"

"Papa will hardly—"

"Papa be damned! I'm going to him!" She was already out the door.

"Then I'm going with you," Lydia cried, following. In all her years, she had never seen such a magnificent sight as Alexandra in a fury with her eyes blazing.

Halfway down the hill, Alexandra said, "Mama, there's something you don't know yet. It's shocking."

"My dear, at this point, nothing you can say would shock me."

"The Cougar's not Indian."

Lydia blinked. "Not Indian! Darling . . ."

"He's English."

"English!"

"His name is Adam. Adam Rutledge. Lord Adam Rutledge."

Lydia laid a hand on her heart, said faintly, "You're right. I am shocked." She looked at Alexandra with concerned eyes then. "Are you feeling quite all right?"

"My brains aren't curdled, if that's what you mean, and nay, I don't feel a bit all right with his being tricked into jail like this."

Lydia watched in helpless wonder as Alexandra, like some beautiful, pale avenging angel, ordered the detail of young militiamen to transport them to the garrison immediately. And once within the blockhouse, she said to the officer in charge:

"I wish to see the commander!"

He gaped at the two women in amazement. "The colonel's not here Ma'am."

"Then take me to the prisoner," Alexandra snapped.

"Ma'am, I don't think—"

"Immediately!"

He was well-aware that these were the colonel's womenfolk, and he was at a loss as to what to do. What the beauty wanted—and she was a beauty—was highly irregular. He could not imagine the old curmudgeon allowing it, except there was such a desperate light in her eyes, it fair turned him into a puddle. Dismissing the youngsters who'd brought them, he said low, "I could let you see him just for a bit, I suppose . . ."

Alexandra almost threw her arms around him. "Oh, sir, would you? Oh, I'd be so grateful. Can we go now?"

"Aye. Come along then."

Alexandra turned. "Mama, will you come?"

"I'll wait." And if Wade came, she would sit on him if necessary to forestall him until the two had had their reunion.

As Alexandra followed the officer, his torch lighting the way through an endless damp black corridor, she was dying inside. To think he was here, imprisoned in this awful place because of her. And when they came to the corridor's end, and she realized that behind the heavy barred doors were cells, she quaked. He could not remain here. She would do anything, say anything to free him. Anything. She watched, scarcely breathing, as the bar was slid back and the heavy door was swung open. The officer held up his torch, touching it to another fastened on the corridor wall.

"There he is, little lady. I'll be back soon."

Alexandra could not see anything as she stared into the pitch-black hole. "Cougar? Are you there?"

"Alexandra . . ."

"Oh, God! Oh, Cougar . . ." She heard the rattle of chains as she reached for the torch and thrust it into a holder inside the cell. She gasped, "Beloved . . ."

Adam rose swiftly and took the vision that had appeared out of the blackness into his arms. She was shining, and she was warm and soft and golden—and she lived. He breathed in the faint lavender scent of her and kissed her mouth hungrily again and again, felt the sweet familiar shape and softness of her breasts and throat and shoulders beneath his seeking hands. Seeing the tears on her cheeks, he wiped them away. "I am all right, Alexandra." It was a fact. He had scarcely thought about himself since his capture except to feel disgust that he had fallen into this damned trap. It was

Alexandra who concerned him. She was going to hate him when she learned . . .

"You're chained! Does Papa think you'll break down the door and escape? And this is a hideous, wet, reeking hole where even a poor animal shouldn't be kept! How could he *do* this?" She stroked his hair, patted his face, kissed his mouth, and tried to cease her weeping. It would not help him to see how despairing she was.

"Shhh. It is all right—I will not be here long." He held her close, stroking and kissing her, adoring her body with his hands and eyes, but he was burning with questions. "Was the last part of your journey a safe one?"

"Hen." She slid her arms around his waist, laid her head on his chest, and held on. She had never expected to be in his arms so soon, and this time she was not going to let him go again. Not ever.

"Jared did not return when I expected."

She whispered, "He rode south to put my journal aboard the *Treasure*. It's going to the king. He knows a man in New York named Charles Hamilton who will take it." Gazing up at his wonderful face and the tenderness in his eyes, she was so filled with love she could scarcely bear it. "I was wildly happy about it, of course, but now"—she shook her head—"now it doesn't matter at all. All I care about is getting you out of this hole."

Adam buried a kiss in her hair. "I will get out, never fear." He had doubted Wade Chamberlain would hold him, and he doubted it especially if Charles Hamilton had Alexandra's journal. The old boy was a force with the king and a stickler for law and order to boot. He asked, "Did you talk to John Stargazer?"

"Mama did. Papa had me under guard, so she went this morn. We learned you were taken last night."

Adam nodded. "Then the Schoharie Mohawks will arrive toward evening." The old brave would have sent word to Silver Hawk immediately.

"To . . . do what?" The look in his black eyes touched her like a cold wind.

"To do what they do best," Adam replied. "They are very fine warriors, Gold Hair."

"Cougar, there mustn't be a fight!"

"It would not be pleasant, it's true."

Tell her, he commanded himself. Get on with it. He was wasting precious time. She had to know who he was before Wade Chamberlain barged in and told her for him. Tell her. He lifted her hands, touched his lips to her wrists and palms, and wondered if she would walk out and he would never see her again. God help him, he had not been this terrified since that night two years ago . . . He drew a shaky breath, heard himself saying, "I told you there were four winters of my life I would tell you about one day, Alexandra. Now that day is here. I must make a beginning."

Alexandra gazed on him, fascinated—ebony hair, bronzed skin, eyes like jet under those frowning black brows, broad cheekbones, that wide forehead and arrogant nose. He looked as Indian as Silver Hawk . . . or Mojag . . . or Akando. He looked more Indian, in fact. Now he was going to tell her that he was not Indian at all, and she saw in his eyes that he feared she would hate him. As indeed she had . . .

She murmured, "You needn't tell me anything. Not here and not now."

"I must. It is a thing I should have told you long ago."

Blazes, she could not bear seeing him look so sad and grim. She blurted, "Cougar, I already know! I know about you . . ."

Adam frowned, tried to clear his confusion. What she said made no sense. She could not mean the same thing he meant. The net in which he was so deeply entangled could not be loosed this easily. Sweet Jesus, he wished his heart would stop thundering. He had scarcely the breath to ask, "What do you know, Alexandra?"

"Promise you'll not slay me?"

He could only laugh. "I'll not slay you, beloved. Just tell me, what is it you know?"

"I know that . . . you have another name, my lord." Alexandra saw the widening of his eyes in astonishment, saw the harsh lines of fear vanish from his face. In the silence, she heard his sharp intake of breath, heard the soft trickle of water down the black walls of the cell.

My lord. The words sent a chill down Adam's spine. God in heaven . . . blessed Sustainer . . . She had called him my lord. She did know. And she was here. She had come to him. She had not run away, nor did she hate him. He threw back his head, and his relieved laughter filled the black hole in which he was chained. But it was not a black hole at all. Suddenly it was a small, torch-lit nest in which he was holding and kissing the woman he loved.

"How?" he murmured finally. "How did you know? Did Lark tell you?"

Alexandra shook her head. "Never. I needed paper. I thought the bedchamber next to mine was a storage room, and I found the key—and saw the portraits . . ." When his laughter turned to a soft chuckle, Alexandra murmured, "Then you're not angry, my lord—and after all of my insults . . ."

"I am not angry—and I am not your lord." He grew silent, seeing that Wade Chamberlain had appeared in the doorway.

Wade had watched the two embracing for several moments. Now he said crisply, "Your mother is waiting in my office, Alexandra. The two of you get yourselves back to the house. This is no place for a woman."

"Nor is it any place for man or beast!" Alexandra flared. "Papa, I'm furious with you! You simply can't keep him in this hole."

"I have told you to go, Alexandra."

"I won't. I'm staying."

Seeing the Cougar's arm go around her shoulders, Wade knew better than to pursue the subject. He had far more important things to concern him—one of which was that this savage was not a savage at all but a member of one of England's oldest and noblest families. It would behoove him not to forget it. It made things damned awkward. He cleared his throat, met the Cougar's inscrutable black eyes.

"These are serious charges, Your, er, Lordship. Leading raids against your own people . . . harassing them . . . destroying property . . . delivering ultimatums to His Majesty's commanders . . . holding a hostage . . ."

Alexandra thought she would explode. "If you'd taken a minute to look at my journal, Papa, you'd know those charges are but half the story. The 'raids' never harmed anyone; the braves only took back the game stolen from their own hunting grounds. 'Destroying property' was removing the stupid fencing that kept the People off their own land. The 'harassed settlers' were poachers and squatters. The Cougar was doing your job for you, Papa! As for the hostage"—she was nearly breathless—"I wanted to stay! As for delivering ultimatums—"

Wade said sharply, "Alexandra, that is enough!" But the wind had left his sails.

"You really should have read my journal, Papa. It was intended just for you, but now it's too late. It's on its way to the king." She had expected to feel triumphant in the telling him of it, but she felt only sadness that such a thing had been necessary.

"Nonsense."

Adam spoke for the first time. "I promise you, Commander, her account of the Mohawks' plight will reach His Majesty's hands. You should know also that my Mohawks are on their way here. I expect them before evening."

Wade bristled, but he felt the blood drain from his face. One Mohawk alone could create havoc, let alone a whole damned tribe of them. "Are you threatening me, Your Lordship?"

"I had thought you would want to know."

Wade stared at the glittering black slits of the nobleman's eyes. Dangerous-looking bastard . . . He wouldn't be surprised if the devil had Mingo blood in him . . . but then he hadn't time to dwell on his ancestry. Not with this news he'd been hit with. Who would have ever thought Alexandra's ridiculous journal would have been sent to that damned ass George? And just how bad had she made him look? Why hadn't he at least glanced at the thing? And now the threat of a Mohawk raid was hanging over his head. Good God. The dampness of the corridor seemed to wrap itself about him so that he shivered.

Seeing it, Alexandra said to the Cougar, "Will your people attack if you're outside to meet them?"

"They will attack only to free me. It is a thing I would hope to avoid."

"Papa, do you hear?" She saw that her father's face was chalky and perspiration beaded his forehead. "If you release him, there won't be any danger. Do let him go. Surely you can see you've no reason to hold him, because everything I've said is true. He's committed no crimes."

He needed time, Wade brooded. He needed to think this through. But early evening was not all that far away. Already he could imagine the scalp-yells and see the devils with their lances and tomahawks and bows and their faces painted for war. He could not subject this town to that, yet how could he back down and lose face? But how could he not? He needed time. Time . . . He snapped his fingers and two men appeared.

"Take my daughter to my office," he ordered, "and escort her and her mother back to the house. The detail will remain there to guard them."

"Papa, nay!" Alexandra gripped the Cougar's arm and felt hope leave her.

Adam bent to her ear. "Go with them, Alexandra."

"I can't leave you . . ."

He pried loose her cold fingers and pressed them reassuringly. "Trust me."

"Very well." She said it for him, made herself smile for him, but her terror had returned. Looking at her father's grim face and the thin line of his mouth, she could already see her beloved on the gallows. "I meant what I said, Papa." Her voice shook. "If you harm him, I'll never call you Father again. I'll hate you, and I'll continue this fight against you as long as I live!"

Wade kept his stoic gaze on Lord Adam, but the image of his defiant daughter hung in his thoughts—trembling, furious, those blazing green eyes shining out of her pale, beautiful face. The face of an angel. A damned pity she did not have the disposition of one. He said gruffly to his men, "Remove her. I tire of this."

He did not watch her departure, but he heard the whispered endearment and saw the burning look Adam Rutledge gave her—and he'd witnessed earlier the passionate embraces between them. Nor had he lost sight of the fact that he'd brought Alexandra to Tiyanoga to meet the nobleman in the first place. Nay, he had not forgotten. He grated his teeth and ruminated that, in truth, he did not need any more time. He had to free the fellow. He had no choice in the matter—but not yet. Not just yet. Let him stew awhile.

"I am not quite as convinced of Your Lordship's good intentions as my daughter is," he said. "I must give this some thought."

Adam's smile did not touch his eyes. "Do not think too long, Commander."

"Surely you understand—no man can be permitted to take the law into his own hands." A dark red flush stained his face. What a damned fool thing for him to say.

"I could not agree more," Adam said quietly, and lowered himself to the damp earth. As the torch was removed from his cell wall and the door swung shut, he called out, "The hours are flying, Commander, and my Mohawks' mounts are known for their swiftness."

Wade had seen the wisdom of not waiting. He had released Adam Rutledge before the sun began its descent. And after the nobleman had greeted the arriving Mohawks and brought them back to the fort, a new and stiffer agreement had been forged, signed by the highest-ranking men on both sides, and riders had been sent out to carry the word—officers of the New York Seventh to the settlers and garrison commanders, and the Mohawks to their Iroquois brethren. And Adam Rutledge had just now left to claim his daughter. He'd not even asked Wade for her hand. He had said only that he was going to wed her.

Wade sank into the chair behind his desk, rubbed his eyes, and poured himself a brandy. He was more tired than he had ever been in his life. He'd not realized until now how sick to death he was of fighting the king and the damned heathen Iroquois and the commissioner for Indian Affairs. And how sick he was of settlers and squatters and hunters and trappers and traders. Give him a good clean war any time and turn him loose. He shook his head, took a swallow of brandy, and thought bitterly of the events of the day— and of what was to come. A reprimand? A dishonorable discharge? Good God. What a way to end a distinguished military life . . .

Chapter 28

Lydia watched sadly through the kitchen window as Alexandra walked to and fro before the house, her gaze turning constantly toward the far end of town where the fort lay. Unable to bear the sight another instant, she went outside and fell into step beside her.

"Darling, do come and have something to eat." She spoke in as soothing a voice as she was able. "It's past dinnertime, and you've not even had breakfast."

Alexandra shook her head. "I'm not hungry, Mama." She doubted she would ever be hungry again, seeing that her worst fears had surely been realized. She had lost him. There was no doubt in her mind.

Lydia took her hand, said gently, "But you need to eat, my precious. Especially now. And I just cannot believe that your father would take it upon himself to punish a peer of the realm. Surely he would not. He would have the entire House of Lords on his back."

"Why haven't I received word, then?"

"Darling, I don't know. I'm just sure that no news is good news . . ."

Alexandra was sick. All she could think of was that black hole and her darling chained to the wall. It was no consolation that she had heard neither war cries nor muskets being fired, for it seemed clear now that the Mohawks had never received John Stargazer's message. She whispered, "I've lost him, Mama. I know I have."

It was then that she heard horses coming at a gallop and saw the detail come suddenly to attention as two

362

riders reined to a halt. One was Lieutenant Hatch; the other had long, gleaming black hair and wore only a breechclout. As she watched, her pulses pounding, the lieutenant spoke to the guard and departed, and the other horse and rider started up the hill at a trot.

"Cougar! Oh, Cougar!" Oh, God, thank you, thank you, thank you! Alexandra lifted her skirts and raced toward him, her feet and her hair and her heart flying. "Beloved!"

Adam slid off Anoki and lifted her up into his arms. He was without words, seeing her in her white gown in the bronze-red rays of the setting sun. She was an angel, a dream come to life: pink cheeks; rosy, laughing lips; her green eyes wide and shining and filled with love; her hair a flame-kissed golden cape rippling down her back and curving over her breasts. Offering up his silent thanks to the Great Sustainer, Adam held her close and took her soft mouth in a deep, possessive kiss. Only when he had drunk his fill of her did he notice the small, pretty woman who was looking on, smiling. He gave her a smile in return, set Alexandra on her feet, and said gravely:

"You must be Alexandra's mother. I cannot believe you are so young . . ."

Seeing her mother's eyes glaze, Alexandra knew well that she was conquered. In addition, no woman alive could look on the Cougar's dark, gleaming skin and ebony hair and those long, hard arms and legs without being conquered. She said gently, "Mother, may I present Lord Adam Rutledge? A-Adam"—how strange to say his given name for the first time—"may I present my mother, Lydia Chamberlain?"

She was in a warm daze of happiness as the two greeted each other, and then her mother was fluttering, murmuring how grand it was that everything was settled . . . His Lordship must certainly join them for dinner . . . She would call them when it was ready . . . She imagined they had many things to say to each other.

She walked toward the house then, leaving them alone to watch the setting sun.

"What do you think?" Adam gave Alexandra a slow smile. "Did I pass muster?"

"You've won her completely." Alexandra kissed his hand and pressed it to her cheek. She was drained, trembling with relief. "Where have you been? I was scared to death. I . . . thought I'd lost you."

"I'm sorry you had that worry. I had hoped you knew that your father was in such a corner that he had to free me. A new agreement has been signed, and the word is now being spread. I'm well-satisfied."

He was satisfied, too, with the unexpected news John Stargazer had given him: It was Mojag who had betrayed him—and now he was dead. He had been slain by a Mohawk in a dispute over a woman. It was not in Adam to wish any man dead, but in this instance, as with Akando, his relief was great.

"Are you saying it's safe for me to go with you when you leave?" Alexandra asked. "And that we can go back to Windfall?" She was yearning to tell him of the babe they had started, but she could not push the words past her lips. Not yet.

"I . . . am not saying that, Alexandra. It will be a while before we return to Windfall." Seeing that he had disappointed her, he said gruffly, "I wish I could give you the answer you crave, but I cannot."

"Just don't make me return to New York or England without you. Please . . ." When she pressed her body against his, pressed her lips against his, he took her mouth in a kiss that was long and deep and hard. It filled her with such heat and hunger, she could only cling to him. "Please, Cougar."

"I'm not going back, Alexandra." He put his arm around her and began to walk across the grounds.

"What?"

"I have told the Mohawks I will not be returning. We

will be leaving here, you and I, and going to live wherever you choose—New York, London, Paris . . ."

Alexandra was dumbfounded. "But they need you!"

"Not as they did before. Better times are ahead for them now."

"Cougar, these people are your life! How can you just forget them?"

"I will never forget them, but you are my life now."

"Not all of it. I'm only part of it. I can't replace the wilderness and Windfall and your Mohawks. You belong there, Cougar. So do I." With peace in the offing, she could think of nothing grander than having the best of both worlds for her babe. The beauty and security and civilization of the manor house, with the freedom and excitement and mystery of the wilderness right outside the door.

Adam said low, "It is time we ceased talking about the Cougar, Alexandra, and talked about Adam Rutledge. You know nothing about him."

The gruffness of his voice widened her eyes. She replied carefully, "I've seen the man the Cougar is. That's all that matters."

"You have not seen the man who lost his wife."

His arm had tightened about her, and she stroked it gently and murmured, "I think I have." She had seen that man those many times his eyes had been clouded with distance. When she was riding with him on Anoki; the night he had stared out into the wind and the darkness with tears in his eyes; the afternoon he'd seen her in his wife's gown and raged at her. Oh, aye, she had seen Adam Rutledge. "If ever you want to talk about Eliza, I'd like very much to hear it. She was very . . . beautiful, Cougar."

"The most important thing you need to know about her is that she died birthing our child. She and the babe are buried at Windfall."

His words went through Alexandra like an arrow. She had imagined some accident in the wilderness, an

Indian attack, throat sickness, the wasting illness—never dying in childbed. And now, now she had to tell him she was pregnant. She leaned her head on his shoulder as they walked, and watched the fiery fingers of sun stretch across the shadowy town. And she prayed for the right words to say.

"So you see, little fox," Adam continued, "I cannot take you back to Windfall. Not just now. When a man and a woman love as we do, a child will follow as surely as spring follows winter." She had been so innocent about lovemaking, he suspected she knew nothing about childbirth as well. He said, "A babe does not just . . . appear, Alexandra. A woman must bear it."

Alexandra replied gently, "I know how babes are made and how they come, Cougar. I'm not afraid, truly."

"I see well that you are not." Nor had Eliza been. She had known there would be pain, aye, but she had gone forth on her last journey filled with excitement and anticipation and joy—just as she had come here with him to this wilderness. She had been filled with the shining prospect of holding her babe to her breast. Instead she had been given three days of mind-searing torture and a grave overlooking the Schoharie. He said gruffly, "Know, Alexandra, I would give all I own to shield you from every hurt and pain. I would bear it all within my own body if I could . . ."

Alexandra sighed, slid her arm around his waist, and slowly walked in step with him. She had to tell him. Now. She could not wait for the right words to come. She said quietly, "Your love is my shield, Cougar. It's all that I need. It's all that either of us needs, our babe and I . . ." She heard his sucked-in breath, felt his hands gripping her shoulders, saw the widening of his black eyes.

"Our . . . babe?" He felt as if lightning had hit him. "You are sure?"

She nodded. "My . . . woman's time hasn't come, and I've been losing my food." Shyly she took one of his hands and placed it on her belly. "It's early, I know, but I'm certain. He's growing in me, Cougar."

Adam could already hear the bells tolling for her as he moved his hands over the small, warm mound of her abdomen. A life was growing within her, a life he himself had planted. He made his mouth curve into a smile. "You seem quite certain it is a buck."

She looked up at him, her eyes shining, but not without concern. "I'm certain, aye. I . . . had hoped you would be happy, but I see now it will only cause you to worry . . ."

Adam caught her close, held her as if he would never let her go, and heard himself saying, "I am very happy. And I am proud, Gold Hair. Prouder than I can say." But his heart was crying. It is too soon . . . too soon . . . I have only just found you. Already his head was filled with plans for protecting her. He said abruptly, "We will leave for New York on the next ship, and since a sea voyage is now out of the question, I will buy us a house there. I will place you under the care of the finest doctors as soon as we arrive—and I will bring doctors from London for you. I will—"

Alexandra put a finger to his lips. She was smiling, shaking her head. "Nay, Adam." For in truth, it was Adam Rutledge she was seeing now, not the war chief of the Mohawks.

Adam frowned. "What do you mean, nay?"

"I want to go back to Windfall."

"Abandon the thought."

She was relieved, seeing the return of the Cougar, but even so, she knew she must tread gently, gently. She slipped her hand in his as they continued walking and said carefully, "You think I'll be like Eliza, but I won't. I'm me, Cougar, and I'm sure I'll be just like Mama. I popped out of her as easily as could be."

Studying her glowing eyes and peaceful face, Adam recalled that only after Eliza was gone did he learn that her own birth had nearly killed her mother. He asked sharply, "You would not lie to me about such a thing?"

"Never. Mama says I came without a bit of trouble. Like a grape slipping out of its skin. Ask her." She lifted his hand to her lips, brushed kisses over it. "I'm not saying I don't want a doctor—I do, I'm not a martyr—but why couldn't we bring one to Windfall?" With Lord Adam Rutledge in command, she knew that anything was possible.

Adam muttered, "There *is* a fine doctor in the area . . ." Damned if her words about her mother had not given him heart.

Alexandra crossed her fingers. He was relenting. She felt it, saw it in his eyes, heard it in the resonance of his voice. He was relenting, relaxing, rethinking. "Then please, beloved, let's go back to Windfall. If a fine doctor is already there, and if Lark and Fox Woman help me, everything will be perfect. And maybe Mama won't go back home right away. Maybe she'll come up to Windfall to be with me! She's helped birth babies. Oh, Cougar, please. And you could bring a doctor from New York if it would make you feel easier."

"I want you to be happy, Alexandra"—God help him, what was he to do?—"but I must give this some thought. Your safety comes above all else." He had known Indian women to slip away, give birth, and be back in the fields the same day. Yet Eliza, with a good doctor in attendance, had perished. He was torn, and confused. "I must think about this . . ."

"I beg you," she whispered, "don't make me live in New York. I don't want that kind of life."

"We can go to Windfall after the babe comes."

"But will we? What if you fear another babe will come—and another? What if we never go back because you fear something might happen to us? Please, don't cage me in the city, Cougar. I want to be free—to wear what I want and do what I want and be what I want. And I want our babe to be free. I want him to learn Indian ways and to live with the land and the animals and to plant and to take only what he needs. I don't want him to have white ways, Cougar. I want him to be just like his father. I want to see him with a bow over his shoulder and his hair free—and I want him to be born at Windfall and raised at Windfall. Please." Seeing the sternness of his face, she knelt and wrapped her arms around his legs before he could stop her. "Please, my lord."

Three days later, Alexandra was at the bow of a keel-boat eagerly watching, waiting for Windfall to come into sight. They had plied the River Hudson on the sailing ship *Treasure,* and transferred to a rented smaller craft when they reached the Mohawk, and now they were on the smooth green Schoharie Creek, and surely it could not be much longer. Cushioned against the Cougar's bare chest with his arms around her, she exclaimed for the hundredth time, "You're my husband! I can't believe it. And we're going to our home, and we're going to have a babe." She turned her head, felt his warm lips seeking, taking hers hungrily. She laughed softly after the kiss. "I'm sorry, I just can't stop telling you how happy I am or how much I love you. You'll tire of hearing it."

Adam chuckled. "I will not tire of hearing it. But I fear I do not speak enough of my own love for you."

"It's all right, you know. Men don't. They show their love. Your bringing me back to Windfall, for instance, and the way you worked things out with Papa." Remembering that black hole of a jail, she added softly, "It was more than he deserved."

"Everyone deserves a second chance." Adam turned her to face him, tilted up her chin, and gave her another long, hungry kiss. God help him, he could not keep his hands or his mouth off her. And what she said was so—after this babe came, he would fear her bearing the next one, for how could he not fill her with another? He loved her, and she was so beautiful, so ravishing.

As Alexandra snuggled in his arms purring, he reflected that Wade Chamberlain was the luckiest devil in the land. Jared, arriving in time for the wedding, had said that Charles Hamilton would not be returning to London until mid-July. If Adam should have a change of heart regarding the journal, he should let Hamilton know. Adam had. After talking it over with Jared, he had decided the commander was now solidly under his thumb, and if things even hinted at getting out of hand again, the journal would be waiting in a safe in London to go to the king. In addition, Adam had no desire for Alexandra or her mother to be disgraced by the old boy's mistakes. He would let the matter lie for now.

Alexandra studied her husband's eyes and ran her fingers through his black hair. "You're Adam Rutledge all of a sudden—I can always tell. What are you thinking, beloved?"

"I'm thinking that Jared will have reached Windfall last night." He had sent him on ahead with their mounts to tell the Mohawks of their unexpected arrival. But he was not quite ready to tell Alexandra the other news Jared had brought him from New York.

"Lark will be so happy! Oh, Cougar." She kissed him again—his smiling mouth, his chin, his cheek, his throat, his big hands. "Have I told you in the last minute how happy I am and how much I love you?" A sigh shivered through her as she felt the velvet glide of his hands over her breasts and buttocks.

"Twenty-five times," Adam replied, feasting on the vision she was in her soft doeskin shirt and leggings, her golden hair sun-glimmered, lips laughing, eyes shining, roses in her cheeks—and his babe in her belly. It gave him such a pang he almost winced.

"Do you think Hawk will be glad that we're wed?"

"Hawk will be glad. He is my brother."

Alexandra felt a shadow touch her as she recognized the familiar distant look in his eyes. She cupped his face. "What is it? You scare me when you look that way. Are you worried about me still?"

"*Iah.*" It was a lie. He would die a thousand deaths until the child arrived, but it had not been the babe he was thinking about. He said, "I had other news from Jared." When she stood silent, waiting, her beautiful eyes watchful, he continued, "My brother, the Duke of Dover, is dead, Alexandra. Charles Hamilton had heard it from a friend just arrived from England. I suppose the word will be awaiting me at the trading post."

Alexandra could not speak. Feeling his grief, she went into his arms and held him, just held him for an endless time. She whispered finally, "I wish I could take the hurt away."

"Knowing you are mine takes much of it away."

"If you should want to talk, I'm here."

"*Niawen.*" Leaning on the rail, gazing down into the green water foaming past their bow, Adam thought how strange it was, knowing that the old boy was gone— and had been for weeks. They were all gone now. His father, his mother, Dover, Eliza. All that he had left was Jared—and Alexandra. His life. His dark gaze brooded over her as she leaned on the rail beside him, pink-cheeked, with her glorious hair streaming behind her. He caught his negative thoughts in a vise then and ordered himself to think only good for her. All would be well with her. Alexandra was not Eliza. Alexandra was going to walk by his side for many years to come, and Windfall was going to be filled with their love and their laughter and their children.

Alexandra laid her hand atop his. "Cougar, are you the Duke of Dover now? The thought just occurred to me."

Adam could not help but smile at the wonder in her green eyes. "I fear I am, little one. Duke Number Fifteen. Add to that the Marquess of Hawthorne; Viscount Harrow; Viscount Staines; Viscount Vauxhall; Earl Rutledge of Cheswick; and Baron Rutledge of Newington, Richmond, Portpool, and Deptford." God help him.

"Blazes . . ."

It took the breath from her, and now she was remembering the meal they had eaten at Tiyanoga with her mother and father. It had been George Adam Christian Rutledge who had sat at the candle-lit damask-covered dining table that night. She had not been able to drag her eyes away from him, seeing that her beautiful savage was indeed an Englishman nobleman. He had been dressed impeccably in a ruffled cambric shirt and satin breeches; his speech was crisp and perfect; and he had handled with ease her mother's silver, crystal, and fragile china. From his gleaming ebony hair, secured at his nape with a narrow ribbon, to the toes of his speckless black boots, she had seen that he was of the nobility. It had almost frightened her.

Now he was the Cougar again, his black hair hanging free, a breechclout and moccasins his only clothing, and a knife at his belt. She felt the same touch of fear, wondering if he had become the Cougar only to please her. For he had wanted desperately to take her back to the world—to London or Paris or New York City—but she had made such a great fuss over staying at Windfall that, against his will, he had relented. And now she feared he had really wanted to go back to civilization, and had given up his heart's desire because of her. For he would. He was that kind of man. She whispered:

"Cougar, maybe we should just visit Windfall a-and return to England to live. I know I can make the journey, and you have all of those titles and all of those places waiting for you to be duke and marquess and earl and baron . . ."

Adam said, gently teasing, "Have you changed your mind then?" He doubted there was a woman in the world who would turn down the chance to be a duchess and live in the ancestral home of the dukes of Dover. "I'll not blame you if you have."

"But I haven't! It's just that I . . . want you to be happy. I want you to have your heritage."

He laughed softly, pulled her close. "It is appreciated, my lady, but rest assured, I am quite happy." She was incredible, this golden vision, and she was his. All his. Her soft, ravishing beauty; the smile that lit her face; the hunger burning in her eyes; the heat of her raying out into his starving body; his babe growing within her. She was all his. He added low, "I have all I want in the world right here in my arms."

"I'm glad," Alexandra whispered against his lips, "because it's what I want, too. You're all I want in this world . . ."

The Cougar turned her around then so she could see it. Windfall. It was just coming into sight around a bend, and Alexandra's heart beat faster as she gazed on its graceful pillars and portico, the shuttered windows, and two tall chimneys. It was a bit of England in this wilderness she had come to love, and it was their home. She was coming home with her husband and their babe. But as their vessel put to shore, she realized that something was missing. She asked, startled:

"Cougar, where are the Mohawks? Has someone driven them away?"

"*Iah,* Alexandra, there is nothing amiss. Hawk talked about moving upriver where there is rich cropland. I'm sure he and Lark will ride down to see us this evening." After they had disembarked with their few belongings, and the boat turned and began its placid way back, Adam smiled down at her. "So, my Gold Hair, we are quite alone. I hope you are not too disappointed."

"I'm . . . not at all disappointed, Your Grace." Seeing the hunger, the promise glittering in her husband's dark eyes, Alexandra felt herself suddenly without strength. In the burning silence between them, she went willingly, hungrily into his arms, felt herself lifted, held close, and then borne, as carefully as if she were treasure, through deep grass to the great house waiting on the hill.

Epilogue

March 1765
Windfall, New York Colony

Adam gazed down on Alexandra's peaceful face as she slept, and then, bending, he brushed a kiss over her softly parted lips. He wanted to cradle her, breathe his life and his love into her, tell her how wonderful and beautiful and clever and strong she was, but he did not. She needed her sleep. The babe had come into the world but two hours ago, and while the three doctors in attendance had assured him that the birth had been normal in all ways, the babe had not slipped out of Alexandra's body like a grape sliding out of its skin. She had suffered as all women must, and he had been by her side every minute, encouraging her, giving her his hands to grip, and hiding his terror. Part of him had died with her every cry, every time she bore down, but now all was well. They lived, the mother and child, and now he himself could begin to live again.

His gaze went to the swaddled babe sleeping in the cradle. He smiled, seeing that already Lark had hung a small dreamcatcher overhead. His heart full, Adam bent and stroked the dark down on the little rounded head, touched the perfectly formed fingers, saw the tiny mouth begin to suck. His eyes grew damp.

"Sekon, little buck," he said low. "You have made me very happy ..." He wondered then, Would Adam Alexander Avery Rutledge ever return to England to

be the sixteenth Duke of Dover? Or would he be absorbed into this great new land as Adam himself had been? He touched the babe's head again, added softly, "The choice will be yours to make, Alexander. All yours."

"Cougar?"

Turning, Adam saw Alexandra smiling at him, her eyes sleepy and her hand reaching for him. "*Sekon, Gold Hair.*" He leaned down, held her in a long, loving embrace before lowering her to the pillows again.

"Where's Mama—and Lark?"

"Your mother is resting. Lark is about. Shall I fetch them?"

"Nay. I want to hold my babe. Is he here? Is he all right?"

"He is perfect. In all ways he is perfect." Gently Adam lifted the swaddled babe from the crib and placed him in his mother's eager arms. He then stood gazing down on the two.

"Do you . . . like him?" Alexandra murmured, stroking the small, fuzzy head.

Adam smiled. "Aye, little fox. I like him."

"He looks just like you." She carefully opened the swaddling and gazed on her son with wondering eyes. "Just see how black his hair is and how square his hands are. And his fingers are long!" She nibbled them, kissed them, breathed in the wonderful baby scent of them, and then looked up at her smiling husband. "He's so beautiful. Just like you . . ."

Adam laughed. "Aye. He is big and strong and healthy, and his lungs are powerful."

Alexandra could not pull her eyes from the miracle in her arms. "Look, he's trying to suck!" She giggled, enchanted by the sight. "How on earth does he know to do that? Look at the little bubbles between his lips. Oh, Cougar, he's adorable . . ."

Adam's mouth twitched. "I think he is hungry, Alexandra."

Alexandra's eyes widened as she heard her child's sudden sharp wail and saw his frantic attempt to stuff his fingers into his mouth. She gasped, "I've been starving him! Blazes." She hurriedly unbuttoned her gown, bared one full breast, and brushed the nipple over the babe's sucking mouth. "I hope you like it, little one . . ."

"He will like it," Adam murmured under his breath. He watched, enthralled, as his son captured Alexandra's engorged nipple and began greedily to suck upon it.

Alexandra looked from her son's contented drinking to her husband's glowing black eyes. She smiled. "Now are you happy, Cougar?"

"Now I am happy, Gold Hair."

"And Adam? Is he happy, too?"

Adam bent over them, one hand cradling his son's dark head, the other Alexandra's pale gold one. He gave her mouth a tender kiss. "Adam is at peace."

Lark stood on the portico gazing out upon the brilliance of the March day—sunshine, blue sky, snow icing the grass and woods and making the Schoharie look jade-green. It was a day for celebration and jubilation. Bundling her bearskin about her tightly, she walked briskly toward the woods.

She had been having tea with the pretty, smiling German girls, the one a nursemaid and the other a keeper-of-the-house, when she had been moved strongly to give thanks to the Creator. And what better place for thanksgiving than the peace of the great woods where the blue jays were calling to one another, tree sparrows were singing, and the gray squirrels were chasing from tree to tree in the sunshine.

She stood quietly, listening, gazing at the beauty, and then she lifted her face to the blue canopy of the sky over her head. Reaching within her warm cloak, she laid her hands on her belly where her own babe was kicking. She gave thanks for it, and for her man, Silver Hawk. And she gave thanks that Alexandra and Adam had found each other and that their babe was a powerful little buck who had come into this world screaming and kicking, and who had given his mother little pain.

Filled with such gratitude for all the mercies received, Lark dropped to her knees in the snow, raised her hands to the heavens, and closed her eyes. When she opened them, the woodland was alive with birdsong, and her father the sun shone on her with such warmth and brightness, she thought spring had suddenly come. It was then that she noticed the slim figure standing quietly in the distance, saw the long brown hair and familiar blue gown.

Lark's breath caught. Eliza! The name leaped to her mind before she could bar it, but surely on such a day as this, no harm would come from it. Surely only good could come. Surely. Marking the little buck as he came then and stood by his mother's side, protecting, Lark saw that he had grown taller and leaner. He was not a soft babe anymore, but bore a quiver and bow across one slender buckskin-clad shoulder. When she saw how dark he was, and how like his father he looked, her heart melted.

Still on her knees, she steepled her hands and asked, begged the Creator to touch her friend and tell her that all was well. Her man was content. She could sleep in peace now; she need walk these woods no more. Scarcely daring to breathe, Lark watched as her friend turned her eyes toward Windfall and gazed long at the great house, now enfolded in peace. She watched as she raised her hand, watched as she and her young buck turned then and walked deeper into the snowy forest. Their heads were high, and they did not look back.

Grasping the finality of it, realizing that it was a farewell, Lark's heart began to sing. Eliza knew! She knew that all was well, and she was at peace. Gazing after the two until she could see them no more, Lark began to weep. For joy.

Glossary

atksia—my sister (older)
khekena—my sister (younger)
raktsia—my brother (older)
rikena—my brother (younger)
onkiatenro—my friend (male)
onkiatshi—my friend (female)
niawen—thank you
oronkene—good morning
okarasneha—good evening
Seknen wasatenkionhe—Safe journey
onen—goodbye
sekon—Greetings
ononkwa—medicine
onekwensa—blood
hen—yes
iah—no
mingo—a derogatory term for the Iroquois
Iroquois League (also called the Six Nations)—a North
   American Indian confederacy comprised of the Mohawks, Oneidas, Onondagas, Cayugas, Senecas and
   Tuscaroras
castle—a large Iroquois settlement surrounded by a palisade
tumpline—a strap or sling passed around chest or forehead to help support a pack carried on the back

Author's Note

Your response to BELOVED INTRUDER and to Firewalker in particular was overwhelming. I'm grateful that so many of you took the time to write and tell me. I'm pleased to give you another Indian romance in BELOVED PRETENDER. I hope that the story of Adam and Alexandra touches you as deeply as did the story of Hope and Firewalker.

Writing these two Indian books has been a fascinating experience for me as well as an eye-opening one. Not only have I learned about the Original People of our land, but your letters have shown me how very much love there is in this country for the Indian people.

My special thanks go to the Akwesasne Library staff in Hogansburg, New York for their friendliness and willingness to help in any way they could. The Mohawk vocabulary which they supplied was invaluable.

As my steady readers know, I love hearing from you and try to answer every letter—except when they have no return address! Write me at PO Box 905, Sharon, PA 16146 and please enclose a self-addressed stamped envelope if you want a bookmark.